A Cycling
Murder Mystery

a novel by

GREG MOODY

VELOPRESS • BOULDER, COLORADO

Two Wheels, A Cycling Murder Mystery Novel, by Greg Moody

ISBN: 1-884737-11-0

Printed in the U.S.A.
Second printing

VeloPress
1830 N 55th Street
Boulder, Colorado 80301-2700
USA

303/440-0601
303/444-6788 fax
e-mail: velonews@aol.com

To purchase additional copies of this book
or other Velo products,
call 800/234-8356
or visit us on the Web at www.velopress.com.

Cover illustration by Matt Brownson

Contents

To

Becky, Devon & Brynn

Your love, faith and ability to play quietly in the next room
made this happen.

For

John Stenner

Also by Greg Moody

PERFECT CIRCLES

CHAPTER ONE:

THE KING OF THE ROAD

"It's good to be king," he thought. Jean-Pierre Colgan stood at the window, staring out over a dazzling Paris on a drizzling late January Sunday. Despite the rain and the gray overcast, it remained a dazzling Paris because it was a Paris that belonged to him.

The city was his to have in any way he wished — women, wine, the very best tables — for at 27, he was the world cycling champion; the French national champion; the first Frenchman with a true chance at winning his own country's national tour in nearly a decade; the first Frenchman in 30 years who truly knew how to ride and truly control the peloton, the press and the fans.

He was a legend in his own mind.

He ignored Fignon. He ignored Hinault. He ignored Leblanc. He ignored them and their mindless followers.

"Tifosi," he snorted, and laughed.

Jean-Pierre Colgan had always liked that Italian term. It made the screaming, kinetic fans of the roadside, so trapped in their nationalism and hero-worship, sound like so many roaches ready to be swept from the path of his heroic effort.

He was not "a king of the road." He was "The king of the road," and he knew it. This was his time in the world, his time in the spotlight, and he was going to make the most of it. The sidewalk cleared for him, waiters treated him with respect, and the world was at his feet — at least, the corner of the world that cared about the demons on two wheels.

Colgan winced and rubbed his eyes thinking back about America. His trip to Disney World had been a disaster. No one knew him. No one asked for his autograph. Goofy had been too busy with a tour group of old ladies from Ohio to take a picture with him. And he had to pay some outlandish admission at the front gate. *Mon dieu*! He hadn't paid for anything in years.

For God's sake, he thought, he had to stand in line. He had to stand in line. He had to wait to ride "Space Mountain," and then, he had thrown up halfway through the ride. That wasn't the mark of a champion. If he had been treated better, he thought, he wouldn't have sent his lunch hurtling toward a cardboard Mars.

He should have gone to Euro-Disney.

No. He wouldn't go to any of their damned parks. I hope Euro-Dis does nothing biz. He chuckled. His American teammates were rubbing off on him.

They were crappy riders, Colgan thought, but the Americans knew business, and they weren't afraid to talk back to the bosses. They had broken the entire industry free from the tight-fisted owners. Now, a champion could get paid like a champion — and, with the right endorsements, could expect a comfortable retirement as well.

But as riders ... pffft. LeMond, maybe. Armstrong. A few others. Hampsten. But so many at the back of the pack.

And the fans. Colgan had ridden once in the U.S., when he was 20, in some Colorado race. A beer company sponsored it, and it wasn't a bad race. Competition was more of a late-season training ride for him, but there was nobody watching. Even the "big crowds," Colgan felt, were small by comparison to France.

The Americans just didn't get it. And they never would. They would never understand the danger, the power, the dedication, technique and desire necessary to make a true champion, even those of their own. American champions were simply huge blocks of meat in pads for football. What finesse did that take, running into each other on a lined field?

Americans.

Colgan looked down and saw his neighbor Yvette on her porch. She looked up and their eyes met. Hers seemed to ask why he had left the night before; things seemed to have been going so well.

He shrugged. *C'est la vie*. I like my own bed, my dear.

Colgan turned and walked barefoot across his kitchen, the largest he had ever seen in a Parisian apartment. Then again, he said — to the wall, to the couch, to no one in particular — this is not just anyone's apartment.

"It is good to be king."

He liked big kitchens. He liked big groceries. Jean-Pierre cut two slices of bread from a fresh loaf and dropped them into his new gift: an American toaster. Quite nice. High-chromed and very high tech. If anyone ever needed high-tech to toast bread, he had it. And he deserved it.

He poured himself another cup of coffee. Another glass of juice. And sat down at the kitchen table with the latest copy of *L'Équipe*, the French sports daily. As he scanned the sports paper, he realized that maybe it wasn't such a good day after all. His name didn't appear until page three. Something was definitely wrong. He would have to talk with Martin about his marketing.

Marketing. Another American innovation. Now, if they could only ride.

The idea that something in the apartment, outside his consciousness, was not quite right, didn't hit him all at once. It came upon him as a quietly ticking clock might intrude on a dream. Nothing sudden. Simply something not quite right.

He sat back and slowly looked around the room. Something. Where? Where?... There, with the toaster. A thin plume of whitish smoke rose from the gleaming machine. Colgan dropped his paper and walked quickly to the counter.

He looked inside the toaster, then jiggled the handle. His bread popped up. Still white. Still cold. Certainly it should be brown and hot by now.

Colgan pushed the handle back down, but found it wouldn't latch. He pushed. He pushed hard. Then he slammed the handle down. The toaster wouldn't work.

Another anchor for the Seine, he muttered.

Colgan pulled the bread out and peered into his new, high-tech, highly polished, chrome American toaster. It had to work for him. Machines always worked for him as if through sheer force of personality. His. And yet, this one refused.

By turning the machine to the side, Colgan could look deep into the appliance. The sunlight showed the wiring, the plating — all in good order, it appeared.

And that: a gray ... something ... at the bottom of the toaster.

Colgan reached for a knife and poked inside. He prodded the ... well ... it seemed to be clay, and it seemed to be all over the bottom of his new American toaster. He scraped it. He poked it. He dug at it.

No doubt. This thing was going back to the store with an angry champion right behind it, wondering in a very loud voice why the clerks let children drop modeling clay into brand-new, high-tech American toasters.

Colgan pushed a bit of the clay away from the handle latch and depressed the key. The wiring along the sides of the toaster slowly began to glow red. Now, perhaps, if he could only get the clay out, this thing would work.

With the toaster plugged in, the clay on the bottom and his wooden-handled knife buried in the machine up to the haft, Jean-Pierre Colgan, champion of the world, the favorite for this year's Tour de France, didn't have the time or interest to notice a small glow coming from a small wire leading from the heating coils to the clay covering the bottom of the toaster.

He didn't notice the glow. He didn't notice the sizzle. He didn't notice the spark.

What he did notice was that, quite suddenly and without warning, the universe expanded in a terrific burst of colors, opened before him, and, as a lover beckoning him home, raised him above the focus of reality and thrust him toward nirvana through, what he felt, in his last conscious moment, was far too small a door for such an important event.

❂

WILL ROSS HAD NO IDEA HOW LONG THE PHONE HAD BEEN RINGING. MAYBE 10 minutes for all he knew. He started to reach for it, but couldn't find his hand. He knew he had brought it to bed with him. But he couldn't find it now.

German beer, real German beer, had a tendency to do that to him. Always had. That's what he loved about Europe. They had a completely different philosophy about getting sandblasted than Americans. And now that he was out of training, for good, there was nothing wrong with some regular sandblasting at that little saloon just down the street from this apartment in Avelgem.

The phone continued to ring.

Maybe, thought Ross, it was his parents. They never did understand the time shift and now were constantly bugging him about moving back to the United States and getting a real job since he wasn't riding a bicycle anymore and isn't that for kids anyway, you didn't make any real money at it, and....

The phone continued to ring.

Ross had fallen asleep again. But he had found his hand. Right where he had left it.

"What? What?"

"And hello to you, too, Will. Where the hell have you been? I've been trying to get hold of you for the past six hours."

"Leonard, I've been indisposed. Not only have I been sleeping, but I've been contemplating the wide variety of job offers and endorsement possibilities that you have provided me over the past six months."

"Sorry about that, Chumley, but somehow the big beer companies aren't dog-nuts crazy about broken-down bicyclists who haven't won a race in six years and exploded off the back of the Tour de France ... how many times? Four?"

"Five."

"Five, thank you. So, sorry, but somehow, I can't see Budweiser dropping Ed McMahon to sign you for the Clydesdales."

"Thank you so much, Leo-nard. What about that Belgian soap — we got anything on that?"

"Sorry, they went with David Hasselhoff. But I do have something for you."

Ross rubbed his face, trying to work the lines and the alcohol out of it.

"What? About now, I'll take anything."

"How about a ride?"

"I'm sorry?"

"A ride, Will. I got you a ride on a team."

He had been lounging in bed. Now he shot up and sat bolt upright on the side.

"Are you out of your damned mind, Leonard? I can't ride. I am broken. Bent. Out of shape. I haven't ridden seriously in six months, and I never was all that good around here when I did — Jesus Christ on a drill press! What were you thinking?"

Will paused for a moment and took a deep breath, thinking about his last season's hatred of the road versus his growing need to replenish a lagging bank account — even if that did mean dropping the life he had come to love in Belgium and moving back to the States to ride for a company team. As much as he hated to admit it, the bank account won.

"Okay. where and when? When do I have to be back in the States, and what team am I riding for?"

"It's not really a domestic team. It's more like a foreign team."

"Whaaaat? Motorola? Why would Motorola have any interest in me? Och' still hates me for throwing up on the team car last season."

"No. It's not Motorola. Look. There has been a wrinkle in the Force. The time-space continuum has torn, my small, out-of-shape buddy. Your dear friend Jean-Pierre Colgan has now become your dearly departed friend Jean-Pierre Colgan. You, my friend, have been requested for service by the Haven team, and I — a true professional, I might add — put aside my grief at Colgan's untimely demise in order to cut you a pretty damned good deal at 15 percent, if I remember correctly."

"Twelve-point-five."

"Whatever. You're in, baby. You're set. You're up for another season."

"Are you crazy? Leonard, I couldn't ride when I was good. I didn't have the long-distance legs. What makes you think I can ride now? Are you .... oh, shit."

"Don't panic, pal. I think you can ride now because deep down, Willie, you have style, power, and the heart of a lion. You also have a signed contract, since you gave me the power to close deals. You're due in Paris day after tomorrow."

Will shut his eyes and tried to shake it off. Of course, it was nothing but a long, nasty dream sparked by the seemingly endless intake of fermented grain beverages. There was still a question to be answered. Will slowly, quite slowly, brought it to the surface.

"I'll send you the particulars by fax — pick them up at that office down the street from your place tomorrow morning. You got anything else? I'm buying this call, so I'm gone."

"Leonard, wait. Colgan. What happened?"

"From what I've heard from Haven and seen on the wires, they're figuring a gas main blew in his apartment — took out the entire corner of the building and a couple of neighbors, too. Pretty bad."

"Was it quick anyway? Was it quick for him?"

"S'pose so. They found him in a cupboard."

"What?"

"Force of the explosion. They found what was left of him in a cupboard. Blew him right across the room. Nasty. Gotta run. Details on the way. Call me when you get the fax."

"Leonard. Len. Are you sure about all this?"

"What — him or you?"

"Both."

"Him, Willie, I'm sure of. The great Jean-Pierre Colgan, the biggest asshole in the bunch, is dead. Dead as a mackerel on my mother's Friday china. As for you, Willie — yes, I'm sure. You've got a contract. You've got a job. Get out there and earn me my 15 percent."

"Twelve and a half."

"Whatever. You've got a training ride to get in, bud. Go to it."

William Edward Ross hung up the phone and glanced at the clock. Four p.m. There would be time for a quick training ride if he got going now; maybe 65 hard kilometers if he didn't have a complete internal collapse and die by the side of the road just outside Roubaix. He glanced outside. It was wet. No. Wet snow. It looked cold. It looked miserable. It looked like Belgium.

He turned to the mirror just over his dresser. What looked back at him looked cold. And miserable.

He ran to the bathroom and spent the next 45 minutes throwing up everything he had eaten since he was 10 years old.

❖

JEAN-PIERRE COLGAN HAD NEVER BEEN RELIGIOUS, BUT HE WAS TRYING TO make up for that now.

"Heavenly Father, forgive me for all my transgressions and for my sins of pride and regular fornication and for sticking that cell' phone in Calabresi's spokes on that turn when the TV motos where out of sight...."

This tunnel wasn't so bad — it was warm and pleasant and seemed to have some sort of walls, even though he couldn't touch anything. That first unpleasant trip through a small door in infinity had led to this and this wasn't so bad at all. The tunnel led to what appeared to be a very bright light, and, as he approached the light, Jean-Pierre Colgan was beginning to discern a figure, which at first was just a form, but now had definition — tall, thin — and more, the most incredibly muscled legs he had ever seen.

Jean-Pierre Colgan was home, and Fausto Coppi was there to greet him.

"Welcome, my brother in peace and goodwill."

"Monsieur Coppi.... "

"Fausto...."

"It is my great and grand honor ... aren't you dead?"

"Yes, my friend ... as are you. I'm here to show you the way. And to thank you for keeping my memory alive in the peloton. You brought great fame to me by bringing great fame to yourself."

It took a second for it all to sink in. Jean-Pierre Colgan had stepped across the line. He had moved to the other side. As that hideous American rider in the striped socks and the back of the peloton had always said, "You bought it, babe."

He took a deep breath — strange, he really didn't feel much of anything other than peace and contentment — and turned his attention back to the gangly figure standing before him.

"You were my hero," Jean-Pierre Colgan said quietly.

"I know my friend. Your other heroes are here as well — they look forward to meeting you?"

"Bartali? Garin? Anquetil?"

"Well, Bartali is still alive, amazingly, given the way he lives, but Anquetil is here ... yes."

"When can I see him?"

"Soon, but ... be patient. Give him time."

"Time ... why isn't he here to greet me into this hall of champions?"

"Well, Jean-Pierre," Coppi paused. "Frankly, he thinks you're a putz."

IN A SMALL HOUSE IN AVELGEM, NEAR THE BELGIAN/FRENCH BORDER, NOT FAR from Roubaix, on a wet and snowy Sunday in January, William Edward Ross pulled on his trademark red-striped riding socks in preparation for a two-hour ride into hell.

CHAPTER TWO:

WELCOME TO SENSELESS

"You're late. Twenty-four hours late." Will Ross looked up from his gear, now spread in what appeared to be an endless sea of unrelated bags around him. Had he really carried that all over the French countryside for the past day and a half? His back ached, his shoulders were rubbed raw, his mood was foul.

"Yeah, I'm late. I have been in Paris for the past day looking for you and looking for transport."

"We've been right here — waiting for you, oh mighty champion, to make an appearance. And now here you are — looking ready to ride."

"You gave my agent the wrong address, Carl. And you told him there'd be transport."

"He just wrote it down wrong, champ."

"Leonard doesn't know Paris. He doesn't know Senlis. He would have double-checked because of that, and because there's money in it for him. Somebody — and I assumed you did the talking — gave him the wrong info. And, by the way, don't call me champ."

"Oh, don't worry about that — hardly a chance you'll ever be called that again, is there? Look, I've scheduled a team training ride for, well, the next four hours, beginning right now. You've got 15 minutes to get geared up. A bike is waiting for you out back. I'll leave a team jersey on it. Get dressed and let's go. You're on a professional team now, Ross, one that, as of last week, anyway, fully intended to win the Tour de France. I liked that intention. And even with crap like you on my squad, I fully intend to have a go at it. Savvy?"

Ross stared up into Deeds's hard, heavy-lidded eyes.

"Me savvy, bwana Carl."

"Screw you, Ross. We're outta racks. Pile your stuff up over here — you're living out of a bag this season. Welcome back. Let's go."

Carl Deeds, directeur sportif, team manager, for Haven Pharmaceuticals, turned on his heels and strode off. Just before he turned the corner out of the changing room, he slammed his fist into a mirror. The mirror shattered. His hand bled. Bad luck. This was one angry dude, thought Will.

Yet, in a way, Will couldn't really blame Deeds. After all, here was a man who had slogged through years of riding and managing the peloton, usually with mediocre teams, mediocre riding talent, and now, on the brink of his own superstardom, leading Jean-Pierre Colgan's team to victory at the Tour, he had seen his champion and his own dreams snuffed out. Richard Bourgoin, his new team leader, was a talent, to be sure, but the champion, the man who would make it all come true, had been replaced, not by another champion, but by an aging mediocrity who hadn't had championship potential even at the height of his powers.

Why, in God's name, was he here?

No time to ponder the question. Will could do that on the road. He tossed his gear in a heap next to a roll of dusty, moldy carpet, changed quickly and pulled on the socks. Red stripes. An ugly affectation, but his bow to the superstition of the riders. He had always worn them. Perhaps for the luck he never had in Europe. He looked at his life piled in a corner.

"Maybe it's time to find a new brand of socks."

Ten minutes later, Will stepped out of the rear door of the locker room and into a large courtyard next to the aged and forgotten velodrome just outside the town of Senlis, 50 kilometers north of Paris. He was alone. The cold whipped around his T-shirted chest, and he quickly pulled on the winter jersey. Haven: black, red and yellow. Well, at least his socks matched. He tucked in the jersey and slipped on a windbreaker and his riding gloves. It won't be enough, he thought. He really had returned to hell. Deeds was one of those "cold makes you tough" directeurs. Will was one of those "warm makes you happy" riders. To hell with riding at all. On a day like this, he ought to be sitting at Hilda's, around the corner from his apartment in Avelgem, sipping a German beer and barking couch-potato oaths at whatever sporting event happened to be on the little black-and-white TV set in the corner.

He threw his leg over the bike and knew immediately it wasn't sized for him. A bad fit would rip out his crotch over a four-hour ride. It was close, he could probably make it work, but he'd certainly have to adjust the seat before today's ride if he had any plans of riding tomorrow.

He rolled out of the courtyard and down the alley toward the street. Maybe there he could find a wrench to adjust the seat post bolt. The team must be out front, he thought, waiting on him. His 15 minutes were almost up.

He came out of the alley and turned the corner next to the velodrome. The street was empty.

A petite brunette wearing a light blue Patagonia down jacket stood by a lamppost and looked up as he rolled to a stop before her.

"I had almost given up on you."

"Hey, right on time. Just like the Super Chief."

"Well, I hate to tell you this, chief, but they rolled out about 15 minutes ago. Deeds said you could catch up."

"Of course I can. Let me just catch the cross-town bus here — uh ... Miss ...?"

"Crane. Cheryl Crane. I'm the team soigneur. And ..."

"A female soigneur — that's a bit...."

"Unusual, I know. And I'd rather not hear...."

"Any of the old jokes ..."

"Exactly. Shouldn't you get going? You're already ... 17 minutes behind."

"I usually am anyway. Especially when I'm given instructions to start 15 minutes after everyone else. I need a wrench."

Nothing.

"A wrench."

"What, do I look like a hardware store?"

"No. More like a small-appliance warehouse."

"Cute, and thank you, and no, I don't have a wrench. The team mechanics are following the team. If you start now, you might catch up with them — about the time they get back here, I figure."

"Your faith in me ... Cheryl? ... warms my heart. Honestly. Where's the mechanic's shed or workshop or wherever they keep their tools?"

"Just inside — what do you need?"

"I've got to adjust my seat...."

"Okay." She turned and walked into the building. Will called after her.

"A seat post wrench — a ring of them if you've got...."

Cheryl stuck her head out the door. The anger shone in her face.

"Look, pal. You don't have many friends here to begin with, so don't piss me off, too. I know what you need. I've been around bikes all my life, and up until last season, I raced them myself. I know the routine, and I know the machine. I know what wrench you need — like this one."

The short, skinny metal bar shot out of her hand. Will put up his hand to block his face. The wrench hit him in the shoulder. He picked it up off the edge of the gutter and loosened his seat bolt, adjusted the seat and retightened it. He climbed on. It felt close. Maybe not right, but close enough that he wouldn't be burning out a new pair of riding shorts and developing a whole new universe of saddle sores.

He got off the bike, checked the line on the saddle, tightened it once again and tossed the Allen wrench back to Cheryl. She caught it with one hand, without moving from where she stood. Impressive, thought Will.

"You think you've got a spare tube and a frame pump in there?" Will asked. "I'm kind of behind the cars at this point."

"About 22 minutes. It's going to be interesting to see where you come in. Hang on, let me see what they've got back here."

She disappeared again into the shed, emerging only a few moments later with a tube, a frame pump, a roll of tape and a sheet of paper.

Will taped the frame pump to his top tube, X-crossed the tube across his back and took the paper Cheryl held out to him. It was a route map. A long route map. A real long route map.

"Look," Cheryl said, her voice softening. "It's shitty what Deeds did to you today. There's a phone number on the sheet. I'll be there most of the day. Get in touch with me if you get in trouble, and I will get help to you. Either I can come or, depending where the team is, maybe I can get Tomas out to help you."

"Tomas — Tomas who?"

"Delgado. Yeah. He already told me. Old buds, right?"

Well, this was certainly something. At least he'd have somebody to talk to on the team. Delgado had followed him, or he had followed Delgado, to any number of teams through their careers. Hell, thought Will, at least four.

That was just the way it worked out, just the way the business operated, but it had certainly made life easier for both of them. They had developed a bond that time, distance and the end of a mediocre career hadn't weakened.

He hoped.

"See you later...."

She smiled. "By the time you get back you won't have the energy to see much of anything."

She was right.

Will kicked his leg over the white Colnago and pushed away from the curb. He knew most of this 175-kilometer route from his days as an amateur ... what, 12 years ago? He pushed the map into a pocket of his jacket and began a long, slow kick to bring him up to cruising speed. Without a pack to pace or break the wind, it was going to be a long, slow day.

He glanced back over his shoulder and watched Cheryl as she receded in the distance. A female physical trainer with a smart mouth. This will certainly make life interesting, he thought. Nice to look at, too. Then he thought about Deeds and the team and any kind of mechanical help, a good 20 to 30 minutes ahead, hitting well over 30 miles an hour.

He kicked a little harder.

Cheryl watched Will disappear around the first corner.

"What a joke ... what the hell were they thinking of?"

*

THERE'S A CERTAIN LOVE, BORDERING ON OBSESSION, THAT MUST GO HAND IN hand with a sport. It's dedication, bordering on fanaticism. A focus that overcomes your sensibilities. A fire that burns hot and deep and long. You know your talents, your abilities, the prize that waits just beyond the 200-meter line, and, somehow, you overcome the pain, the heat, the lack of desire, the sheer, stultifying boredom, to reach across space and time and put yourself at the head of the pack — just at the moment you have to be at the head of the pack.

Amazing, men in love with machines that bring them such pain and agony.

Men in love with bicycles.

❁

"INSPECTOR."

Inspector Luc Godot of the Paris police pulled the collar of his torn and battered trench coat tight around his neck. There was a bitter breeze in the apartment, which made sense, as the apartment no longer had much in the way of walls.

"Watch where you step, Inspector. Portions of the flooring are weak or missing. And ... this is still an active crime scene."

Godot glanced at the young evidence technician through heavy, red-rimmed eyes. Every year, he thought. They get worse every year. And younger. This child must be 10, and he was the oldest of the three. Where was Claude? Claude should be the evidence technician on a case of this magnitude, not some snot-nosed Young Pioneer.

Godot shuffled through the debris of what used to be the apartment of Jean-Pierre Colgan. Three technicians were busy at an outer wall, carefully examining a gas pipe, ripped from its well and twisted into a cat's cradle. There were scorch marks around the wall where it burned.

Godot lit a cigar. Cuban. It helped him think.

The technician who had lectured him as he entered the apartment jumped to his feet and yelled excitedly at Godot. "Don't smoke that here, Inspector! This is a gas-explosion site and a crime scene! You are putting us all in danger and the evidence in jeopardy!"

Godot simply stared. He took a long, deep breath and sighed heavily. How far away was retirement? He ignored the skinny weasel in the white lab coat and turned to the other side of the apartment, what appeared to be the remains of a kitchen. Through the wall of smoke he generated, Godot took in a magnificent view of the city, one that had been blocked by red bricks until just a few days ago. I love Paris in the springtime, he thought. Too bad it's still winter.

The technicians chattered at the gas pipe on the other side of the room. Godot had already seen their initial report on the explosion and on the death of Jean-Pierre Colgan. It didn't wash. At least, not with him. Godot gingerly tested the flooring, which gave a bit, like a hard mattress, and stepped carefully onto an exposed joist next to the wall of Colgan's kitchen. Two days ago, he thought, this must have been a countertop. He could still see an outline of wood and tile in what remained of the floor around him.

And then he looked up.

Godot reached toward a chunk of ceiling plaster, hanging on a piece of reinforcing wire just above his head. The wooden knife handle was buried to within an inch of its tip. He grasped it carefully and pulled. The plaster came down with the knife. Godot brushed the debris from the sleeve of the trench coat, then slammed the plaster against an exposed wall stud, freeing the blade. It was warped and burned, its tip shredded. He looked around. Straight up ... this butter knife had flown straight up.

From his precarious position, Godot turned slowly. The angle of debris and destruction in the room radiated away from him, from the point at which he was standing.

Godot smiled.

This was no gas explosion.

✵

WILL HATED THIS BIKE. HE HATED THIS DAY. HE HATED BEING WHERE HE WAS and what he was doing. He would love to get his hands on that critic who had written in *VeloNews* about the lyricism of bicycle racing.

"You bet, pal, let's see you get your fat ass off the couch and on a bike for six hours."

He had already been through one flat. He had changed out the tube and then stopped to get a patch kit and a water bottle at a bike shop en route. It had been a necessity that turned into an embarrassment.

An older, white-haired man with the physique of a man who had known the sport in his youth but had ended the friendship years before met Will at the counter.

"I see, monsieur, that you have a Haven jersey. The team rode past perhaps 45 minutes ago; you just missed them."

"I'll see enough of them. I need, let's check the money supply here, a tube, a patch kit, a water bottle and a couple of Haven Power Charge Bars."

"You should be more prepared when you ride."

"Well, I left in a hurry. You said the team was through about 45 minutes ago?"

"Forty-five minutes. Maybe an hour. You'll never catch them. They were bookin'."

"Bookin'?"

"Bookin'. I heard it on 'Place de Melrose.'"

Ross suddenly wasn't sure that American cultural influences were a good thing in France. Coca-Cola might be a big Tour sponsor, but this was getting ridiculous.

He carried his gear outside and loaded up. At least he'd be able to finish the ride. Outside the time limit, perhaps, but finish nonetheless.

"Are you wearing that in honor of Colgan?" the shop owner asked.

"In a way — I am wearing it because of him. After he died, I took his empty spot on the team."

"You're on Haven? You expect me to believe that you are a Haven rider? Forty-five minutes behind the team? In a ratty jersey from, what, three years ago? Riding a bike with no support, so far from the team?"

Suddenly, the shopkeeper caught the look in Ross's eye.

"Yes, my friend. *Mais, oui*, you replaced Colgan. Now I remember. I read about it in *L'Équipe*. Yes, of course. *Bonne chance* — now, you must fly. You have a lot of distance to make up. And yet, it shouldn't be difficult for you, as you are a champion, eh?"

He pushed Will off and watched as he rode down the main street of the village. As soon as he was out of sight, Jean Jablom ran into the back room of his shop and dialed a number he always kept close to his heart. Within five minutes he had changed his bets on the entire racing season. He had always bet on Haven. He won a lot of money thanks to Haven. He believed in loyalty.

But there was no reason to be stupid about it.

*

HEAD DOWN TO BREAK THE WIND, WILL STRUGGLED ON. HE HAD BEEN ABLE to capture and maintain a quick pace early on, but now, with the changing terrain and the afternoon breeze beginning to kick into a wind, he found he had to focus more on just keeping the pace up at all. He had looked at the map a few kilos back, and had noticed a farm road. It was a shortcut to the return leg. He could cut across that, make up at least two hours, come up in front of the team, let them pass, roll out as soon as they were out of sight and arrive at the velodrome maybe 15 or 20 minutes behind them. God, he thought, wouldn't Deeds shit? The entire team would. That would certainly win him some respect, until the next ride, which was the next day, when he blew off the back 20 klicks in. Maybe they'd think that he'd blown himself out the day before so they'd be sympathetic. Maybe not. Even if they were, it would only last until they saw that he didn't have it anymore and no amount of training would give it to him.

Had he ever had it, even as a kid, even when tearing off on that cast-iron bike with the huge tires, driving his mother crazy as he rode down the country road to Hickory Corners — what, four miles away? — through blind corners and high-speed country turns, on that little bike ridden by a little kid who couldn't be kept off two wheels once he learned how to stand up on it? His brother had taught him. One large bike. Not his, but his sister's. No point in ruining his. One large hill and one push. It was the most magnificent feeling in the world, the wind, the speed, the fear. The crash had dented the fender, but not his feelings toward bicycles. He couldn't get enough. When he was told to stay off the road, he pedaled in fields and ditches and even had a neighboring farm pal cut a path through the fields with his dad's tractor.

Will wasn't sure of the cyclometer. It blinked on and off and didn't look like it was working. It was saying he had been riding for three hours, which should have put him past the turnaround. In his reverie, he had missed the shortcut at least 20 klicks before.

Head down into the wind, he found something inside him to keep him going, not a burning desire, but simply a memory of finding a copy of *L'Équipe* in the classroom of the high-school French teacher in Delton, Michigan. His father was assistant superintendent there and had taken him along to gather little frogs from a window well for fishing. As Will waited for his father, he wandered into the classroom and there he was — the fiercest person he had ever seen staring down at him from a tattered newspaper tacked against a concrete-block wall. He didn't have the slightest idea what it said, but the page spoke to him, reaching out across thousands of miles and an incomprehensible language to touch the soul of a kid in the heart of Michigan. Somewhere in the world, someone wrote about bikes and racing and fierce men on two wheels who felt the same way he did whenever he felt the wind in his face.

Anquetil: It was the only thing capitalized in the caption, so Will figured that had to be his name. And this was a French class so this had to be a French guy. And there was something about a Tour. Tour. Tour de France. He'd have to ask. Tour de France. Commit it to memory. Make it stick. Have to remember what it is....

It wasn't easy to find his answers on the western side of Michigan in the mid-1970s. The area had never been a hotbed of cycling or champions. It was farming and furniture and religion. Sports were the Tigers and Cubs and the Lions and Bears. Basketball was high school. Hockey was Canadian. Cycling was something kids did.

But Detroit, two hours across the state, was a different story altogether. The library said there was a track, a bicycle track in Detroit. A track they called a "velodrome." And there were clubs. Clubs that actually raced their bikes on weekends. And there were stores. Bicycle stores. Stores that sold something other than balloon-tired Western Flyers with coaster brakes.

A bicycle had always meant freedom to Will. Now, it meant something more. Speed. Speed a kid his age and size wouldn't attain until the magic age of 16 and driver's training. And danger. Speed. And danger. And Anquetil, staring out from the page with those eyes. it meant that he might learn, finally, what was behind Anquetil's eyes.

❁

CHERYL CRANE SAT DOWN HARD IN A TATTERED EASY CHAIR IN A CORNER OF the mechanics' room. A cloud of dust, accumulated over the decades, rose up around her. She closed her eyes and held her breath for a moment until it subsided. It smelled like her mother's basement. She opened her eyes and focused on a row of low-profile time-trial bikes, their paint and titanium polished to a high gloss. They looked deadly. And she missed them. She missed the speed and the rush, the thrill and the bump and the grind of the pack. The challenge from inside and outside.

She wanted to be back on the bike, back in the pack, rather than wasting her life playing nursemaid to a team of semi-talented egos and bullies and chumps.

And Ross. God only knew where he fit in.

✻

WILL ATE AND DRANK AS THE MILES BEGAN TO FLY. THE HEAD WIND THAT had dogged him the entire outbound leg now pushed him home. The pace was easier to maintain, if not build, and, after checking the map quickly, he picked it up. Mentally, he set the metronome that he used every winter on the wind trainer. In his mind, he set the pace higher, and his legs pumped in time to the mental clock.

Click. Click. Click. Click. Clickclickclickclickclickclickclickclick.

The first trip to Detroit had been a near-disaster. They didn't know what or who they were looking for, and his father's hatred of driving in a big city had brought the search to a halt before it had barely begun. They wound up at Tiger stadium two hours before game time.

But it wasn't wasted time. Armed with a handful of dimes, Will walked into the tunnel, found a phone and what appeared to be the majority of a phone book and began calling. The velodrome, the bike clubs, stores. Anyone he could find to give him the answers of where, when and who. Where was the best store, when was it open and who should he talk to about riding, racing and that Anquetil guy?

Within 20 minutes, he had an answer. Two Wheels, in the 'burbs — Romulus. Open till five tonight. Ask for Stewart Kenally. Not bad for a 13-year-old. Now, if only the Tigers could make short work of the Orioles.

In fact, it was the other way around, but the game was over and they were in the car by 3:45. Dad had wanted to shoot home and beat the traffic, but Will had won him over. After all, the game had been the afterthought of the trip. Not the cycling shop.

It took them nearly an hour to find the way — but as afternoon stretched into evening, they turned a corner and Will saw the battered wheels hanging over a dark green sign. Two Wheels. He damned near peed, he was so excited.

Indulging a habit he had picked up from his grandmother, Will opened the door and leapt from the yellow Ford station wagon as it rolled to a stop.

"Dammmmiiittttt...." came from the front seat, but Will was already on the run. He turned the corner and ran up to the door. They were closing in on five o'clock, and who knows? Maybe on a Saturday they would simply shut the door a few minutes early and head home for dinner. He reached for the door handle and depressed the latch. The door opened, and he stepped into wonderland.

William Edward Ross was home.

THE FOOD WAS GONE NOW. HE HAD EATEN HIS LAST ENERGY BAR AN HOUR AGO His legs felt like lead. His focus shifted, and he couldn't hold his own pace. He had plenty of water and kept drinking, but now he needed something more solid. His brain was beginning to feel like it was packed in cotton. Bonk. He was bonking. He figured there were 20 klicks to go now, and he simply determined to keep going. Deeds was going to have a field day when he got back into that rundown velodrome near Senlis. What was that place anyway? Some old dump the team had hired out for the early-season team training sessions before everyone got into the race schedule and team units found themselves spread out all over the Continent racing like madmen to try and win the heaps of praise from bastards like Deeds who knew nothing about racing other than putting crap in your way putting people down and.... Stop it. Use the energy to pedal. Don't use it to gripe and whine and moan. Just keep your head down and go under the wind — it had shifted again, or had that last section of road turned him back into it? Just pedal. It will be done soon. Just think of the shower at the end of the road and Deeds. You'll have to deal with Deeds. But that is survivable even if the ride isn't. And, oh, my God, I've got to do this again tomorrow....

❋

"HAVE YOU SEEN HIM?"

"Not for the past three and a half, four hours, Tomas." Cheryl Crane shrugged. She didn't even know this Ross guy, but Delgado's concern was beginning to rub off on her.

Tomas Delgado kicked the pavement outside the Senlis velodrome and cursed. Somewhere out there, along a 140-kilometer route, was his friend. New to the team, and so far unseen by him. The team had returned 30 minutes before, and already, like the end of a factory shift, vans were pulling up and riders streaming out for lifts to their apartments around Senlis and the northern suburbs of Paris.

He'd wait for Will. Except that the entire team was out now. And Deeds was locking the door to the velodrome building.

"Hey ... what about Will?"

"Who?" Deeds seemed genuinely confused.

"Will. Will Ross. The new guy. He's still out on the road."

"Well, that's his problem."

"I'll wait for him."

Deeds sighed. "No, you go on Tomas. You and Crane. I'm team manager. It's my responsibility. I'll wait for Ross. Not used to having him around yet. Just didn't think of him."

"He's doing it alone — it could be a while."

"I'll wait. Don't worry. You go home — get some dinner and a rest. See you tomorrow."

Cheryl Crane climbed into the van. Tomas Delgado hesitated on the step.

"Go, Tomas. Just go. I'm here. I'll wait. As long as it takes."

Delgado paused for a moment, then climbed into the Haven team van, shutting the door behind him. The van pulled away from the curb and quickly disappeared into the evening traffic of Senlis. Carl Deeds watched it go, then slowly walked to his own car, climbed in, and began the long drive home to the bottle of wine that waited in his apartment in downtown Paris.

❖

HE PASSED THE MARKER. HE WAS ON THE OUTSKIRTS OF SENLIS. SENLIS. SENSE-less. This whole damned thing was senseless. Ten kilometers out. The next turn would take him into traffic and he'd have to focus all the more unless he wanted to wind up as a hood ornament.

Ten. Not far. What — six miles? He hadn't lost certain Americanisms despite years of living in Belgium. He converted kilos to miles. He converted Flemish to French and French to English, even though it took him forever to order dinner. It was stupid and it was parochial, but it was just the process he had developed in the first year to get through the day, and now it was the way he did it. It wasn't fast, and it wasn't pretty, but it worked for him. Eight out. Seven out. Six out.

Cars were racing past him now. He should be focused on them, but he couldn't raise his head. He saw his feet. He saw his pedals. Shouldn't they be moving faster? He blew through a traffic light and got lost in a turnaround. Which way. Which road? If he took the wrong one he'd be heading back. The map didn't make any sense anymore. And now here, here was the street because there was the store the cab had passed on the drive into the center. The velodrome should be right around the corner, which it was in all its brown, ancient ugliness. What a rat trap. How could anyone ride in this place, this hellish place? God, I'd never do it, never do it never do it.

Will braked in front of the gate. He looked at the cyclometer. It had stopped. How many hours in the saddle? Too many. Had he really lost that much out of his life, and for what? He lifted his leg over the bike and stepped on solid ground for the first time since the store. Where was that store? How long ago was that? His legs were shaking. He walked like Grandpa Ross did after his stroke. Dragging the bike behind him, almost a comic-book sheriff dragging in an unconscious desperado, Will stumbled to the door. Deeds would be shocked to see him.

Maybe. Maybe not. The front door was locked.

Will turned, and, holding the bike by the front wheel, pulled it behind him around the end of the building, through the alley and into the courtyard next to the track. The locker-room door was locked as well.

He might have collapsed at that point if the growing anger inside him hadn't kept him upright. He leaned against the door for support and began to bang on it, slowly then harder then faster, with his fist.

"Son of a bitch!"

Bang!

Now he was even more exhausted, and the door had not opened, and no one, it seemed, had heard him.

Looking up, Will noticed that one window about six or seven feet up was open. He pushed his bike next to the wall, climbed to stand on the saddle and looked in. It was a hellish drop to the floor on the inside, but if he could just get himself up, up and in, in, in ... the corroded aluminum frame grabbed his ass and started to cut through the Spandex and skin, and still he pulled himself in and down the wall until gravity took over.

Ross tried to slow himself with his feet but he couldn't catch them on the lip of the window before they had already shot by. His outstretched arms hit a covered wooden crate first, then slid to the tiles. He tried to roll out of the fall, but it was already too late, and he was too tired for that anyway.

His head turned and he slammed his collarbone into the floor. Will yelled as the pain shot down his entire right side. He lay on the dirty floor and tried to catch his breath. He didn't think it was broken, but it would certainly bruise like a mother.

He sat up. This was a drying room of some sort. He thought he remembered it being just off the changing room. He stood up and tried to stretch out his right arm — ack — not yet. He kicked off his riding shoes — he didn't need to go slip-sliding around on a tile floor now — and padded over to the back door, released the latch and stepped outside to retrieve his bike. It was their damned bike, and he should have just left it and let Deeds deal with somebody stealing it, but cycling equipment had always come so hard for Will that he just couldn't bear to treat it with anything but respect.

He rolled the bike into a corner and relocked the door. The building was quiet as a newsroom an hour after the final edition had rolled. He could hear an occasional creak, the throated rush of an overhead heater. He was alone. Dead alone. Had he just broken into the wrong building? No. There was his equipment, loosely piled in a corner. There was a note attached.

He pulled it up and read what he could of the chicken scrawl on the notepad: "Welcome home. 8 a.m. tomorrow. Team meeting here. Deeds."

He needed a shower. No shower and he stood the chance of getting saddle sores or mushrooms tomorrow or a week down the road. He stepped in, letting the hot water cascade over him. He scrubbed nothing. He simply stood there, uniform, socks and all. Slowly, ever so slowly, he stripped down and scrubbed off the more odious parts of his body. Will didn't know how long he was there. He may have slept, leaning against the shower wall. He may have passed out. He only knew that when he did realize what was going on, his fingers were delightfully prunish.

He stepped out of the shower and reached for a towel. There were none. Only those the team had used, still wet with that slightly moldy smell that only athletics can impart to everything. He took a towel, the least wet, the least disgusting, and dried himself as best he could. He stumbled over to his gear and dug into his travel bag for one last Haven bar. He always kept one on hand. You never know when you're gonna bonk.

The unopened bar fell from his hand. Will was asleep, naked, against his gear, before the food hit the chipped and grimy tile floor.

His last thought before passing out was a memory. What he fell in love with that day in Detroit when he opened the door of Two Wheels moments before closing time. It was a memory to last a lifetime. It had brought him to this place, this job, this moment in time.

It was the smell.

And once he experienced it, for real, in that moment, he was forever lost.

CHAPTER THREE:

HAVEN IS IN YOUR MIND

"It's a painting I've been working on. I call it 'Morning — With Coyotes.' " Will instinctively rolled to the side and covered his nakedness. He covered it with a Haven Power Charge Bar, but he covered it nonetheless.

"I said, I call it 'Morning...."

"Yeah, yeah — I got it. I'm awake."

"No you're not. If you were awake, you'd say, 'Delgado — any relation to Pedro?' and I'd say, 'Distant ....' I can't remember. What movie is that from?"

" 'Plain Clothes.' Hello, Tomas."

"Hello, Will. No offense, my friend, but you look like absolute hell."

"Feel it, too. Thank you very much."

Will stood and stretched, wrapping the now-dry, but stiff-as-a-board towel around him. Tomas shook his head, both in sympathy and dismay.

"You'd better get your act together. There's a team meeting in less than an hour and Deeds was steamed you weren't around yesterday."

"Well, he should have thought of that yesterday when the bastard left and locked the back door."

"He said you were all settled and there wouldn't be a problem."

"I wasn't — there was and now I'm a mess. Is there a café or something near by? I need to get some breakfast."

"Half a block down. Marie's. Expensive, but good. And you'll get a lot."

"Money I got. Lot I need."

"You've got about 45 minutes ... and ... make the meetings. Deeds'll shit when he sees you up and around."

Ross smiled. Nothing would please him more. Tomas told him to hurry and perhaps they could set up his bike before the morning team ride. He also promised to scrounge Will some team gear — perhaps something of more recent vintage.

Will thanked him and stepped back into the shower, quickly scrubbing himself down. He dried with a fresh towel Tomas had brought him, then rubbed himself down with alcohol. He didn't know if it really did any good, but he remembered Izzy telling him that it toughened skin and killed "them little saddle-sore guys." He shaved quickly and dressed in a loose sweat suit and riding slippers. It would do until Tomas could find some gear. Will glanced at his watch. Seven minutes start to finish. No doubt. He was, is and always shall be the fastest stripper in the eighth grade. At least there was one talent he had never lost.

He stepped out the back door and walked the alley to the street. He hadn't noticed the small, human touches that even this back alley next to an ancient velodrome in Senlis seemed to have: detailed grillwork, flowers, cobblestones with just a hint of moss growing through, and a courtyard that would actually be a place to sit a spell, take your shoes off ... y'all come back now, hear? "Beverly Hillbillies." This stuff just jumped into his mind at the strangest times. Lines from old movies, cartoons, TV shows. His mind, he liked to say, "was a true suppository of useless information." As long as he didn't begin quoting "Gilligan's Island," he figured he was safe. One Gilligan line and he'd commit himself.

The café was two buildings down, set back just a bit from the street. It carried the stereotypical tables and chairs along the sidewalk, which had always fascinated Ross. Why would anyone want to sit out, even on the most beautiful day, while an army of poorly tuned cars stood bumper to bumper five feet from you, not moving, not shifting, not doing anything except filling your lungs with exhaust?

He loved the French, but knew he'd never understand them.

Marie's was small, but immediately appealing. A bar stood off to one side, capped by a gigantic espresso machine, surrounded by what appeared to be hundreds of bottles of wine. My kind of place, thought Will; lots of wine plus lots of espresso made him the most wide-awake drunk on the Continent.

A woman he assumed was Marie stood behind the bar, cleaning and arranging glasses. Strangely enough, she looked more German than French. Graying blonde hair, pulled back in a severe bun, an outfit that looked something like a collision of Dorothy Gale of Oz and the Hitler Youth, gingham lederhosen draped over a zaftig frame. There was a good 240 pounds to Marie, he thought, which meant that he was likely to eat what she cooked. Perfect.

This was his kind of place.

"Monsieur...?"

This was the best part of riding, thought Will, as he ordered coffee, juice, fruit, müsli, yogurt, buttered croissant, four eggs and a waffle. "And don't bring it all at once, please. Just when you've got something ready, bring it on — I'll be eating in shifts, and I'm in a bit of a hurry."

Marie smiled. Having a bicycling team next door was good for business.

✯

WALKING BACK TO THE VELODROME, WILL WISHED HE HAD A BIT MORE TIME before the morning ride. Even at 32, he could no longer eat everything and anything in the world, leap on his bike and ride until dawn. Now, he needed his quiet time — for an hour at least — or a handful of Tums. Now he realized where the "don't swim for an hour" idea came from. If he stepped into a puddle today, he'd sink like a stone.

Will checked his watch. Right on time. Ten minutes until the meeting and he was ready to go. Tomas had left a fresh uniform on his bags. Along with the uniform, Will found a helmet, gloves, even sunglasses. All coordinated. All with the Haven logo and a world of smaller sponsors. Not bad. Big teams had their perks.

Ross suited up as the rest of the team began to wander in. No one took much notice of him. In fact, the only thing said to him was in answer to his own question of where he could find the mechanics' workshop. He knew these things took time, especially when you were the body replacing the guy at the top. There would be resentment, cynicism ... and quite a lot of just plain pissed-off. But here he was, for good or bad, for God knows what reason.

He picked up his shoes, glasses, gloves and helmet, and walked through a partially carpeted tunnel toward the sound and the smell he knew so well. The sound of wheels being trued and wrenches being dropped, and the smells of grease and leather and light machine oil. Maybe he should have stayed a mechanic. No. He wanted to ride. And even the most wonderful thing in the world can become hell if you do it too long or with the wrong people.

Tomas looked up from the workstand as Will walked through the double doors.

"Perfect. I just got your bike up on the wind trainer. Let's check your fit and cleats."

Tomas was an Old World kind of mechanic. He eyeballed a lot of things. Seat height. Cleat angle. Stem height and length. He didn't go in for computers or calipers or even tape measures. If he couldn't see it, or feel it, it didn't exist.

Will had been close the day before, but Tomas put a final tweak in the seat height and angle that Will could feel immediately. Maybe this machine wasn't such a lost cause. Maybe he wasn't. Whoa. One thing at a time.

"I spun out the wheels. Did you hit something yesterday? Your back rim was way out. I'm amazed you made it around. I cleaned out the bottom bracket and adjusted the derailleur. Trued the handlebars, too. Sort of surprised they'd give you this bike. It was pretty much ready for the junk heap yesterday morning, but it will get you around today."

Will smiled. This was the Tomas that he knew and loved, the man who would begin talking about a bike, slowly, then would talk faster and faster until he was rattling off facts at a rate difficult to keep up with, especially if he leaned heavier and heavier on his native Basque accent.

Tomas was one of the true characters Will had met on the road through the Continent. The sport was filled with them. Tomas, Colgan, even Deeds. Though, as he thought of Deeds, any sport would be better off without some of them.

The team meeting was in one of the few remodeled rooms in the collapsing velodrome building, dark blue floor and pale blue concrete walls, sprayed with an epoxy-based paint. Hard to use, easy to clean, thought Will, recalling his days as a painter in a local hospital, working the graveyard shift in order to train while it was still light. He ran his hand across the cool, smooth surface. Yep. He might not know the capital of South Dakota, but he knew paint. That was epoxy. Nicely applied, too.

He realized then that he couldn't put it off any longer. He turned to face his new team.

Will was the last into the room, aside from Deeds. As he looked around, he realized that he knew a lot of his new teammates, some from simply a general knowledge of the peloton. Others he had ridden against over the past four or five years. One or two, he only knew from articles in *L'Équipe* or *VeloNews*. There may have been no personal knowledge, but he knew the reputations. Richard Bourgoin, the new team leader, was a shark: steady and powerful in the mountains; solid, if not spectacular in the sprints; and an anchor, a dead weight, in time trials. No one was convinced he would ever be able to put it all together for a Tour win, especially without a powerhouse team behind him. Until Colgan's death, Bourgoin had been the able lieutenant, ready to marshal forces, dictate tactics, control the pace of the peloton ... or, if necessary, destroy himself in a spectacular blaze of glory, all in order to place Jean-Pierre Colgan on the top step of the winner's podium. Now, that glory was his, if only because the leader had died and there hadn't been the time or opportunity to sign a championship replacement.

Only Will.

Only me, Will thought. Bourgoin should be thankful. It's because of me that he will get his shot.

There was Anthony Cacciavillani, the sprinter. He had been one of the top three in the world for the past five years, but a horrific crash last year seemed to rob him, not of his jump, but of his "death come hither" attitude when bumping and grinding toward the line.

Hans Merkel was the new team lieutenant, as Cacciavillani didn't have the legs to stay with the leaders in the mountains. Besides, sprinters are a breed of rugged individualists. Number two needed to realize the needs of the team. Tony C would never have that, but Merkel had it in spades, submerging his own talents and personality in order to put Bourgoin over the line.

There was Miguel Cardone, the Basque, and Masenti and Mooria, the Italian tandem champions, who acted as if stage racing was somehow a vacation from the track and somehow beneath their contempt and John Cardinal, the American mountain biker, who had returned to the road after he lost his ride on an Italian mountain-bike squad.

And there was Cheryl. She looked at him with sharp gray eyes that focused his attention and bore right into him. He didn't know how to break a spell that was undeniably cast upon him. He tipped an imaginary hat and turned to the door as Deeds walked in.

"Ross — fifty-dollar fine for missing yesterday's team ride. I'd make it more, but I'm told there were extenuating circumstances and you did ride the course."

"About two days behind us," Cacciavillani snorted. The team laughed. Deeds joined in.

"How to win friends and influence people, huh, Ross? Okay. Same course today, but I want the pace up. You bunched yesterday and got lazy. I want the same pacelines as we had yesterday — the three squads. Ross, you'll work with the B squad. Henri, make him keep up — he'll be slacking."

Henri Bresson looked up from his issue of *L'Équipe.* He glanced over at Will and smiled.

"*Oui.*"

"And, Ross," Deeds said, almost in closing, "I want you to pee in a bottle. Team requirement ... and frankly, I don't like to hear about my riders popping pills before a ride."

"They were Tums. Stomach trouble."

"Pee. I don't trust you."

"Fine."

"Welcome to the pros."

Will smiled. "By the way, Carl. Anal-retentive does have a hyphen."

"Screw you, Ross."

As the meeting broke up, Will stepped across the hall to the team doctor's office. He wasn't there, but an assistant, Luis-something, said he'd handle everything. Will filled two specimen bottles, then took a third and filled that as well. Luis taped the two and initialed and dated both. Will took a third tape and sealed the extra bottle. He dated it, signed the label and told Luis to do the same.

"I only need two."

"That's okay. I need the third — party favors."

Luis scrawled a signature on the label. He didn't seem any too happy about it. Will carried the bottle back into the changing room and pretended to put it in his bag. He then carried it, with his gear, out to the front of the building. He emerged to see the team rounding the corner in the distance. Tomas stood before him with his bike. Cheryl stood off to one side, watching the team disappear around the turn. Will handed Tomas his sample.

"Put this someplace quiet, will you?"

"Sure, buddy." Tomas slipped it into the pocket of his coat. With a sudden realization, he glanced up at Ross.

"It is sealed, isn't it? Real good sealed?"

"Real good sealed. Thanks, pal. I have just never trusted the testers."

Cheryl turned as Will pulled his bike over to the curb and threw his leg over the frame.

"Deeds said you were late again. This time, you've got to catch up."

Ross looked down at his gloves, pretty much beat to hell over the past few years. He looked at his legs, pretty much beat to hell over the past few years. He looked at Cheryl through eyes that had been pretty much beat to hell over the past few years.

"No problem," he said, as he pushed off in pursuit of a multilegged animal that might already be out of his reach.

❖

"I AGREE WITH YOU, LUC. BENEDICT AGREES WITH YOU. THE PROBLEM IS THAT the Chief Inspector does not agree with you — nor does the kiddy corps of evidence technicians."

Inspector Godot stood in the middle of what had once been Jean-Pierre Colgan's apartment, on the one, small, solid area of tile that remained in a floor which was now a series of hills and valleys of buckled tile, or broken and exposed joists. It was difficult to move through the room. He stood with Stephen LaSarge, like Godot, a veteran of more than 20 years with the force. And yet, he was only half listening to LaSarge, as he was eyeing a mountain of debris, shards of metal, splinters of wood, tatters of cloth, searching for the elusive something he needed to throw the investigation in his direction.

This was no gas explosion.

Godot stared at a vase holding a single, wilted flower. The blast had not touched it. Just above, a framed poster of Jean-Pierre Colgan, French racing champion, had been nearly obliterated, leaving only a corner of the frame, a torn fragment of the photo and the wire hanger on a wall now punched through with shrapnel. He kicked over a pile of half-burned newspapers on the floor. Next to them was a box for a toaster. Two-slice, American-made, but designed for French electrical systems. There was still a bow on the box. A gift?

A burned and battered butter knife and a gift toaster.

After months of pushing paper in his office, usurped on each and every case of the Children of the Chief, he was on an active crime scene and his mind was working again. He liked the feeling.

"The evidence technicians won't back off on the gas explosion because that was their first idea," LaSarge continued. "They have been touting it for two days. They would rather be wrong than embarrassed."

"And what about the Chief Inspector?" Godot mumbled.

"Ah ... the Chief Inspector. He hired them. He did not hire us. You always stand by your own children."

"It doesn't matter that the Chief Inspector was only recently named to the board of Haven Pharmaceuticals?"

"I don't see why it should. Jean-Pierre Colgan is only a small part of the Haven company."

"Was."

LaSarge shrugged. "Was."

"He was the champion of France," Godot said quietly. He stamped his foot hard, causing a rat that was climbing up through the floor joists to drop the treasure he carried in his mouth.

"I'm not a cycling fan," LaSarge muttered. "Don't really know the champions. I'm more of a football fan. Our football."

Godot continued his quiet search through the room, then stopped. Something was nagging at him, sitting in the back of his brain. What? He had to bring it forward. He carefully stepped over the exposed joists, back to where he had seen the rat. Crouching, he reached into the space between the beams and, out of the accumulated dust and muck of 60 years, picked up the piece of wire and metal the rat had been holding in its mouth, along with a second treasure that sat beside it.

"Stephen. You know about explosives. What do you make of that?"

Godot tossed it across the room.

LaSarge caught the burned and gnarled metal strip and turned it in his hand. "I can't be sure until I get it to the office," he said, "but it could be — appears to be — part of a very simple electrical device."

"Device?"

LaSarge took a deep breath. "An electrical detonator. Where did you find it?"

"Right here, in the flooring. It had been gathered up by our good friend, Monsieur Le Rat, along with other treasures."

"Such as?"

"Scraps of paper ... a bit of bread ... and this." Godot tossed a pencil-thin object to LaSarge, who reached forward to catch it. "What appears to be the remains of one of Monsieur Colgan's fingers."

❁

THERE WAS NO WAY WILL SHOULD HAVE FELT THIS GOOD, NOT AFTER YESTERDAY, not even after a decent meal, not even after a decent sleep. He should have bonked in the first hour, but it flew, it honest to God flew, along with him. His bike felt reborn. A pickup truck yesterday, a sports car today. Tomas had worked a miracle. Will felt good and strong and just angry enough with Deeds and his treatment to find the strength to push his pace. Alone. And keep it up. This was flying. This was why he got into racing in the first place.

This, and the smell.

Two Wheels was closing. Ten minutes to five and the lights were already shut off in what appeared to be a workshop in the back of the store. Will just stood in the doorway and stared. This was no bike shop. There were only one or two balloon-tired flyers. The rest of the machines on the floor and on the wall were pure danger: thin-tired, lean-framed razors on wheels. He walked across to a row of bikes, red, black, purple and a green, the most amazing light green in the world.

He was transported, he realized, as much by what he smelled as what he saw. It was grease and it was rubber and it was light oil and it was sweat and it was wool and it was exotic.

He supposed for a moment that this is what drew his brother to the Ford garage downtown day after day, even though that never captured Will. That was vague and overwhelming, this was sure and sensual. That was a world of six-thumbed Neanderthals. This was a world of mechanical surgeons. It was addictive, and he, with one true hit, was now a junkie.

The bell rang on the door behind him as he and his his father stepped inside. A white-haired head popped out from behind a curtain leading to the back of the shop.

"We're closing. That's it today."

"Just dropped in for a look. Sorry. Come on, Will. They're closing. Let's hit the road."

Stewart Kenally wiped his hands on the grimy coveralls while he watched Will stand beside the line of racing bikes. He walked over and looked at him hard.

"You like to ride? Ride fast?"

Will looked up and started, broken from his reverie. "Uhhh, um, yes, sir."

"You like to ride faster than anybody else?"

"Yes, sir."

"You ride an old fat bike?"

"Yes, sir."

"You need a real bike."

"Yes, sir."

Will's father, realizing that his checkbook was suddenly being discussed, spoke up.

"We're here to look. That's all ... we're here to look."

But even Will's father saw in his son's eyes something that hadn't been there before that moment. His son was captured in something. And it was bigger than anything or anyone in the room.

❁

COMING AROUND THE LAST TURN, INTO A LONG STRAIGHT, WILL COULD HAVE sworn that he saw the team up ahead, perhaps a quarter of a mile, making a turn into the first section of rolling hills. If he were going to catch them, this was the place to do it. He focused his energies and picked up his pace again. He was in the big gears and kicking hard. He had been chasing for the better part of an hour, and, even alone, was feeling good about it and himself. This was what riding meant, deep down. As much as it was a team sport, to Will, racing was the kick-ass feeling of doing it yourself, putting what you had in your legs behind what you had in your head.

Into the turn that led to the first hill, Will shifted his weight and pushed through the corner, taking it easily. He could now see the team ahead of him, and he reached down again to find another boost. This was a good day, because he found it.

He was pushing hard now, reaching the end of what he had to offer. It felt as if there were plenty more where that came from, but even the greatest riders, Merckx and LeMond and Indurain, find a brick wall that they can't break through — as if physiology and physics conspire to push them back into the world of reality by making the laws of the physical world apply to them. How unfair, how unreal.

Will kicked his right leg up to the top of a stroke and pushed through a hard right turn. It always amazed him that he could do that. He must have been hitting 45 degrees or better on that turn and had control straight through. He was sailin'. And had to be coming up on the team. Over the next rise and they were directly ahead. One of the new Italian domestiques had fallen behind with chain problems. Will picked him up, and the two, without saying a word, began a two-man paceline, each taking a pull at the front to break the wind for the follower, set a harder pace, and make up the lost time to the group without killing one another.

And the gap closed.

Deeds was rather surprised to see Will not just pull up to the rear of the group, but burst through to its head; shocked might be a better word. He looked long and hard at Will.

"All right, ladies, echelons ... let's pick it up."

The pack split into three groups of eight riders each, then immediately fell into echelon to counter a sidewind. The lead rider broke the wind and pulled for the rider just to his left and a half wheel behind, and for the next, to his left and half a wheel behind, and so on. It formed a rolling wall and a faster pace, especially for Bourgoin, who, as team leader, pulled less often and not as long as the Italian who had helped Will bridge the last gap up to the group.

For the next 10 minutes, Haven was a rolling barricade, a well-oiled machine. But as the team rode together in silent rhythm, Will gradually became aware that he was falling out of synch. Bridging the gap from the Senlis velodrome to the pack had been the easy part. He had felt strong, powerful. He had felt in the pipeline, "five by five." Now, in the group, where he should have felt the ease of working with the team, being pulled in the paceline, even in the echelon, he felt the first stirrings of a drag on his legs, as if someone were slowly pouring sand into his calves, into his shoes, into his thighs. He downshifted to keep on the pace being set by the team, missed the shift and found himself falling out of position, spinning madly to keep up. The derailleur had jumped two gears. He shifted again and pushed himself back toward the pack. This shouldn't be happening. It couldn't be happening. He could think beyond it and make it not happen. And yet it was. And it did. And he couldn't stop it.

Will had blown. He had tried too much, too hard, too soon. The chase, so strong at the outset, had consumed his energy and dug too deeply into his long-ignored reserves. His legs began to burn with an incredible fire. He had to stretch — just stop and stretch them out for a moment. The powerful rhythm he had, so strong just moments before, was gone. His thighs began to scream. He knew he couldn't keep up the pace for the remaining four hours of the ride. He couldn't keep up the pace for the next hour. He tried to draw strength from his arms, from his lungs, from his upper body. Think your way through it. It can't last forever. And yet, he knew. He knew.

He broke gear and fell out of line. He broke ranks. He sat up. The great experiment, the great challenge, was over. He had faced the enemy: his age, his talent, his recent lack of training, his head, his ego, his confidence. The enemy was him. And the enemy had won.

He rolled to a stop outside the bike shop he had passed only the day before. The white-haired owner stopped cheering for the passing team and stared at Will for a long time before turning back into the darkness of the shop.

The trailing team car pulled up beside him.

"Deeds said to ride back to Senlis and clean out your gear. You're finished."

Ross stared at Philippe Graillot, the minor team functionary, with unseeing eyes. Who the hell are you, he thought, and what right do you have to talk to me like that — I'm a rider, damn it. I'm on the damned bike every damned day. No matter what the weather, or what the challenge, I'm here and you're not. You're sitting in a damned leatherette bucket seat, chatting and munching away on something and trying to think how you can make the girls at the bar believe that you ride for the team so you can get laid, you little bastard. Who are you to talk to me like that, you damned worm?

Ross looked through the bland face gaping at him out of the window of the battered team Peugeot. He hawked up a great wad of snot and spit it on the road beside the car.

"Tell Deeds I haven't got anything to clean out, you twerp."

"You can't talk to me like that." Philippe's voice was heavy with menace.

"Move your ass or the next one will land right between your eyes. If I'm fired — I don't have to listen to you, now, do I?"

Gravel shot across the shoulder as the team car spun back onto the road and into a game of catch-up with the team. Will could see the round, bald head speaking frantically into a radio. Deeds was getting the word. Perhaps he should have thrown some choice ones in for him as well. No need. Deeds knew how he felt, just as Will knew how Deeds felt about him. No secret in that, either way.

His chance was over. The die was cast. And yet, somehow, dismissal from Haven had lifted a great weight off his shoulders. He could be packed and gone before Deeds and the team returned.

He launched one more oyster toward the bike shop and quickly regretted his anger. The owner took riding seriously. Will didn't. Not anymore. And as he turned to ride alone back to the training center at the Senlis velodrome, for the life of him, he could no longer decide who was right.

A little more than an hour later, he pulled up to the dilapidated racing bowl. A tail wind had pushed him along. Cashing it in was always hard, but getting home, it seemed, after you gave up, always seemed easy — something like the road to hell being a slight descent with a tail wind and little or no road resistance.

He stepped off the Colnago, almost wanting, for a second, to shove it out into the street as a sign of defiance, but he didn't, because he kept hearing Kenally in his head telling him that you never blame your bike, you can never blame the machine, even when it breaks. For the fault lies with the rider or the mechanic or the forces of nature and the peloton. Never with the bike.

It had been a good ride, even if for only two days. A good ride. He crouched down on the curb, holding the stem with his left hand, and looked at the angles of the bike. The lines were sharp and true, and even while it could use a coat of paint, you could see the beauty the designer and the builder had been seeking. This was not a toy. This was not a commuter's bike. This was not a yuppie's showpiece. This was, very nearly, a weapon of war — a machine that reached deep into the soul of the man atop the saddle and captured his heart.

And Will felt, for a moment, quite unworthy of it.

He stood, and, rolling the bike behind him, stepped into the building. He saw Tomas in the mechanics' room and slid the machine over to him. It was his now. Nothing to be said. Tomas knew, either by instinct, or by Deeds having gleefully radioed ahead.

Nothing left to do but strip down, shower up and make tracks.

Will walked into the changing room and pulled off his jersey. He hadn't even had a chance to get a rider's tan: dark arms, pale white chest, pale hands with tanned circles on the back, deep burgundy neck. Everything was still fish-belly white.

He tossed the jersey in a corner and picked up a towel. Inside, out of the chill, he was starting to sweat. He rubbed his face hard, burying it in the rough nap of the towel. It felt almost like sandpaper, yet, almost sexual, too.

What a day.

❂

DEEDS HAD TOLD HIM TO LEAVE. AND WILL HAD TRIED. AN ASSISTANT TEAM manager, however, told him to stick around until the team returned. Will didn't see any percentage in staying, so he showered, packed his gear and piled it near the front door until he could get a taxi into Paris and to the Gare du Nord.

The assistant manager had it moved back to the locker room. Will moved it out onto the street. The manager had it moved back. The taxi arrived. The driver and Will tried to load the gear into the car, and, still, the assistant manager unloaded the car, paid the driver handsomely and told Will he had been ordered to keep him on site until this afternoon, when everything could be cleared up.

Will rubbed his eyes to work the growing frustration out of them. What now? What was this game? One last shot to the head before he was sent away in disgrace? One last humiliation? Will was too tired to worry about it anymore. He walked into the trainer's room, put his feet up, and quickly stepped through the wall into sleep.

Later, he had no idea how much later, Tomas woke him urgently.

"You've got to see this."

Will stretched his face and stood, following Tomas down the hall in a drunken half-sleep. He hated feeling like this, never knowing where he was or who he was until he was fully awake. When he stopped behind Tomas and looked where he pointed, Will awoke immediately.

It was Deeds, on the phone, not having a very good time of it. His face alternately went bright red, purple and then ash white. Whoever was doing the talking wasn't buying what Deeds was selling. Wheedle. Cajole. Rage. Beg. Plead. Nothing seemed to have any effect. Will was watching a master destroy a bully. It was a marvelous performance. He wondered where he could send the thank-you note.

Deeds was only listening now. Whatever he said had fallen on deaf ears. He listened quietly for a few more moments, then slowly put down the phone. He covered his face with his hands. Under the fluorescent lights, Deeds looked positively green.

He looked up and saw Tomas and Will, now joined by a few others, standing outside his office door. It was as if all the energy had been drained out of him.

He motioned.

"Will. Come in, will you? Shut the door."

Will stepped through and quietly closed the door behind him. He sat in the straight-backed chair opposite Deeds rather than the overstuffed chair in the corner. You never knew when you'd have to get up fast.

"We've had our differences, you and I," Deeds said, "but you've got to understand where I've been coming from — I want to win. And you know as well as I do that you're no replacement for Colgan."

"Well," Will said, starting to get up, "if that's all, I'm.... " He made a gesture for the door. Deeds waved his hands.

"No, Will. That's not it. I'm sorry for what I've said to you." Deeds took a very deep breath. This was tough for him. "I'm sorry for how I've acted. Locking the door last night. Leaving you behind on the training ride. The drug test this morning. I wanted you out of here any way I could get you out."

Deeds paused. He was looking for something he had to say. Will was just looking for a ride to the station.

"The fact is, you are a part of this team. Whether I like it or not" — Deeds saw a look of surprise on Will's face — "and whether you like it or not."

"You're telling me...."

"I'm telling you we're married, Ross. From here until the end of the season. You can't leave — we've got the options. And I can't can you — because the company says it wants you. I don't know what the grand plan is, but you are part of it. So am I. We're in — and from here on, I'll try to make the best of it." He paused for a long time, having hit the hardest part of his speech. "Will you?"

Will thought for a long time. This wasn't what he was expecting at all. This wasn't what he wanted at all. He was, he knew, legally bound to Haven until they pulled the plug on his option. But why, in God's name, would they want him around?

Today had told him. Deeds. His teammates. Everyone. He was a broken mediocrity. But he was a mediocrity with a contract. And now, he was being backed into a corner. He didn't like being in a corner. He didn't like being told no. He didn't like being told you can't, you're not good enough, you're not this enough or that enough, even if he wasn't. Perhaps now a contract had finally worked in his favor, forcing him to stay in the pocket and do what had to be done for one more season, one more ride, one more trip down the tarmac. Maybe this was a blessing, his chance to give it one more shot, and perhaps shove it up Deeds's ass along the way.

And maybe it was all egotistical bullshit.

Will sighed, almost painfully. He thought about the season ahead. The interminable rides along the roads of France and Italy and Belgium, through rain and cold and snow and angry fans and down an endless road toward a finish line already being torn down by the time he got there.

He surveyed his body. The feelings and the future. He savored the fact that, at least at this point of the season, his knees didn't scream and his hands didn't ache and his lungs didn't struggle. Perhaps, he thought. Just one more time. Just to show them, and perhaps himself, something. That was his ego talking. But his ego had gotten him this far. Maybe he could listen just one more time.

Just one more ride.

He looked Deeds square in the face.

"I'm in," was all he said before standing, turning and walking out of the room without a glance back. Deeds didn't say anything to anybody for a very long time.

❖

NOW, THE SAME TEAM ASSISTANT WHO HAD BEEN BEHIND THE LAUREL AND Hardy luggage routine earlier, was helping him gather gear and move it out to a team car for the ride to one of the team apartments scattered between Senlis and Paris. Tomas rolled the Colnago out to the curb and strapped it onto the roof of the white Peugeot. He turned to Will as Will carried out the last nylon gear back and launched it into the trunk.

"We've been friends for a long time, right?" Tomas looked uncomfortable.

"Sure," Will replied. Now what?

"Remember something, okay? I am just a messenger."

Tomas dug into his pocket and pulled out a scrap of white paper. He shoved it over to Will as if he was attacking him with a knife.

Now, Will was worried. He took the scrap and opened it carefully. The unease of Tomas had transferred to him. He read the note.

"See me. Tomorrow. Deeds's office. — Kim."

Amazing. It had been a knife. And it struck him in the heart.

CHAPTER FOUR:

RIDING THE WALL

The apartment wasn't the worst thing Will had ever lived in. An apartment in Milwaukee had been the worst. But this one certainly was close. It was a forgotten street in an ancient industrial neighborhood north of Paris, west of Aéroport Charles de Gaulle, 20 kilometers south of Senlis, a second-floor efficiency with bed, tub, toilet, hot plate, table, chair and phone all in the same room. Well, at least the toilet wasn't a hole in an upstairs corner of the hall. Will had seen those in Parisian apartment houses and hated to think where they might lead. At least here he had a little thinking room and a little privacy. And, better yet, with the showers at the velodrome, there was no need to shower while balanced over the hole on a rickety wooden frame that could give at any time. Was this, Will thought, where kids originally got the fear of going down the drain with the bath water? In these, they really could. So could skinny, clumsy adults.

He usually didn't sleep well in a new house or a new bed, but he was dead to the world within an hour of moving in. He had stepped out for a quick pasta dinner, then crashed heavily on the paper-thin mattress. Out.

As he slept, a rush of faces roared through his dreams, Deeds and Cheryl, Bourgoin and Cacciavillani, but mainly Kim and her friends, the mysterious men who paid so much attention to her and elbowed him out of the way at parties and whose suits he found in the closet after he got bumped from GelSchweiz just before the Tour of Lombardy and arrived home four days early. *Quelle surprise! Quelle horreur!* The proverbial straw.

He woke at six, disciplined to the hour, unless, of course, he had been straining fermented grain beverages through his nose the night before. He hadn't, so the biological alarm clock struck the hour perfectly.

A quick bath and a one-man rubdown with alcohol, followed by a quick breakfast of noodles and eggs he whipped together on the hot plate, and into his gear. Today, he thought, he would be first on the line.

He slung the duffel over his back and the bike over his shoulder and carried both out to the street below. This was going to be a good workout in itself, he thought: a long hall, three tight turns and two flights of stairs, morning and night, with 75 extra pounds on his back and shoulder. How did fat people do it? God, he thought, it must just kill their knees.

It was only about 20 kilometers to the decaying velodrome in Senlis. He could kick that out in no time and arrive with a bit of a stretch and warm-up already under his belt.

As he rode through the morning traffic north of the city, Will's mind began to wander back to his dream of the night before, and back again across the miles and the years to a day in Toulouse when he had seen an American student in the criterium crowd and felt his heart split right there and then. What was it, "The Godfather," where they said, "He's been struck by the thunderbolt?" Yeah, Michael Corleone, struck by the thunderbolt. That's what had happened when he first saw Kim Grady standing in the crowd, strawberry-blonde hair lit up by the sun. He had won that race, damned near killing himself to do it. But he had to. He had to win. He had to show off on the podium. He had to finish before she got bored and decided to wander off to another café.

She hadn't left.

In fact, she had seen how he looked at her on each lap. So she worked her way up to the podium, watched him receive a bouquet of slightly withered roses, 500 francs and a bottle of red table wine, then stood in a strategic position so that as he scanned the crowd for her, those around her parted like the curtains of opening night and there she was, alone, available and absolutely stunning.

She told him all this later at the café where he bought her dinner with his prize money. She told him, quite confidently, that it had never been his choice to win her. It had been her choice for him to win her. She had seen him in the race, willed him to look at her and pointed him toward his destiny.

"What — the destiny of spending my money on your dinner?"

"Exactly," she replied.

This was great, he had thought: a real smartass who likes me. Life is sweet, isn't it?

His first real impression, on the podium, was almost as if this had been a gift from God, for the crowd had parted and he felt like Moses looking at

Israel for the first time. Oh, yeah. Milk and honey.

How did it ever turn so sour?

Will turned the corner, and the training center loomed before him. Vans had pulled up earlier with the leading riders. Bourgoin. Merkel. Even Cacciavillani got a ride in. It meant nothing that he had ridden in, but somehow, he felt better for it.

"Hi there, survivor."

Will pulled up to the curb next to Cheryl.

"Survivor?"

"I hear you pulled quite a Lazarus yesterday over the objections of Herr Deeds. Must have been something to see."

"Oh, it was, it was." He suddenly felt himself lost in her face, the shape, the tones, the smoothness of it. She frowned, and he shook himself away.

"Don't get any ideas, asshole."

"Whoa ... whoa ... I'm sorry. I was just unconscious for a second, but I'm back now. Brain lock. I suppose you get a whole ration of crap for just being who you are — what you are — a ..." he searched for a word that wouldn't make him sound like a complete doofus.

"Woman, I think is what you mean," she said, smiling at his discomfort. "Yeah, frankly, I do. I'm a professional. I know my job, and I do it very well. But, on the other hand, it's tough enough to be a woman in Europe without being a woman in what the Europeans still consider a man's business."

She looked around quickly, to see who might be listening in on what was partially an emotional catharsis, but also, given the situation she found herself in, a revelation of her own vulnerability. Why was she telling this guy, another leaker in the pack? Just because he was American? Cardinal was American and Cheryl knew she wouldn't tell him shit. This guy ... gads ... no more late nights. Lack of sleep was making her an emotional goon, ready to talk to anybody.

"The wives look at me like I'm some kind of pincushion, the men treat me like the first thing I'd like to do after a long day of chasing them ass over teakettle through France is to bop their ears off. I don't think so. I've worked too hard and too long to get here."

Will listened carefully to a speech he had heard in many forms, any number of times, even spoken himself, since he had begun racing in Europe as an amateur. Culture clash between the American ego and the European. Then again, next to nobody had ever wanted to bop his ears off.

"I understand," he said.

"Do you? You've been here? I don't think so."

As quickly as it had opened, the door closed in front of Will. She stared at him a long time in silence.

"When you ride today, don't try to stick with the head of the pack. They'll try to bust you just to watch you bust. Stay quiet in the middle until you get your sea legs back. Focus on staying right in the middle. If you fall back, you're dead, because the neo-pros will explode off the back and you'll go with them. Stay in the middle."

"I know. I used to be a pro, remember?"

"Just a reminder. You haven't been acting much like one."

"Thank you. I'll do better, I promise. For God, Haven and country."

"Screw you."

He paused and looked closely at her. There was a fire in her gray eyes that he hadn't noticed in all the banter.

"I'm sorry. Thanks for the advice."

"Don't mention it."

Will heard the door of the velodrome tower open behind him. That's all he heard. And yet, he shuddered involuntarily, feeling some kind of wall going up around him, a barricade against any hurt from the outside. As if it could. Kim Grady Ross stepped in front of Will and immediately breached the wall. She knew the words. She knew the looks. She knew not only where the holes in the armor were, but how rusted they had become.

"Good morning, Will. And you must be ... Sharon?"

"Cheryl," the soigneur replied stiffly.

Will was impressed. What — five seconds? — and already Kim had pissed her off, gotten inside the defenses and set off a small grenade.

Kim ignored Cheryl and turned her attention back to Will.

"You've missed the meeting. Deeds is upset again. But don't you fret, Will. You're safe. Just get back into shape as soon as you can. Will you? The team needs you and that ability of yours to simply destroy yourself for the team leader."

"Well, gee," he said sarcastically, "kinder words ain't never been spoken to me. I don't mean to be rude, Kim, but ... why should you care? There's no alimony. There's no support. There's no tie between us. Why should you care about how I do?"

"Don't flatter yourself, Willie. I care. But I don't care for you. I care for the team. You see, they're mine. So, what you do impacts on how much I make, and how much I make impacts on how you spend the rest of your life: comfortably, in this business in some way shape or form, or out on your ass as a bike bum. You always said that everybody turns into the kind of person they hate most. You're on the cusp, now, Will. You could very easily be that bum if you piss me off too much. Don't screw it up."

She had reached forward during her monologue and was holding his chin in her fingers. Will froze as he felt the fingers tighten, then almost snap away, turning his head to the side.

"Ride hard today, Will. The team — and your employer — fully expect you to."

Kim turned on her heels and walked off. The scent of her Lagerfeld hung in the air. Cheryl watched her walk to a silver Mercedes, slide into the back seat, and roar off in a cloud of diesel and suburban street grime.

"Jesus. What a bitch. Friend of yours?"

"Sort of. Ex-wife. It's the kind of thing that drives men to drink."

"She's not all that beautiful."

"I'm not talking about her looks."

"Ahhh."

"I lived with that attitude for three years. It was like walking on bottles of nitroglycerin; you never knew when one would go or if that one would take up the whole warehouse."

"Sounds like fun."

"Oh, yeah. The only woman I ever met whose period lasted three weeks out of four every month."

"Gee. And not even bitter. Let's see, a keen marriage and now living in a Belgian dive ..."

"It's not a dive."

"... while working for a cycling team that puts you on the roster as an afterthought. Gosh, Ross," she said with heavy sarcasm, "some folks really know how to live. Given your sparkling repartee, I gather you didn't know that she owns a chunk of the team and runs it for Martin Bergalis?"

Will shook his head.

"I didn't think so," Cheryl said, "you don't often see such a great imitation of a basset hound hit by a car."

Will smiled, then laughed out loud. Maybe he and Cheryl had found a common enemy, and the rancor of these first meetings could be finally pushed aside for at least a friendly relationship. He could use a friend along with Tomas. There was still too much to say and be and simply get out of himself. He had reached a point where he needed someone to talk to other than Leo, the barfly in Avelgem who didn't understand a word of English unless he was smashed to the gills.

Will was about to say something to Cheryl when the slow whir of wheels and gears and chains and derailleurs rose up behind him. The team was rolling out on the morning training ride through the countryside north of Paris. They would block traffic, they would run down pedestrians, they would be a rolling barricade. In America, they would be shot, but here, they were Haven. And they ruled the road.

Cheryl looked at him.

"Stay in the middle. Get your legs."

He smiled. A thousand one-liners popped into his head, and he knew that if he said any one of them, she'd likely haul off and give him a shot right across the chops. He had spent his life in the world of one-liners, and suddenly he wanted nothing to do with that world anymore.

So he didn't. For the first time in his life, he didn't. He simply looked up at her and quietly said, "Thanks."

He pushed off the curb and joined the team, moving smoothly into the middle of the 20-man pack.

❁

THINGS WENT BETTER FOR HIM THAT DAY, AS WILL WAS BEGINNING TO FIND A rhythm, a focus on the bike. He kept pace, took his pulls at the front, quickly regained his feel for riding in a controlled pack, and was always ready to jump off the front when Deeds called him up for a breakaway and chase. It felt good. It wouldn't always, he knew that. There would be days on the bike when he wouldn't be able to sit down, mornings in his hermit-like apartment when it would take 15 minutes just to unlock his knees and arches to the point where he could stand and walk without crying out in pain or leaning on the door frame, days in the pack where he wouldn't be able to stay with anyone for any reason.

But today, today he felt good.

Today, he belonged on the bike.

GODOT WAS BORED.

He had filed his report on the Colgan "incident" weeks before, complete with forensics results on the site as well as notes from LaSarge on the wire and metal shard found in the exposed floor joists. LaSarge was good: "85 percent probability exists that the debris noted and found on site is part of an electrical detonator for an explosive, most likely *plastique.*"

The daily papers were slowly forgetting Colgan and the devastation. Reports on the continuing investigation were now deep inside the paper, lost in a forest of low-paying ads. They still said it was a gas explosion.

Gas explosion my ass.

And so Godot waited. He waited to hear from the Director of Homicide. He waited to hear from the lead investigator on the Colgan case. He waited to hear from the Chief Inspector of the Paris police and any of the assorted bureaucrats and politicians who sat in summary judgment above him.

I don't know, he thought. I don't care. I don't even want to catch the murderer right now. I simply want someone to admit that a murder has been committed. That would be a victory in and of itself.

His phone buzzed. Godot snatched at the receiver.

"Luc."

"Stephen. Any word? Have you heard anything?"

"Yes. But ...." The long pause sent a chill down Godot's spine. "They don't buy it. The Chief Inspector's secretary told me the Chief feels a 15 percent probability on the detonator is too great a chance to take — especially when it would mean smearing one of the great teams of France, sponsored by one of the great companies of France."

"A company whose board of directors includes himself," Godot added.

"Uhhh. Yes. Yes, it does."

"So ... I'm sunk?"

"Yes, Luc. I'm sorry. They're sticking to the gas line. It's simple. It's clean. And Colgan's family is already looking at a multi-million franc settlement from Gaz de France."

"It's so nice they waited. Are they suing to get his finger back, too? They were, after all, so close."

"There was no love lost, true. But the finger ... that is out of reach."

"Destroyed evidence?"

"No," LaSarge said quietly. "It's sitting on the desk of the Chief Inspector, encased in plastic. I think he intends to use it as a paperweight."

Without a word, Godot quietly hung up the receiver. He had been backed into a corner by the department. He didn't like being in a corner, concerning anything. He saw two ways out.

First, he called a reporter he had known from murder cases spanning the past two decades. Could we meet? I have something you might like to hear.

And second ... he'd just plain do it himself. Meet the suspects. Interview the suspects. Squeeze the suspects. Without authorization.

And he'd start with the man who replaced Colgan.

❂

AS JANUARY FLOWERED, WILL FOUND MORE GOOD DAYS, A REAL BURST OF ENERGY and enthusiasm as the team began to form into a cohesive unit, reacting, almost without thinking, to the needs of Bourgoin and the other team leaders. Will worked his legs hard, then worked his upper body in his dingy apartment, with weights and push-ups, remembering Stewart Kenally's nostrum that energy flowed from the whole man, not simply from the legs, but from the arms and the chest and the waist and the heart and the mind and the soul.

And there were days when it was there.

But then came the reminder, that moment that Will had faced so many years before, when he knew, knew, clear as crystal, that he would never be a champion. He could go and he could fly and he could make things happen, but he couldn't fly fast enough and far enough with enough consistency to make things happen when they needed to happen. The champions always could. And they could make it look easy. They might have their off days and their slumps, but it was like comparing minor-league baseball to the bigs. There was an invisible wall that, until you confronted it and passed through, kept you in your place, in the second or third or fourth tier of the peloton.

Domestique.

The word was banging in his head on the days when the energy just wouldn't come, when the power needed to turn the cranks at pace had taken a quick vacation at the shore or had simply failed to get up that morning.

He made the rides. He never gave up. But he would fall off the back of the pack half to three-quarters of the way through the training session. Sometimes, it was slowly, as if quietly drifting away from a ship in a rolling sea. Other days, he would simply explode off the back: one moment in the midst of it all; the next, looking up to see the last car turn the corner half a kilometer in front of him.

There were days it almost worked better for him that way. Will would return to the training center 10 minutes to an hour behind the team, and by the time he was ready, Cheryl had worked through the team leaders and was ready to rub down any of the lesser lights who needed it. At 32, he needed it more than he would admit.

"What happened?" she'd ask, probing a rock-hard muscle in the middle of his back.

"I ... just ... fell ... off ... thhhhhhheaaaaaa the pace. It was there — and then it wasn't — and everybody was moving just too quickly for me to catch up."

"That's going to happen, but watch your focus. When you start to daydream in the pack is when you hit trouble."

"An expert on the pack now ... ooowwwww ... are we?"

"Yes, I'm sorry. I forgot. Only men ride bikes. Only men race bikes. Only men fly down a mountainside at 60 miles an hour with their ass in the air and

Jeannie Longo three inches off your back wheel. Yes, of course. I forgot."

"Sorry."

"Not good enough." She dug hard into his shoulders and hit a trigger deep inside the muscle. Will jumped and tears flooded his eyes. He buried his face into the opening on the headrest.

"Let me know when the pain starts releasing."

Through gasps, Will tried a joke, "Uh ... try to ... ugh ... morrow."

Great, he thought. Not only had he insulted her, but now he sounded like Beavis and Butthead.

"There," he said, "there, now it's releasing."

He felt the rush of blood back into the muscle and the freedom from that little point of pain and stiffness the trigger had produced. She might be mad at him, he thought, but, brother, does she know what she's doing. And with those hands, she could probably snap his neck like a twig. He chuckled. Better make nice.

"I apologize. I had no right to say any of that."

"Accepted. Sorry I took it out on you like that. But goddamn it, I worked my ass off in the saddle for nearly 10 years. Age 13 to 23. And all I get from you jer ... members of the elite ... is diminishment. Yeah. You diminish everything I do. And that's crap. In training, I can keep up with you most times, and there are a lot of guys on the team that — you know what? — I could beat. Yeah, me. And you are one of them."

She turned and walked out the massage-room door. Will watched her go. He was growing more fascinated by the moment. This, he thought, was a woman who knew who she was and knew where she had been and where she was going.

He wished he did.

She looked back in, no smiles, all business. Will was snapped back from his reverie to a cold table in a dilapidated training center on the north side of Paris late in a frosty January. He covered himself quickly with the tattered training towel.

"Like I said. Focus. You've shown you've got the legs. Use them."

❁

THAT NIGHT, ROSS DREAMED OF STEWART KENALLY AND THE TWO WHEELS bike shop of Romulus, Michigan.

Stewart hadn't been able to talk his father into buying a bike that first day, almost acted as if he didn't want to, but he had persuaded him to bring Will back the next week, early, so they could talk some more and Stewart could see if Will was really interested in riding, rather than just looking for something shiny to buy. To seal the deal, Stewart had sent home a number of French and Italian bicycling magazines.

Will hadn't the slightest idea what the magazines said, but somehow, he loved how they said it with pictures. Later, by stealing his sister's high-school French/English dictionary, he was able to pick out a word or two, and figure out what was going on, though for the life of him, he couldn't understand the something called Paris-Roubaix.

"Dad, look at this: they ride in the rain and mud and on bricks for 200 miles."

Harold Ross didn't even look up from *The Kalamazoo Gazette*. "Kilometers. In France, it's kilometers. About two-thirds of a mile. And they do it just because the French are like that."

Will had no idea what his father meant by that last remark, but Dad had been there during the war, the big one, WWII, so, he must know.

The drive back to Romulus, two and a half hours on a late summer Saturday morning, gave Stewart the answer he needed. Will's father had been worn down over the week, bit by bit, into making the trip and taking his checkbook, but deep inside he had a vague realization that he didn't have the slightest idea what he was getting into or what it was going to cost. When they reached the store, Kenally pulled Will's father aside, sending the boy out to look at bikes and gear. The two men were gone a long time, discussing, Will figured, him and bikes and racing and the dollar signs attached to them all.

"George — watch the shop for a bit, will you?" Stewart called from the office. "I've got some ridin' to do."

Kenally walked briskly out of his office and motioned for Will to follow him, back past the open office door where his father sat, somewhat white-faced, looking through a huge scrapbook of clippings and programs, back through the workshop and a sea of wooden boxes and drawers holding what looked to be all the bike parts in the world, back to a room where Stewart pulled out a tape measure and ran it along Will as if he was selling a suit.

He walked into a back room and walked out with a battered black bike, small, and a pair of black, woolly shorts.

"Here — put these on." With his Scottish burr, 'these' sounded like 'thuz.'

Will did as he was told. "What size shoe do you wear?"

"A six, sir."

"Never heard of a foot so small," he grumbled. And yet, the sounds of digging through the boxes of unrelated effluvia that had collected in the back of the shop over the years didn't stop for a very long time.

"Here. This is the best I can do. It's an 8, but we'll stuff the ends with newspaper for today."

"Are we going riding?" Will asked, the prospect at once thrilling and frightening.

"Not we. You. And not here — there." He pointed up at a photo on a wall. Will looked at what appeared to be a concrete loop, flanged at each end. Under the photo was a caption scrawled in white: "Winterset."

"We're gonna see what you got."

Within 15 minutes, they were at the Winterset track, stuck behind a warehouse in an untended field just north of the town. A few young men, obviously from the University of Michigan, were just leaving, so the concrete track was empty, which helped Will. He was nervous in new situations, and being able to make his mistakes in private would be a big help. Stewart set him up and rolled him onto the tar-over-concrete track. The shoes didn't fit, but the bike, he thought, was perfect, except for the fact that he couldn't coast. Every time he tried, the pedals kicked his knees back up into his chest.

"It's a fixed gear," Stewart yelled, as Will rolled past him, obviously fighting the pedals all the way. "They just keep going — no coasting. And don't try to back-pedal to brake!"

Will had already tried that, and found that the pedals simply wouldn't let him. Yeah, wait a minute. Where were the brakes? There were no hand brakes, no foot brakes, no way of any kind to stop this thing once you got started. All you could do was pedal, faster, or slower, and simply roll to a stop. Or crash.

There was always that option.

Will rolled around the bowl-shaped track on a red line a few times, slowly getting his bearings on the bike, realizing that with one gear and no brakes, there was really only one way to go: forward, the faster the better. Then Stewart shouted, "Ride up the wall!"

There was no way to ride up the wall. The law of gravity said you simply couldn't do it. But, each time around the bowl, Will rode a little farther, a bit more, a little higher up the 33-degree angle of the track. It was frightening, it was exhilarating, it was — my gosh, it was high. And then at the top of the bowl, he fell out of turn two and swooped down the back straight, pedaling furiously like a man, a boy, possessed. There was no stopping, there was no slowing, there was no way to control himself or the bike other than to simply look straight ahead and lean, the natural curve of the track taking him smoothly around the corner in a thrilling rush.

The wind roared in his ears and brought tears to his eyes. He tried to catch his breath. He wanted to stop his legs, but simply couldn't — because of the bike, and because of himself.

This ... this was ... this was fun.

Every now and then he tried to coast and was brought up short, the fixed gear quickly reminding him by jamming his knees up to his head and jumping the back wheel up off the track. He slowed his pedaling and found the bike slowing with him, enough, so that, as he came around turn four and back onto the main straightaway, he could roll up to the wooden railing that surrounded the track and, by running his hand along it, slowly bring himself to a stop.

Will looked over the railing, past the dilapidated grandstand, to the parking lot, where his father was just pulling up in the family car. He turned back to the infield and pedaled back to the starting line, where he noticed another boy rolling back and forth on a bike next to Mr. Kenally. Stewart introduced him as Raymond, another racer, making Will think, what, me, a racer? Cool. But Raymond didn't say a word. He just stared at Will, a look that froze his insides and suddenly made him wish he was anywhere else, even at the Ford shop, anywhere else but here.

"Raymond will ride with you a bit," Stewart said. "Why don't you roll out?"

Will slowly began to pedal away, with no idea what to expect or how to expect it. His first indication, the first thing that annoyed him, was Raymond hugging his back wheel like he was stuck there. Will didn't like the feeling of this guy running up his back, so he rode a little faster, but Raymond held on, never losing his concentration, glued to his Will's wheel. Twice around the track, and Will couldn't break Raymond's hold, so, running into turn one, he broke high on the wall, then shot back down and found himself about four feet behind Raymond. Raymond was starting to add coal now and Will, alternately angry and ecstatic, kicked up his efforts, pulling onto Raymond's wheel. He can do it, I can do it, thought Will, sitting maybe four inches right behind him, exactly as Raymond had been doing to him, and realizing that it was suddenly easier. He was riding faster than he had ever ridden before, but he wasn't putting out half the effort he had been earlier.

As they passed the line again, Stewart screamed, "Pick it up!" and Will felt a surge from Raymond. Without warning, the stream that had held him behind Raymond broke, and Will found himself falling two, four, six feet back. He didn't like this guy, and he wasn't going to lose to him. Will surged once more and pulled up again to Raymond's back wheel, but too quickly; he tried to turn away, tried to brake, tried to back-pedal, but he had pushed too hard to make up the gap, and their wheels touched.

That was all it took. Will felt himself thrown forward over the handlebars, and the front wheel of the bike shoot back and forth, out of control. And then, he simply started to go over, head over heels, nothing to be done as the hard black surface reached up to meet his shoulder and his head and his face and his knees and whatever else it could find of him and the bike. His shoulder hit first, and he felt an explosion in his neck, and then, it was not feeling so much as simply sound, the sound of a phonograph needle being shoved back and forth, back and forth, over an old Bobby Darin record. And then he was up.

He had almost completely rolled out of the fall and was still holding onto the handlebars of his bike, staring blankly down the short straight into turn two. Raymond, he saw, was just pedaling slowly into turn three.

Harold Ross had just reached the wooden railing when he saw his son crash. He was already up and almost over the railing when he saw Will stagger to his feet. He looked to his left, to see Raymond making it through turn three, smiling in triumph.

Against everything in him as a father, everything that told him to run to his son, he stayed in place, half on, half off the rail. He looked at Will and muttered under his breath, "Get up ... get up .... get up...."

Stewart Kenally hadn't moved. He saw the accident, saw the roll, saw Will come up with the bike in his hands and blood in his hair. This was not the time to say anything. This was the time to see everything.

Will was already beginning to push the bike forward and run beside it, a hop, and he threw his leg up and over the seat, wobbling into the turn as he tried to fit his feet into the clips holding his shoes. By luck or miracle, his right foot dropped perfectly into the clip and he felt the cleat on the bottom of his shoe slide onto its runner. He couldn't seem to get the left shoe engaged, so he just ignored it. There was no time, he was falling farther behind.

Will felt his blood rise along with a deeply seated anger he had never experienced. He threw himself down on the pedals and slammed the bike back and forth, trying to gain speed, while Raymond continued to pedal smoothly on the other side of the track. Will kicked again, this time with his focus on how hard and fast he could push and pull the pedals, push and pull, without throwing the bike as much, and he was gaining going into turn three, sliding through without a pause on the turn.

Raymond continued his leisurely roll. There was simply too much distance to be made up, and, this wasn't racing, anyway. Stewart had just asked him to come out and blow off another wanna-be. Done and done. Raymond sat up on his bike and leaned back, hands off the handlebars, to stretch. He glanced ahead, through turns two and three and four to see where "Crash Boy" might be, but he was nowhere to be seen. Hmph. Raymond thought, his daddy must have pulled him off the track. And then, Raymond glanced over his shoulder. There, behind him, was the wanna-be, with blood streaming down his face, and a fierce look in his eye.

Will charged up behind Raymond. He hadn't been looking, Will thought, he hadn't been thinking! Well, here I am! Here I am, pal! There was no room below Raymond, and Will knew he'd have to go above him on the track, onto the wall, before his front wheel came up on Raymond's right, before Raymond had a chance to see him and really react.

But surprise was out of the question, Raymond had seen him and with a panicked intensity, flailed his bike back and forth to regain the speed he had let wither away after the crash. Will pushed again and started to draw alongside, both boys in a frantic rush to the line. But not this time, Will thought, not this time, as he began to scream, almost a howl, as everything he felt in him, all the anger and frustration and fear that had ridden with him on those first laps, the pain in his shoulder, the embarrassment of falling flat on his face — on a bike! on a bike! — came pouring out in a torrent of rage as the line shot by.

And, suddenly, it began to fade.

Crossing the line had been like opening a safety valve; Will had felt the power and speed and pure emotion slip away quickly and quietly. He tried to stop it, to bask in that rush of pure energy and strength, but it was no good. With every labored breath, with every heave of his chest, every turn of the pedals, Will felt it all slip away, as he became the same kid who had stepped onto the track, what, 30 minutes before? Only 30 minutes?

By the next turn onto the back straight, what had seemed a race for life or death was now little more than just a comfortable country jaunt with Raymond. The two rode silently, only passing their labored breathing between them. Finally, Raymond looked over as the pair rode side by side and spoke the first words Will had ever heard him say: "Nice ride."

The two rode two more laps comfortably, to cool down, then rolled to a stop in front of Stewart.

"Well, Raymond, what do you think of him?"

Raymond merely smiled.

Stewart smiled as well. "You're right. He'll do."

Stewart probed through Will's hair and examined the cut on his scalp. "You'll be needin' a stitch and a hairnet," he said, "We've got to try to keep in what's left of your brains — you'll be needin' 'em." He then looked up over the apron of the track. Will followed his eyes and saw his father sitting on the rail, his face bright red.

Then Stewart smiled once more and spoke, this time to Will's father. "I hate to tell you this, Mr. Ross, but you'd best prepare yourself for a life of this — I do believe we've got a rider on our hands."

❀

WILL'S EYES SNAPPED OPEN. HE HATED WHEN HE WOKE UP LIKE THIS, SUDDENly and without a chance in hell of getting back to sleep. Usually, it only happened when he was really stressed, maybe the night before the start of a race. But this, he didn't know why, maybe it just happened. The squads would be posted tomorrow for the first of the early-season training races, the Étoile de Bessèges and the Ruta del Sol and the Tour Mediterranéen. Those would take 21 riders with one in deep reserve and one on the back burner to continue his training. Will figured that had to be him, so why worry?

He rolled over and looked at the clock his grandmother had given him 25 years before. It had certainly taken a lickin' and kept on tickin'. Five-thirty. He sat up on the edge of the bed and rubbed his face, stood and walked to the window, looking out over the first gray streaks of a late-January morning in France.

Whatever happened to that boy at Winterset? he wondered. What happened to that boy who raced with his heart and head as well as his legs?

He rubbed his eyes again. He didn't know. And yet, for the first time in four years, he suddenly began to care about the answer.

CHAPTER FIVE:

PIECE O' MY HEART

Truly bad days rarely begin that way, Will thought. They don't begin as an average day, either. They begin with a heightened sense of awareness, easily mistaken for a biorhythm high, as your emotional phase senses what is just around the bend in the road, the turn of the clock, and sets you a notch higher to deal with the day ahead.

Will used the extra half-hour that morning to stretch luxuriously, and to take a little more time in his morning preps; bath, rubdown, breakfast, dressing. He looked at himself in the mottled mirror over the kitchen sink. If he angled it just right, he could see himself down to his knees, ratty and browned, but that was him all right, down to the knees. Maybe it wasn't the mirror, he thought. Maybe it was the fact that at 32, he was turning mottled and brown. He turned to the side and glanced at his profile. The Ross belly, that tendency toward weight that his father and brother so enjoyed and that he had seen for the first time in his six months of retirement, was virtually gone now, the weeks on the bike doing their job, no matter how many calories he took in during the day. Even after his next retirement, he would keep riding, he promised. No more Mr. Nice Gut. You can't ride against razor-slim 22-year-olds and expect to keep up with an extra 20 pounds in your fanny pack.

He rode over to the velodrome through the blustery morning, with the wind sounding like the blast of the TGV train roaring past in the northern French countryside. It proved to be a workout getting to the front door in Senlis, the gale pushing him two strokes back for every three he took on the big ring. A workout was fine, though. This was a rest day, officially, a day for team meetings and regrouping, letting the muscles rest and tuning up the bikes, stretching a bit and eating a leisurely, long-winded meal.

Will thought he might also get in a workout in the small, poorly stocked weight room, hone his triceps and forearms, maybe some heavy duty with his thighs. He might even go a few rounds with the heavy bag to work out a few aggressions. For some reason, he always saw Deeds's face on the bag. He used to see Kim's, but as the bitterness faded, so did the image just below the Everlast logo. Now it was Deeds, and it was satisfying. Maybe, if there were time, he thought, he'd see if Cheryl could work his lower back. It wasn't giving him real trouble, but it would give them the time to talk.

He rolled his battered team Colnago to the mechanics' work room. Tomas was nowhere to be seen. He put it in the work frame and spun the front wheel. He'd just mention it to Tomas and see what could be done to keep "The Beast" on the road and in the pack. This was his 24th "Beast." Maybe he'd just stay in the game until he hit 25 and then he'd hang it up, making a living out of selling photo montages of his 25 racing bikes. That — now that — would be a big seller.

He turned into the hall and walked a little faster. The wind had slowed him down to the point where he would be walking into the room just as the clock hit 8 a.m. and Deeds started the meeting. No matter how he tried, it seemed, punctuality was not his strong suit. He broke into a little jog-trot, came to the door, grabbed the doorjamb and whipped himself around the corner into the room. Fifty or 60 eyes were on him. Well, maybe 59, since that one team assistant had one Will didn't think was real.

"I'm not late. Even your clock says I'm right on time."

Deeds looked up at the clock over the blackboard. "I must have started early. Take a seat."

As Will walked to an open spot on the couch, right beside Tony C and Ricardo Paluzzo, the Italian neo-pro, he realized that everyone continued to watch him. Some, it seemed, in amazement, others in horror, one or two, in a painfully unconcealed anger.

No doubt about it. In his inimitable way, Will had missed something. Something big.

He looked for the first time at the blackboard and noticed three rows of names — the team layout for the first three races of the season, all within the next two weeks. The first, Étoile de Bessèges, was only three days down the road. A seven-man squad would be leaving to stage for the race tomorrow. Will's eyes ran down the list. Just as he had expected, his name was nowhere to be found. Nor was it on the second list, for the Tour Mediterranéen, a five-day stage race the next week. They were interesting races, to be sure, but too early in the season to cause much of a stir among any but the most fanatical tifosi.

And then, there was that third list, the one for Spain's Ruta del Sol, a five-day, early-season run in Spain. This, because of the weather and competition, was where the big boys would really go to play: Bourgoin, Cacciavillani, Merkel, maybe Cardinal, the names and faces that would form the centerpiece of the team come the classics, the late-spring stage races, and then the big guns, the Vuelta, the Giro, the Tour.

It was what he expected, as his eye ran down the list: Richard, Tony C, Hans, John, Miguel Cardone, a Basque domestique of proven power and temper, and, at the bottom of the list, one word: Ross. Will felt the air sucked out of him as if by a five-horse shop vac'. No wonder the looks! His teammates were either in a state of shock or out of their minds with anger. Here was a newcomer to the team, and not much of one, bumping the rest of them, even if only in their own minds, from the last slot on the A-team, from a ride in sunny Spain in February with the big boys and the first of the international media attention.

Will raised his hand.

"I think we've got a bit of a mistake, there, chief."

Deeds looked at the board and looked at Will with undisguised disappointment. "No mistake. You're up and you're on."

"But I'm not ready."

"You're never ready for the start of the season. Nobody is."

Paluzzo spoke up from the back. "I am."

"Nope. The Ruta ride is Ross's. That's the way it is, that's the way it will be. Any problems, you come to me after the meeting and I'll tell you exactly the same thing."

Cardinal spoke up. "My ex-wife would never do that for me."

The room rippled with laughter. Cardinal waited for the pause and continued, "Then again, I guess I just don't have the right ex-wife."

Will turned red as the room quietly grumbled its agreement.

Deeds spoke up. "This wasn't her choice. This was my choice. This was the way I wanted to play it for training and team development. I don't want just one or two leaders and the rest as drones. You all have a job to be the best in the pack and to lead the way when necessary. That's what you're going to do, and the squad breakdown gives you that chance. It was my idea."

Someone in the back quietly sang "... with a little help from my friends."

THE REST OF THE MEETING DID NOT GO WELL AND WILL WAS HAPPY TO LEAVE it behind, getting a break in mid-morning before individual race squad meetings after lunch. He needed a break. He needed a friend. Tomas was busy spinning out the wheels of Bourgoin's time-trial bike; he didn't have time. Besides, the other mechanics were friends with other riders in the pack, and weren't at all happy about Will's impossible addition to the A squad.

But Cheryl was available. She had just finished a morning run for Bourgoin and Merkel, gathering the special foods and ointments they needed during the race season. The team supplied a lot, but superstition and tradition told both the riders which things they needed, personally, to make sure the machine was always ready to go.

"Got a minute?"

"Sure, what do you need?"

"I've got a knot the size of Cleveland right beside my spine, upper back. Could you hit it for me?"

"Sure, lie down."

He stretched out on the table that smelled of years of sweat, ointment and liniment. This table had been around the track a couple of times.

"Is it ... let's see .... that one? Right there?"

Holy smoke, she was good. Her thumb drilled into the knot and hit the trigger dead on, first time. It snapped Will's head down into the headrest.

"Awwwwwwuuuuuggggghhhhh." He sounded like Homer Simpson drooling over a doughnut.

"No, no. I think the Mets will do fine if they catch some pitching along the way," Cheryl replied sarcastically, giving the trigger another thumbnail shove.

Will squeaked, he honest to God squeaked, then burst into rolling laughter. Cheryl did the same.

"I have taken control of your spinal column. I control the vertical. I control the horizontal ..." another poke, another spasm "... you will do as Simon says."

She sat next to the table, smiling. Will was still laughing and breathing hard, panting, as if this had been the next best thing to energetic sex.

"Thanks, I needed that."

"Don't mention it. A bit concerned?"

"About what?"

"Well, given the way you came in here right after the team meeting, I'd say it was the team meeting. And given that you were chosen for the A-squad, to back up Bourgoin, Merkel and Tony C, I'd say it was flop sweat. And, given that you aren't universally adored in Haven's little corner of heaven, I'd say that you're a bit strung out because you don't have a whole lot of allies. How close am I?

"Ten outta ten. The amazing Kreskin."

"I'm taking my act on the road." Silence. She knew he was concerned, and deeply so, and rightfully so, but she wasn't sure what she could say that would break the fear that had eaten into a corner of his soul.

"Look. You think you're not ready. Maybe not. But then again, maybe so. You've been in the middle of every practice. You've ridden hard. You've worked out. You've been in the thick of it all ever since you got here. Pretty much, anyway. No one expected you to be chosen. Now you are. And you should just make the best of it. If it works, great. If it doesn't, then the team will know soon enough before too much damage is done. That's what the early season is for, anyway. You're not riding the Tour de France, for God's sake."

"Problem is, I've always looked at every race as if it were the Tour. Every time I climb on the bike, it's a life-or-death situation. Every time I ride through a corner I'm thinking, 'Break away, leave 'em behind, win this thing...."

"But ..." she asked.

"But I haven't got the heart for it. I've been sliding so long in this business that I don't know how to pull myself out of the skid any more. "

"You'd better find a way."

He stared at the floor. Yes. He had better find a way. And he had about a week to do it.

"What a charming domestic scene, Will. You must play it for me, sometime."

Both Cheryl and Will turned quickly. The woman at the door changed the warm atmosphere in the room completely and suddenly.

"Hello, Kim."

"Sorry to intrude, Sharon...."

"Cheryl."

"... but I need to talk to my ex-husband and current employee for just a minute. Alone. I won't be long, Sharon."

"Cheryl."

"And then you can get right back to having your pants charmed off, all right?"

Kim took Cheryl by the elbow and walked her to the door, maneuvered her outside, and shut it behind her. On the other side, Cheryl produced the international monodigital symbol for rank disagreement.

"For heaven's sake, Will. What do you see in that?"

"I see a friend, Kim. What do you want?"

Just want to make sure you're happy with the Spanish vacation I've planned for you."

"You've planned? Deeds said it was his idea."

"Male ego, I suppose. Mr. Deeds is in an uncomfortable situation." She opened a solid-gold case and extracted a long, black cigarette, lit it, despite the hundreds of "*défense de fumer*" signs throughout the training center, inhaled deeply and blew the smoke directly at Will, who, though he had lived in Europe for years and dealt with smoke regularly, felt suddenly sick. "He's got to preserve what he can of his reputation with my team."

Will rolled onto his back and stared at the ceiling, as much to take him out of the line of smoke as anything else.

"Kim, just how in the name of Fast Eddy did you wind up with this team? I mean — you hate riders. You hate the egos, you hate the smell, you hate race day, you hate...."

"The grease."

"All right, the grease. The travel. The Tour. Roubaix. The classics. You hate everything about this sport except the media and the parties. I'm sorry, but what the hell are you doing running a team?"

"Bringing a sense of business to the sport. American business and marketing savvy. Haven liked what I had to offer," she said, pausing for a second and smiling, "and they're making the most of it."

Will turned his head to look at her. "And screwing your way to the top doesn't hurt, does it?"

"Oooh, that's a cheap shot, even for you, Will. You didn't used to be so bitter."

There. There it was. The opening shot in her argument. If he had nailed her on a point, she'd always try to throw him off by making him wonder if he was fighting "unfairly," if he was being "defensive." He'd get so muddled in wandering through his head to recheck his arguments that by the time he emerged the argument would be long gone and his ego would be in a heap in a corner next to the cat's bed. Was he still affected? He sat up, swung his legs over the side of the massage table, and looked first at the floor, then at her. Time for a shot across the bow.

"Not bitter. Hard realities. Look, I don't care what it took for you to get where you are, Kim. Everybody does it in some way or another. But don't try to tell it me it's the love of the game, okay? I don't particularly appreciate what you did for me on the team roster. I should be with the C-squad getting in a backwater race, or here getting more miles under my belt. I don't belong with Bourgoin and the big boys at the Ruta."

"Such modesty," she said sarcastically, "and after all the nice things I've told Martin about you."

This was the first time she had mentioned him. What did Bergalis, the head of Haven Pharmaceuticals, care about him, except in a passing, oh, you must be one of my nameless, faceless, employees kind of thing?

"And how is the boss?"

She suddenly realized that she had given Will an opening that she didn't want opened. She quickly backpedaled, a bit nonplused, but still, quite clearly, in charge.

"He's fine, pleased with your progress, and sure you'll do your best for Haven at the Ruta. He had to sign off on my team roster and liked the breakdown. It's like Little League, Will. Everybody gets a chance to play. The second level of the team gets to win something. The A team gets to work together. The neo-pros get to win for good ol' Haven. You see, despite what you might think of my accomplishments, I have a solid idea of how this sport and this business and, yes, how you work. I am in charge of the most powerful cycling team in the world since, what, '86? La Vie Claire? Now, about that little comedy you're playing with Sharon...."

"Cheryl."

"I like 'Sharon' better. It gets a better reaction. Whatever. It seems to be softening your brain. Maybe we should set her free so you can concentrate on the business at hand."

"What?"

"You heard me. Maybe I should fire her."

"Fire her and I'm gone."

"Ahh. What about your contract."

"Fire Cheryl and I am out of here on the next train."

"You're out of here on the next train and in the next mail you've got a lawsuit on your hands for illegally breaking your contract. I'll own your life," her voice started to rise, "everything in that little place in Avelgem on that shady street between the warehouse...and is that a whorehouse right next door?"

"So, own it," he said, quietly, holding his shock at how much she knew about his life after their split. "The plumbing's bad and the wiring's a firetrap. Bottom line is," he stood up and looked at her hard, "she's gone — so am I. Take whatever you want. Take it all. There's not much. Here, I'll even call your buddy Bergalis right now and tell him the same thing."

"My, my. I didn't realize it was such a big deal to you. Or that she was such a big deal to you."

"She isn't a big deal to me, Kim. The fact that she's not a part of yours and my equation, whatever that is now, means it just isn't fair to kick her off the team because she talks to me. Okay, so you run the most powerful team since La Vie Claire. Well, she's a part of your most powerful team since La Vie Claire. Keep her because she's good. You need her more than you think. Keep that in mind."

"And you should keep something in mind as well," Kim said, picking up her fur coat, her voice coolly venomous. "Your ass is mine. All right? If you try, even try, to make a move I don't like, on the team or off this team, I'll squash you so flat that it will take the street sweepers weeks just to get your eyebrows off the pavement. You are on this team, whether you like it or not. And you will ride for this team, whether you like it or not."

She smiled. Will felt a chill run down his spine. This was not a friendly spirit.

"And you will do what I say, whether you like it or not."

She draped the flawless red-fox coat over her shoulder and turned to the door. "See you in Spain next week, Will."

He shuddered at the thought. He had worked for some real jerks in his life, some painfully bad managers, but this was going to be new. Even for him.

Just before she was out of the room, he said it. He didn't know why. It was just there. Like his subconscious knew what to do, even if he didn't.

"Say 'hi' to Marty for me."

It wasn't a big reaction; more of a pause, a break in her movement, that he noticed, as if her natural rhythm had been displaced for just a fraction of a second. She never looked back, just stepping into the hall and striding away, hard, perhaps more than just a bit angry.

It was silent in the training room as her steps disappeared down the hall. Will leaned against the training table and noticed that he had been shaking, his stomach in a knot, from the argument, from the threats, from the stink of her cigarette and perfume in the air. She always wore too much damned perfume. It got so that it smelled like bug spray.

All the elements were combining to making him sick. The smell, the smoke, the stress. Time to get out of here. His gorge rising, he strode out of the room and down the hall, feeling sweat break out in a prickling sensation along the top of his skin. He had to run now, he might not make it to the front door. As he flew past Deeds, Carl put out a hand to grab him, yelling, "Who the hell was smoking in...." Will broke his grip and rolled, almost drunkenly, toward the door. It was one of those old wood-and-glass fire doors from the 1940s and '50s, maybe if he missed the bar he could shove his hand through a glass pane and be done with this season and these people once and for all. Why did such a great sport have to have such a bunch of knobs running it? At the last moment, he turned his back to the door and hit the fire bar with his butt, automatically, a reflex left over from junior high, rolling out on to the sidewalk, stumbling to the curb. He pushed his shoulder into a lamppost and retched. It wasn't a pretty sight. It wasn't a pretty sound. Smoke or stress or jerks on their own, he could take. But all at once, they cleaned him out. In a particularly ugly, noisy way.

"You see what I have to work with, Henri?"

Will looked up through red-rimmed, rheumy eyes. Kim stood just feet away from him, at the door of her Mercedes. The tail pipe of the car burbled with diesel exhaust, which made Will feel sick again. With her stood a tall, bookish, somewhat intense young man.

"That's littering, Will. The team won't pay your fine."

She pulled her coat up around her throat and stepped into the car. The young man watched, with sympathy, as Will pulled himself erect on the lamppost.

"I hate smoke, too," was all he said, in halting English, before he turned and climbed into the car, closing the silvered door behind him. The engine revved twice, shooting a small black cloud of exhaust toward Will, then pulled away from the curb and disappeared into the late-morning traffic of Senlis.

Will leaned against the post, exhausted, clammy and, at least from the inside, he felt, white as a ghost. He breathed hard, trying to steady his stomach and his mind.

"Great," he said, to no one in particular, "just fucking great."

❁

AT THE AFTERNOON MEETINGS, DEEDS WATCHED HIM SUSPICIOUSLY, BUT NEVER mentioned the morning, the smoke or the argument with Kim. People had heard something, and Will wondered how much they heard, but everyone, it seemed, was too careful to bring it up. Only Tony C mentioned anything at all.

"Never ... eh ... vomit ... in front of a woman, my friend," he told Will, "especially after you win a fight. It makes them think that they won, and then they're impossible to live with." He smiled and patted Will on the shoulder.

Strange. Out of a surprising and wretched morning had come the first glimmer of acceptance from the team. Even Deeds had acted a little more friendly toward him. Wait; let's not get carried away. Deeds had only pointed out where there was a seat down front. That's not friendly. That's organizational anal-retentive.

The C-squad would leave that afternoon, Deeds announced, for the Étoile de Besèges. "B" would leave Friday for the Tour Mediterranéen. "A," including Will, would leave Saturday for Spain to work in the sun, finally, out of the cold and overcast of the Parisian winter. Why did they work here, anyway? Because Deeds is one of those guys who thinks it toughens you to suffer, Will thought.

"Gather your gear, gentlemen. Bourgoin, I want to talk to you before we leave tomorrow. I won't be joining you until next week. So, you'll be in charge of things. I'm sending Philippe down with you as your assistant manager. Feel free to run him into the ground."

Deeds smiled crookedly. Everyone in the room turned to Philippe, the round-faced, balding, rather weaselly character with whom Will had already had plenty of arguments. Philippe smiled weakly and shrank back into his rotund little shell. Obviously, Will thought, there was a lot less love lost between Deeds and the weasel than he had thought. Wonder what's up there. Plenty to ponder tonight. Over a beer, perhaps.

The meeting broke up about two and the squad split up to pack, train, talk or simply go their separate ways. There was time, Will thought, for a two-hour stretch ride, if he started now. It would help settle him out, he thought, after his morning, blow the stink off him and keep his legs in tune, at least closer to tune, over the travel days that stood ahead.

He walked to the mechanics' room and pulled his battered Colnago off a storage rack. He was no giant, and it had been put almost out of his reach.

"Hey, come on," Tomas shouted from the other side of the room. "I'm shorter than you are. It took me all morning and a stepladder to get that up there."

"I appreciate your efforts," Will said, bowing dramatically, "but I need a ride and a few hours in the air and a shower and a beer and a woman and a million bucks...."

"You dream good. But put that piece of shit away."

"Yes, it is a piece of shit, but it's my piece of shit."

"Ride your new one. I've got it measured and everything. Just give me your pedals and you're on your way."

"What?"

"It's Christmas, Will. When you ride with Bourgoin, you get the good stuff. New uniform, new bike, new headband, new shorts — even new socks. You still wear those things, don't you?

"Good luck. See? They work."

Will stepped over to the new Colnago, white, pristine, just out of the box. Oh, man, what a bike. Top-of-the-line Campagnolo gearing, Ergo' levers, the whole magilla. Man, oh, man. This, Will thought, was what techno-dweebs lived for in the States.

"Great bike. Do I hafta?"

"Do you hafta what?"

"Do I hafta take it? I mean, I like it, but I like this one, too. It's a lot like me. A little older, a little battered, a little outta style."

"It's got tube shifters. Next thing, you'll have toe clips and straps and cleats on your shoes like Kelly."

"A race ain't real to me unless I miss a lever and shove my hand into the spokes at least once. Nice bike. I'll keep this one."

"Deeds won't like it. He's big on image. Especially for Bourgoin's ladies-in-waiting."

"So keep it as my backup bike. I'll stick with the Beast, here. We understand each other."

"I hope you understand I'll be patching that thing together all season with glue and spit."

"That's why you're the miracle worker," Will said over his shoulder.

He rolled the Colnago into the hall, changed quickly in the locker room, and stepped outside. As he tightened the last strap on his shoe, Cheryl quietly walked up from behind. Her face was flushed, as if she had been out in the weather for a long time, walking, or running, hard.

"I hear you had quite a conversation with the Dragon Lady."

Will smiled. "Well, at least we agree on something. Yeah. I did."

He didn't go any farther with it. He left the conversation at that. They were both quiet for a long time, so long that Will's mind moved onto other things, like the sheer stupidity of riding alone on a day when a 23-kilometer-per-hour head wind would beat him up for the first hour of the ride, then mysteriously shift to face him again on the way back in. That's the way it always was. That's the way it always will be.

He swung his leg over the bike and snapped his right foot into the pedal. As he moved to push off, Cheryl spoke up.

"Thanks."

Will paused. He realized that anything he said at this point, any reaction at all, would simply be an embarrassment to her.

"Just thanks."

He looked at her for a moment, then pushed away from the curb.

"I just hate bullies," he said, and quickly moved into the flow of traffic, leaving Cheryl alone on the curb, the late-January wind blowing her hair in a thousand different directions.

✿

THE RIDE HAD BEEN GREAT, ONE OF THOSE GREAT CLEANSING WORKOUTS IN which he found himself with an angry energy to spare throughout the ride. It was an unfocused anger, spinning out at real and imagined slights from real and imagined enemies. But he also knew that it had all been sitting just below the surface, and if he didn't get it out on the road it would spill out at someone or something when he least expected it.

As he had predicted, the head wind had battered him on the outbound leg and then mysteriously turned to face him once more on the inbound. God. Everything in his life seemed to be like that lately — the wind always in his face. My, my. Let's feel sorry for ourselves now. The self-pity flushed out of him as the anger had before, all part of the emotional rush that made up his solitary rides. He had no idea where his mind would go when he started pedaling alone. It took him to euphoria and into hellish depression, back up into wild sexual fantasies and back down into arguments with whomever was giving him grief at the moment, wars fought over and over again in his imagination, until he had to force himself to turn away from them.

It was an odd way to ride: furrowed brow, mouth moving with insults and one-liners, and what he felt were reasoned arguments. And it had to frighten the casual observer who wondered how the mentally unstable got hold of such bikes and why they were allowed on the roads of France to frighten passers-by. But it always accomplished its magic, for by the time he arrived at his apartment, Will's mind was clear and focused and the day's events and missteps had fallen into their proper perspective. He would have to ride the Ruta. Perhaps he could be a help to Bourgoin. Maybe. Maybe this wasn't such a bad place to be after all. Besides, Kim seemed almost crazed about not letting him off the team, so, why not make the best of it? Show her up by proving he still had — well, if not it, then something like it.

He stepped into his apartment, which, after the cold wind of the ride, felt like a steam bath. He was almost overcome, for a time, by the warm blanket of heat, but he realized that if he sank into a chair it would be over. They'd find him there days from now, still passed out and stinking, with a stupid-ass smile on his face. Will turned on the water in the tub — hot, please let it be hot today — and stripped down, tossing his gear into the corner. He'd wash it tonight for packing tomorrow. Tomorrow, Spain. Sunny Spain. With the big boys. A rush of happiness came over him. Hey, maybe there was something left in his old bones. Maybe a few more miles and a few more sprints and a few more mountains and a few more ..... aaaahhhh ..... the water burned his chilled skin and reached deep into his muscles. He should have warmed up more first; this was almost too painful. But somehow he sank down into it.

He turned to look out the window of his apartment. The first gray streaks of dusk were appearing over the building across the street. The young girls in the dance studio on the second floor were at the bar, some stretching, some pointing at him through the windows and laughing. He hadn't turned on any lights, but maybe they could see him. He waved. They waved back. They could see. Oh, well. He was beyond caring. Beyond modesty. Beyond consciousness.

He didn't know how long he had been asleep. But now it was fully dark in the apartment and in the dancing academy across the street. The water was cold. Very cold. But it wasn't the water that had awakened him. It was the knocking on the door. Steady, rising and falling, sometimes hard, sometimes gentle. But damned persistent.

"Yeah. Yeah. *Une minute*; *une minute*," he shouted.

He dragged himself out of sleep and climbed out of the tub. The warm apartment that had greeted him was gone, now it was cold in here, too. Damned cold. Oh, man. Was the heat on?

The knocking on the door was louder.

"Just a minute! Christ! Keep your shirt on!" Shirt. Yeah, shirt and sweats. Will pulled them on over his nakedness and walked to the door. He leaned his head on it for just a moment, to clear the last of the cobwebs. A last hard knock bounced his head off the wood. Will twisted the lock and threw the door open.

"Yes! Yes. Hello. Yes. What can I do for you?"

A short, rumpled man in a gray, rumbled trench coat stood in the doorway. His face was as gray as his coat, and all of him smelled of old cigars and ancient sweat.

"Monsieur Ross? Weee-lee-um Ross?"

Will rubbed his eyes.

"Ummm. *Oui. Et vous*?"

"Monsieur Ross, I am with the police." The wrinkled, gray little man reached into a seemingly bottomless pocket and produced a wallet, flipped it open and revealed a photo I.D. He spoke his English very slowly and distinctly. "I am with the Paris police. I am Inspector Godot."

Will almost laughed, but managed to say very seriously, "Come in. I've been waiting for you."

The inspector rolled his eyes. He had heard it all before, too many times.

"I am not here for jokes, monsieur. I am here to investigate a murder."

CHAPTER SIX: I LOVE MY BABY, MY BABY LOVES ME

The night was growing late and cold around Will as Inspector Luc Godot installed himself in the one comfortable chair of the apartment, lit what would seem to be the most foul-smelling piece of dung-soaked rope in the world, and spent the better part of the next two hours pumping him for information — the who's, what's, when's, why's and wherefore's of a life Will really hadn't been paying much attention to at the time he was living it.

"Have you ever been in the military, monsieur?"

"I thought it was a gas explosion."

"Worked with explosives in any way, monsieur?'

"The papers said it was a gas explosion."

"What was a gas explosion, monsieur?"

"Colgan's apartment. Wasn't it a gas explosion?"

"It was explosives, monsieur."

"I thought it was a gas explosion. That's what the papers said it was."

"No. Have you ever worked with explosives, monsieur?"

"M-80s. A few sticks of dynamite on my uncle's farm. So, it wasn't a gas explosion?"

"*Plastique*. Have you ever worked with plastique?"

"Plastique?"

"Plastique."

"Plastique?"

"Plastic explosives. It looks like clay and blows up like dynamite." Godot wiped the sweat from his brow. This was going nowhere in a very large hurry.

"No plastique. M-80s. Firecrackers with an attitude, but that's about it."

"Where were you the week prior to the incident?"

"The incident?"

"Oui, the incident."

"What incident?"

"The death of Monsieur Colgan."

"Oh, yeah. Sorry. I've never done this before. I've only seen it on 'Dragnet.'"

"Dragnet?"

"Dragnet."

"Dragnet?"

"Yeah. It's a cop show. Like 'Kojak' with hair and cheaper suits."

"Ah. American TV."

The way Godot had said it made Will believe this wasn't really a subject to continue. There were, he knew, certain Frenchmen who detested the American cultural infection of France, through TV shows and burger chains. Godot was clearly one of them.

"I was in Avelgem for that whole week before the, uh, the 'incident.' Before that I spent three days in Brussels and looking for work."

"What kind of work?"

"Any kind of work. Day labor to pick up a few bucks, something to do."

"Do you have friends in Brussels? Could I have their names?"

Will gave him the numbers of anyone he could think of in Brussels. It wouldn't do him much good, though. He had crashed on Angela's and Ernhart's couch and they were traveling through India on some sort of parapsychology retreat. Tia had left for New York. And no one ever knew where Rick was sleeping. Will then gave the inspector Leonard's phone number in New York, thinking that, now, that, would be a conversation to listen to, and gave him the address of Hilda's pub in Avelgem, probably his best alibi. Did he really need an alibi? And if he did, wasn't it a sad statement for him that his best one was the bartender and Leo the barfly in a hole-in-the-wall dive in a small Belgian town? Stewart would not be pleased with how he had turned out. If he stopped to think about it, neither was he.

"Am I a suspect?"

"A suspect?"

"Yeah, a suspect. This is a murder, you say, so am I a suspect?"

"I suspect everyone. I suspect no one."

Godot was deadly serious again.

"Have you ever met Jean-Pierre Colgan?"

"Not officially. We knew each other."

"How so?"

"We rode many of the same races. I knew him when I saw him. He may have known me. I don't know."

"Did you ever talk?"

Will thought back to the number of times in the peloton they had passed. Colgan going forward, Will going back.

"Once or twice is all I remember."

A long pause. Godot leaned forward.

"And...?"

"Oh. Sorry. Uh, once he told me that I wouldn't be such an embarrassment on a bike if I didn't wear such ugly socks."

"Ugly socks?"

"I wear ugly socks — well, some people think they're ugly — striped socks, when I, uh, ride."

"Why?"

"I dunno. Affectation. Superstition. They were a gift from my mother just before she died. Tradition. Stupidi..."

"Fine. So. Your mother is dead?"

"No. "

"You said your mother was dead."

"No."

He looked into his notebook.

"You just said she gave you the 'ugly socks' just before she died."

"She's alive."

"Then why did you say she was dead?"

"Because she says she's dead."

"Why does she say she's dead?"

"Because I'm riding bikes for a living in Europe and not making a dime at it rather than living two miles from her and teaching school in the same school system as her and providing her with tons of grandchildren."

"So, it's a joke."

"Not to her, it's not."

"She wanted you to be a teacher?"

"Well, she wanted me to be a priest."

Godot sighed heavily.

"You said she wanted you to be a teacher."

"That was only after the church told her I'd never be a priest."

"But why would the church...?" Godot suddenly caught himself, shook his head, and looked back into his black notebook, trying to regain the thread of his original line of questioning.

"Colgan," he said, pointing at his last meaningful question, "you and Colgan. There was ... another occasion you say you talked. And what was that?"

"Well, I guess it was last year's Tour de France. He had punctured, uh, had a flat tire, on the approach to Mont Ventoux and was chasing the pack. I was falling back a bit ..." (Falling back a bit? Jesus! You liar! You were exploding like a Roman candle!) "... and he just told me to get out of his way."

"Do you recall what he said? Precisely."

"Yes."

"And?"

"And what?"

"And what did he say?"

"Oh, uhhh, 'Get the hell off the road, you fucking amateur.'" Will looked over Godot's notebook as if to make sure he was getting it all down.

"Ahhhh," Godot said, scratching a long note to himself in the tiny black book.

"No other contact?" he asked

"No, not really. Those were my two big moments in the shadow of greatness. Otherwise, I was there. He was there. But we were essentially in two different worlds — different teams, different nationalities, different languages, styles and ... well, he was a champion. I was a serf."

"A serf? Ahh," Godot said waving his hand before Will had a chance to begin another session of '20 Questions,' "by serf, you really mean domestique?"

"Well, if there's nothing below that, then, yes, I was a domestique."

More notes in the tiny black notebook. Most people would fill that with a light week's shopping list, but Godot had been writing in it for nearly an hour. Solid. His handwriting must be the size of molecular structure. And then, how the hell would he read it?

"Inspector, if I may — why are you talking with me?"

"You profited, monsieur, from untimely death. I have a rule with my investigations — *trouvez l'argent.*"

" 'Find the money?' "

"Oui. You went from looking for day labor in Brussels two months ago to one of the top cycling teams in the world, with a very pleasant paycheck. All it took was the death of Jean-Pierre Colgan. You profited. Perhaps others did as well. I am simply finding the trail of the money."

"Well, yeah, I profited, but I couldn't anticipate that. I mean — he was Colgan. You replace a Colgan with a champion. I don't consider myself a champion."

"And wisely so, monsieur. Perhaps it is a 'stretch'? Yes, a stretch. But you had contacts on the team. You were looking for work. You still can ride. Just before the season begins — a champion dies, and there you are. A stretch, perhaps, but a possibility as well."

He flipped the book closed and dropped it into one of the seemingly endless number of folds in his rumpled raincoat.

"I will want you to be somewhere you can be reached. You can continue your normal activities with the team, but you should be ready to return at any time if we need more from you."

"You can get me through Haven, they'll always know where I am."

Godot hunched forward and scratched his eyebrow. He turned suddenly on Will.

"Do you know anything about toasters?"

"Toasters?"

"Toasters."

"Toasters?"

"Oui!," he said, exasperated, "Toasters!"

"Not really. Put bread in, take toast out, that kind of thing. Toasted tea cakes. Muffins. Never put a knife inside while it's plugged in...."

"What?" Godot looked up from scratching his eyebrow, and the notebook reappeared, "I ... there's something here I don't understand."

Will was suddenly on edge.

"Uhhh, basic safety, isn't it? Common sense? Never put a knife inside a plugged-in toaster, unless you wanna curl your hair."

Godot frowned. He thought he had something. But he only had an American clown who talked too much. He folded the notebook again, and once more it disappeared into the coat. His hand re-emerged clutching a business card.

"If you think of anything else that might have any connection with Jean-Pierre Colgan. If you hear anything from your teammates. Call. I am always there."

"Is this your home number?"

"The police are my home."

"Who picks up your socks?"

"Eh?"

"I mean, does your wife ever see you?"

"She understands."

"I'm sure."

Will took the card and walked Godot the three steps to the door.

"I will be in touch."

Will shut the door behind Godot and leaned against it until he heard the roar of a badly tuned engine on the side street next to his apartment. Walking to the window he looked out to see a battered Peugeot rattle away and turn the corner in a cloud of blue smoke.

This was an evening to ponder. Colgan murdered. The way Godot reacted. Him a suspect. And Godot — the eyebrow, the coat, the car, the way he talked. My god, thought Will — I've just been questioned by Columbo.

Hollywood. It really was everywhere.

❋

"MERCI."

Across Paris, a cellular phone was snapped shut and returned to the jacket pocket of an Armani suit.

"The police have just left. I'm told we'll be interested to hear the conversation. I am in your debt, my dear."

"You should have more faith in me," Kim said, pulling the red-fox coat tight around her neck. She settled back into the leather couch and smiled.

"He has no idea what he is in, or why he is in it. I've got everything we need on disk. Letters. Phone logs. Contacts. By the time he figures it out, he'll be starting his third year in the big house."

"The big house?"

"Prison."

"You watch too many movies. American movies."

Kim knew it to be true.

"I learned this at the movies," she said, leaning back into a corner of the couch and slowly pulling her coat open. She was naked underneath. She loved making love on this couch in front of the wall of windows that overlooked Paris, especially at night. It was like a gigantic stage, and she was in the center of it all, the Paris of money and power, fashion and ... well, yes, why deny it? Sex.

"He won't catch on?"

"If he does, he won't know what to do about it. If he does, no one will believe him. If he doesn't, we catch him without a struggle and both our plans proceed without delay. In either case, he is a sitting duck. By the time anyone realizes what is happening, if, in fact, they ever do, the deed will be done — and we will be rich." She paused. "Rich-er."

The room was quiet for a long, still moment. Kim could only hear the muffled sounds of city traffic, at this height and through this much glass, like the sound of a distant rushing stream.

"Can he still ride?"

She laughed, took his hand, and pulled him in to her.

"No, my dear. I'm not sure he ever could. He hasn't got the brains, the heart or the balls."

CHAPTER SEVEN:
STOPPING POWER

Godot had been busy.

It seemed as if the scruffy police detective had talked with the entire team, from Tomas to Cheryl, Deeds to Kim, Bourgoin to the dog that slept in the window well beside the back door of the velodrome. Where were you? Were you friends? And, the question that interested Will the most: Why did the team replace Jean-Pierre Colgan with William Edward Ross? A champion with a mediocrity? A Frenchman with an American? A dazzle with a dolt?

Groups of teammates, the press and the curious surrounded Will as he approached the circular track in Senlis. "Did they talk to you?" "What did they ask?" "What did you say?" The rapid-fire questions sounded as much like accusations as inquiries. With his grade-school French, Will swore one of the questions had been, "When did the frog eat the croissant and when did he do the tango?" It was impossible to get away from it all: the talk, the looks, the stares and now, suddenly, the headlines. Cacciavillani was buried in one of the cheesier morning papers of Paris as Will walked in the door. The headline reached out and slapped him across the face: Colgan Murdered! Haven in Disarray! And there was Will's picture, along with Colgan's and Deeds's and a guy identified as Martin Bergalis, the big-cheese deal maker of Haven. God, when did they take that picture of him? He looked like crap! And what was that ... aw, man! It was one of those cold-day training rides! That was a snot stream on his lip! Why didn't they use a promotional picture? They did with everyone else.

What did it say ... what did it say?

He reached over and unconsciously pulled the paper out of Tony C's hands. Cacciavillani didn't move at first, just sat there with his arms extended and his face focused on the article he'd been reading. He slowly lowered his arms and turned a wry smile toward Will.

"I had to win a stage in the Tour to get my photo in the paper," he said, "you get one just by getting hired."

"Huh ... wh ... oh, God, Tony, I'm sorry...." Will handed the paper back to Cacciavillani, who waved it away.

"No, no. That's all right, Will. You need it more than I do. I was already on the puzzle."

Will shook his head and wandered off, as in a daze, returning to his clumsy translation of the story. It was Colgan and exploding toasters — toasters? No, his translations was wrong. No. Yes. "Griller?" To grill? To toast? That was the whole toaster bit last night with Godot. And look — right next to the story inside after the jump — a department store was having a sale on high-tech American toasters. Tasteful.

Oh, yeah — Bergalis was saying that it was a terrible tragedy. Deeds was saying it was a personal loss and a team disaster. Kim admitted that it was a great loss for France and a horrible situation for the team, especially with Colgan and Haven anticipating such a tremendous season. Will noticed that he was added as an afterthought, as the rider filling the empty space on the team. Bourgoin, Kim said, was the team leader and destined for greatness with the help of Merkel and Cacciavillani and the rest of Haven.

"Haven," the paper quoted Kim, "has great 'bench strength.'"

The French would be pondering that Americanism over their morning coffee. Rolling the paper and stuffing it under his arm, Will realized it wasn't as bad as it had originally looked. It was a crappy picture of him, but he wasn't being dragged into the papers as Colgan's killer. Godot's questioning had shaken him. Did they actually think he had done it? No. How could anyone think that?

He turned the corner and stepped into the large room used for team meetings. The looks he saw, the looks he felt, were the same as the first day he had stepped into a Haven team meeting: cold, empty, contemptuous. Whatever he had built over the past few weeks had disappeared in a headline.

"Come on in, Ross. Grab a seat." Deeds pointed to one down front. Will wished it was back a bit, out of the glare of the team, someplace he could hide a bit, but it wasn't to be. Tony C walked in behind him. Room was immediately made for him on a back couch.

"Look around, gentlemen. Today we break into squads and cover the Continent. Some of you will not see some others again this season. We will be here, there and everywhere," Deeds said sarcastically, "carrying the Haven banner to new heights."

The team marked for the Étoile de Bességes would leave that morning.

The B- and A-squads, set for the Tour Mediterranéen and the Ruta del Sol, would lcavc Saturday: B by team bus, A, the big boys, by commercial jet. Gear up and get ready was the gist of the speech. Make your name or expect a ticket home in a hurry. Deeds said he had no room or patience for people who didn't produce.

Will wasn't sure, sitting in front as he was, but he could swear he felt every eye in the room turn toward him. It was a good question. Could he produce? Could he survive something other than training rides? And beyond survival, could he make things happen for Bourgoin and Merkel and Tony C?

He wasn't sure.

And sure as hell nobody else was, either.

❂

BY THREE, THE C-SQUAD WAS PACKED AND GONE TO THE ETOILE DE BESSEGES. Everyone else was in the weight room or the mechanics' workshop or huddled with Deeds, planning last-minute strategies, or out on the road winding out a few miles. The headlines of the morning were fading into the background noise, and Will was beginning to feel like he wasn't quite the suspect he had originally envisioned.

He rolled The Beast, his battered white Colnago, onto the road for a one-hour workout and a few speed intervals. He ran through his program and pedaled easily back to the velodrome. He handed his bike over to one of the mechanics and walked back to the locker room.

No matter what he did, or how he did it, Will knew, there would be angry reaction to him all season long. He had upset the apple cart. Colgan's death had changed a lot of plans, few for the better. Will was the daily reminder of that change. He passed a copy of the morning newspaper thrown atop his duffel bag. Of the five photos associated with the story, someone had spit on his picture.

As Will stared at the newspaper, his concentration was broken by a voice behind him.

"It's very realistic, don't you think, almost 3-D?"

He smiled at Cheryl. "Hi."

"No, really. It you look at it just right, it's almost like they planned the spit to be the snot coming out of your nose."

"Look, I ..."

"By the way, who chooses your publicity pictures — your ex-wife? This is a doozy."

"Fine! Okay?"

He looked again at his picture in the paper, now darkened by the spittle. She was right. It was a doozy.

"Did you talk to Godot?" he asked.

"Godot?"

"Godot. The policeman. Little guy. Sleeps in his clothes?"

"Oh, Columbo. No. He only talked to the big fish. One of his flunkies talked to me. I didn't have much to say. Colgan had a personal trainer. I never really saw him. What did they say to you?"

"They wondered what I knew about Colgan and toaster bombs."

"Oh, man — wasn't that the weirdest shit? I had a coffee maker burn a hole through a kitchen counter once, but I never had a toaster explode."

"Me neither. Wonder if it's a design flaw? Anyway — this Godot said I profited from Colgan's demise, and so I get to spend some time in the hot seat."

"Some profit. Peanuts for a paycheck and an ass full of saddle sores."

"My, how romantic you make my chosen sport. When are you leaving?"

"For the Ruta?" Cheryl screwed up her face. "We pack and leave tonight. Lucky me — I get to ride in the equipment van with Philippe, my favorite traveling companion."

"No love lost?"

"Well, I'm sure you two would have a great trip, given what you said to him when Deeds fired you. Would you like to switch? I'll fly Air France."

"No, that's okay. Philippe doesn't serve little bags of peanuts in the van."

"Why me, that's what I want to know; why me! The trip will be long, the

Pyrenees will be a mess, Philippe won't bathe and the only place I'll have to stretch out is the back of the van on top of the gear. Put your soft stuff on top, okay? Be a pal?"

"Done. I don't envy you."

"I don't envy me, much, either. But that's the story of, that's the glory of bike racing. Crap rides, crap hotels, crap food and no end to the glamour."

"So why do you do it?"

Cheryl looked at the floor for a moment, blew out a sigh and said, "Because ... because ... I can't get enough, I suppose. I love the speed and the sound and the people and those few moments — the one or two minutes in a six-hour race where everything happens. The rest of the time is all a build-up to that moment when somebody makes a move. Parry, thrust, reposition, fake, thrust, counter, breakaway, sprint, block — it's magic to me." She laughed. "It's better than sex. And you?"

"I dunno — I don't remember sex all that well."

THE NEXT TIME WILL SAW CHERYL WAS SATURDAY MORNING, IN FRONT OF THE hotel in Spain. She was pale, rumpled and in an obviously crappy mood.

The squad had arrived that morning on Air France. Fancy-schmancy. Leather seats, lots of room. Great food. The works. He liked playing with the big boys. The last race he had ridden had been along the southern coast of Sicily, and he got there on a cattle boat.

As the company equipment van pulled up to the hotel, Bourgoin led the squad into the drive from the other side, finishing off a three-hour training ride along the country roads of southern Spain. They were here early to acclimate, Deeds had said, but also, clearly, to step away from Paris and the constant questions about the death of Jean-Pierre Colgan. They had brought the basics with them. Now Philippe had arrived with the rest of the gear and Cheryl in tow.

"Hi, stranger," Will chirped.

"Piss off," was all she said, in a deep, guttural, "I've been living on coffee and whiskey for the last few days" kind of voice.

Bourgoin walked past, head down, pace quick, a man with a mission. This was his first time leading a team with Deeds occupied at the Étoile de Bessèges until tomorrow at least, and then the Tour Mediterranéen.

"Philippe," Bourgoin snapped, "take the gear around the back of the hotel. Delgado already has a storage area set up for everything. Crane — you set up where the hotel tells you. They have a room set aside for our needs. And do it now — a few people need to be adjusted."

Cheryl looked over at Tony C, busy impressing two young Spanish girls, certainly not over 16, with his riding power and prowess.

"Adjusted is a good word."

She turned to Will.

"No rest for the weary, eh?"

"I guess not."

Bourgoin turned to Will.

"Ross — I want you to check with Philippe. Make sure all the arrangements are made for cars, support vehicles, feed zones and the like."

"Shouldn't an assistant manager be doing that?"

"You aren't busy. I want everybody busy."

Will looked over at Tony C. He was posing for photos with each of the girls. As he put an arm around each, his fingers lightly dangled over their breasts.

Will shook his head. "Everybody is, Richard. Everybody is."

Cheryl had already pulled her gear out of the back of the truck, and was busy hauling it up the steps to the front door of the hotel. Will walked up to the driver's side, hoping to catch Philippe before he drove around back, but the driver took one look at Will, sneered, and pulled away in a blast of diesel exhaust.

"Philippe! Awwkk. Little bastard."

Will made sure one of the mechanics had The Beast in tow, then slowly walked around to the back of the hotel. This was one of the great moments of the season: the early spring, before the classics, before the northern cold and the southern pain set in, getting ready to ride in warm weather. After the conditioning Deeds had insisted on around Senlis in January, this was a wonder.

Will walked up toward the open loading dock where he saw the van parked. Just inside, out of the sun, Philippe was talking on a phone. As Will approached, his shoe scuffed some gravel. Philippe turned with a start and quickly hung up the phone without finishing his call.

"What?"

"Sorry to interrupt, bud — but Bourgoin wants to make sure that you've made all the arrangements for the cars and the feed zones."

"It's taken care of."

"I hope so — he's pretty squirrelly about it."

"Squirrelly?" Will noticed Philippe was sweating more than usual.

"Squirrelly. Rocket J? Anxious. Tense. Out of sorts. Look in a mirror — you'll know what it means."

Philippe's eyes squinted to slits. Will didn't know why — but it was suddenly cold in the room. He had no intention of sticking around. His laugh was amazingly unconvincing.

"See you, Smiley. Don't forget. I don't want an empty musette when I come flying through the zone."

"You don't fly."

Will stopped and turned back to face Philippe.

"Maybe not, asshole, but I sure as hell walk fast, have big feet and can step all over you."

Philippe smiled. Showing sharp teeth.

Will backed out of the room. Never, he remembered his father telling him, never turn your back on a wabid wabbit.

WITHIN THREE RACES OF THE START OF THE SEASON, THE TEAM, WILL KNEW, would be in some semblance of order. Deeds would have returned to manage the A-squad, jobs would be known or remembered or simply done, and with some racing under their belts, the riders would finally be calmer, seasoned horses rather than colts waiting out their first thunderstorm.

But that first race was always interesting, mainly because nothing in the world went right.

The organizing committee, no matter what the race, was trying to catch lightning in a bottle, without a bottle stopper. The teams, no matter who or what they were, arrived in disarray. The support services were slow on the uptake. Everybody forgot something. And the riders were manic-depressive. The older riders signed in on day one and sat at the starting line, staring down a long, gray road to October, while the neo-pros raced around, driving everybody crazy. They wanted to go. They wanted to be. They wanted to fly. The realization never struck them that clearly 90 percent of them would explode off the back of the pack by the end of the next five days and spend the rest of the year explaining to their parents how in "just one more race, I'll regain my form." They might have been the amateur provincial cycling champions from across the Continent, but these were the pro ranks, a whole different world with a whole different style.

Will wiped the last bit of sleep out of his eyes as he mounted the steps to sign in for the first of the five stages He never slept well the night before a race and last night had been worse than normal. The short stretches he found had been littered with dreams of Stewart and Godot and his dog, Hiram, and Fausto Coppi all watching Kim, Will's ex-wife, digging a hole in the middle of a French country lane.

"What's in the hole, Fausto?"

"Sign your name."

"Huh?"

"Just sign your name."

Fausto Coppi raised an arm and pointed toward the hole like the Ghost of Christmas Yet to Come pointing at the grave of Tiny Tim. "Yoooouuuurrr nnnaamme!"

Will knew he should be paying attention to this, whatever the hell one of the greatest riders of history was trying to say to him, but hell, did you ever notice his arms? Everybody always screamed about his legs: Look at that femur! What a lever! Look at that musculature! He could pound a bike up dirt roads in the Alps like he was riding new tarmac outside Des Moines! But his arms, Will thought, look at those arms! He could snap a pair of handlebars in two with a twitch. Wow. He looked like a bird — but he rode like a T. rex, eating everyone and everything in his path.

Stewart, he saw, was staring at the hole Kim was digging. Godot was scratching his eyebrow furiously. Hiram was crying. God, what a great dog he was ... wait a minute — dogs can't cry. Especially dogs who have been dead for 10 years. What the hell was going on?

And someone else was there. Jean-Pierre Colgan. In a white robe and holding a mangled collection of chrome and wires. God, Will thought, it's an exploded toaster. Maybe you have to wander through eternity with whatever killed you. What do the people do who were run down by buses and trucks?

Colgan looked like hell, tired, depressed, angry. He stared at Will and pushed the bits of the toaster forward. He was mumbling, trying to say something. Will leaned forward. He couldn't quite hear what Jean-Pierre was saying slowly, over and over again.

"What, Jean-Pierre ... what ... for Chrissakes, speak up!"

In response, Colgan screamed, "Anquetil says I'm a putz!"

And then, Jean-Pierre Colgan exploded in a puff of MGM Wicked Witch of the West smoke. Will turned away from the blast — which, honest to God, made no sound — just in time to see Godot filling in the hole Kim had dug with McDonald's wrappers and Coca-Cola cans and pieces of what appeared to be a '94 Chevy Lumina. Meanwhile, Will noticed, in the distance, his high school English teacher taking off her clothes in a forest of parking meters.

Oh, man, Will thought. This is too weird. No more cheesy crackers before bed. No wonder he felt like something off the bottom of his shoe.

Will signed in. He was at an odd angle, but was still able to get his signature on paper. He hated doing that. He had developed that signature for a reason, and, had to admit, it was pretty flashy, but he had to be sitting down to do it, not standing up, rocking back and forth on racing cleats, trying to hold a flapping piece of paper down with one hand while creating signature art with the other. Will looked at it from one side, then the other. It wasn't beautiful, but it would do.

Cheryl was standing at the base of the stairs when he came down.

"Do you have everything?"

"I've never had any complaints yet."

"What?"

"Old Marx Brothers line." Pause. "Forget it. Uhhmm ... yeah, I think so. Why weren't you at the team breakfast?"

"Stuff to do, and I'm not particularly welcome. Bourgoin is like an old sailor — my radically different genetic makeup brings him bad luck. It's just easier to stay away and grab something on the road."

The road. Will turned and looked across the town square and saw the orange pylons marking the turn that took them out of the center of town and into the countryside for nine months of pedaling. He sighed. Good God in heaven, why was he doing this again?

"Good luck."

"Huhmm?"

"Good luck." Cheryl smiled. "You've worked hard, you've given a lot, and now here you are and ready to go. It might look like hell out there, but once you're on the road you'll be fine. You're strong — you're flexible — you're ready to go. You were a champion once. Be one again."

Will smiled.

"Thanks." He walked back toward the team cars to get his bike and push out toward a new, seemingly endless season.

Tomas walked up behind Cheryl, wiping the last-minute race-day grease off his hands with a rag.

"I heard what you said — he'll appreciate it."

"I hope he believes it."

"Yeah — I'm sure he does."

"I only wish I did."

✲

THE FIRST DAY OF ANY RACE IS ALWAYS THE SAME. THE RIDERS LINE UP, RECOGNIZE old friends and foes, and jostle for position behind the line to talk, which continues right through the ceremony and the speeches and the starter's gun and the first 50 kilometers of the day. Nobody is going to kill himself this early in a race, this early in the season. This is a stretch run, a chance to relearn all the rules and names on the road that three months back home or on the criterium circuit have purged from the soul.

❁

EVEN NOW, A LITTLE MORE THAN AN HOUR INTO A NINE-MONTH SEASON, THE class lines had already been drawn in the peloton. The big guns, the Tour and Giro and Vuelta and Classics champions, were riding en masse near the forward center of the bunch. The neo-pros, including Paluzzo, were leading the pack. The laughing group, the stragglers of every race, the roster padding on every team, was already falling toward the back. Realistically, that's where everyone expected Will to ride, especially once things started to wind up.

Tony C was angling himself toward the other sprinters. If somebody decided to make a break, which likely wouldn't be for another 90 kilometers, he didn't want to be sitting behind some first-year pro with no bike control who might freak as he flew past and bump him into a ditch. Merkel was beside Bourgoin. Right and maybe half a wheel back, awaiting instructions, just as Bourgoin had done with Colgan last season.

Cardone and Cardinal were in the bunch, meeting old friends, chatting, discussing Haven's tough luck and the ascension of Will. Given what he heard, Will knew it wasn't complimentary. He'd never had a great deal of popularity in the peloton, never aroused a great deal of notice. He was one of the faceless rabble who rode, helped the leader and disappeared into the general classification, the race standings, without sound or fury or media attention. There was room at the top for only so many Anquetils. And that demanded a talent he didn't have.

At about 75 kilometers, just past the halfway point, the pack began to break up. Some of the neo-pros near the front decided to make a break for the too-distant finish. They raced up the road with their minds set on the glory at the end of it, with Bourgoin and Cacciavillani and the champions with any experience at all just watching them. There was no experienced riders in the breakaway to fear, no one who couldn't be hauled back. Just to be sure, the pack picked up the pace a bit, ensuring that the breakaway could be easily reached and controlled. Will felt the pace grow, his own cadence increasing in the big gears with ease, as if the pack of unrelated riders had become a single beast, a collective singular. How, thought Will, could anyone ever consider walking away from this? The wind, the sound, the feel. This was life. This is what Stewart had promised Will he'd someday find at the end of every hell-on-wheels training session. For 140 kilometers, it was nothing but sailing.

Stage one had been flats and long straightaways leading into the finish. Sprinter's heaven. The peloton had easily captured all but one rider in the inexperienced breakaway with 10 kilometers remaining.

Moving past the five-kilometer marker, the pack began to spread out into single file, triple bunches, single file and a large group at the back, as everyone took their unspoken positions for the final sprint. Coming around a turn, Will saw the remaining breakaway rider ahead, pedaling furiously for the finish line. Will realized the guy didn't have a chance in hell of making it. The power of the group was too strong. He had been away too long. He was going to get swallowed up.

But it wasn't an easy meal. The rider on point stayed there, gamely trying to keep his lead for those last few kilometers. With a burst of speed, the corps of sprinters reached out across the distance to touch him, meet him, beat him. Will fell in behind Bourgoin in the second major pack, picking up the pace and protecting his team leader from potential blockers, thugs and troublemakers coming up from behind. Merkel sat just ahead of Bourgoin's front wheel, clearing a path for his No. 1. Tony C and the other sprinters were already far ahead, putting the touch on the neo-pro. Just before the one-kilometer mark, he was ahead and alone. Just beyond it, his exertions of the afternoon had been for nothing, as he realized the futility of the battle he had waged against the beast. He sat up in his seat, riding the crest of the wave down toward the finish that only moments before had seemed his and his alone.

The wave broke at the 200-meter line. The first few sprinters began to string out toward the line, wholly aware that the rest of the world's best were sitting on their back wheels, looking for nothing more than a whip-around toward the finish line. One-hundred-fifty, 100, 50 meters. Cacciavillani, riding the left side of the street, broke low and cut right, diagonally slashing the pavement, throwing off the other riders. From 20 and then 10, there were now three pounding hard for the line, throwing their bikes back and forth in a frenzy, trying to find any ounce of power still remaining, while keeping their trajectories to the line clear. Just short of the finish, a Portuguese rider in the center, threw up his arms in a victory salute that was a second too early. A

Russian pushed through just ahead of him, with Tony C on the other side. Jumping his celebration, while racing these two in particular, had just won the Portuguese third place.

Merkel and Bourgoin had surged ahead in their final sprint, catching some of the inexperienced sprinters napping and pushing themselves higher on G.C. Will had tried to hold on, but lost Bourgoin's wheel in the final 200 meters. He noticed somebody coming up on his left and drifted that way just a bit to discourage any thoughts of passing. He pushed hard and kept pushing right across the line, then braked hard to avoid doing a body, mind and bike meld with the crowd that had already formed just across the line around the winners of the day and the heroes of the bunch. Will had grabbed enough of a jump to shove him into 43rd place, 14 seconds behind the leader, but those were first-day standings. He was two seconds ahead of Cardone, and five ahead of Cardinal. That would change with the terrain and with each rider's ability to race 151 kilometers today and then turn around and do 174 tomorrow and then turn around and do it again the day after tomorrow and the day after that and then yet again.

Rolling up to the Haven van, Will handed The Beast to Tomas.

"Take care of it — it was a good ride today."

"Take care of yourself, my friend. You were a good rider today."

Yeah, Will thought. Not bad. Not bad at all.

❀

FAUSTO COPPI DID NOT RETURN THAT NIGHT. NO ONE RETURNED. NOT EVEN the teacher doing the striptease in the parking-meter forest. There were no melting clocks or exploding toasters or ghostly images of people wearing Peterbilt spelled backwards on their foreheads. Will didn't dream that night. Race nights, he slept like the dead. He couldn't stay awake.

❀

STAGE TWO WAS HILLS. NOTHING SPECTACULAR. THEY WEREN T THE ALPS OR THE Pyrenees. They weren't Mont Ventoux or L'Alpe d'Huez. Rides so long and so steep they were beyond the ability to describe and categorize.

He thought back to his last ride in the Tour, up the slopes of Mont Ventoux, an extinct volcano in the south of France. He had experienced death climbing a mountainside many times on a bicycle, but nothing like that. Each pedal stroke had been a hot poker behind his eyes. His lungs couldn't capture enough air. He had reached the point of hallucination in his dehydration, and as he passed the monument to Tom Simpson, an English rider who had died on the slopes of Ventoux in, what — '67? — all he wanted to do was join him.

But now, today, along the southern coast of Spain, he would simply curse his way up the hillsides. He wouldn't die here; not on these hills. Not this early.

It was a beautiful day as the peloton rolled away from the starting line, a light breeze stirring a few clouds. It was a tail wind for the moment, which was nice, thought Will, enough to push a bit and dry the sweat from your back. He just hoped it didn't pick up and turn into his face during the final hour when he needed it least.

The hills began almost immediately, after a left-hand turn out of town, just past a little tavern where toothless, unshaven working men waved morning glasses of wine at the riders before draining them. Two months ago, that might have been me, Will thought. Toothy, but sloshy.

The undulating terrain was pleasant at first, the peloton pulling and dropping along the hills like a rolling sea. There wasn't a great deal of effort for himself or any of the other seasoned pros. The neo-pros were beginning to wise up and drop back into the bunch, including yesterday's breakaway king, who had come close to summary execution last night at the hands of his team leader for racing off without him, and not listening to the directeur sportif when told to pack it in. He was looking properly chastised this morning — and a little wiser as well.

Deeds had joined the B-squad at the Tour Mediterranéen, so Bourgoin was still in charge. He was still finding his managerial style, still finding, essentially, what he wanted to say about what had happened in stage one, but, frankly, there really hadn't been much to say at all. Everyone had met the challenge. Nothing exciting had happened. Support crews had done their jobs. Philippe had put the team's lead car right where it was supposed to be during the race. Nobody missed the feed zone. Everyone finished on time and on schedule. Even Will, much to Cardone's surprise.

"You finished ahead of me."

"Yes, I know."

"You finished ahead of me."

"Yes. I know." Will leaned forward. "It was nothing personal."

Stage two was playing out much like its predecessor. Nothing terribly exciting; everybody stretching more than racing, trying to pace themselves for the big-money, big-media prizes that lay ahead. No one seemed even terribly interested in posing for the photographers on the motorcycles. The neo-pros kept making determined faces, but the lead riders were quiet, settled back in the pack, just trying to regain their form. It was quiet, it was sunny, and the clouds were rolling in. The sprint to the finish line would be into a head wind.

At 85 klicks, life suddenly got interesting.

Bourgoin punctured a front tire on a 55-kilometer-an-hour descent and fought for control along the tarmac and then into the gravel along the edge of the road. For an ugly moment, Will was convinced that Richard would shear his leg off on the guard rail, but the man was simply too good, too cool, to panic and lose control of the bike. Bourgoin pulled up along the rail, his face now dirty from the sweat and dust kicked up in the battle with the gods of disaster.

Merkel frantically waved Will over.

"We don't know how far back the cars are — we need your wheel."

This was it. This was payback time. Will sacrificed whatever faint chances he had in order to supply his leader and get Bourgoin back on the road. The rest of the day would be catch up for Will, just so it wouldn't be for Richard.

In seconds, the wheel was off The Beast and on Bourgoin's mint-condition Colnago. Without a look back, he and Merkel were pounding away, leaving Will on the side of a road in Spain, holding a dead bike with a deader wheel.

It had all happened so quickly that the last of the peloton, which had remained fairly tight up to this point, was still passing by as Merkel and Bourgoin finished the descent. The stragglers of the laughing group rolled by and waved at Will. One, an aging Frenchman whom Will had passed, forward and back, for years in the pack, shouted out to him: "Eh! *Chaussettes rouges*!

Bonne chance!"

They passed quickly, chuckling, and, then, for a moment, all was quiet on the road. Then, the squadron of team cars began to roll past. As the peloton splintered, they'd quickly pass the stragglers and race forward just behind their team leaders. Things were still too tight for that now.

Will caught a glimpse of the lead Haven car, maybe fifth or sixth in line. What were they thinking? They should have bullied their way up front.

Will stood perpendicular to the road to accent his jersey and waved the dead wheel over his head. This, he knew, would be a quick turn-around, maybe 15 or 20 seconds with the mechanic out of the car and the wheels changed and him back on the road with little time lost. It was an easy pickup, even at this early, somewhat clumsy time of the season.

He waved slowly. The mechanic in the passenger seat saw him and turned to Philippe, asking for a pull-over. Philippe stared straight ahead and drove right past Will. The mechanic was shouting "*Arretez!* Philippe!" as the car rolled past. But Philippe didn't budge. He stared straight ahead into the trunk of the car ahead of him.

Will suddenly realized that he was shouting, too. "What the fu....hey, hey ... hey! Philippe! Son of a bitch!"

He was running along the roadside next to the guard rail, running down the hill trying to catch the driver's attention. He had the driver's attention. He could see that — Philippe was looking at him in the rear view mirror, watching him run down the hill dragging a disabled bike in one hand and a dead wheel in the other. Running in cleats, Will caught a piece of road shit that sent him ass over teakettle over bike into the sand burrs along the guard rail.

Will lay there for a second trying to catch his breath and his anger. Under his breath, he said, "Son of a bitch. Son of a bitch...." Over and over again. It didn't do any good. It didn't make him feel better. But it was all that came out.

He was still sitting there, less than a minute later, when Tomas and Cheryl pulled up in the van.

"Good God, man, what happened to you?"

"Honest to God, Cheryl, I don't know. One second I'm giving a wheel to Bourgoin and the car is right behind me, and the next second that two-bit son-of-a-bitch Philippe is driving by me without so much as a look, and I'm chasing him down the road like a 13-year-old in high heels and fall on my butt here...."

Tomas looked at his old friend. This guy never failed to amuse or amaze him. "You're ready." For during Will's 15-second rant, Tomas had stopped the van, removed a wheel from the rack, put it on The Beast, closed the brakes and spun it once to check the true. Will was on the road again.

"What?"

"Time to play catch-up, my friend. Earn your paycheck."

Will threw his right leg over the saddle, and Tomas gave him a push down the road. Will looked over his shoulder and shouted, "I owe you one."

"You still owe me one from the Vuelta four years ago."

Will did. He was horrible at paybacks. But he sure as hell appreciated what his Spanish magician could do.

The last of the trucks and vans were passing now. Everything had been so bunched up at this stage of the race that Will would have to fight his way through motor traffic just to catch up with any part of the peloton again. It was like riding through Paris at rush hour, he thought, pedal hard, inhale exhaust, spit it out, pedal hard, inhale exhaust....

This would take some work; he had lost a lot of time, thanks to Philippe, and would never be able to reach the head of the pack again today. Still, as they scattered across the Spanish hills, he might be able to catch the stragglers, maybe that asshole in the back, making fun of his socks and his dilemma.

Will put his head down and set the metronome in his head. Concentrate on the sound, he said, concentrate on the beat. Click. Click. Click. Pick it up now. Click. Click. Click click click click click clickclickclickclickclick. He was pacing well. He could feel it. As time spread, out he could feel the power in his legs as the kilometers passed beneath him. This is what racing was all about, he thought, not just the sprint and the win and the battles up front, but the struggles in the back of the pack and the coming from behind and finding an extra bit of something from somewhere that kept you going when everything else seemed lost and all you had left realistically was a shot at the lanterne rouge, the red lantern, last place in the race, the last car on the train. Head down, cutting the wind alone, Will paced himself on, not paying attention to the cars, avoiding them with a sixth sense and peripheral vision, paying attention to the road alone, the center line that he kept for himself, click click click click, without any concept of how long he had ridden or how far he had come, passing the vans and the cars emblazoned with team logos and sponsors from soft-drink manufacturers to framebuilders, TV networks to food giants, and now the stragglers, the last few in the race, the laughing group, with someone saying something to him, he didn't know what, not hearing anything but the metronome, Stewart's metronome, click click click click, passing the team cars that had now become a part of the peloton, click click click click, moving back in it now, even at the back of the pack, click click, feeling the euphoria of being back in it, even at the back, click click, maybe saving himself in the standings, the G.C. for one more day. Picking up the pace again, clickclickclickclick, he was not aware of the riders or the cars he passed, not aware of the weather, the new rain slicking the surface of the road, not aware of the slowing of the stragglers, clickclickclick , not aware that the lead car of Haven had fallen back and was directly in front of him, clickclickclickclick, not aware that the driver of Haven's lead car just slammed on his brakes, clickclickclic....not aware of the back of the car.

Not aware.

The lead Haven car, with a dented trunk and cracked back window, quietly pulled back into traffic. After all, the leader might need them.

*

KIM HUNG UP THE PHONE AND LOOKED INTO THE MAIN ROOM OF THE hotel suite.

"He's down."

Martin Bergalis showed no emotion when he heard the news. The team was down one. The clown in the red-striped socks. Lose one more — especially someone like Merkel — and the team was crippled. The champions would have to regroup and struggle and pull together, which their egos would not likely let them do....

Martin Bergalis showed no emotion when he heard the news. Now, he smiled.

"Perfect."

✿

GODOT HAD BEEN BUSY. THE RAIN OF A FEBRUARY EVENING BEAT AGAINST THE ancient windows of his office, the same office he had stepped into as a homicide detective some 20 years before. A single, crane-necked lamp illuminated his desk, piled high with papers and notes and leads on the death of Jean-Pierre Colgan.

There was no computer. Computers, Godot thought, made a cop lazy. Better do it yourself and think it through.

And he had thought this through. With the evidence from the apartment, the information he gathered from Haven and the interviews he had already done, his investigation pointed solidly in one direction. And that direction, the evening paper said, had just dropped out of the Ruta del Sol in Spain.

Godot scratched his eyebrow, sat back, and lit a cigar. Not his usual brand. A Cuban.

It made for better thinking.

CHAPTER EIGHT: SEEING THINGS

Stewart had told him there would be days like this, days when his legs wouldn't work, his head wouldn't clear, and he couldn't ride to save himself.

They were racing near Flint that Sunday, through a little town called Birch Run, and Will knew he just didn't have it. Raymond and the rest of the Two Wheels team had ridden up the road and he was fighting for his very existence in front of a bunch of older riders who acted like they were riding an easy century rather than a race. They kept telling Will to hook on with them, they'd all get to the finish line together and make whomever was left think they were really racing to get there. Will didn't want any part of that — but the harder he rode, the farther behind he fell, as if the cranks were working in reverse. The older riders passed him, laughing, as he struggled to make it up the last hill, a long, grinding climb up to the final descent back into the plaza parking lot on the southern edge of the city.

His legs burned, his back hurt, and his mouth was dry and aching. He had run out of water miles before and didn't want to lose time by stopping to pick any up. Maybe, he thought, that hadn't been such a good idea. But, more than anything else, Will's face hurt. It must be sunburned, he thought, the way it ached. It was so burned, that each time he touched it, it didn't feel like his face anymore, but like a mask in front of his face.

He focused on the road. And on the wheel. And on the crank. Around. One more time. Around. One more time. Around. One more time. And each revolution, he saw the socks. Red-striped socks. They were his sister's socks. When he and his father had left at four that morning for the race, he hadn't been able to find his short socks — his racing socks — so he took a pair of hers. Around. One more time. Around. one more time. He focused on the socks. Around. One more time.

His face burned. His mouth ached. He wanted to scream. Around. One more time. No. No more times. He hated this. He couldn't do it. Around. One more time.

And then Stewart was there, holding him up, pouring water on his face and it was so cold and cool and wet and in his mouth and wet and yes and yes and yes.

He had been dead last. Far behind even the old riders who didn't care. But the whole team was still there. Waiting for him. And the whole team was cheering.

"DOROTHY ... DOROTHY ... DO YOU HEAR ME, IT S AUNTIE EM. WAKE UP, SWEETIE."

"What the fu.... what ... what's going on?" Through eyes that felt like they had just been through the spin-dry cycle on a commercial washer, Will saw Cheryl.

"What happened?"

"How were the lion and the tin man?"

Will laughed. He stopped. His head banged like an A-bomb in a soup can.

"The tin man is a weenie."

He shut his eyes and opened them hard, stretching the lids, in a feeble attempt to push them to the point where they'd stay open.

"Nice to see you back, Tiger. I thought we were gonna lose you for a while there."

"Not me. I've got a skull made out of solid Michigan Walnut."

"Not so solid anymore. Appears you've got a few cracks in it."

Will reached up and touched his face. It felt like a relief map of the lower Mississippi Delta.

"Geezo peezo. What happened?"

"A Peugeot happened. You were pounding along, head down, eye on the road, when Philippe stopped dead in front of you. You hit the trunk and the back window, leaving a wonderful imprint of your face, I might add. At which point, Philippe, claiming not to have noticed anything, simply drove away. We were like three cars behind it all, and, scraped you up."

"How's the bike?"

"I knew you were going to ask that. I knew you were going to ask that. A real rider always asks that. You know that? God, I oughta go into show business. It's a gift, I tell you." She saw that he was waiting for an answer. "Well, it's not trashed, but you do need a new front wheel, fork and headset. Aside from that, you can ride that antique again when you get up. That is, if Deeds lets you. He heard you were still riding that third-year reject and wants you on new equipment for the next race."

That was something, anyway. The Beast Lives. He'd worry about Deeds and any kind of racing when his eyes could focus on something other than those 15 little Desi Arnaz autographed conga drums flying around the room and through his ears. It was a long time before he pieced together his brain and talked again.

"The stage. How'd we do?"

"You mean the race."

"Huh?"

"It's Sunday afternoon. It's done. We're done. We're going home. You've been in and out for about 72 hours."

Will started to rub his forehead in exasperation but the pain and the stitches and some kind of medicated goo stopped him.

"So how'd we do?"

"Bourgoin hung in — you woulda been proud of him. Caught the breakaway in the next to the last stage and took fourth in the G.C. Cardinal and Cardone did nothing, really, they just showed up. Treated it like a training ride. Tony C. won a sprint but lazed out in the last stage. And Merkel pulled a hamstring and dropped. No, really, even with Merkel gone, Bourgoin did the job. I didn't think he could do it. Surprised just about everybody. He's really taking this team-leader business seriously."

Of course he was, Will thought. Bourgoin had been good, never great, for years, always in the shadow of Colgan or somebody else with a big paycheck and a bigger ego. Now, Bourgoin had been given one chance to reach for the next level of riding, a level of greatness, and no one was going to hold him back, even if he had to do it all himself.

Will smiled. He liked that in a rider, in a leader. This was the kind of guy to work for, and work for hard.

"When can I get out of here?"

"Now that you're awake, I don't know. They were going to transfer you tomorrow to Paris ... but maybe you can walk out. I dunno."

"Not walk out — first class all the way." Kim stood in the doorway.

"Jesus," Cheryl carped. "Don't you ever knock?"

"I didn't think I had to with my ex-husband, Sharon. But from now on, I suppose I should."

Cheryl was holding her rage in check, mainly because, Will felt, of the need for a paycheck. But someday, this was going to explode and Will didn't want to be anywhere close when it did.

"I'd better be going." Cheryl said. "Things to do. People to see."

"No, no, no," Kim cooed. "Stay. We're just here for a moment. Wanted to pop in and see if Will was awake before we all headed back to Paris. And here you are." She pulled his chin up with her fingers and studied his face through the bottom of her eyes, like a jeweler with bad glasses examining a ring. "None the worse for wear."

The pain of twisting his head up was causing Will's eyes to tear.

"I miss you too, sweetie," she said with a smile. "I've got some friends down the hall who'd like to see you. Do you have a minute?"

She let go of his chin and Will's face fell forward. That hurt, too. Kim walked to the door of the room and waved down the hall. Presently, she swung the door back to reveal three men: a grizzled old man in a wheelchair wearing the most beautiful suit Will had ever seen; a young thin man he had seen somewhere before, wearing a Haven jacket and pushing the wheelchair; and, the man from the picture — Martin Bergalis, Italian suit, perfectly manicured, bejeweled and all.

Martin spoke quietly, but, it seemed to Will, with great force.

"I am very glad to see you awake — alive, Mr. Ross. You had quite an accident."

"Thank you, sir. I owe my recovery to Haven Pharmaceuticals."

No one in the room laughed. Cheryl had slid to a back corner, quietly, as if to remove herself from the line of fire. Kim and the thin young man had done pretty much the same. The floor was held by Martin and the man in the wheelchair.

"This is my father, Mr. Ross, Stefano Bergalis. He is the founder of Haven Pharmaceuticals — the man who built an empire from a simple interest in helping cyclists perform to their utmost. Interesting, isn't it, how an entire fortune has been built because of cycling, but without it?"

The old man in the perfect suit turned to Martin on that comment. He raised what looked to be an electric shaver to his throat and began to talk in a slow and distant voice of buzzes and clicks and pops and starts.

"Myy ... son has it wrong ... Monsieur Rozzzzzz. Cycling hazzz made this company ..." He pulled the device from this neck, obviously exhausted by the effort. He waved over his shoulder and the young man stepped forward, quickly, from the darkness of the corner to continue his father's thought.

"No one has introduced us, Mr. Ross. I am Henri Bergalis. I run the athletic-supplement division of the company."

"Excuse me, have we met?" Will asked.

"Yes, Mr. Ross. You, eh, were unwell...." he waved his hands, clearly distressed.

Will remembered. The velodrome. The silver Mercedes. This had been the young man who commiserated with Will about cigarette smoke while Will retched on a lamppost. Will smiled. At least, he felt, he might have one ally for some reason somewhere inside Haven.

"My father believes, Mr. Ross, that Haven would be nothing without cycling. As a young man, he loved to ride and to race. He knew many of the early greats of racing — Octave Lapize, after he gave up the game, Ottavio Bottecchia, in his prime...." The old man nodded happily at the memories. "Henri Desgrange, Coppi, Bartali, Kubler, Anquetil, Poulidor, Merckx and many others, right up to Jean-Pierre Colgan."

At this, Will noticed, the old man closed his eyes, blew out a bit of air in exasperation, and shook his head, as if to say, "What a waste; what a waste."

"Cycling was his life, Mr. Ross — but love for a game doesn't necessarily make you good at the game."

"You're telling me."

Will looked at Stefano Bergalis. The man returned his gaze. The two were suddenly locked at a point of understanding. Will had been there, through it all in cycling, met the heroes and the characters and the duds, but Stefano Bergalis had been there first and had found a way to stay.

"He studied as a chemist," Henri continued, "determined to find new ways to make riders stronger ..."

Stefano pulled the electric wand to his neck. "And ... to find a way ... to support a teeeeeam."

"Yes, papa. To find a way to support a team. Even though it has become a very expensive proposition to support a team as principal sponsor, my father is determined to be a part of the cycling world, which never left him — which never leaves anyone, I suppose."

The old man nodded.

"And so, Haven Pharmaceuticals was born. To support riders and support my father's dream. It has survived."

Will smiled, thinking of the multinational giant Haven had become.

"Survived quite nicely."

Martin Bergalis stepped forward.

"This is all very nice," he said, "but it is time to...."

He stopped dead in his tracks. Will looked over at Martin, still as a statue, and followed his eyes to the right. Stefano Bergalis had his right hand up in the air. It shook, he couldn't hold it up long, but it was up, and it commanded attention.

Henri looked at his father and then looked at Will.

"My father believes you should rest — but perhaps in Paris. He was very impressed with your fire on the bike earlier this week. And he hopes that in more comfortable surroundings, you will continue to improve."

"Thank you, sir." Will nodded to the gentleman. He nodded back.

"You need to rest now. I'll handle all the arrangements and will be in touch."

"Thank you."

Will looked at the old man. Of all the people in the room, they understood each other. They understood the beauty of life on two wheels, the need to be it and touch it and hear it and see it, even if you weren't directly a part of it. That's what Stefano Bergalis still had, even in a wheelchair. That's what Will had lost. That's what Will was getting back, slowly, ever so slowly. The old man smiled and nodded. He knew. Henri rolled him past the bed and out the door into the hall.

Kim and Martin stood on one side of the room. Cheryl stood on the other. Will was trapped in his bed. In an effort to make himself more comfortable and give himself a more powerful position while reclined, he had been playing with the electric motor on the bed and now sat in a position with legs and arms and elbows up in the air. He looked like the foothills of the Italian Alps.

Martin waited a long moment before speaking. With the old man's departure, the power in the room had quickly shifted back to him. He knew it and wanted to make sure everyone else in the room knew it as well.

"My father believes in bicycling. And in cyclists. He's been around them his entire life. That is why Haven Pharmaceuticals has always sponsored a team — amateur or professional. That is why Haven has always sponsored a team — even in a changing world that doesn't understand or care about bicycling anymore. American TV knows. It's American football and baseball and basketball — possession of a ball or a field or a goal — action that has plenty of planned breaks perfectly designed to sell to sponsors."

Will broke in. "But the game matters ... at least to the players. To the fans."

Martin Bergalis smiled at Will, as if smiling at a naïve, idiot child.

"None of it matters, Mr. Ross. Your training. Your pedaling. Your winning. What matters is my ability to sell product based on your performance. That's what it is all about, Mr. Ross. As the world changes — I don't know if you can sell that anymore. Not on a bicycle, anyway."

Bergalis turned to Kim and whispered something in her ear. She nodded. He then pulled her close. She wrapped her arms around his neck and kissed him lightly, burying her head in his shoulder. He moved his hands down and up her back rhythmically, and then settled them on her derriere, cupping both cheeks and gently squeezing. Involuntarily, Cheryl and Will both leaned to the side to get a better look. This was quite a show. Bergalis slowly turned to both of them and smiled. Cheryl and Will slowly leaned back upright, hoping that no one really noticed they had been peeking.

Bergalis said only, "Het Volk," stabbed a finger at Will, broke his grip on Kim and strode, purposefully, out of the room. Kim watched him go, smiled, and turned a smug and satisfied, though slightly flushed, face to Will.

"The doctors say that you shouldn't race for two weeks at least. We'll send you back to Paris for that time. You'll leave tomorrow on the company jet. You have just over two weeks to get ready for Het Volk, the first of the classics. You will be on the A-squad for all of them."

Will closed his eyes. Oh, Christ! That meant Paris-Roubaix.

"Yes, all of them. Everyone likes your spirit. You will be there, Will. I have faith."

She walked over as if to kiss the top of his head. She couldn't find a spot that wasn't bandaged or stitched or covered with some kind of goo. Kim looked up at Cheryl and smiled. She leaned over and kissed Will full on the lips, sliding her tongue quickly into his mouth.

"I kind of miss that," she said with a wicked smile. "See you in Paris, sweetie. You, too, Sharon." She picked up her Italian leather jacket and swept out the door.

Will didn't move. He was in shock. Cheryl only said, "Good-bye, Kimber-ly," emphasizing each part of the name. They could hear Kim pause in the hall for just a moment, then stride on, her heels echoing in the empty hall in the distance.

❂

JUST DOWN THE HALL, KIM STOPPED AT A WATER FOUNTAIN. SHE TOOK A QUICK mouthful of water and then spit, disgusted, into the drain. God. That was hideous. He hadn't brushed his teeth in days.

❂

CHERYL BROKE THE LONG, SHOCKED SILENCE THAT FOLLOWED KIM'S departure.

"My, my. That was an interesting little psycho-drama."

Will shook himself out of his coma. "I'm ... I'm sorry. What do you mean?"

"Oh, come on. Didn't you see it?"

"No, what?"

"Martin was fuming when daddy was in the room. He was like a caged tiger watching his handler."

"I didn't notice. I was watching the old dude."

"Well, as soon as the old dude left, Martin made damned sure everybody knew who was in charge. That football speech and that whole business with your ex just before he left."

"I thought...."

"Please ... it was all for your benefit. It was a show. I control your life. I could dump cycling and own a football team and make millions. I control your woman...."

"She's not my woman."

"To him she is ... or was." Cheryl knocked on Will's head. "Hello! Anybody home in there?"

The pain rang down to his toes.

"Oh, sorry. But come on — you've gotta tell me you saw it. And then that business with Kim."

"Maybe she wanted to make up for the four months she wouldn't kiss me before we split."

Cheryl shook her head.

"You're a loony. Man, he's a snake. She's a snake. They're all pretty much snakes except maybe the brother. I dunno about him."

"He rides. At least he rides. That's something."

❖

THE STRETCH LIMO PULLED ONTO THE RUNWAY AT THE AIRPORT AND UP TO ONE of two gleaming corporate jets, both of which bore the Haven logo.

Stefano Bergalis had not made a sound since the car pulled away from the hospital. He talked as little as possible. Since the stroke and his throat cancer, every move, every word had been an effort. Now, he felt he had to speak.

"Wwwhy? Why him? Whyyy did Martin hire Rozzzzz?"

Henri Bergalis turned a sympathetic eye to his father. He loved this hard man who had built so much and been through so much, but since the operations and the stroke, the hardness and the bitterness, the frustrations, had overcome the man inside.

"Martin didn't hire him, Papa. Kim hired him. She's in charge of the team."

"Kimm izzz a *prostituée.* Martin callz the shozzzzz."

Stefano Bergalis shook his head. "Why? A rider who hazzz lozzzt his heart?"

Henri Bergalis placed a hand on his father's frail leg. What did his father understand that he didn't? There was still so much to learn about the world and about business, but he could spend his life and never learn what his father knew about people.

"Maybe, father, Martin simply couldn't find a rider, a champion, to equal Colgan."

Suddenly, Stefano Bergalis exploded in a paroxysm of coughing and sputtering and wheezing. Henri grabbed his father's shoulders to calm him and realized, that for the first time in months, if not years, his father was laughing.

The old man struggled to regain his breath. He raised the electric wand to his throat and croaked, "Colgan ... Colgan ... wazzz a puzzzz. Heh. Heh. Heh. Heh."

He took a long, shattered breath.

"Anquetil told me."

❁

IN PARIS, INSPECTOR GODOT WAS FEELING THE FRUSTRATION OF TRYING TO apply the law to the rich. He was ready to make an arrest in the death of Jean-Pierre Colgan, but the Chief Inspector had told him to wait. There was plenty of time, the Chief Inspector had said, Haven had asked for some relief and, besides, the suspect wasn't going anywhere. After all, there was a racing season to consider.

Perhaps, thought Godot. But there was also a murder to consider. And despite the orders from on high, perhaps it was time to squeeze just a bit and see which of the mice squeaked the loudest.

CHAPTER NINE:

J'ACCUSE

The velodrome at Senlis was no longer a training center; it had returned to its former identity as a crumbling and forgotten corner of the cycling history of France. But the Haven Pharmaceuticals team still had privileges there, and Will still had a key, so he determined to make the most of it. After all, there was no other place he could take a shower, a stand-up-no-end-to-the-hot-water shower. Besides, the velodrome made a good starting and stopping point for his rehab rides, and who couldn't stand the adoration of a hundred little French girls at the dilapidated boarding school on the other side of the cul-de-sac for whom you were the pinnacle of athletic achievement?

Will x-crossed a spare tube across his back and straddled The Beast, his battered, white, ancient Colnago. He pulled the balaclava down over his ears and up onto his chin as best he could. The headpiece was worn and torn after years of Michigan riding. He had to dig for it in the box of assorted gear his mother had sent last week. Before his face plant into the back window of a team car, cold-weather riding, even below zero centigrade, had never bothered him, but now, even a slight breeze made the rivers of stitches along his face sing and ache. Today, it would be worse than usual. Today was bitter. There was even a touch of snow in the air. But Will knew that he'd have to keep riding no matter what his face or the weather or his legs or the wind said.

He was in the soup, big time, and the marbles were on the table. His "who gives a rat's ass" attitude was slowly giving ground to the tug of the crankset, the pull of the diamond geometry, the call of singing tires. And besides, that's what his contract called for. Everything outside and inside him said that he had to ride again, ride hard, and get some good results in the one-day spring classics. It was what Haven wanted. And for the first time in years, it was what he wanted as well.

But did Haven really want his effort? That was the damnedest thing, he thought. He was pushed and prodded and told to go out there and do it, ride hard, but deep down, it was without conviction, like the last days of his marriage to Kim. There was nothing said. Everything seemed normal, a part of life, the quiet moments in a long-term relationship. But it was her tone that first told him something was wrong. The times when she said, "I love you," and he suddenly realized that he didn't believe what she said about her feelings and where she went and what she did. By the time he finally realized there was a problem, it was all too late. He was fighting for closet space in his own house with her boyfriends.

That's the tone he was hearing from her now.

The wind shifted and burned his face. There were a million reasons not to do this today. He could climb off the bike and take a cab back to his apartment and sit in a café all day, alternating between wine and espresso to give himself a distinctly different perspective on the world around him; he could stay in the shower all day, or the team whirlpool, still set up in the corner of the changing room; or he could simply go somewhere, hide in a chair and read. There was a new *L'Équipe*, a new *VeloNews* and a thriller sitting on his chair at home. Plenty to keep him busy until tomorrow morning when he could step outside and see if the weather was nicer and he might try to do this again.

He looked up at the school. In the second-floor window, he saw a half-dozen 12-year-old girls watching him carefully. Now that he was looking, they started waving madly. Another girl ran up with a can of Diet Coke. He curled his arms over his head and flexed his rather stringy muscles, at the same time pooching out his belly. The pose reminded him of his dad rolling his overhang to make the neighbor kids laugh. It had the same effect in any language. Now the girls were laughing and pointing and waving. Will smiled. He knew he was stuck. He had to ride. His fans demanded it.

Will pushed off and pedaled smoothly toward the cross street and traffic. He'd use the next few minutes to warm up and stretch, then kick into his training routine when he crossed outside the town and hit a few country roads. This was a different course from the one he usually took with the team.

About half an hour into the ride, he turned off the main road onto what was listed as a country lane, but was little more than a cow path. Any moisture at all on this thing, Will thought, and the training ride would become a cyclo-cross. The lane provided a shortcut across a field to a newly paved secondary road. As Will hit this, he decided the warm-up was over. He shifted into the big gears and started to work against the machine and the wind and himself. His face burned like charcoal briquettes working overtime, his legs felt stiff, and his mood was foul, but the pace slowly grew, and with it, his desire to be on the bike.

There were days when he loved to think about riding, and to prepare for riding and he loved having ridden, but hated the ride itself. Today, it was the best of days. Over the indecision, the hurdle of the first few kilometers, he had found his legs, and with his legs, his spirit, which, after the trials of the Ruta del Sol, had slowly begun to revive.

Even the burn of the wind began to energize and invigorate him. He pedaled harder and turned on his heart-rate monitor. It was harder to get into his training zone now, as his fitness improved, but he took that as a challenge, sprinting into a section of hard intervals, trying to find where the edge of his personal envelope was hiding today.

The wind burned. His eyes teared. And the last few cobwebs that had clouded his head for so very long began to clear away. Will Ross had given up years ago. He had lost his desire to ride, his sense of fun on a bike, his urgency to get up front, his hatred of seeing anyone pass him, the touch of death on his shoulder when he abandoned, until it all became the same: one feeling, one sensation, tedious, tiresome, dull. Then, there was nothing to lose. He got on the bike. He rode the bike. Each race, the same as before. Each day, the same as the next. But now — now, he felt the bike beneath him, the power in his legs, the sense of anger and fire and challenge growing inside him. Maybe it was the competition, maybe it was the team, maybe it was himself or his personal life or just the world around him in general, but he felt it again for the first time in years. The fire in his belly.

He had found what he had lost. And he planned never to let it go again.

He reached down with his right hand and pushed the gear lever of the index shifter until he heard the click and felt the extra drag on his legs. He stood up on the pedals and began to slide the bike back and forth beneath him, back and forth, all the time watching his speed slowly climb along with his heart rate.

The wind burned the stitches on his face.

And he felt alive.

✵

JEAN JABLOM STEPPED OUT OF HIS BICYCLE SHOP FOR A MOMENT, TO CATCH some air, to catch a smoke. In the distance, over the rolling hills, he could see the rider approaching. He was still, what, maybe two or three kilometers away? Who would ride on a day like this? It was too damned cold. Jablom cupped his hands and lit the unfiltered Gauloise. The smoke burned his tongue and the back of his throat. He really should give these up. They weren't good for him at all. He spit out a few errant threads of tobacco. They went against everything he had ever trained himself to do. But, God, they were good at the end of a long day of fixing the wheels of clumsy bicyclists who bought high-priced mountain bikes, thank you, only to ride them straight down a cliff and into a pile of rubble, thank you again, after which they would pay dearly to see them in working order again.

It is good to have a reputation, even though it was frustrating to see how people treated these machines. But, eh — it was a living. Not much of one, but he had never raced in the big-money days. He had ridden when riders were warriors as much as tacticians and business men. He had carried bikes up dirt roads in the mountains right next to Fausto Coppi. He had ridden beside and behind Koblet and Bobet and Geminiani and Ockers and Bartali. He knew what it was like to ride in a different world, when just crossing the line made you a champion. But that was before American television and the big world sponsors and all the rest. A different world. A much different world.

The rider was much closer now, making much better time than Jablom had considered possible. This wasn't a tourist, this was a rider who had to be on the road, because someone told him to ride, or, simply because he was driven to it. That need to ride each and every day was one monkey it had taken Jablom years to finally get off his own back.

He took one last drag on the Gauloise and flipped it out toward the street. The wind suddenly shifted, picked up the butt and blew it right back at him. Jablom ducked and brushed the ashes off his work vest. Dirty habit. Have to give it up.

The rider, he saw, could also feel the change in the wind. His pace had slowed, and he seemed to be struggling. Always bad, thought Jean, fighting a bitter wind on your homeward leg. He was much closer now. Jean could see the Haven winter jersey and the yellow sunglasses and a black balaclava and a bright red face and two heavy streams of snot pouring out of the rider's nose and around the edges of his mouth.

This rider, Jablom thought, was in a bad way. He took pity and waved him toward the shop. The Haven rider rolled gratefully to a stop.

"Come in. The shop is warm, and I have some wine."

The rider's face, Jablom could see, was crisscrossed with bright red streaks, ugly slashes, covered with sporadic black stitching. With his wind burns and the cuts and bright blue lips from the wind, the rider looked like the Frankenstein monster after stealing a bicycle.

"Merci."

"*Non. Entrez, s'il vous plaît.*"

"Merci."

It was about all that Will could say at that point. The personal drive he had felt earlier hadn't been quite enough. Time and nature had conspired against him and slowly worn him down. Each direction he turned, it seemed, the wind had been there, head on, steely cold and slowly growing in ferocity. The ancient man in the tattered apron waving at him had seemed to be an angel, sent down to earth to save him. He should have kept riding. He had maybe 45 minutes back to the velodrome and no end of hot water. But there was no reason in the world to be stupid about this — he had trained and proved his point.

It was Miller time. Or coffee time. Or just sit in a warm room and wipe the snot from your lip time.

The door opened into the shop, and the bell rang fitfully, almost as if it was as tired as Will. Then the heat hit him; the heat and the smell. Both washed over him in a wave. The heat quickly caressed his face and made him realize that his nose was running in a gush down his face, while the smell of the grease and the oil and the parts and the tires made him realize he was in his safe place once again. He always felt safe in a bike shop. He always felt safe on two wheels.

"Please," Jablom said, "have a seat."

He pointed to a worn and tattered couch in a corner of the shop. At the same time, he offered Will an oily rag for his nose. Will gratefully took it and cleaned himself. God, he hadn't realized how plugged he had been. A full breath of air, through his nose, damned near made him faint.

Will collapsed into a corner of the sofa and looked up at his benefactor.

"Merci. *Merci beaucoup*."

"Ah." Jablom pointed at Will. "Aha. You're the Haven rider — the one with the car ... didn't you see the car?"

"Non. I did not see the car."

"Ahhh. It was right in front of you."

"Oui. I know."

"But you did not see it."

Will started to laugh. "No. I did not see it."

"Ahh. You should have seen it. You were doing well."

"Yes."

"It is too bad you did not see the car. You should watch more."

"Oui."

"You should have seen it."

Will didn't say anything in response, and the room grew uncomfortably quiet for a moment, the only sound coming from an overhead heater in the back corner of the shop.

Suddenly, the old man slapped his hands together as if inspired. He reached behind the counter, failed to find what he was feeling for, then hopped up onto the counter, his legs hanging off one end, his butt in the air, his head and arms on the other side of the counter, searching for his inspiration. With another "Aha," he found it. He twisted his arms into an almost unnatural position and held up two bottles, one, whiskey, one, red wine. Will could hear a muffled, "Choose!" And he replied, "*Le vin rouge*."

He wasn't sure it was the proper usage, but it got the point across.

The old man twisted himself into a sitting position and hopped down. He pulled the cork from the wine with his teeth, spit it across the room, and handed the bottle to Will. He took the cap off the whiskey, toasted Will, and took a long, satisfying drink.

So, thought Will, why not? He took a long hard slug of the wine and felt it burn and twist its way down to his stomach, then expand in a circle of warmth as it hit. Yes, indeed, he thought. The French just can't be beat.

"I'm Will Ross."

"Oui. I know." He extended a grease stained hand. "Jean Jablom."

"We've met?"

"I know you from the newspapers, of course, your adventures in Spain. But, you also stopped here, your first day with Haven." The old man settled into a wooden chair and began the long, slow deflate from the day.

"Ah, yes. I guess I did."

"I've followed you since, in *L'Équipe,* from friends still riding with the peloton."

"Still riding?"

"Oui. Some are trainers. Some drivers in races around France. One helped shovel you off the pavement in Spain and put you in an ambulance."

"You rode, then."

"Oui. I rode. I raced. I won. Nothing that mattered really, but I won. I got the girls. I got enough money to survive, with help, but yes, I did ride."

"What teams?"

"Oh, the national teams. A lot of national teams. Some small trade teams with the bicycle companies. I was too old for the big-sponsor trade teams when Geminiani started them 40 years ago and the real money, I was too early for that. I did it for the love of the game and the love of France, and," he laughed a low and dirty chuckle, "the love of the girls. There were always girls and much wine. The girls loved us, no matter how dirty and sweaty and stinking we were. Those were great days. Do you know — do you know," he said, swinging his arms in the air, trying to conjure up a world that no longer existed, "we were the kings of France when we rode. Even the bad riders were kings. Everyone knew us, everyone respected us — some even adored us. But today, pfffft! Even a French winner of the Tour today is no longer the king of France.

Coca-Cola is the king of France. Ahhh!" He waved his arms again and his vision disappeared before Will. "There are too many sports, too many people who don't know, don't care about racing anymore. Too bad. Your friend, Colgan, for instance...."

"He wasn't my friend," Will mumbled, the wine working its way deep inside his skull and rewiring his brain pan.

"He strutted, like a peacock, he acted like he was a king — and he did win some races — but, he was nothing to France. Easily ignored. The children didn't even know him. The children, they don't care anymore. They don't race. They don't ride. They watch. Football, eh? Your soccer. And American football, with its jerseys and its hats turned backwards and its printed coffee cups on MTV. And CNN — I don't care what happens in Atlanta, Georgia. I care about France. And, Euro Disney!" He upended the whiskey bottle. "What is Disney doing in France? Disney does not belong in France. Disney belongs in Hollywood."

"Anaheim."

"What?"

"Nothing."

The warmth and the wine and the letdown from the ride were slowing Will down. He suddenly realized that while he listened to Jablom continue his diatribe about Disney, Will was staring at the floor, trying to find a pattern in the stains on the wood. If he didn't leave soon, he'd never make it back to the school before dark, before it got really nasty outside, before he got really nasty inside. Jablom was starting to stare now, too. The whiskey was working its magic on his concentration.

"No one wants to ride today in France. Now, it's watch somebody else do it. Watch television and play fat-man sports one day a week and spend the rest of your life trying to recover from your injuries because you didn't know how to play." He spat with disgust into a corner of the room.

"Weekend warriors," Will mumbled.

"What?"

"Nothing."

"Even the big companies," Jablom continued, "the companies that have made their fortunes with cycling, like Peugeot, or Haven — your Haven, yes, your Haven...." He shook his head up and down pointing a gnarled finger in Will's general direction. "They made their fortunes with bicycles and racing and on the hearts and backs of men like me, and you. But they all leave and abandon and ...," he searched for the word, "... bail out."

Jablom's head began to bounce a bit like a spring-loaded pottery dog in the back window of a car.

"Bail out — yes, bail out."

"Haven won't bail out. They're in too deep," Will said. He took another deep drink from the bottle of wine. "Haven's whole history is cycling. The old man loves it. His kids love it."

Jablom snorted, sounding like a horse. He took another long slug from the whiskey bottle.

"They all bail out, eventually, my friend. Haven is no different. It costs too much and brings in too little because the people don't line the roads like they used to ... and even if they do line the roads, nobody buys a ticket, do they? They just watch. They just watch. For free. Better to get them into a stadium. Get their asses into the seats. A hundred francs a seat. Buy my hats. My shirts. My trinkets. Watch the game. People running into each other. Watch them get hurt. That is the future, my friend. Watch somebody else do it. Watch them get hurt. No finesse. No tactics. Just watch them run into each other. Kaaaa-boooom. Then go buy the hat."

He spat across the room into the corner, again, and took another drink from the soon-to-be-empty whiskey bottle.

"Go buy the hat."

"Go buy the ticket," Will said, "Then go buy the hat." He was starting to poke at the air like Jablom.

"Whoever is running Haven right now...." Jablom was oblivious to Will.

"My wife." Will crinkled his face, "my ex-wife...."

"... is putting the final strokes on Haven. No offense, my friend, but replacing Colgan with you was like telling the world that this was the last season for Haven."

"Thank you. Thank you very much."

"No offense, my friend."

Will shrugged. He was beyond caring about insults. Besides, puffing himself up to defend himself would have taken way, way, way too much energy.

"I'm sorry, Rozz, but ... " Jablom looked like a dual windmill, waving both arms through the air as he tried to make his argument, "you are a sacrificial lamb."

"*Excusez-moi*?'

Jablom looked at Will. Hard.

"A sacrificial lamb. You are the rider they bring in, bring along too fast, put in too many big races he's not ready for or able to ride and then ... pfft ." He waved a hand absently to the side. "You and the team are history. The owner looks like a wonderful guy — 'I juz wanted to keep the tradition going, but business is bad ... I am sorry about the riders.' And then the Haven jersey is history. Forty-eight years, how many champions? All gone. Gone. Gone. Then he sinks all his money in New Jerky bogs."

"New Jersey swampland."

"Eh? Swamp. Yes, swamp. Swamps and American football. Football and American swamps. Don't do — watch. Just watch. And grow fat. I hate Americans. I should be a waiter so I can show Americans how much I hate them."

"I'm American."

"But I like you."

"I like you too, Jean. But don't be my waiter, okay?"

"You know something? You know I took all my bets off Haven when I saw you in the store that first day? I always bet on Haven, but you made me change all my bets."

"That's okay. I don't mind. Any man with any brains would have done the same thing, given the way I looked."

"I'm thinking of changing them back."

"Invest in New Jersey swampland — it's a better potential return."

"Potential?"

"You buy five acres in Jersey and I can promise, that, within a year, there will be at least six New York mobsters per acre buried on your property."

"Six?"

"Six."

He thought for a second. "That's good," he mumbled, "that is 30 mobsters per year buried on my property." Jean Jablom smiled and fell face first onto the carpet.

Will sat for a moment, then slowly pulled himself off the couch and tugged on Jablom's inert body.

"Oh, man, don't die on me."

He pulled the old man up into a sitting position and bent over, wrapping his arms around him in some sort of drunken fireman's carry. He pulled and tugged and lost his balance, moving the man slowly, ever so slowly, toward the couch. With one last bit of exertion, he pulled Jablom up and over the edge, dropping him, in some semblance of relaxation, onto the middle of the sofa. Will picked up a torn blanket that was piled in a corner and draped it over the now snoring man.

"Thanks for the wine. And thanks for the warmth. And thanks for the talk. Even the stuff about Americans."

Will smiled and walked, in more or less a straight line, back to the door. His gear was dry now, but there was no way he wanted to put it back on. He checked his money and decided that if he saw one along the way, he would hail a cab. He needed the ride to clear his head, but there was no reason in the world to be stupid about it.

He slipped on the balaclava and the helmet. He didn't know if his skull could take another bounce on anything harder than the threadbare pillow back at his apartment. Before pulling on his gloves he walked to Jablom's counter and snitched a Haven Power Charge bar for dinner along the way. He'd make it up to Jean somehow. He then stood before the door and took one last deep breath of the warmth. He pulled open the door, felt the blast of cold night air hit him, wrestled The Beast outside, snapped the lock and shut the shop door behind him.

He didn't want to do this at all.

But the ride wasn't over. There was still work to be done. And miles to go before he slept. This was the downside. This was the reality. Turning the crank in the dead of evening while the world reeled around him.

IT HAD TAKEN HIM OVER AN HOUR TO RIDE BACK TO SENLIS AND THE velodrome. It was easy: just follow the white line, follow the white line, even when there were 12 of them. He had left the road only once, wandering off into a field, but he found his way home, and into the training center and then, into a shower.

Now, he was on the downward leg of the drunk. He always hated this part of it, so much, in fact, that he tried to plan his blitzes so that when he hit this part of the alcoholic haze, he was in a place and position to simply pass out and sleep it off. No such luck here. At least he could zone out in the middle of the shower and let the water cascade over his forehead and his eyes and the back of his head and his neck and his back. The stitches and cross-cuts on his face didn't need this and burned to gain his attention, but it felt so good to the rest of his head that he ignored the doctor's orders and let the water pound his face. He tried to ponder the afternoon with Jablom, but there was still too much wine in his system. He couldn't focus much on the tile in front of him, let alone anything that had been said. Usually, it all came back to him the next day, once he had sobered up, had some strong coffee and stared at a wall for 45 minutes or so, but, you never know. Maybe he had finally succeeded in killing off the three brain cells that constituted the last lick of sense in his body.

The water ran over him. He leaned his head forward, against the cold tiles of the shower. In the heat of the steam and the warmth of the water and the hiss of the shower, he fell asleep.

He awoke sometime later. He was disoriented; unsure where he was, when he was, who or even what he was. Will shook his head and moved out of the stream of the water. It had grown cold in the time he was there. He looked around, slowly, then, more frantically, trying to find a familiar landmark that would reacquaint him with the conscious world. Nothing. Where the hell ... no ... who the hell ... turning toward the entrance to the huge changing-room shower, Will noticed a man in a faded gray trench coat and battered hat, smoking a cigar.

Will flushed. He covered his nakedness and shut his eyes, trying to clear his head. His name. His name is.... "Inspector Godot."

"Pardon me. I did not mean to startle you."

"Sorry. I don't always wake up well."

"It happens. Please." He motioned Will toward a towel.

Will turned off the shower and walked over to the table near the door. He picked up a towel and wrapped it around his waist, then picked up a second to dry himself. Ignoring Godot for the moment, he rubbed the rough towel up his face, then down, then up, then down, avoiding the stitches and cuts with the pressure of his fingers, while letting the rest of his face feel the pleasure of the cloth. He tried to wake up and collect himself in the moment he was separated from Godot's gaze.

He lowered the towel and stared at the policeman.

"So, Inspector Godot. Fancy meeting you here."

Godot had planned his conversation with Ross carefully. His superiors had told him to back off, to give Haven some room, that none of the suspects in the case were going anywhere and the company needed a successful season without a scent of scandal. But Godot wanted some action. His hero — Columbo — could solve the crime of the century in an hour or two. He didn't see why he should wait two, three or six months until Colgan's murder was forgotten and the killer simply walked away. He had everything he needed in his files to spring the trap on a killer. And that was exactly what he was going to do right here, right now.

"You did well at the race in Spain."

Will chuckled. The last chunks of grape from the wine were floating in the veins behind his eyes.

"I suppose. Kissing a car ended it early."

"The team is happy with you?"

"I dunno. They seem to be."

Will sat up on the edge of the training table and began to dry his feet. Godot walked over to a locker and casually leaned against it.

"Will you continue to ride in the lead squad?"

"I think that's the plan, but you never know in this game."

"No, you never do know, do you?"

"Uhh, no. You never know."

"You never know when the breaks will find you, do you?"

"Uhhh, no."

"Or, when you will find the breaks. Or make the breaks."

"Guess not. You just have to keep your eyes open."

"So," Godot said, pulling at his eyebrow, "there is something I do not understand — you have never had much of a career in racing — correct?"

"Well, not in the last few years, no."

"In fact, you had retired, no?"

"Yes."

"Yes?"

"Yes, I had retired, yes."

"So, you — an admitted mediocrity — had retired."

"Let's not get carried away with this mediocrity business, okay?"

"You had retired, but somehow, you become a player on the leading squad of the most powerful racing team in Europe — the world. How does this happen? That's what I ponder."

"Do you lose sleep?"

"What?"

"Pondering like that. It makes me lose sleep." Godot did not react. "No pondering needed, inspector. I was just lucky, I guess."

"Was it luck, or design?"

"It was luck. They called me. Hell, they didn't even call me, they called my agent in New York. I didn't have anything to do with getting the job. I didn't even sign the goddamned papers. My agent did that."

"Your agent?"

"Yeah, Leonard Romanowski, agent to the tarnished stars. Times Square, New York City, USA. He did the deal. I didn't even know about it until it was signed and he called me."

"He called you?"

"Yes, he called me."

"And you had no contact with the team?"

"None."

"Or your ex-wife?"

"What? Kim? No. The last time I talked to her, before getting here, anyway, was at her lawyer's office when she demanded the dog."

"The dog?"

"Yes, the dog."

"What dog?"

"My dog."

"What, 'my dog?'"

"*Mon chien*. Woof woof. Dweezil. He belonged to me, and I lost him in the flood."

"The flood?"

"Jesus! The flood. The divorce. I call it the flood. And that was at least two-and-a-half years ago. I haven't had any contact with my wife since."

"None?"

"None."

"Then, please, Monsieur Ross, explain these."

From some pocket deep inside his coat, Godot produced a large, clear plastic bag. Inside the bag were photocopies of letters and envelopes. Will looked close. They were letters to Kim — from him.

"Yes, monsieur. You had quite a successful Ruta del Sol. You rode well. You rode with strength. You helped your teammates and you were helped by them. I have followed this game — this cycling — for many years. and I have decided that many a marginal rider can achieve at least a measure of success with the proper team, the proper support, the proper teammates. You have found that."

Will continued to read the letters through the plastic. What they said, when they said it, and what Godot was beginning to imply, chilled his blood.

"I ... I ..."

"Yes, Monsieur Ross, I have often said that given the proper opportunity, even a marginal rider can have a championship year. And all it took for you to achieve that opportunity were a few well-timed letters to your ex-wife and a few well-placed grams of *plastique*."

Will began to hyperventilate. He could feel his throat close. It was becoming difficult to breathe. His face flushed hot, and he could feel each gash on his face and each stitch within each gash. His eyes wouldn't focus on the letters. He could feel the blood pounding in his neck and temple and forehead. He was going to faint or have a heart attack or stroke out right then and there. He couldn't talk, he couldn't think, he could only feel every system in his body go into overload.

"So, Monsieur Ross. Before you fall, why don't you sit down, perhaps get dressed, catch your breath, have a drink of water and tell me all about it? Tell me about the toasters and plastique and Jean-Pierre Colgan and mailing these letters to your wife."

Will's eyes raced across the letters, across each word and phrase and sentence. All very business-like, all with a slight tone of pleading: please give me a chance, please consider me if ever there is an opening, I've been training, I'm ready, for old time's sake, just one last shot, I can produce, I can still work and help and ride and let's forget the past, for just one more summer in the sun. Love, Will.

That was his name. That was his tone. That was even his letterhead. The old stuff, but his letterhead. But that wasn't his letter. He looked up and saw Godot staring at him.

"Get dressed," the inspector said, sharply. "We have much to talk about."

Will carried the letters over to the lockers and dropped them onto a chair. As he dressed, he stared at them. He turned to Godot.

"I didn't write these."

"Just get dressed. We will go to the station, and I will take your statement. Do you have a lawyer, Ross?"

"Only agents. That's it."

Will couldn't think. His mind was panicked and blank. What was there? There had to be something there. Some word. Some phrase. The typing. Whose typewriter? Didn't the FBI check typewriters?

"I didn't write these, and I sure as shit didn't kill Colgan."

"You had motive. You had opportunity. And you profited from death."

Think, damn you, thought Will. Think. He doesn't have you in a box, but he sure as hell wants to put you there.

"What about the bomb? I didn't do any bomb."

"That will come. Get dressed."

Will pulled on his pants and began to pull his shirt off the rack. It caught on the hook, and he began to wrestle with it. In his anxiety, he couldn't seem to get it out of the locker. The shirt ripped at the collar as Will finally pulled it clear. He stood there for a second, looking at the torn shirt, then threw it hard into the back of the locker and turned on Godot.

"God damn it! I did not do this! You are barking up the wrong fucking tree, inspector, and I'm being framed...."

Godot had been pleased up until now. His fish had taken the bait and was running with the line. He had set the hook beautifully. He would have this case wrapped up by tomorrow, and then he'd watch the headlines trumpet his name while his superiors tried to explain why they had held up the investigation of the murder of Jean-Pierre Colgan. He would be a national hero, catching the American criminal and putting an end to the case. They might be baffled, but he wasn't. And yet, now, his suspect was beginning to rankle him, break the beautiful harmony of the moment. He was taking too long to get dressed. He was holding up Godot's parade. He was making him wait. And Godot never waited. People waited for Godot. For a moment, the facade broke and Godot shouted, long and slow, trying to regain control of the moment: "Get ... dressed!"

He pulled himself up to his full five-foot-five and pointed at Will's scattered clothing, popping his eyes wide for effect. The shout broke Will's rambling diatribe. He stopped, frozen, and stared at Godot. Godot felt the pride of power grow within him. He was, once more, in control.

Will did not move. He stared hard at Godot. What, what was the memory? He desperately brushed the last strands of alcohol from his mind. What? What was it? What had somebody said, where had they said it? He stared at his feet. At the floor. Where and what was the memory?

"Oh, my God."

Godot stared. This was not the reaction he had expected. From a sweating, rambling, incoherent, panic-stricken suspect, suddenly, Will was scrambling through his clothes and grabbing the plastic-covered letters. He was ripping the plastic off and pulling the letters apart, closely examining each one.

"Those are only copies, monsieur, you are not destroying evidence, I have the originals."

"I'm sure you have, Monsieur Godot. I'm sure you have," Will said, realizing he was smiling. "In fact, I'm counting on it."

Through the fog and the haze of a long morning ride and a long afternoon drunk and a long evening accused of murder, Will Ross had reached up and caught the ball on the warning track, just as the son of a bitch was flying over the rail into the cheap seats and out of his hands forever.

There. And there. And there again. His mind was working. Check them out. Check them all. He scanned the letters, then the envelopes. And there. Again. Two, not one, but two ways to prove. Oh, yeah. Whoever you are, you are clever. But you are so dumb. So fucking dumb.

Will laughed. A deep, evil laugh that caught Godot off guard. His suspect was cracking. Time to restrain him and take him in.

"Now, Monsieur Ross. It is time to calm down. Put your jacket on and let's go for a ride ..."

Will continued to laugh. "I don't think so, inspector. You and I have already been taken for one. We're both being played for suckers. Saps. Morons."

"Morons?"

"Id-i-ots. One look will tell you why." Will thrust the letters toward Godot.

"You charge me based on this and your career is over, inspector. And, I suspect, my ass ain't worth the change behind the pillows of my mother's couch. And — to top it all — the bad guy walks."

He stared at the letters and felt his spirit rise.

"Oh, man — thanks for the clue, inspector," Will said euphorically. "I couldn't have done it without you."

Godot walked quickly across the room and grabbed the letters out of Will's hand. He stared at them without comprehension. What did this man see — or was he simply trying to buy breathing space?

"Look closely, professor. Each signature. They've been scanned. And look at the name — it's mine. It's something I wrote. But it's not my signature. Want to discuss it? Over a beer?

"I'll even buy."

CHAPTER TEN:

THE RETURN OF WILE E. COYOTE

Omloop Het Volk.

The 198-kilometer race through Belgium wasn't considered an official start to the season. That began in two weeks with Milan-San Remo. But this was where you began to see more of the faces that would make up the season.

Despite the preponderance of Belgian and Dutch teams, more of the major teams were jumping into the mix now, their early-season training sessions leading here, to the first real challenge. Here, you found the conservative directeurs sportifs, who — unlike Carl Deeds — believed you eased into the season and built toward the big races; not for them the fiction of top dog now, top dog forever, there is no such thing as bicycle burnout.

Will Ross knew differently.

He also knew that early-spring burnout could affect one race, or a series of races, or, as the rider tried to find his way out of the slump, entire seasons and careers. In a way, he had been almost grateful for his high dive into the back window of the team Peugeot. Despite the pain and the fact that it had made him look like a zipperhead, the accident had given him time to continue his quiet build-up to the real start of the season, even in the crappy, late-winter conditions north of Paris, and allowed him to pass by the low-wattage excitement of Trophée Laigueglia, Monte Carlo-Alassio, Sicilian Week, Haut Var and the Giro dell'Etna.

Besides, he thought, standing in the town square of Ghent, the start for the day's event, he had been able to have his little showdown with Inspector Godot, enough of a showdown that the real-life French version of an American TV detective had backed off, driven off into the night without Will in tow, and had, for the first time, Will thought, begun to question his own powers of deduction. The two had seen each other many times since that first night, but it was days before Godot seemed to regain any of his old confidence. Perhaps he had found an old episode of "Columbo" in which much the same thing had happened to Peter Falk: following up a phony lead almost to the end before realizing, backtracking and nailing the real killer just prior to a cheese commercial.

Yep. Life was pretty much back to normal. Godot was in Paris scratching his eyebrow. Deeds was pushy. Tomas was grumpy because he was up all night fixing broken bikes that "good riders wouldn't break." Cheryl's hands were cramping. Bourgoin was sullen, convinced he was blowing his season in the first few weeks. Merkel was upbeat, convinced of Deeds's training philosophy. Cacciavillani was in his element, hitting on 16-year-old girls. And, somewhere in the background lurked a killer who liked to sign Will's name to cheesy correspondence. Just another day in the peloton.

"Hey, Rozz," Cacciavillani yelled, his arms draped over a black-haired teenager with extraordinary dark eyes and light skin, "Deeds wants to see you."

Will waved and started to walk back toward the team van. Cacciavillani put his hand out and caught Will by the chin. He turned the scarred face toward him, examining it closely. The girl looked at the bright red streaks running across Will's face and turned away. Tony C smiled. "I dunno," he said. "I think it gives you character."

"Well, character's keeping me up at night." Will replied.

He broke Tony's grip and smiled, continuing his walk back to the car.

Let's get this going, Will thought. Let's get on the road.

Will always hated the first few kilometers of a race, when the pack spun out of town, bumping and grinding for position, warming up, trying to find its rhythm. It was tougher, still, with the races like Het Volk. This early in the season and everybody was still out of synch. The major teams, the real pros, still weren't in full force in the peloton, and the pack was filled out by local or national teams that saw this as a chance to show off, riding beside the big names while making a name in their bicycle-crazy hometown. To top it all, conditions were usually horrible. Cold. Wind. Snow. Rain. Sunshine. Always there. Every race. One after another after another. Riders layered on clothing that make them look like Spandex sausages with arms, then shed them as the race progressed, then pleaded for something, anything to cover themselves as the weather changed, again, and frosted the little hairs on their arms and necks and between their legs.

And the roads. Paris-Roubaix was the worst, but Het Volk and the Tour of Flanders had their moments as well, whole sections of hell known as *pavé*, or cobbles, or Belgian bricks. There were fewer sections of these now, as Belgium, the Netherlands and northern France looked beyond tradition and decided that smoother roads were more necessary to the advancement of civilization than leaving the pavé in one piece so race directors could shatter bicycles and racers' spinal columns on it once a year.

The race sponsors would be sad to see it go, as would the automobile underbody shops that repaired the cars shaken to bits by the roads. But that was progress. That was the future.

Will couldn't wait.

Pavé made his skin crawl. His hands hurt. His teeth chatter. His ass ache. His mood foul. His eyes rattle around in his skull like dried peas in a gourd. He didn't like it. At least at Roubaix, he would be on the road with people who knew what they were doing, who knew how to handle a bike under any conditions. Even when things were treacherous, with a proven bike handler in front of you, you had a good idea of what was going to happen. They might fall, but they usually knew how to fall and where to fall to protect themselves from having the rest of the peloton fall on them. You knew what they were going to do. Not always, certainly. You never did know when a moron would step out in front of a screaming sprint pack to snap a picture and cause a 20-bike pileup, or when even the best would lose control on a wretched descent, but those moments were the exception. The rule was that you wanted somebody who could handle a bike in front of you. They were predictable. They were professional. They were ... they were putting The Beast back in the truck!

"Whoa ... whoa there, gentlemen. That's my bike. Unless you somehow expect me to roll Eddy Merckx for one of his display bikes over there, I'm going to need that."

Deeds stepped out from behind the van.

"Not today, Ross. Today, you ride team issue."

"But that is team issue, Carl."

"Yeah, four years ago. Today, you get a new bike. Just like Christmas. Think of me as Santa Claus."

"Nope, I'm sorry. Santa for me is a little short guy with a pot belly, white hair going in eight different directions and boxer shorts saying, 'Nobody touches nothin' till I have my first cuppa coffee.' I know Santa. I'm Santa's son. You're no Santa. Give me my bike."

"Lock it up, Delgado, and throw away the key if you have to," Deeds said to Tomas. "Ross doesn't ride that bike today."

"You know this is bad luck, don't you, Carl?"

"Gee, Ross, I didn't know you were superstitious."

"Not bad luck for me, Carl, bad luck for you. It's difficult to direct race tactics through a mouthful of bloody Chiclets."

Will stepped forward and raised a fist. Deeds's eyes went from stern slits to wide surprise.

"Hey! Back off, Ross!"

Will smiled and lowered his fist. "Gee, Carl. I didn't know I had that effect on you."

"It's those damned scars. You look like some kind of Chicago hit man."

"Look, Carl," Will was somewhere between conciliation and pleading. "I've trained on that bike. That bike is set up for me. It is right for me. If I try to ride that new one today without any kind of break-in, I'm going to be in hell's own shape by tonight. Besides, you know me, Mr. Back of the Pack — come on. I won't even make it on the live coverage, let alone the videotape. So, who's gonna know I'm riding last year's model?"

"Last decade's model."

"We're big on tradition in the South."

"South of what?"

"South of Michigan."

Deeds rubbed his forehead. He didn't need this, not today. Today was the official start of his season. He went against tradition and always mentally started his season with the Het Volk. And now his team would, too. Before, we were just spinning. Now, we play for the marbles. And today, of all days, he didn't need this roster-padding telling him that he wanted to ride a four-year-old piece of shit rather than the top-of-the-line, team-issue bike. Not today.

"Not today."

"Shi..."

"No. Final word, Ross. Not today. We can worry about you and your love affair with that bike later. Not today. Today, you ride the new team issue. Get your ass on board and get with the program. Team meeting in five minutes. Delgado, don't, if you value your job, listen to this bastard. He rides team issue. I don't want to see that bike on the course today."

"*Si.*"

"Si?"

"Si."

"Stop it." Deeds stamped his foot. "Five minutes. And don't waste them doing that old Jack Benny 'si, sy, sue' routine. You've got work to do, Delgado. You've got to sign in, Ross. You ride the new bike. Put a chain around that other thing, Tomas. And everybody," there was now a crowd, "get the hell away from me!"

Deeds lowered his shoulders and bullied his way through the sea of fans now surrounding the van. Tomas turned to Will with a smile on his face.

"Ohh, man, I haven't seen anything that prime in two years. Not since Bartoli slammed Hendricks's face into the side of the van. See, you can still see the dent here."

"How have you been? I really haven't had a chance to see you since I got in."

"Me? Fine," Tomas said, "especially with this marvelous Belgian weather to help my mood. I don't know what it is about this place. Why in hell would anybody want to ride here?"

"It toughens you up, the cold, the wet, the snow, the roads."

"Why do you live here?"

"The cold, the wet, the snow, the rent. What's been going on here?"

"I dunno. Merkel is hurt all the time, which means that Bourgoin has to pull on his own because Tony C is looking out for his own ass and Cardone and Cardinal aren't doing much of anything. Sicilian Week was a mess, an absolute mess. Deeds was screaming at everybody and Bourgoin was riding his heart out, just to land somewhere decent in the G.C., which surprises me, because you expect him to hold back until the Vuelta or Giro or Tour. He keeps riding at this pace, without any help, and he's gonna have nothing left come June 15." He looked over Will's raw face, the stitches now gone, the gashes pink lines running through a two-day growth of whiskers. "How's the face?"

"I'll never win Miss America."

"Tragic."

"It is, because I always thought I was a lock for Miss Congeniality. Speaking of whom, have you seen Cheryl running around?"

"Yeah, in fact, she was looking for you."

"Probably wants a brass rubbing of my face."

"Not unless she wants a road map of the Pyrenees."

"Thank you. Thank you ever so."

"There she is, man. Talk at'cha."

Will realized over that the years spent with Tomas, he and an army of Americanisms had rubbed off on the Spaniard. Too bad. He wished that more of the Continental style had rubbed off on him rather than the other way around. Maybe it had. He was sounding an awful lot like Godot.

"Americans. I hate Americans."

Cheryl looked at him quizzically. "I'm sorry?"

"Oh. Uhhh. Nothing. Nothing."

"For a second there, you sounded like Peter Sellers doing a bad French accent."

"Sorry. How you been?"

"Better than you, it appears. How's the face?"

"It only hurts when I ride."

"Perfect. Especially with the roads you get to deal with today." She was quiet for a moment, tossed her head to move the brown hair away from her eyes, and looked hard at him. "I've missed not having you around. There's really been no one to talk to since I left you in that Spanish hospital."

"Left me in a heap."

"True, but that was your own doing, wasn't it? Brakes are designed for stops. Not back windows."

"True enough." Will smiled. This was getting to be okay. Then, the smile froze on his face. He tried not to react, but he knew that he must have. Philippe appeared about three meters behind Cheryl, just over her right shoulder. He appeared to be looking over the race bible, the route map, but the cant of his head and shoulders told Will he was moving in for the eavesdropping kill. Will shifted his stare to Cheryl. She noticed that Will's smile had changed from soft and friendly to something you might find on a corpse that had laughed itself to death.

"What the ..."

Will put a hand on her shoulder. "Don't react," he said, "just smile. Smile friendly. And laugh. Go ahead."

She did, more out of concern for his sudden change of mood than anything else.

"Look," he said, never changing his expression. "Philippe is just over your right shoulder. Don't look! There are things going on that you should know about."

"Making a little too much about this accident, aren't we?"

"Look. I've gotta race. Tonight, let's find someplace quiet and I'll bring you up to speed."

"And we'll run outta gas, right? That was old when my grandmother...."

Will laughed obnoxiously. Philippe quietly smiled and turned away. Will looked back at Cheryl, the most insincere smile in the world on his face.

"You gotta trust me on this one, okay? I don't really know what's going on, but we've got to talk. Okay?"

"Uh, okay."

Tomas ran up.

"Deeds is starting the meeting. Better get a move on."

Will looked at Cheryl for a long moment. The look in his eyes told her that he wasn't kidding about any of what he had just said. It intrigued her. And frightened her as well.

"Okay," she said. "I'll see you tonight."

"Thanks."

Will turned and joined Tomas in the walk across the concrete parking lot to the small klatch of red, black and yellow Haven jerseys. Tomas was smiling broadly.

"The kid shoots ... the kid scores."

Will looked over his shoulder at him in mock disgust. "You know — I'm feeling guilty as hell for the way you're turning out."

A PELOTON HAS A SENSE OF POWER. ONE OR TWO HUNDRED RIDERS, in unison, if everything is going correctly, moving through a city, a village, a field. One rider draws the next, who draws the next and the next and so on, until the entire mass feeds on itself. Race off the front toward the finish and glory, and often you will only go as far and for as long as the peloton permits. The lieutenants within the pack increase the pace, and the creature with 400 legs closes in on you, the beast reaching out over meters or kilometers, seconds or minutes, to hook your back wheel and slowly pull you back. A breakaway is a desperate act, an attempt to split the pack, steal the power from the beast, race off alone and draw off a few to help you, or, simply race far enough ahead so that even as your power extinguishes, you are crossing the line, the group still chasing, the lieutenants and tacticians caught napping because they underestimated your power or your will.

It happens often in the spring classics. In the stage races, you have less than 24 hours before you have to race again, but in the classics, you have one day to explode, and then one, two, three or even seven days to recover, depending on your racing schedule.

Here, in Het Volk, racing through the Belgian countryside over the devil's own roads and nine, nasty, cobbled *monts*, it happened 30 kilometers into the 198-kilometer day, as four young Belgian and Dutch riders sailed off the front of the pack, looking for glory, headlines, a trophy for mom, and a better contract and more respect from the directeur.

See you soon, kids, thought Will. This pack will have you for lunch.

He wiped his nose again on his glove. These were the snot rides, he had concluded years ago, the wet, gray, cold, overcast days that forced you to dress like a kid in a snowsuit and hardly allowed you to breathe, while your face was exposed to every element spring in northern Europe had to offer. Inside, you were generating God knows how many kilowatts of heat energy, while your face met the bitter cold and wet and snow and rain head-on.

Snot happens. Rivers of the damned stuff. And there was no place to put it but the back of your glove. Which meant that the winner's picture was always the same: a wind-burned rider with a frozen stare and at least one mustache, usually green, to set off the upper lip and two gloved hands tucked discreetly out of sight. A disgusting reality of racing in Belgium in March. Luckily, most of the big photographers, the ones with the international reputations and circulations, didn't always show up en masse until Milan-San Remo, the unspoken season start, meaning that your mother wouldn't find your glistening lip staring back from her hometown paper on a slow sports Sunday back in the States.

Will wiped his nose again and laughed. He could have called in sick, stayed home, bought a box of tissues, wiped his nose there. But this was the season, this was his business, this was his sport. It had chosen him as much as he had chosen it. And now, they were stuck with each other. Will wiped his nose again. Everyone near him in the pack wiped theirs with the same hand, at the same time, in the same way.

Fifty kilometers of this and Will had had enough. He looked over at Bourgoin. It was mad, but what the hell, it was an idea.

"Hey, pal, what's say you and me blow this popsicle stand?"

"Eh?" Bourgoin looked like hell. The cold had flushed all the color out of his face, leaving a gray complexion and bright red-rimmed eyes. If any photographers were here today, Will hoped they were shooting black and white.

"I'm sick of this — let's boogie. We don't have to work again until Wednesday. Schiller and Van Dryden have just jumped. We can latch on to them, climb the Kwaremont, shatter the pack and break free."

Hans Merkel, Bourgoin's lieutenant, his leading assistant and second-in-command on the team, pulled up between them.

"*Nein.* No break. Deeds would not want it. We break later. I have my instructions."

"Deeds is sitting in a little car, way back there, with the heater turned all the way up. Come on, Richard, what do you say?"

"It's too early to break. We have a race plan," Merkel said, defensively.

"I'm sure we do, Hans. Let's get out of this rat race before all this snot gets airborne and gums up our chains."

Hans fell back a bit and talked frantically into a radio. Even with the hum of the peloton around him, even through the tiny earpiece Merkel wore, Will could hear someone shouting instructions back at them.

"Deeds says no. Stick to the game plan."

Will looked over at Bourgoin. He was in turmoil. He knew, as well as Will, that as safe as you were in the pack, you were trapped as well. The velvet lining soothed you, protected you, warmed you, kept you at speed. Then, without your noticing, the lid closed and once again you were left behind, second, third, fourth, 10th, whatever. None of those rankings mattered to Bourgoin. Only first. And he hadn't been there often enough to his liking. Bourgoin looked over at Will Ross, the American clown in the red-striped socks.

"Can you keep me out, ahead of the pack?"

Will looked at Bourgoin, then Merkel, and back to Richard.

"Yeah. If you can cut a deal with the two up ahead, I can keep you free. What do you say? Let's throw ourselves off the cliff and see if we bounce."

Bourgoin didn't say anything for a second, as he debated the time needed, the distance to cover and the power they were going to have to generate to leave the pack behind once and for all on the climbs and the long straights. Without a word, he touched a button at his waist, then reached across his handlebars and shifted. Will smiled and reached toward the down tube to shift. Shit. This wasn't The Beast. Will fumbled a bit with his brake-lever shifters and shifted. Dear Lord, don't let me screw up with this in a sprint, he thought. They'll be picking bits of me out of a lamppost. The gear kicked in and Will stood on the pedals, pushing through the crowd, making a path for Bourgoin, and reaching out beyond the grasp of the peloton.

Back in the pack, Merkel shouted desperately into his radio, listened to the angry response, then sighed, shifted and raced forward to catch his team leader and drum some sense into his head.

Cacciavillani started laughing at the suicidal breakaway. Cardinal and Cardone, the two other members of the Haven team, watched the three red, black and yellow jerseys streak up the road toward Schiller and Van Dryden, followed by a smattering of secondary riders from other teams who didn't like the thought of Haven stepping out, even this early in the dance.

"Deeds'll be pissed about that."

"Don't worry," Cardone assured his teammate. "We'll see them all again. It's too early in the day. The Kwaremont is only the first climb. The last are the worst. Look, it's so early nobody is reacting — last year they would have gone nuts if Colgan had stepped out like that. It's a long way home ... and Bourgoin will realize there is hell to pay for breaking the rules."

The peloton did not respond to the Haven attack. One simply did not react to such stupidity so early in the day.

❂

BACK IN THE CARAVAN, TOMAS AND CHERYL LISTENED WITH ONE EAR TO THE race coverage over a Belgian radio network, and, with the other to the team radio as Deeds tried to regain contact with Bourgoin.

Cheryl rubbed her eyes and leaned back in her seat.

"What the hell?" She looked at Tomas. "And you're smiling. They're acting stupid, and you're smiling. They're going too early — they're going to kill themselves ... Jesus. It's Will, isn't it? It's Will's idea, isn't it?"

Tomas was laughing now.

"You ever hear of a cartoon coyote?"

"What? Yeah, of course, Wile E. Coyote. Warner Brothers. Never caught the damned Road Runner."

"Yeah, he never caught him. But he always came up with the damnedest ideas to catch him — throwed himself off a cliff all the time."

"But he never caught the Road Runner. He never won."

"No — but who was more fun to watch?"

Cheryl looked far down the road at the back of the pack and beyond to the head of the pack and beyond to the backs of her teammates breaking away, far too early, in far too small a group, with far too many kilometers and climbs and cobbles to cover before the finish line.

She smiled.

"You always watched the Coyote."

"You bet. Wile E. Coyote lives and breathes and rides for us."

"I just hope Deeds likes cartoons."

BOURGOIN CUT THE DEAL WITH THE TWO DUTCH RIDERS. PACE US. HELP US get to the line. There was TV exposure and a cut of the prize at the end of the road. The five of them, working together, pulled away strongly and cleanly from the peloton, still somnambulant in its pace. A few hangers-on from the other teams fell in behind, conserving their energy, leeching off the riders at the front. They weren't there to help Haven win, they were there to keep in touch, hold down the pace and make sure that their teams, their sponsors, were always represented in the photos of the leaders.

It was madness, breaking away from the peloton so early in the day, before the climbs, against orders, against all common cycling sense and, yet, Will was having a great time doing it.

"Carl Deeds's body lies a-mould'ring in the grave...." Will was singing at the top of his lungs.

Bourgoin started laughing, then Merkel spit, "Stop ... you're breaking our rhythm."

"You're breaking my heart, man."

Jeez, Merkel was a downer, Will knew the guy was supposed to be the voice of reason for Bourgoin, his contact with Deeds, ready to throw himself in front of a speeding train for the guy, but this was getting ridiculous. It was like racing with your mother.

"Hans — is you wearing new underwear? You should be wearing clean undies."

"What? What are you talking about?"

Will laughed and kicked up the pace. Today, he thought, he felt great. His legs and lungs were strong, Godot was off his back, maybe, by now, even on his side, and he was beginning to get the feeling that he didn't care much about what Deeds or Kim or Martin or the team as a whole felt or wanted. Somebody out there wanted him to take the rap for Colgan and had been quietly manipulating Will all along. The job? Certainly. That meant Kim. The A-squad? Maybe. That meant Deeds. The accident? You bet. That meant Philippe. Somebody up top wanted him on his ass and out of the picture, carrying all their baggage to Bastille Station. But not this kid. He didn't need strings to hold him up. And what the hell? Now he felt like he wanted to win. Even if that meant winning through Bourgoin. What would that do to their plans?

The five kicked up the pace again, just prior to the Kwaremont and the cobbles. There weren't many on Het Volk, but there were enough Belgian blocks to make life miserable ... mainly because they always seemed to cover the climbs. The cobbles varied in size, from thin, knifelike slices that could slash a tire, hand or head, to great slabs at odd angles that could bend a rim into a million-and-one new designs. Even at their best, when, for seemingly instantaneous stretches, they were aligned perfectly to actually form a usable road, they bounced the bike and sent shudders through a rider's hands and arms and shoulders, up to the penthouse apartment of the skull, down the spine and through the bottoms of the feet right back into the road, where the energy was stored to drive through the next rider. Paris-Roubaix was the worst. This, certainly, was bad enough.

Through the cobbles and onto a smoother section, Will looked back. Bourgoin was right on his wheel, the look in his eyes telling him that Richard hated the cobbles just as much as he did. The Dutchman Schiller sat in the hole behind Richard, while Merkel continued to talk madly into the microphone strapped to his wrist. He looked like Dick Tracy with a runny nose. Van Dryden had just finished his pull and brought up the rear. The latter two were slowly, however, falling off the pace set by Will, Bourgoin and Schiller. And losing the pace was like throwing red meat to the peloton, slowly uncoiling in the distance behind them.

"Hans — come on, me bucko! Pick it up!" Will yelled. Merkel looked up with a disgusted look on his face. Ross had usurped his position today. That's what Hans should have been telling Ross, not the other way around.

"I'm here. I'm here."

"No, you're there. We're here. Get your ass in gear."

The five rode silently for the next hour, focusing on pace, power and energy. Merkel was eating frantically, trying to keep his energy levels up, while Will and Bourgoin ate slowly and steadily, trying to stretch their food and water supplies until a car could get through the pack to pass them fresh supplies, or until they hit the feed zone. They caught and passed the four early breakaway riders on the Kruisberg climb, 89 kilometers into the race, passing them as a pickup truck would pass a horse on a country road. Yes, indeed, meet the pros, kids.

But there were problems in paradise as well. Van Dryden exploded, the last bits of his energy disappearing as suddenly as Will's last paycheck. He fell quickly behind the quartet. Merkel was fading. When the lieutenant took his pulls at the front, Will noticed the pace dropping quickly.

"Come on, Hans, you're losing it."

"*Ja, ja*. I'm here. I'm here."

He spoke as much to convince himself as Will and Bourgoin. The next time through the line, the pace dropped again as Merkel took the pull on the Mur de Grammont. This, Will knew, was where the pack could begin to suck them back into its fold. Bourgoin and Schiller were still strong at the front, as was Will, but Merkel was falling off — hard. It was decision time. Somebody was going to die here, and Will decided it was going to be Hans.

"Bring up the rear, Hans, sandwich Richard and let's take this thing home. We're halfway there. How far back are they?"

Merkel smiled thankfully. As he dropped to the side and fell back to the rear, he said, "Two-twenty-five," then climbed on Bourgoin's wheel and hung on for dear life.

Two minutes and 25 seconds. Not good. They had fallen back after a strong breakaway and the peloton had picked up its pace. It could eat up 145 seconds in a matter of minutes. Yet, even past the halfway mark, there was still a chance that they still weren't taking the Haven breakaway seriously. Maybe someone had seen or heard of Van Dryden exploding or Merkel falling off the pace or the inconsistent efforts of the group. Then again, perhaps the bunch still had confidence it could reel in its errant children whenever it damn' well pleased.

Bourgoin said quietly, "Merkel's gone."

Will looked back when he heard Bourgoin's voice. They were just three now, Hans falling back quickly, carrying the burning shells of other breakaway riders with him, as if a wave bore them away from a life raft. The pace, the climb, the cobbles, had destroyed them. Merkel looked up, then spoke into his radio.

"Well, what do you think, chief? You want to win this pup alone, or you want to take your chances with the pack?"

Bourgoin stared back at him. Schiller nodded. The deal was still good with him. Bourgoin turned and looked at Will and sighed. Will nodded. The three understood each other completely.

Together, they shifted into the big gears, picked up the pace and disappeared around a blind turn heading toward the final, ugly climb of the Molenberg and the finish that beckoned only 34 klicks beyond.

REACHING THE BASE OF THE MOLENBERG CLIMB, THE PELOTON HAD FINALLY reacted to the breakaways of the day, and like a whale straining plankton through its teeth, began to swallow them all: the Belgian and Dutch breakaways, Van Dryden, the neo-pros, Merkel, Will, Schiller ... and yet, not Bourgoin. Will didn't realize what happened until the last moment. He was focused only on the road and the pace and the finish line. In the last five klicks, as Will felt his legs and arms and head explode, he gave Bourgoin a whip-round and sent him on his way, then hung back, staying as far ahead of the pack for as long as he could, sliding across the road, muddling the pace, obstructing traffic as surreptitiously as possible so as to not raise the suspicions of the UCI commissaires. It wasn't much, to be sure, but it seemed to be enough, for as the pack roared around the final turn onto the long straight beside the Ghent Watersports Center, Will broke focus long enough to aim high in traffic and see Richard, arms high, break the invisible wall just ahead of a stream of Dutch and Belgian sprinters. This was a national tragedy, a Frenchman winning their race. It didn't happen. It had never happened. But it had happened today. And the Frenchman was damned happy about it.

But his directeur sportif was not.

Nevertheless, Deeds stood and smiled with Bourgoin for pictures, knowing that his smiling face would grace the cover of *L'Équipe* tomorrow along with stories and commentary about his dynamic, "no-holds-barred" race tactics. Deeds waved to the photographers and what spectators were left — in what had become an icy downpour within 10 minutes of the finish — and then marched back toward the team area.

Will had just delivered his bike to Tomas. It had gone well. A nice machine. Not The Beast, to be sure, but a nice bike nonetheless. One could get used to it, especially when you got to the mountains. God, Will thought, I bet she's a mother on a fast descent. And not bad, 64th. First to 64th in, what, five kilometers? Not bad at all. The way he was feeling in that last stretch, he never would have made it if it hadn't been for the bunch carrying him along, pacing for him. God, he thought, that was fun. And Bourgoin! Wild man. He was a wild man.

One second, he was looking at the ground, lost in his thoughts, smiling, the next, he felt his head slam into the back of the van and he was looking at the sky, the rain catching light like so many cold, falling diamonds in the air.

Deeds had him by the hair, jamming his forearm across Will's throat.

"Don't you ... ever ... fucking ... dare ... disobey my instructions again, you son ... of ... a ... bitch!"

Will was close to passing out. He was still recovering from the race, and now, he was being choked to death.

"Auwwk — but ... we ... won...."

"Not my way, damn you!"

"Ack — ack — ack — why ... didn't ... you just tell ... ack ... Merkel?"

"Because I don't talk to Merkel! I talk to Bourgoin, asswipe — and he turned off his radio because of you. He's lucky he won. Otherwise, I'd have his hide, too. But you ... you died. And if you ever pull that shit again — you're gonna die big-time."

Deeds pulled his arm away from Will's neck, leaving him to drop to his hands and knees on the muddy ground. Deeds marched off as Will tried to catch his breath.

The rain beat down. The cold enveloped Will. He yanked the soaking balaclava off his head and gasped in the mud. He stared at the water gathering around his hands. He should have been thinking about kicking the living shit out of Deeds. Nobody deserved to be treated like that, especially after a win. But that wasn't on his mind at all. What Deeds had said was on his mind.

If Deeds wasn't talking to Merkel, who was? And why? And my, oh, my, he sure as hell had a lot to tell Cheryl tonight.

The rain of Belgium surrounded him and he was lost in a wall of water.

❂

IT WAS RAINING IN PARIS AS WELL THAT EVENING, THE GLOOM OF THE OVERcast bringing dusk early to the city. Martin Bergalis stared out the windows of his office across the horizon as the lights began to come on one, after another, after another. He stared for a very long time, then looked again at the fax message he had received.

"He did well today, your friend."

"Yes," Kim said from the darkness surrounding the couch.

"You said he wouldn't."

"I didn't think he would. He certainly had enough obstacles. But not to worry. I know he can't keep it up."

Martin smiled and reached out his left hand to her. Kim quietly rose and walked across the room to him. She took his hand gently, then screamed as he crushed her fingers. Martin turned and brought the full force of his right hand down on the side of her face.

Kim fell to the floor, and, breathing hard out of shock and surprise, looked up at the man who was her employer, her lover, her ticket into a world of which she had only dreamed. His face was alive with fury.

"Martin...."

"Enough games. The police have the letters. Call our friend. End this —" he looked at a calendar, "— by Milan. Two weeks. Shatter the team."

CHAPTER ELEVEN:

GOIN' SOUTH

Ghisallo sits just south of the fork in Lake Como, some 50 kilometers north of Milan. A sharp and steady ascent into the lake country brought them to little more than an indentation in the road, a turn-off, an overlook, upon which sat a small church, a statue and a bust atop a granite column. Will pulled off the road and turned off the rental car.

"I've got to admit: A Fiat is a much nicer way to get here than a bike."

Cheryl threw open the door of the rented compact and wrenched herself out of thc rump-sprung leather seat.

"I'm not so sure. I've been sitting on that all morning and I've been sucking up exhaust fumes off the engine through the glove compartment. I'd rather be riding."

"We would have, but you don't have to ride nearly 300 kilometers tomorrow and then wrap it all up by descending the Poggio."

"All you guys do is whine. The Poggio is fun."

"Screaming downhill in heavy traffic where one wrong move or an inch too wide will paint you onto a carved rock wall. Yes, I guess you're right. Fun is what it is — you betcha by golly wow."

Cheryl looked around.

"What is this place? I know my mother would be happy to know I'm at a church on some day other than Easter, but, really — why are we here?"

"This isn't just a church — this is the cyclist's church. Here, come here, look at this."

He pulled her over to the bronze bust on the granite piling. A hawklike visage stared back at her.

"Fausto Coppi. Great Italian rider. The best. Amazing man. He could generate a tremendous amount of power."

"I've heard of him."

"But you're not impressed."

"I'm sorry. Statues just don't do it for me."

Will turned in mock disgust.

"Hey," Cheryl said, looking around him from behind. "I'm sorry. This is a nice place, and these are nice statues, but, I dunno, churches and professional cycling don't really mix, do they?"

"This one does. Come on." He took her hand and pulled her toward the church, across the gravelled parking lot. He pulled the heavy wooden door, hoping it wasn't locked. It gave easily, swinging open to reveal darkness and calm within.

"Come on."

They stepped into the cool dark, both, by inbred reflex, dipping a hand toward a holy-water font they could not even see. As their eyes adjusted, Cheryl could first make out little splashes of color, and then, slowly, a sea of jerseys and trophies and bicycles were revealed to her.

"Oh, my God."

Will laughed. "Exactly."

Cheryl slowly walked around the room. It was like a museum, a collection of bicycling memorabilia that collectors in California would give their fortunes to possess. Through the dim light, she peered at the names — Bottecchia, Coppi, Merckx, Bartali, Hinault — the whole history of Italian and European professional cycling was here, from Italian professionals who long ago lived their 15 minutes of fame, to young men of the Continent whose faces were now selling everything from bicycles to processed cheese spread on European TV.

"This ... this is marvelous," was all she could say.

"Impressive, isn't it? The Madonna is the patron of cyclists, and the Madonna del Ghisallo is the patron church of cyclists. Winners offer up their jerseys or their trophies, even their bicycles, to the church, for posterity, for display — for a tax write-off, I suppose — or, just in thanks for getting them across another finish line. The Holy Mother is our lady."

"Bet she loves the way her children talk."

"She understands. She's ridden with us. She knows what it takes."

"A heart of gold, an ass of lead."

"Exactly." Will looked toward the altar and murmured under his breath,

"And Holy Mother, please, give me legs tomorrow."

❁

WILL TOOK THE HAIRPIN TURN A LITTLE TOO FAST ON THE DESCENT TOWARD lunch in Bellaglio. The Fiat groaning with resentment, Cheryl was thrown into Will's side.

"Yeow. Hey, this isn't a racing bike and there is oncoming traffic, so why don't we power down a bit here and survive until the weekend? My favorite TV show's on Saturday; once I see that, then you kill me, okay?"

"Sorry. The brakes in this thing aren't that great."

"Oh, that's good news. Accelerator seems okay. Lighten up on it."

So, maybe he wasn't Mario Andretti, Will thought. Stephen Roche could run off from the peloton and build a second career as a rally driver ... but Roche was different from Ross by more than a few consonants. Will couldn't find the line on the descents quite the way Roche or Kelly or Indurain or LeMond could. Rockets. Ass up, head out over the front wheel, no brakes, 65 miles an hour easy on skinny tires. Hah. Nothing easy about it. At least for Will.

He lightened up on the accelerator.

"Thank you. The rest of my life appreciates it."

"What is the rest of your life?"

"The way it's going, visiting you either in the hospital or in prison every month. Have you heard from your rumpled little buddy?"

"The French answer to Columbo? No. Inspector Godot hasn't called me since last week. Before Het Volk he wanted to put this baby to bed as soon as he possibly could — even if that meant giving me an all-expense paid trip to the guillotine. But now he's taking his own sweet time about it, trying to convince his bosses it is a conspiracy."

"A conspiracy of who?"

"Haven Pharmaceuticals. Martin, Kim, Deeds, Merkel, Bourgoin, God knows who else."

"Just not you."

"I really wouldn't ... hang on." As he had been talking, his speed had built up again and he wrestled the Fiat around another tight corner, nearly scraping the molding off the door with a tree trunk. "I really wouldn't say that. You never know what else might come up as he builds his little airtight case. He had it airtight once already, and look what happened."

"So you...."

"Just sit tight until something pops. Until Columbo sees the final credits approaching and makes a bid for detective glory."

"Scratching his eyebrow all the way?"

"Of course. Scratching his eyebrow and convincing his bosses at police headquarters, all of whom own — hang on." The car slid through another hard turn. "All of whom own Haven stock, or do lunch with Bergalis at the club and the like, that dropping a curtain of scandal and murder at Mr. Marty's doorstep is really the right thing to do, even if it does mean they'll take a bath on their investments."

"So nobody's moving."

"Everybody's moving very carefully."

"So what is Godot up to? Sheesh ... watch it."

"It's not me, it's the car."

"Go ahead, blame something else."

"No, really, the brakes in this thing are like mush."

"The Italians don't like brakes much, anyhow."

"If I don't find a little back pressure here, you're going to be opening your door and sliding your foot along the ground, kid." He madly pumped the brakes. "Come on, Jasper, come on." Will felt his palms start to sweat and tighten on the wheel, almost peeling through the imitation leather steering-wheel cover. As the next turn came up, he downshifted, hearing the engine scream a high-pitched whistle, pounded on the brakes for all they were worth, went wide and cut in across the turn, convinced his left elbow had been hanging off the edge of the road. The road suddenly flattened in Bellaglio, the engine caught, and they rolled to a slow, but very satisfying stop. For a moment, neither spoke a word. Then Cheryl turned and hit him once, twice, three times on the shoulder.

"Goddamn you! You could have killed us!"

Will jokingly cowered in his seat. "Hey, hey, hey! Jeez, what did you say? And you just coming from church."

She hit him again.

He put the car in first and rolled away from the stop, across the street toward the trattoria. Will turned to Cheryl and smiled.

"You'll be happy to know this: the brakes work again."

She stared at him in angry silence.

"Look. Godot has told me, flat out, to keep out of the police business. He's doing what he should have done in the first place — running a computer check on everybody connected with the team to see what kicks up in motives, backgrounds, experience with plastic explosives. Since Jean-Pierre had so very many friends, the list of possibilities must be endless. He figures that since somebody took the time to forge letters and try to frame me, that there is something being aimed at the team, from inside or out. With Merkel and the radio business at Het Volk, he thinks inside. His bosses think out. Can't have Bergalis getting his skirts dirty, not if they've got a tennis date with him on Tuesday. Anyway, he's looking over stuff and just waiting for something more to pop."

He shot her a quick, stupid grin.

"I don't really care about that now. You can tell me all that at lunch. You damned near killed us!"

Will opened the door and began to get out of the car in front of the trattoria. He popped his head back in the Fiat.

"Just trying to get your mind off it. You know, you might really think about cutting down on caffeine in the morning."

Her fist shot out and caught him beside the nose.

❦

BEHIND THE SMALL HOTEL IN MILAN, INSIDE A CYCLONE FENCE, TOMAS DELGADO and two other mechanics continued to work on the bikes for the next morning's run from Milan to the coastal city of San Remo. This was one of the races Delgado enjoyed most of all, a one-day classic, brutally long, covered by good roads and capped with a smashing finale: the blast down the Poggio. There were some great finishes here: Kelly streaking down the Poggio, his elbows millimeters away from disaster on the walls, streaking past a startled Argentin at the line to carry off the day. Bugno. Fignon. Vanderaerden. The crash on the Cipressa — in '89? No, '88. No other sport gives you that, he thought. No other sport gives you men, one on one, reaching into themselves to push away the fear of death and find the last ounce of themselves — not of a machine, but of themselves — that might push them across the line to glory.

Delgado smiled. Almost poetic tonight, aren't we?

He eyeballed Bourgoin's lead bike for what must have been the eighth time, looking, checking, peering, trying to find anything that seemed off or over-tweaked or just not right. He didn't measure. He didn't use computers. He had the feel. He could touch a bike or see a rider and simply know what was, and what wasn't, and where it had to be taken in or let out.

Bourgoin's bike went back on the rack. He pulled Will's new Colnago from the rack and rolled it over to his work stand. He looked at the bike for a long moment, then looked back into a corner where Will's old bike, The Beast, stood waiting.

"Don't worry," he called back, "you'll get your chance. Either that, or you'll get a free ride to San Remo tomorrow. Not bad for a bike your age."

He laughed. Tomas realized he was becoming as bad as Will. He had given the bike a personality, and he didn't want to hurt its feelings.

Will and Cheryl had returned from their day trip in the late afternoon, stopping in and checking on Tomas, the bikes, the daily team chatter. Nothing new, they're fine and so am I, he had told them. He watched Will pass by the bike he would actually ride tomorrow and work his way back to his older machine, checking it, stroking it, speaking to it in a kind voice. Tomas understood. He understood how his great, if goofy, friend could identify with an aging, rusty machine held together by spit and wire and sealing wax, because his friend, he knew, was held together much the same way. Tomas turned to the new Colnago, white, fresh, right out of the box. Will had to love this machine as well, he thought. It had everything — top-of-the-line framing, geometry, gearing, shifters, wheels, tires. It was an ace, a deadly machine that could take the Poggio like nothing else. It had taken him through the battering of the Het Volk cleanly, had performed very well at the eight-day Tirreno-Adriatico, even though Will was riding closer to his old form than his new. That wasn't a true test anyway, Tomas thought, Deeds had used the race as a final warm-up for Milan-San Remo, the official start of the season, allowing everyone to coast, to stretch, to not worry about the final standings. By the final day, most of the team was gone from the race for real or imagined injuries: sores, pulls, headaches, brain-aches, toe-aches, ass-aches and simple lack of motivation.

That's why he never rode himself. Lack of motivation. Every time he had found himself in a bunch as a kid, he hung back and looked at the bikes. He listened. He saw. He knew who had a top machine and who had a dog. It wasn't that he didn't like to ride, he simply loved to feel and know and fix. It had begun with his own bike, a rusty cast-off his father had found in a city dump and brought home for his second son. Within a week, Tomas had pulled it apart and cleaned and greased everything down to the last ball bearing and rebuilt it and had it up and running. Within a month, it was painted, and restored and humming and sold for another bike, which was sold for another, and another and another, until the baker's son was riding beautiful discards of the rich boys and repairing top-of-the-line racing machines for the local champions. It wasn't a hobby. It wasn't a talent. It was a calling; a need to touch a top tube and, with a glance, know that there was something out of true, out of order, out of whack.

Like with this bike.

Tomas ran his hand along the frame, once, twice, three times. What? He spun the front wheel. Clean. He spun the rear. Clean. He stepped back and looked over the entire frame, centimeter by centimeter. Where, what, why? No answer. The bike wasn't talking. He loosened the chuck on the work stand that held the bike in place and lifted it out of the clamp, then lowered it to the ground. There. He found the balance point under the top tube and lifted the bike with one finger. There. The weight was off. Not by much, it couldn't be more than a few grams, but it was off. The bike was heavy. He put it down and ran his eye along the bike from above. Nothing. He reached under the titanium seat to lift the bike back onto the rack and felt his fingertips slip into something cold and giving.

He pulled them out quickly, disgusted, and lifted the bike back onto the work stand by the top tube. He locked the stand down, released the back clamp and spun the bike up on end. He pulled a screwdriver from his apron and peered at the titanium rails under the seat. Between them, molded to the seat frame was a five-millimeter covering of what had to be children's modeling clay. He poked into it with the screwdriver, peeling some off with the tip, then rubbed the clay between his fingers, forming a ball that he tossed over into a corner near his gear. Looking back under the seat, he noticed something in the center of the clay, a small, triangle of black plastic or metal. He pulled his knife from a pocket of his apron and began to scrape the clay away from the centerpiece. Whatever it was, it was in there pretty good. He turned the knife to the side and ran it along the edge of the triangle.

And then the press arrived. Cameras and flashbulbs. There were flashbulbs everywhere. It was all Tomas Delgado could see: flashbulbs popping with a series of bangs that were almost unreal, otherworldly, and too damned noisy for the rear courtyard of an Italian hotel at this time of night. Who was the celebrity that rated so many flashbulbs?

They blinded him.

❁

IN THE MIDST OF HIS DREAM, DEEP IN THE FOLDS OF SLEEP, WILL FELT THE shift in air pressure, the whump of the explosion, the shifting of the windows. He drifted to the surface for just a moment, then slid back into the depths, while Cacciavillani snored quietly in the next bed.

It seemed instantaneous, but it could have been two minutes, 10 or an hour later, when Will awoke to the banging on the door. Hard, insistent, someone trying to yell his name.

"Will! Come on, man! Will!"

It was Cheryl.

Ross rolled out of bed and tried to focus his eyes on anything. He struggled into his sweats and workout slippers, losing his balance while trying to dress. He was pulling on his Howdy Doody shirt when he opened the door.

"This had better be real...."

He stopped in mid-sentence. Cheryl's face was flushed and puffy and her eyes were bright red. She appeared to be very nearly in shock. Will woke up immediately.

"Jesus, kid, are you okay? Come on in...."

"No. You've gotta come. You've gotta come." She tugged on his arm and began to pull him down the hall toward the stairs, toward the lobby, toward the alley and toward the hell that awaited them just behind the hotel.

"What? God damn it, what, Cheryl? Just tell me, all right?"

"Tomas. Tomas...." she burst into tears again, her face growing bright red again.

"What about him?" Will said, quietly, almost dreading the answer.

She didn't answer; only looked at him through tear-filled eyes.

He began running now, down the stairs, through the small lobby and through the service hall behind the front desk that ran through the back of the hotel and to the back door. As he ran, he put his hand up to push open the edge of the door, but it was locked and his arm collapsed as he ran into it and he shoved his shoulder through the glass. He pulled himself free and fumbled with the silvered lock, swinging the door open as it rained glass and bits of wood framing on the ground. He ran across the courtyard in the darkness, kicking bits of wood and tubing and cyclone fence to the side. He ran toward the lights, police lights and ambulance lights and hotel floodlights and the lights of the mechanics' work area, now hanging in the air at crazy, unreal angles.

The last line of the fence, bowed out like an open milk carton, finally stopped him. He knotted his fingers inside the wiring and tried to catch his breath. He was hyperventilating as he looked through the fence at the carnage before him. Wheels were everywhere. Tubing was everywhere. Blood was everywhere. Giuseppe, one of the secondary mechanics, an apprentice of sorts, was sitting to the side, wrapped in slapdash bandages and covered with blood. He was in shock. Eyes wide. Mouth open. Staring. Blindly. Not seeing. Not hearing. Ears bleeding. They began to lead him away to an ambulance. Will turned his head back to the center of the pit, back to the place he had left Tomas. The white work stand was in three pieces, head, tube, feet. The bike that had been on it was shattered beyond recognition. The entire area was nothing but blood. And ... and ... he couldn't breathe. And ... pieces. Pieces of people. And one of the pieces wore a blue work apron. And the blue work apron had a name on it. And the name. And the name. And the name. Will stared at the apron and what was inside it, and his breath came in short, shattered blasts across his gritted teeth. He had never seen anything like this — he had never seen a friend like this — his friend, his best friend....

"Will, come on. Will!" Deeds shouted to get his attention. "Will! Come on, Will! Will! There's nothing you can do for him. Come with me, Will. Come on." Will struggled for a second, pulling himself back to the fence and another look at the shattered pile of flesh that was Tomas Delgado. "Let's get out of their way and let them do their jobs. Come on, Will, come on, Will."

The officer in charge kept waving people away, including Deeds and Will. He grabbed Will by the sleeve of his Howdy Doody shirt and roughly pulled him away from the scene, finally pushing him back toward the hotel. Will didn't fight. He didn't argue. He didn't struggle. He didn't know where or what or why he was. Deeds led him over to a corner of the courtyard and forced him to sit down next to a tree.

"Take it easy, Will. Take it easy." Deeds was telling himself the same thing. "Deep breaths, not too fast, easy. Easy."

"What ... what?"

"Nobody is sure, Will," Deeds spoke quietly, calmly. The two had their differences, but this was not a matter to fight over; this was a situation in which to pull together. "The chief of the *polizia* over there thinks it may have been a terrorist attack of some kind, but he's not sure, he's just guessing. But — he never knew. He never knew what happened. It all happened too quickly, Will."

Deeds himself leaned back, exhausted. He was breathing hard, too. He was in danger of going into shock, if he wasn't there already. Members of the team, now alerted to what had happened, were wandering out of the hotel, one after another, surveying the carnage and looking to Deeds for answers. He didn't have any — except one: No. We would not be riding Milan-San Remo today. There was no heart for riding today. And there was nothing to ride on.

He looked over to the lights surrounding the shredded cyclone fence. The last ambulance was pulling away, carrying Giuseppe. A black, enclosed truck pulled up and replaced it. On the side was written, in official-looking letters: *Magistrato Inquirente*. The meat wagon. The coroner. Quincy. It was going to be a very long night. And a very long day. And a very long time before anyone on Haven felt much like themselves.

❖

ABOUT FOUR IN THE MORNING, THE POLICE FINISHED ROPING OFF THE AREA and the coroner completed his grisly task of finding, labeling, and packing the pieces that once made up the earthly vessel of Tomas Delgado.

Deeds had watched it all from under the courtyard tree, surrounded by Merkel, Bourgoin, Philippe, Cardone, Cheryl and Paluzzo. Cardinal had returned to his room. Cacciavillani had never stirred from sleep.

The directeur sportif turned to his team. "Let's everybody go get whatever sleep we can. Tomorrow, as you can well imagine, is off. Rest and recover. We'll have a meeting about noon to discuss what we know and what ... will happen."

Cardone spoke up from the crowd. "What will happen, Carl?"

"No idea. I've got to call Paris. Talk to Ross. Kim Ross. She'll probably have to talk with Bergalis. I dunno. We'll see what they want to do. But they've got to know."

Deeds looked around the small group in the darkness. The mercury vapor lamps of the hotel gave their faces a ghostly pallor. And there seemed to be a face missing from the crowd.

"Where's Ross?"

The spot Will had been sitting, next to the tree, was empty. He wasn't in the courtyard. He wasn't near the cyclone fence. Cheryl looked over to where he had parked the Fiat earlier in the evening. The car was gone.

"Oh, shit." She sighed.

❧

FATHER ALFREDO DINI OF THE CHURCH OF THE MADONNA DEL GHISALLO GOT the call about 5:30 a.m. A man from the village had passed by the chapel and seen someone trying to break in. Should he call the police, *Padre*? No. Just watch him. I'll be right there. This had happened before. Someone got drunk and fought with his wife and needed the Lord in the ugly hours before dawn. He could deal with it. No need for the police. Father Dini pulled on his clothes and drove to the shrine. Even from the road he could hear the crying at the church door. This was bad. It was the sound of a wounded animal. Someone had died, Father Dini thought. He had heard these sounds too many times before. He walked to the front of the church and carefully approached the figure huddled at the base of the door.

In the first streaks of morning, the face that looked up at Father Dini frightened him, red-eyed and puffy, with terrible red streaks running across the cheeks, forehead and nose. A criminal. A criminal here to rob the shrine of its treasures. The face turned back to the door and raised his hand up to the door handle.

"*Por favore, Padre.* Please, Father, have mercy."

Father Dini looked long and hard at the man in the Haven Racing jacket kneeling at the door of the shrine. Something in the face, he thought, was familiar. Something he knew. The scars. Haven. The scars. This was *Il Cicatrice*. The Scar. The rider who had flown into the back window of a car in Spain. He was very famous for his crash — and very frightening because of it.

The priest reached into his pocket, pushed the small can of pepper spray to the side, and pulled out his keys. He opened the door to the church and held it for Will.

"*Grazie, Padre. Grazie.*"

The priest waved him in, then locked the door behind the scar-faced rider. He thought he knew who this man was, but there was no percentage in taking a chance. Losing even one of these artifacts would mean the end of his calling. Better to let him in, let him face his God, and then let him out when Father Dini was ready to open for the daily business of saving souls and selling souvenirs.

❁

A SINGLE LIGHT IN A SHUTTERED FIXTURE LIT THE CHURCH. EVEN ACCUSTOMED to the darkness, Will could only just make out the jerseys, the bikes, the museum collection that made up the shrine. He sat near the back and felt the quiet grow around him, until the silence very nearly had a sound all its own. Suddenly, he realized he was crying again, the frustrations, fears, grief and terror all rushing out of him in a flood of emotion. He leaned forward in the chair and simply let everything go.

❁

FAUSTO COPPI RAN HIS HAND ALONG THE COOL GREEN METAL OF HIS BIANCHI top tube, then looked up at his jerseys — donated pleasantly, but without great enthusiasm — to the church.

"So why did you do it?" Anquetil asked.

"The church. The team. They said it would be good for the team. I did it. It was my decision. But this bike, this bike I should have kept. This bike I should have kept."

"You'd still be dead, and the bike would likely still be here."

"True enough. But I could have looked at it a while longer. Ridden it. Touched it."

"Ahh," Anquetil waved his hand in mock disgust. "You love it too much. You never realized, Fausto, it was just a sport, like any other sport. It ate up your talent, took your best years, then malaria killed you. Alone and dead. Star athlete or sickly grandmother — we all go alone."

"So yours was better?"

"Stomach cancer. Maybe genetic. Maybe lifestyle. I went before my time, too. But — I had a great deal of fun. The bicycle let me have that fun, gave me the money to have that fun, to pay for that fun. But, eh, that led to the grave, too. I have no regrets. And I have some great memories."

"Of races?"

"Of races. Of beating Poulidor again and again. Of champagne and marvelous meals and beautiful women and Janine." He smiled. "Janine."

There was a rustling of papers in the corner and Jean-Pierre Colgan drifted past, still carrying his handful of wires and chrome, what was left of his beautiful, high-tech, high-explosive American toaster. Jacques Anquetil gave him a disgusted look, then dematerialized in a puff of bright Tour de France yellow smoke.

Colgan turned to Coppi.

"Why does he hate me?"

"That — that is Jacques. And he will tell you why when he is ready to tell you why, and not a moment sooner. Live with it. You have all eternity to discover why."

They both turned as Tomas Delgado walked through the wall of the church, gliding through a Bottecchia jersey to stand at the side of the altar.

He was holding the seat and seatpost from a bicycle in one hand and a knife in the other.

"Welcome, my friend," Coppi intoned, "in peace and goodwill."

"Where am I, and — excuse me," he said, glancing at Jean-Pierre Colgan, "What are you doing here?"

"You have joined us, friend Tomas," Coppi said. Colgan merely sneered. He and Delgado had never gotten along. He was still convinced Delgado had misadjusted his seat at the Tour last year, leading to saddle sores that forced Colgan to abandon.

"I take it, then," Tomas said, "That I am dead. Gone over."

"True," Coppi replied. "You had the same problem as our friend here," motioning toward Colgan, "tampering with an explosive."

Tomas shifted the knife to his other hand and rubbed his eyes. His sensations were all screwed up, as in a dream. Maybe this was a dream and he was simply sleeping next to his work stand behind the hotel in Milan. But, as he looked around, he realized that as much as he had heard about this church, he had never been here ... so, how did he know how it looked and smelled and felt?

"No," Coppi told him, "it's not a dream. You are here. You will be with us. If it is a dream, Tomas, it is not yours, anyway. It belongs to your friend, there, in the back of the church, sleeping on the chair and drooling down the back of that pew."

Tomas turned, and in the lightening gloom, he could make out a figure collapsed in a chair near the back door. As he walked over to it, he realized it was Will Ross, curled and broken and looking more dead than even he felt at the moment.

Tomas Delgado looked down on the living, breathing face of his friend. He thought for a moment, then raised up both hands.

"Beware, my friend, it was your bike. Whatever it was, it was on your bike. And if you find it as I did, don't play with it. Don't poke it. Don't scrape it."

Colgan jumped in from the front of the church.

"Yes, for heaven's sake, don't play with it."

Tomas turned back to Ross. "Beware, my friend. This was meant for you. For you."

Tomas turned and walked toward Coppi and Colgan.

Coppi smiled. "Come, my son, let us walk together. I have much to tell you." He put his arm around Delgado's shoulder, and together they walked through the wall in the back of the church. Colgan stood there for a moment, looking out over the world he had left what seemed to be an eternity ago. He took a deep breath and felt nothing. He hated that most of all: he could never feel or taste a cool breeze.

This place certainly took some getting used to.

Colgan turned, faced the wall that Coppi and Tomas Delgado had just stepped through, and walked quickly toward it.

"Delgado, you must watch out for Anquetil. He is a bastard...." His voice disappeared as his body flowed through the stone and plaster wall of the church.

Will Ross slept quietly in the chair, surrounded by the silence and peace and safety of the Madonna.

And that is where Cheryl found him.

❁

DEEDS HAD BEEN DRINKING STEADILY FOR THE PAST HOUR AND A HALF, TRYing to settle his nerves and screw up the courage to call Paris. They had to be told. They had to know. He threw back the last half of his fourth glass of cheap cognac and winced as the fire tore down his throat. He rose unsteadily and stepped toward the lobby desk and the phone that had sat silently, staring at him, for the past hour. They had to be told. They had to know. Deeds picked up the phone and asked the operator to connect him with Paris.

But Paris had already been told. Paris already knew.

CHAPTER TWELVE:

SHATTERED

Martin Bergalis was unhappy.

Here he was, 43 years old, on the brink of controlling Haven Pharmaceuticals International and the lives and destinies of thousands of employees worldwide through praise or damnation, and he was afraid of his own father; afraid of what he was about to tell him.

It was a simple concept, but Martin's future was tied to its success. So many other companies had been able to do it, so many other corporate executives had been able to do it ... so, why not him? Why not Martin Bergalis?

One reason: Stefano Bergalis.

Martin turned in his deep leather desk chair and looked out a window of the headquarters of Haven Pharmaceuticals. He could gaze over Paris from his vantage point, or, by changing his focus, see the bubbles in the pane of blue-green glass, formed sometime near the turn of the century.

The office was traditional, the office was elegant. The chateau had been built as a mansion for a member of the landed aristocracy during the reign of Louis XIV. It was No. 2 on the list for Martin Bergalis. Once he had passed the first hurdle, the second — abandoning this elegant, opulent, drafty and crumbling chateau for a major office building downtown — would be simple. He wanted the amenities of power. He wanted the trappings of power. What he needed now was the power itself.

This morning's conversation with his father would determine when the power would be his — today, tomorrow, perhaps never. Dealing with his father was dealing with the devil incarnate.

He looked over the headlines of the papers strewn across his desk from the past week and smiled. The pictures showed the devastation at the hotel in Milan. They showed the devastation on the faces of the members of the cycling team. They showed Kim, slightly tousled and rough, yet, still beautiful, in the thick of the investigation, answering questions, comforting the team, making decisions as to the future. Perfect.

Wrong target, and, yet, better result.

His friend deserved a raise.

◎

GODOT STARED AT THE COMPUTER SCREEN. HE HATED COMPUTERS. They made him feel lazy, doing all his calculating and legwork for him. But his secretary Isabelle had told him that they could find things that he couldn't, that they could make connections that he couldn't, so she signed him on the library computer and punched his ticket for deep section searching. He was cruising the information superhighway in a battered and broken Renault, but at least he was on the road. That was something.

The problem was that as he stared at the blue screen and saw the information blink back at him, one name, one face, one record after another, there was one person on Haven who did not exist. There were no tax records, no employment files, no police entries, no military histories, no deeds, no footprints, tracks or traces of any kind.

One person did not exist. In Paris. In France. In the world at large.

So, if this person did not exist, Godot wondered, why was he taking up space on the planet?

◎

WILL LISTENED TO ANOTHER PLANE TAKING OFF FROM CHARLES DE GAULLE. It was low. For a moment, he couldn't quite hear himself think, for which he was grateful, then the sound went over the gate and began to Doppler shift.

A shadow fell across the window of his apartment, then, over the wall of the dance studio across the street, then disappeared with a roar into the distance. Moments later, an express a few minutes out of the Gare du Nord roared behind the apartment house, the scream of the whistle and the thunder of its passing shaking the building to its foundations. It, too, began to fade.

He should be on the bike, he thought. He should be riding this off, riding to bring his emotions back into line. He stared out the window and considered it for only a moment. Then he leaned his head back and finished the final third of the bottle of hideously cheap red wine.

As it burned his throat raw, Will could only think that a lot of Americans would be surprised. The French could make crappy wine, too.

❀

"YOU'VE GOT TO FACE FACTS, FATHER. THE TEAM HAS BEEN DECIMATED."

The old man held out his hand and waved. Henri Bergalis reached into a pouch attached to the side of the wheelchair and pulled out his father's electric voice box. Henri handed it to Stefano, who put it up against his throat and rasped, "We had some early succezz. Some stage wins in Ruta del Zol. Het Volk." He dropped his arm, clearly exhausted by the effort.

Martin smiled. This might turn out to be far easier than he imagined.

"True, but, even you must admit, father — those are not important races. They are warm ups for the season. Little solid competition. Even the champions hold back."

"A shh-amp-ion never holdz back."

"Perhaps in your day, father, but not today. The season is too long. There are only a few races that merit international attention for the rider or the sponsor. Some champions only target the Tour de France. Others the Tour, the Giro, the World Championships. Others, the classics, Paris-Roubaix or Milan-San Remo. No one goes all out anymore, father. Not for everything."

"Zean Kelly does."

"He retired, father."

"Bourgoin, Cash-e-vy-oneee — even Rozz in Bel-chee-om."

"Perhaps, before the accident — the incident, father. But not anymore. It will take time and money and effort to rebuild this team — essentially, from the ground up. Bourgoin needs a fierce lieutenant. Merkel has been injured all season. Cacciavillani can't really be positioned without a team to help him. Everyone has lost part of his desire, his jump in the peloton. And, Ross, according to Kim, has simply lost his heart. He's drunk in his company apartment."

"Wish company apart — ment?"

Martin opened his desk and checked a sheet in his team folder. "I believe it is the old Navarre building? North of the city along the tracks — next to the N17? It's just west of Charles de Gaulle now. Basically, warehouse and industrial and ... lesser housing."

"Hzzz. I alwayzz meant to tear that down. Maybe I should now and throw his azzz on the street."

"Then we shall, father, we shall. It's time for Haven Pharmaceuticals to change, isn't it, father? Time to do away with some of the old ..." The old man shot his son an unseen glance. "... and welcome in the new: new marketing, new diversification, new focus."

"What new focuzzz?"

This was the chance Martin had been waiting for, the opening he had anticipated.

"Father," he said, coming around the desk and dropping to a knee beside the wheelchair to bring himself to his father's eye level, "sports and sports medicine have always been the key to the growth of Haven. In your day, that sport was cycling. Today, that sport is everything." He waved his hands in the air to create a universe of imagined opportunities before his father. "European football. American football. American basketball. Hockey. The Olympics. Franchises, merchandising and marketing. We control the image, we control the sponsorships, we control the product usage, we control every tier of franchise sales from parking to tickets to stadium concessions to logo merchandising to media contacts and broadcast rights. It becomes ours, father, a new sea of revenue to enjoy — fed by a growing number of revenue streams as our investments bring more success to the franchises which bring even more media attention than we have already developed."

"And the pricezzzz of thizzz?"

"Well, honestly, the end of the cycling team. We take the 55 million francs saved from there, and reinvest it as seed money to attract the American professional leagues — especially football. The investment grows from there — as we support a team — then the investment drops as the team begins to support itself and thrive."

"And cycling?"

"We continue to support it as a product sponsor — we supply the energy drinks, the power foods, the necessary vitamins. But not just to one team — all teams. Haven logos everywhere. Our visibility increases, while our costs drop."

"Drop to whhhhat?"

"Perhaps three million francs — mainly in product supplied rather than direct fees."

Stefano inhaled sharply. What was said was good business sense. But it tore at his heart and everything he held dear — the entire meaning behind his company.

"Caaan't we ddooo bothhh?"

"We need the seed money from somewhere. As you have said, father, you don't find money on the inside of your shoes."

Stefano Bergalis was quiet for a long time. Henri desperately wanted to speak, but knew that voicing his opinion now would insult his father's position and give his brother a greater sense of where Henri stood and how he could be blocked within the company.

"There is wizzdom in your plans, Maaarteeen. We will zzzeee — after Roubaix."

The buzzing stopped. The old man had turned off his electronic vocal cord, spun it once, like a gunfighter from an American western, and dropped it into the pouch on the side of the wheelchair. He smiled. His life hadn't been much lately, not since the stroke, so he enjoyed what small games he could.

"Till Roubaix then," Martin said, trying to control his excitement. "I'll call the team."

Henri broke in. "What — and tell them the bad news? Have your bags packed by Roubaix, the team is finished? I think we should keep this from the team. They sink or swim on their talents. No surprises — no sword of Damocles hanging over their necks. They perform, based on their talents. They recover, based on their strengths. No threats from the great glass office."

"That will be a challenge for them," Martin said, smiling. "Fine, then, no surprises."

"No surprises." Henri stared hard at his brother. You're destroying this company and this man, he thought, you are throwing everything we believe in aside. But the sprint was up, the jostling for position had begun. And, Henri thought, the finish line in Roubaix was still a few weeks away.

Despite what he had just promised, Henri Bergalis fully intended to talk with the riders he knew and trusted.

Despite what he had just promised, Martin Bergalis fully intended to talk with the riders he knew and trusted.

Despite what he had just heard, Stefano Bergalis smiled. This should be an interesting battle. The cycling team as pawns and control of the company to the victor.

❀

IT WAS A STRETCH. WAS THE BANGING INSIDE HIS HEAD OR OUT? INSIDE OR out? Don't know. Don't care. Will slipped back into sleep and Tomas reappeared, sitting on the ledge next to the window. Will kept saying, "I miss you, pal, I miss you," while Tomas, continually frustrated because he couldn't seem to convince Will of much of anything, said, "Ride. You've got to ride. The only way you can win is ride. Ride, Will, get back on the bike, Will — listen, Will."

Bang! Will sat bolt upright, awake, slightly disoriented, slightly hung over, but awake. Oh, Jesus. Saints preserve me from the chunks of grape that get stuck in my brain. The door was being beaten down. God, he thought, it's Godot again. The banging stopped. A voice outside shouted: "Monsieur Ross — we are coming in."

Hmmmph. He was being raided. Never had been raided before. He sat in stunned silence while someone worked a key into the lock, slipped the bolt and opened the door. It was the largest person he had ever seen in France, at least six-foot-six of solid muscle. God, it's the hit man. The hit man that got Tomas is here for me. He stared at the mountain of humanity in a stupor.

"Get it over with ... I've got more drinking to do after I'm dead."

The huge excuse for a human being looked at him quizzically, shook his head, and walked back out the door he had just opened. Will threw the now-empty wine bottle at him, missed completely, and shattered the tube of the black-and-white TV his mother had bought for him.

A thin young man walked into the room. I know this guy, thought Will.

Who is he?

The young man kicked at a piece of the picture tube lying on the floor in front of him. "Are you always so far off in your aim, Mr. Ross?"

"No. Normally, I'm far worse."

Henri Bergalis stepped forward.

"Mr. Ross. I am concerned in talking to you, because you are drunk."

"I'm not drunk. I'm sober. Grumpy and half asleep, but sober. Give me 10 minutes and I can be drunk again."

"I need to talk with someone who can understand what I say. Are you that man?"

"I have no idea. Who am I talking to?"

"I'm Henri Bergalis, Mr. Ross. You may remember me from ..."

"Yes, the hospital and the street in front of the velodrome. So, what's up, kid?"

"Do you like racing?"

"Not particularly. Not anymore."

"Since when?"

Yes, Will thought, since when? Tomas? Before that. Het Volk had been an aberration. A rush. A caffeine high. He had spent one day wired for sound, and that one day had been on a bike. Before that. Training? Joy riding around Senlis? That was touring, that wasn't racing. Last year? GelSchweiz? That had been work. Drudgery. Punch the clock, work the time. Barker-Hartman the year before had been an English-language joke, with the exception of Webster, who raced like he didn't realize the rest of the Anglo-American team was made up of burnout cases.

Will looked at the floor, ignoring the man before him, thinking back, cataloguing his life. The teams began to wash together, the faces running and bleeding in his mind, a great meld of unrecognizable humanity. When had he last felt the competitive fire, for real? Maybe never. Raymond had it. That's what killed Raymond. But him — perhaps he really was one of those Americans whose only reason for being involved was that he got to wear bright uniforms and get some attention. God. He felt like a high-school sophomore trying to decide if he really wanted to go out for varsity football next year. Since when? Since never.

"This was a mistake." Henri Bergalis turned and walked toward the apartment door.

"Sure was. Say hi to your brother and his girlfriend when you see them."

Henri Bergalis turned, covered the distance between him and Will's collar in two steps and pushed him down into the overstuffed chair.

"Don't you care about anything? Don't you know what is going on?" He shook Will hard. Will reached up under Bergalis's hands and, grasping the thumb, turned it out hard. Bergalis yelped and broke his grip. Will was filled with an anger he hadn't felt in years — an anger over Tomas and Raymond and Kim and Haven and Deeds and Hans and Godot and Philippe and the Ruta and a whole world of emotions he hadn't sorted out.

"Look, Henry — I have just about had it with everybody in this goddamned city pushing me around whenever they goddamned well felt like it! Do you hear me! I slingshot a winner at Het Volk, and Deeds damned near strangles me; I catch the goddamned peloton at the Ruta del Sol and Philippe decides to park in the middle of the road; my ex-wife has threatened to fire me; and my friends ... Godot wants to arrest me based on a couple of forged letters, and someone decides that the best mechanic on the Continent needs to play with fireworks!" His face was bright red now, his voice high, his emotions completely out of control.

"Don't you dare ever touch me again, or all the pills in the Haven warehouse won't put you back together! You or any of your two-bit corporate buddies!"

Henri Bergalis backed off. He stared at Ross silently through the entire tirade. When Will paused to catch his breath, Henri unloaded the corker.

"It was your bike," he said quietly.

"What? What bike? What bike?" Will slowly began to catch his breath, his blood pressure returning to normal.

Henri Bergalis gave Ross a moment to calm down, to set him up for the kill shot. Do this right, he thought, and he had a loyal soldier to his cause.

"Delgado wasn't the target. You were. He simply found the device."

Will was poleaxed, slammed backwards into shock, suddenly staring off past Henri Bergalis, toward the window, the street, the dance academy and Paris and Italy and a cyclone fence in the rear courtyard of a hotel in Milan and a shrine in the mountains and a dream in the shrine.

"Don't ... Don't play with it ..." Will mumbled, distantly. "Don't play with it. Are you sure — sure it was my bike?"

Bergalis nodded. "Yes. I've seen the final report. It was your bike."

Then it wasn't a dream. It wasn't a dream. Tomas and Coppi and Colgan and Anquetil wandering across the altar of the Madonna del Ghisallo. And was it a dream with Tomas telling me to ride? Was it a dream? He grabbed his eyes and forehead with both hands, pushing the memories away. He dropped his hands and stared at Bergalis in rage and confusion.

"Damn. Damn you. Damn your brother. Damn all of it."

Henri Bergalis wanted to smile, but showed no emotion. Time to bend a will toward his, as gently as possible.

"My brother wants to disband the team."

"I know."

"You know? How do you know?"

"You guys are amazing. You sit out there playing your little corporate shuffleboard matches without realizing that the people whose lives you are screwing with might actually figure some stuff on their own."

"So what did you figure out?"

"Me? Nothing, I'm a bit of a schlub on stuff like that. But a fan told me." He thought back to a drunken evening with Jean Jablom. "A great and loyal Haven fan laid it all out, even putting me in a central role. Am I in a central role?"

"Now that someone is trying to kill you, I'd say yes."

"Your brother?"

That was the question, Henri thought. The question that could bring down the House of Haven and put only the shattered remnants directly in his hand. Time to tread carefully.

"No."

"No? Who else? Kim? Deeds? Luis, that medical assistant? How about that flight attendant on Air France who gave me all those extra drink coupons? How about her? Jesus."

"Then, perhaps. Perhaps. I can't believe that about my brother, but perhaps. But whoever it is — we have to move quickly, and yet carefully."

"You and Godot. Quickly — so we make mistakes. Carefully — so more people wind up playing second base like Tomas. Great. You guys handle it.

I'm gone."

Will walked to the dent in the wall that passed for a closet and pulled out the nylon bags that carried his life. Without care or concern, he began throwing whatever he owned into them. With any luck, he'd be on the street within 10 minutes. At the Gare du Nord in 20. And on a train to Brussels within the hour. Good-bye, Paris. Good-bye, Haven. Good-bye to all that.

"Don't you care?"

"No. Frankly, no." He turned and jumped into the face of Henri Bergalis. "I don't care. I care that one of my friends is dead. But I don't care about you or your family or your company or the fact that the Paris police are letting people get blown to bits because they don't want to ruffle any feathers of the president of the Chamber of Commerce. No. I don't care, Henry. I don't care."

"Henri."

"Henry. You remind me of that cartoon kid with the bald head, cleft chin and little dotted lines to whatever he looked at. I never liked him, either."

The two stared at each other for a long, hard moment. Then, Henri Bergalis smiled.

"How does it feel to be alive again?"

"It's easier to be dead drunk."

"True. But then, dead drunk, you can't help me — and you can't help your friends. And you can't put the killer of Tomas Delgado into the Bastille."

"Even if it's your brother?"

"Even if it's my brother."

Will realized he was breathing hard. He realized that he felt angry and frustrated and vicious and ready to bend the headset off a brand-new Bianchi. He realized he did feel alive. And he felt used. Which made him furious.

He looked at Bergalis. He smiled, a smile that caused Henri to take one step back and away from him. No, thought Will, I wouldn't cross the street to piss in this guy's ear if his brain was on fire. But Tomas had said ride. And this chump was offering a ride. A chance. An opportunity. To beat these knobs at their own game.

Frankly, he was sick and tired of being used.

And, now, he was going to let the users know it.

❂

GODOT LEANED AGAINST THE DOOR OF HIS OFFICE. HE STARED AT THE MESS that was his desk, the desktop computer that sat at an angle atop the pile of files and photos and evidence sheets. The computer printout, the first he had ever run, fell out across the floor from his hand. He gathered what he could and threw it, hard, into a corner. His frustration was clear. His superiors, his chief, his fellow inspectors, didn't see what he was beginning to see in the Haven deaths. Two deaths. An employee with no past. Obvious attempts to cast the blame elsewhere. But no. Don't move on it. We'll talk to Martin Bergalis about it. We owe it to him to let him know where the investigation stands.

Unless, thought Godot, Bergalis was behind it all, pulling the strings like a master puppeteer. But, thought Godot, what if the puppets knew of the strings? How would they react?

It could make for an interesting puppet show.

✶

HENRI BERGALIS STOOD IN THE CENTER OF THE APARTMENT. THE AFTERNOON sun ran across the floor, warming it far beyond the temperature outside. He watched as Will Ross silently dressed in his riding gear, then rolled the old Colnago out into the center of the room. As Will checked the tire pressure, Henri noticed that the frame was pitted and scarred, a survivor, he thought, of the bomb blast in Milan.

"We should get you a new bike."

Will turned hard and pointed a finger at Henri. He pumped it twice before saying, in a strained, quiet voice: "No. This is my bike. This is what I ride from here on out."

Bergalis held up both hands. "Fine. I'm sorry."

Will began to roll the bike toward the door.

"Thank you. Thank you for doing this," Henri said.

Will turned and stared at the young businessman standing in the center of what remained of his life.

"I am not," he said, slowly and deliberately, "doing this for you."

CHAPTER THIRTEEN:

A WEEKEND IN THE COUNTRY

Will was obnoxiously early for the race. With four hours to go before the starter's gun and the ceremonial procession around the square, his only companions in the city center were the workmen who hammered and sawed and tacked the sign-in podium together. Except for that, it was a silent morning, even the birds taking their business elsewhere. He sat on the steps of the ancient town hall of St. Niklaas, and watched a motley gang of errant leaves and papers skitter across the town square in the freshening breeze.

That would drive the Belgians crazy, he thought. They were a fanatically clean people. They would spend hours debating why those papers were tossed on the ground and why those leaves hadn't been corralled and done away with late last year.

Will smiled. This was a country to love.

He looked skyward through slitted eyes, the brilliance of the coming day forcing him into a ball on the granite steps. It would be another glorious spring ride in Belgium, a day at the edge of bitterness, when the skies were a shattering blue that hurt your eyes to look at them. Then again, Will's eyes hurt anyway. He felt he had golf balls in his sockets. The last few days had been a blender load of training rides and bad dreams and frantic phone calls from Deeds.

"Are you ready? Are you ready? Can you ride? I won't give you the ride unless you can ride. Have you put this Milan business behind you? Can you ride?"

Yes, Carl, I can ride. I can also walk and talk and shit and eat nails.

Which is why he couldn't sleep. Everything within him had been on the rough and ragged edge since Milan, since "the incident." At first, it had taken the form of depression, the world's worst case of Churchill's "black dog." He had been floundering, he realized, with nothing much to live or work for remaining in his life.

Then, slowly, he had found his will to ride once more, yet again, as much out of his resentment toward Haven and the little corporate games that had brought everything to a point over his anger toward the death of Tomas Delgado behind a Milan hotel.

The face of Tomas haunted his dreams. As did that of Jean-Pierre Colgan, who, oddly, actually looked hurt that no one in the ether between Will's dreams and reality gave him the kind of respect he felt he deserved. Tomas, on the other hand, was always hanging around with Fausto Coppi. They appeared to be close friends, holding each other in the highest respect. And Anquetil was always there, never saying much, yet always making his presence felt, always finding time to stride up to the camera that was Will's mind, make a fierce face and say, "This *visage* is what got you into this mess in the first place!" before strutting away laughing obnoxiously.

Yes, that face is what got him into cycling in the first place. Although, as time went on, Will had moved his hero worship a number of times, always into the more emotional riders, those who exploded in a burst of raw human effort, rather than those, like Anquetil, who coldly controlled timing, tactics and pace. Both achieved their aims, the top step of the podium; in fact, Anquetil did it far more often than many of the others. But the human cannonballs were always the most fun to watch.

Was he fun to watch? He didn't know. Lost in the peloton, scrambling to hold any kind of position, nobody really watched him in the first place. Stewart Kenally had always told him that people only see the locomotive and the caboose on a train. Long ago, Will realized he was merely a boxcar.

Chugga-chugga-chugga-chugga.

A rusty boxcar.

As much as he loved this countryside, the rolling hills and endless seas of green, the forests and the villages and the cities with their small town atmospheres, he knew today was going to be hell on wheels, and he was going to feel that rust. Nearly 300 kilometers. Seven hours in the saddle. Sixteen climbs, most with cobbles, all with hellish angles. Back to the Kwaremont, the Muur, the Bosberg and the Patersberg, which a farmer had actually built so his hill could be a part of La Ronde van Vlaanderen, the Tour of Flanders.

Soddy bastard.

At least the Patersberg had replaced the Koppenberg. That was the devil's own design. With a 22-percent grade, it was like riding straight up in the air. With the cobbles, you couldn't get a grip. With only about two-and-a-half meters side to side, you couldn't maneuver in traffic. With the cars and bikes intermingling, there was always the chance of getting run down. In fact, they finally did shut the damned thing down after Skibby slipped on the Koppenberg and nearly got his feet squashed when the race director's car immediately drove over his bike. Amazing.

This whole country was amazing. So wonderful to tour, so hellish to race. This was where cycling lived.

Will looked at the cheap, plastic Sportsman's watch he wore on race days. The green and purple face told him he still had three hours before the race. But even now, so far to go before the start, the square of St. Niklaas was beginning to come alive with activity. The workmen had finished. The first representatives of the teams were beginning to set up their stations. The first fans were beginning to claim their spots. The mood of the square, quiet and thoughtful only moments before, gave its first stirrings of ceremony, life and celebration.

Race day had begun.

✷

WILL STARED AT THE RECTANGULAR PAVING STONES AND COBBLES STRETCHing out across the square. They were roughly the same shape the race would take, a great, 276-kilometer rectangular ride from St. Niklaas to what would likely be a lone-wolf finish in Meerbeke. There had been some great sprint finishes here, some won by less than the width of a tire, but the cobbled bergs often busted up riders and the pack to such an extent that whoever made that final right turn first, merely had to pedal smoothly to cross the line in high style.

Will's eye followed the line of the brick. There, about halfway, the first berg. Then there, and there. The Kwaremont, fourth. 10-percent grade. Only a taste of what is yet to come. The Patersberg, twice that in grade. One-hundred-and-six kilometers to go. The Molenberg. Bad news. Follow the course. Berendries. Not horrible. The Muur. God, I hate that one. And, as his eye came up to the finish, the Bosberg. Hammer time. Watch them split and fumble and crawl to the line from there. Amazing athletes. He snickered. Let's see one of those hormonally endowed linemen do that!

Outside his consciousness, he felt that someone was calling him. Will looked up and scanned the square. No one. Then, he felt it again. He looked back across the square and directly opposite him, he saw Cheryl, her black, red and yellow Haven jacket meshing with the multicolored background. She was waving. He waved back. She waved him over. He waved her off. She shook her head and began the long walk across the square toward Will.

It took her a long time and she was clearly frustrated with him by the time she arrived.

"Why do I have to do all the work?"

"Because you are the serf, and I — I am the star," he said, sarcastically.

"Jesus, you've got that right." She sat down on the granite steps beside him. "All except the 'star' part. I'm not sure about that 'star' part."

"Well, I'm sure. I'm not. How you doing. How are the little charges?"

"Deeds is hung over. Bourgoin is deeply depressed, convinced he can't win. Merkel is anxious as hell, pacing like a cat on cough medicine. Cacciavillani is sleeping, as per usual. Paluzzo, the neo-pro, is so excited about riding the A-squad for this that I've had to pull him out of the ceiling tiles for the past two days. And, Cardone and Cardinal are playing hurt — they want to ride Ghent-Wevelgem next week and don't want to ride today."

"It's not that. They just don't want to spring-board from here to Paris-Roubaix."

"Oh, please. That's probably the one race of the year with the most mainstream international media attention, outside the Tour. Why would they want to skip that?"

"Tell you what. I'll give you a shitload of francs. You go to a laundromat, fill up a dryer with mud and water and rocks, turn it on high heat, climb in, and then let it run, with you inside, for five hours. Then you tell me why they want to ride Ghent-Wevelgem rather than Paris-Roubaix."

"Don't they want the attention?"

"Sure. But the paycheck's the same. Hey, even some of the greats won't ride it. Hinault won it once, then turned his back on it. He thought it was cyclo-cross rather than a road race."

"Well, they're stuck. Deeds told them they're riding today. Which means they're riding next Sunday as well."

"A Sunday in Hell."

"How colorful."

"Thank you."

They sat quietly for a long while, Cheryl staring off across the plaza, Will staring at the cobble he envisioned as the course. The freshening breeze of the morning had stilled again, though Will knew it would reassert itself whenever it was least expected or wanted.

Cheryl looked carefully over both shoulders before she asked, "Have you heard anything more from brother Henri?"

"The night before last. He called, just to say, 'Remember what's riding on all this.' Yeah ... my nuts are riding on all this. And I've gotta say, I care a lot more for my nuts than his little bicycle team."

"What about your paycheck?"

"Paychecks you can find. Nuts, once lost, are so very hard to replace."

"Terrible. And they're never on sale."

Will shot her a sideways glance out of the corner of his eye. And smiled. He hadn't smiled, honestly smiled, since Italy. It was a good feeling.

"Godot called, too. Caught me on the way out the door."

"What did Columbo want?"

"He said he needed to see me as soon as I returned to Paris."

"That's it?"

"Yeah, except to watch my back."

"Swell — watch your back and your bike seat and your small American-made appliances. Too bad he didn't tell you what you were supposed to be watching for."

"Or who."

Cheryl looked at her watch. A little over two hours to the race.

"Gotta run. We're down a few people today. Luis is sick. And Philippe is a no-show. So, I get to handle everybody's job. Fun, huh? Things to do, people to see, nerves to soothe."

"Gotcha."

"Ride good today." She leaned over quickly and kissed him on the cheek, then jumped up, and without a glance back, strode strongly across the square toward the Haven staging area. Will watched her grow small in the distance. He slowly moved his hand up and gently rubbed his cheek.

"Now, what the hell was all that about?"

❁

PART OF THE CEREMONY OF LA RONDE WAS TO ROLL UP ONTO THE OFFICIALS' platform, and, while on your bike, sign in for the commissaires. It was a bit of show, a bit of athletic glamour, a bit of balancing act. Though first in the square that morning, Will was one of the last to sign in. He had checked every nut and bolt on The Beast carefully, as Tomas might, looking for inconsistencies, looking for surprises. He found none. Geared up, he pedaled over to the podium in the square of St. Niklaas, rolled up the ramp and brought himself to a stop right next to the sheet. He had kept his right foot free of the pedal to avoid the risk of losing his balance and riding the bike to the ground while trying to free his foot. He had done that, once, in Belgium, after his last criterium win ... hell, he thought, his last win, period. He had caught some fearsome mud in the pedal and the damned thing just wouldn't release. As he rolled to a stop before the crowd and assorted photographers, he fought with his foot, wrenching it back and forth, then fell over in a heap, to the delight of everyone in attendance.

Not this time. Not with everyone in the world looking on. He reached over and scribbled his shorthand signature, one of the three he had developed for various and sundry purposes. He looked down the list of names on the sheet and realized that the season was truly underway; more of the big guns had arrived.

It hadn't been easy to begin with, and, now, it could only get worse.

Will rolled off the podium and toward the circle of Haven riders. Cacciavillani was grinning ear to ear at a dark-haired woman in the crowd. Deeds had Paluzzo by the shoulders and was grilling him on tactics. Bourgoin was staring out of the square, down the course, trying to stir himself to the day's efforts. And Cardone and Cardinal, the Doublemint Twins, were off in their own little world, grousing about the injustice of their lives, the injustice of having to ride Paris-Roubaix. Merkel, Will noticed, was nowhere to be seen.

"Hey, Richard. How you doing, bud?"

"*Bonjour*, Will. *Comment ça va*?"

"*Bien, merci.*" Will looked out of the square and toward the turn that would take them out of the city and through the Belgian countryside for the next seven hours. "Are you ready for this?"

"*Oui et non*. I am always ready — and I am never ready. I cannot wait for the start, and I dread it. I love being on the road, and I cannot wait for the finish line. I am anxious to bump and grind and tear into the pack — and I want to do nothing more than leave them behind. Maybe forever."

Will nodded. "Been there. Done it. Seen that. Felt the same damned way."

"*Et vous*? Are you ready for this?"

Will took a deep breath and kicked at a loose stone in the square of St. Niklaas. Was he ready? He had trained. He had felt his anger push his emotion, which pushed his power along and strong. He had stopped at Jablom's shop near Senlis for a pep talk. Everything was there — except for a hole in his heart. He had felt this before, and it had kept him off the bike for nearly a year.

"Yeah, Richard. I'm ready," he said, lying, perhaps, but maybe not. He wasn't sure.

"Hey, Ross!" Deeds was shouting at him from five feet away.

"What?" Will shouted back.

"Why are you yelling?"

"I dunno, I just picked it up somewhere."

Deeds shook his head. Management had insisted on Ross again for the lead squad. He still wasn't sure about it, especially after Milan, but they were signing the checks and he was an employee. He looked around the group quickly.

"Where's Merkel?"

Will turned, looked in a full circle, and stopped when facing Deeds again, feigning concern. "I dunno. It's not my day to watch him."

"Well, find him."

"I'm mentally preparing for the day at hand. Can't one of your pack mules go looking for him? What about Eek and Meek over there?" he said, pointing at Cardone and Cardinal.

"You don't have to mentally prepare to follow orders. Follow orders — right? So, you've got the time. Last time I saw him he was near the team buses."

Will pouted and stomped off to find Hans. Why me? he thought. Christ on a Colnago, I've got work to do, too. I've gotta mope around and worry about what I'm going to do today.

Will hobbled across the square, the cleats on his shoes slipping and clacking on the stones. He kicked them off and gingerly walked toward the buses in his red-striped riding socks. He could rip the hell out of them, he knew, which would rip the hell out of his feet during the race, but at least he had some traction now. He quickly covered the distance to the team buses parked at the side of the square. No Merkel. He strained to see over the heads, but still couldn't pick Hans out of the growing crowd. The two team vans, which would not be making the trip today because of the narrow roads, were set off the side. Will walked over there, figuring, if he couldn't find him here, he doesn't exist. He was simply a figment of our imaginations all this time and the team would have to wait for him to rematerialize, like Brigadoon.

But, no such luck. As Will turned the corner of the lead van, there was Hans, talking quietly into a cellular phone. Hmm. Didn't know we had those. Have to ask Deeds for one, he thought. Will stepped up behind Merkel and stood uncomfortably, trying, pretty much unsuccessfully, not to eavesdrop, waiting for a break in the conversation when he could tap Hans on the shoulder and tell him that his carriage awaits.

Will looked at the ground. He looked at the sky. He looked at the side panel of the other van. He listened to the quickly growing crowd of enthusiastic Belgian bike fans he could hear but not see from his position within the maze of vehicles. He tried. It was hard not to listen to Merkel, but he tried. And then he heard his name.

"*Nein*. Ross is not a problem. I can control Ross."

Now, Will listened with interest, staying far enough behind Merkel not to set off his proximity alert, but straining his head at a variety of angles to pick up the thread of the conversation.

"I can counter Bourgoin ... (unintelligible) ... the pack splits after the Patersberg and I can keep him in the lead chase group through ... (mumble) ... *Nein*. There is no chance for him to reach the breakaway if I am not there to sling him forward. Tell them not to worry. I must go, you're breaking up. *Ja*. *Ja*."

Will reached across Merkel's shoulder and touched the power button. The phone beeped and went dark. As Merkel began to turn in shocked surprise, Will brought his left elbow across Merkel's neck and, holding his head in a pincer, drove him back against the van with a bang. Merkel frantically tried to gain purchase with his feet, but the hard plastic cleats merely skittered on the cobblestones.

"How much, Hans? How much is it worth to you? Francs? Marks? Pieces of silver, you son of a bitch, how much," he banged his head back against the wall of the van, "how much?"

Merkel gagged and tried to shake his head side to side to break Will's grip. "Listen, you two-bit whore," Will spit the words into Merkel's face. "Today, I don't care what deal you've made, I don't care how much you've been paid or what you've been promised or who your chums are, you ride. You hear me? You ride. Hard. And you get Richard up to the lead group when he needs to be up there. When he needs it — not before — not after. You ride this race like you're gonna win it. Got it?"

He popped Merkel's head against the wall of the van for emphasis.

"I've wondered about you, pal, since Het Volk and that damned radio of yours. I was one of those naïve goofs who believed no rider would sell out. Yeah, right — or use drugs, or cut deals or hold back. Well, I've seen in that pit, pal, and I don't intend to go back for another look. Or let my team suffer because somebody else has — you hear me? You hear me?"

Merkel stared back with wide, frightened eyes, his lips turning the blue of a polyester leisure suit.

"Yes, indeed, Hans, you are staring at your worst nightmare. I am the Angel of Death on Two Wheels. And I will be riding that bike up your ass to make sure you don't slide." He popped Merkel's head against the van. "And — if you do — if you even consider playing your little game for your cell' phone friends, you'll have to deal with me — and Deeds and the UCI — because I'll squeal like a stuck pig to make damned sure they come down on your head in hobnailed boots. And — when they're done ..." he smiled, "... I will beat the ever-lovin' crap right out of you. Got it?"

Will looked hard into Merkel's face.

"Understand?"

Merkel simply nodded. Will pulled his left elbow away and Merkel crumbled to the ground. The cellular phone fell by his side. Will looked at it for a moment, and then, in his stockinged feet, stomped on it, once, twice and again, for Milan, and again, for Tomas, and again, for Colgan, and again for the Ruta del Sol and again, until the main unit was a mass of pieces and plastic and wire held into some vague shape by the battery pack on the back. Will picked it up and shook the electrical mess at Hans before tossing it through an open window into the back of the Tordant Computer team car.

"Oops. Sorry 'bout your phone."

Merkel looked up at him, his face flushed with anger. "Screw you."

Will laughed. "Well, while you're busy being snarfy, remember this: Buddy, no matter what they're paying you — double it and it still ain't worth half the hell I'm gonna give you." Will reached over and grabbed Merkel by the edge of his jersey. Merkel began to squirm and resist, but the adrenaline still surging through him gave Will the strength to yank Hans to his feet. "Come on, Adolf, we've got a race to ride." He shoved Merkel forward around the front of the van. As he passed the front window, Will caught his reflection. His face was flushed bright red, the mass of scars from his accident in the Ruta del Sol standing out in sharp relief. Will grinned — a death's head smile.

Il Cicatrice, The Scar, had returned ... but damn, did his feet hurt.

*

THE PELOTON MADE ITS TRADITIONAL CEREMONIAL CIRCUIT OF THE SQUARE OF St. Niklaas, then rolled leisurely out of the city. Within 10 kilometers, the pace had picked up dramatically. From city streets and wide secondary roads, the course quickly turned onto country lanes, paved, at least, but still not much wider than an American bike path. Teams and individual riders bumped and ground and sped ahead to try to put themselves in a position from which they could jump themselves or counter any attacks or big-star breakaways.

Surge and slow, surge and slow, through the first hundred kilometers, the riders jockeyed for the spot in the pack that made no difference now, but could make every bit of difference when the world began to splinter over the next 16 climbs. Bourgoin, Merkel, Cacciavillani, Ross and Paluzzo had stayed together, reaching into the front of the pack, sliding to the middle, then working their way back to the front. Paluzzo raced ahead, the colt free of his lead; then, frightened by the pace at the front, fell back into the safe company of his teammates.

Merkel hadn't reacted to Will at all in the bunch, but simply played out the game as the good and loyal lieutenant to Bourgoin. What do you need? Watch out for this. Pick up the pace. Watch the Flemish riders — this is their turf — they'll break first. All good advice, but then again, Will assured himself that Vidkun Quisling had good advice for his fellow Norwegians as well.

La Ronde was nearing its halfway point with the bergs, the climbs, fast approaching. Teams continued to work their way forward on the narrow roads, trying to place themselves in front of the potential traffic jams if — but more likely, when — a team or rider collapsed on the Kwaremont or Patersberg. Haven had timed its move perfectly, reaching the front fifth of the pack just before a section of cobbles. Will felt The Beast shudder and fight the road. He forgot Merkel for a moment and concentrated on the wheel in front of his, watching the line, the road, don't touch, whatever you do, don't touch. A rider sitting just behind Paluzzo, two riders behind Will, wasn't nearly so careful. Looking to his side, he failed to see the gap between two cobbles that reached out and grabbed the front wheel of his bike, holding it fast, stopping him and throwing him over the handlebars at an oblique angle into his teammate. The two went down like collapsing college bank accounts, splintering on the *pavé* and spreading themselves and their gear over the entire road. The pace had been fast, and for the next 20 riders behind them there was no stopping and for the next 60 behind them, there was no getting around. Twenty riders, some of the biggest names in Belgium and the peloton, were now clear.

Bourgoin looked back and saw the carnage behind him. He shifted, picked up the pace, and began his long break with the riders ahead. Merkel looked back as well, almost wistfully, wishing that they had been just a few riders back, just enough to be involved. It would have solved both his problems.

Will shifted and began to pass Merkel on the outside, reaching out to catch the breakaway that was already beginning to string out on the smooth concrete lane.

"Sorry you missed the fun, Hans?"

Merkel turned an angry, bitter face toward Ross.

"Oh, now, Hans, you shouldn't feel like that. If you think about it, I'm really saving you; your career, your honor, your self-esteem. You should thank me."

"Fuck you."

"No, I don't think so. Let's ride, shall we?"

❁

DEEDS WAS STUCK IN A TEAM CAR BEHIND THE ACCIDENT AND FAR BEHIND the action. The size of both the roads and the peloton would mean that he'd spend most of his day out of sight and communication with his team. It drove him nuts.

"Where are they? Dammit, where are they? Are they in the crash or were they ahead? Where are they?"

Cheryl leaned her head back against the head rest and closed her eyes.

Lord in heaven, she missed Tomas on days like this. In fact, she'd rather put up with snarfy, smelly Philippe than listen to Deeds go ballistic every five minutes. Really? No, it was a tossup, but Deeds would still win. You can shut your ears. You can never really shut your nose.

✷

THE FIRST FOUR CLIMBS, THROUGH THE KWAREMONT, HAD NOT REALLY AFFECTED the leading group. The day was still young, they were still relatively fresh and the grades were not overwhelming. Coming into the Patersberg, however, Will could feel the anticipation and the fresh moves for better positioning. Don't want to get stuck behind, don't want to lose the front. Bourgoin had the same thought.

"Let's move up."

Will nodded and looked at Merkel. Hans was fumbling with his gears, looking like he wanted to fall back a bit and attack the 20-percent grade from the rear. Will growled, "Pick it up, Dweezil, we've got a long way to go before we toss you by the side of the road." Merkel looked at Will angrily for a moment, then stood up in the pedals, moved ahead of Bourgoin and led him out toward the front of the pack and the Patersberg.

It had been two years since Will climbed the Patersberg. The little bastard hadn't gotten any easier. It was a short climb, not really long at all, but it was steep and it was narrow and it was cobbled and about 170 kilometers into the game. A lot of riders packed it in on the Patersberg and carried their bikes to the top. There was no dishonor in this, but it certainly didn't help the possibility of standing on the podium.

Bourgoin wanted that possibility. Paluzzo wanted that possibility. Cacciavillani wanted that possibility. Will and Merkel didn't care about the possibility. They simply wanted to survive the day.

This, Will knew, was ugliness personified. The climb reached into his legs, his lungs, his feet, still sore from the cell' phone, his arms and his head to rip and tear at everything vital within him. One more stroke. One more stroke. One more stroke and you're over the top. One more stroke and you're on pavement. One more stroke and the worse is over. One more. One more. One more stroke and I'll have a stroke, he thought.

And then, they were over. Will looked up and struggled to pick up the pace and regroup with Bourgoin and the others. As he rode up, Merkel snapped a look at him. He had hoped they had left Will behind on the climb. Will could read his mind.

"Sorry to burst your balloon, butthead," he wheezed.

Seven kilometers more and they were through the Hotond, a mild, 8-percent climb; no problem, and some of the smoothest pavé he had ever ridden. Too bad this was an exception to pavé, rather than a rule.

They crossed through the center of the course, over the Valkenberg, the Kerkgate, the Leberg, short 11-percent grades. No fun, but nothing terrifying. It was the Molenberg next, Will thought, and then the three doozies in the last 50 kilometers: Berendries, the Muur and the Bosberg. Those, he thought, would give you nightmares.

Haven was falling off the pace. A 12-rider breakaway speared ahead, leaving a 20- to 25-second gap to cross. Bourgoin told Cacciavillani and Paluzzo to bridge, which is what the Italians had been hoping for all day. Paluzzo took the lead and sped ahead, while Cacciavillani calmly dropped in just off his back wheel and rode the neo-pro's draft up to the leading group.

That left the three, Bourgoin, Merkel and Ross, sitting in the growing gap. A car horn beeped and they pulled to the side. A neutral support car drove past, called up by one of the motorcycle commissaires. Merkel tried to grab a ride, which would have meant disqualification, but Will touched his brakes and dropped into the space between Hans and the car. Rather than grab a car window, Merkel grabbed Ross's shoulder. As the car pulled free, he gave it a hard shove. Will weaved over to the side of the road, caught a tire, wobbled a bit, then regained control and dropped back into the group.

Bourgoin watched it all with surprise. "What the hell is going on with you two?"

Will grinned. "Hans is just giving me practical training in bike-control techniques."

"Well, save it for Senlis. We've got a race here."

"Gee, I thought it was just a family trip. Look, Dad! A Stuckey's! Can we stop?"

Will rolled to the front of the trio and took his pull on the pace line. Now that they were out of the climbs for a few moments, he was beginning to get his strength back. All he had to deal with now was straining the oxygen molecules out of air heavily scented with manure. The countryside was a rich green and brown. And Will knew what that brown was.

Thirty-two kilometers from the finish, about 20 miles, and they hit the first of the final three climbs, Berendries. Will was finishing the last of his food from the feeding station and hoped he could keep it down while climbing the last bergs. Two hundred and forty kilometers were behind them. They had already spent six hours in the saddle. And now, with the pace picking up yet again and the climbs in the next 27 kilometers, Will prayed for power in his legs, faith in his heart and lunch in his stomach.

Merkel had been pulling strongly for the last 20 kilometers. He led the way over the 13-percent grade of Berendries and picked up the pace on the country flats leading up to the Muur, the Wall. They regained contact with the lead group on the approach to the Muur, even picked up Paluzzo and another Italian neo-pro as they fell back at the base of the Wall, but their gain was nullified on the short, steep climb. The lead group, including Cacciavillani, popped over the top and raced ahead toward the Bosberg and the finish in Meerbeke, while Will and the others groped their way over the top of the climb. There would be no win this day for them, but it had been a solid effort. The peloton was quickly closing in, finally recovering from the early crash, while the lead group began the long, tactical surge toward the line. Haven was still in the gap, still pedaling hard, but, with victory out of reach, simply trying to finish the day as best they could.

Over the Bosberg, the final climb and you could see the day of effort in everyone's face. Bourgoin had turned ash gray again, Will could feel the flush of red in his scarred face, while Merkel merely seemed resigned to his finish. Around the final right-hand turn into Meerbeke and the five spread out across the wide street. Paluzzo and his fellow Italian neo-pro jumped first, and Bourgoin dropped in hard on Paluzzo's wheel. Forty meters from the line, Bourgoin jumped, came around on Paluzzo's left side, brought himself even, then threw the bike across the line, beating a Belgian pro by half a wheel, while his leadout man finished third. The race might have been hell, but the sprint sure was fun, Bourgoin thought.

Will half-heartedly followed another Italian in, slipstreaming and breaking at the line. That was okay for him. Whatever final enthusiasm he had felt for the day's efforts had finally left him on the Bosberg. Merkel ignored the sprint completely and simply pedaled across. It was not a win, but it was a solid team finish.

Tony C found himself on the winners' podium with third. Bourgoin was 10th, Paluzzo 15th. Will had gotten muddled in the sprint, yet crossed 22nd, his best finish in years, and Merkel rolled in behind at 35th. Not bad, Will thought, not bad for a guy who seven hours earlier had been looking to sell out his team.

Will worked his way through the crowd and grabbed Merkel by the arm.

"Nice work. Nice pull in those last 50 klicks."

Merkel turned to Will with a face red and filled with tears.

"You've killed me."

"What, the ride? Hey, I might have pushed, but that was you all the way."

"Not the ride, you fool." Merkel pushed Will hard, back into the crowd. He turned and disappeared in the throng.

A large Belgian woman helped Will regain his balance. He thanked her and turned to look for Merkel. Hans was nowhere to be seen.

"You did the right thing," he said, to no one in particular.

❂

DEEDS HAD BEEN LARGELY OUT OF TOUCH WITH HIS TEAM DURING THE DAY'S race, but he took great pains to let everyone in the bar that evening know that he deserved the credit for this one. A high finish had eluded him in La Ronde over the years, so even placing third, and placing much of the rest of the team in the top 40, was thrilling for him. It was his team, he told everyone in sight, his tactics, he told everyone at the bar, his riders, his great riders, he said, hanging on Will and blowing vodka-scented breath that could have caught fire into Will's face.

"That's nice, Carl."

"No, Will. You're nice. You're nice. A good rider. I'm sorry I was such a bastard."

"You weren't a bastard, Carl. You were merely a son of a bitch. There's a difference."

"Thank you, buddy," Deeds said, not hearing and slapping Will's shoulder. "Yer okay."

Amazing. Will shook his head. Times change. People change. Even Deeds. Maybe Will himself had needed a two-by-four beside the head to get him in gear. Maybe that's what Merkel needed today. Deeds got results from Will. Will got results from Merkel.

Amazing.

Will had turned himself back toward the bar and was staring at a row of bottles with barely indistinguishable labels when he heard the quiet explosion. He saw a few bottles wobble on their bases. Now, what the hell? A touristy couple sat at a corner table and held the edges of the furniture waiting for the next shock. Californians, thought Will.

Moments went by with nothing, and the tenor of the room slowly regained its stride.

The hotel desk clerk stuck his head into the bar, scanning the crowd. He saw Deeds and hurried over to him, taking him by the shoulder and hurriedly whispering in his ear. Will watched Deeds as his expression changed from celebration to shock to abject deflation. Whatever had been said, the life had just been squeezed out of Carl Deeds.

Deeds slowly walked to the bar and gently put his glass down. He turned to leave when Will put out his hand.

"What's up?"

"Maid. A Maid. Was in the hallway when she heard a bang. Opened the door to Merkel's room to see what was going on and bumped a soccer ball. Problem was — it wasn't a soccer ball."

Deeds, in a vague and distant shock, turned and walked toward the door. Will simply watched him go, then turned toward the bar. He put his glass of juice down slowly, next to three half-finished drinks, lined up, one after another after another on the finished wood. And that was the order in which he drank them.

He looked at himself in a small mirror. Il Cicatrice, The Scar, was now *Il Seccatura*, The Peeved.

"Oh, shit," was all he managed to say.

✵

JACQUES ANQUETIL WAS UNHAPPY. MAYBE, HE THOUGHT, HE SHOULD HAVE gone to hell. Heaven, it seemed, was getting far, far too crowded.

CHAPTER FOURTEEN:

ONE WORD: PLASTIQUE

Godot had key-stroked himself into a corner. His secretary, Isabelle, had gone home hours before, and now he was stuck, but good. He had the face of his mystery Haven employee filling the screen of his new computer and he didn't know where to go from there. The computer search had been helpful, he had made great progress on his investigation. He had brought his suspect full screen and stared at the face, trying to find a clue to the identity. Who are you? Where are you? Isabelle had accessed Haven's personnel records with the UCI, professional cycling's governing board. They were as bland and empty as Godot's files. Who are you?

And now, he was stuck. The name tied to the face staring back at him from a photo in a driving record was as false as Charlie McCarthy's teeth. Clack. Clack. Clack. He was clicking his teeth together. He didn't know how long he had been doing it. He looked up to notice Stephen LaSarge, a companion in the investigator's office, leaning against his doorway.

"Cigars. And rumpled raincoats. And smoky cars. And beeping computers. And now, clacking teeth. You are, truly, one of the most annoying human beings I have ever encountered."

"Yes?"

"The sound of your bridgework symphony drew me here. I take it you have a problem with your computer."

"I'm stuck."

"Yes, perhaps in the 1950s." LaSarge sauntered over behind Godot, reached across him and, tapping a function key, brought down an escape menu.

"Do you want to save this lovely photo?"

"Yes."

LaSarge moved the cursor and tapped a key. "What do you want to call it?"

"Call it?"

"Title it." There was a long pause. "So you know where to find it again."

"I don't know."

"Well then, let's just call him by his name...."

Godot was about to say, "Which I don't know," when LaSarge began typing with one finger onto the title line of the file.

"... which ... is ... La Bombe."

❋

"WHERE ARE YOU GOING?"

"I'm not really sure," Will said, ignoring Cheryl and stuffing his gear into the trunk of the battered team Peugeot.

"Does Deeds know? He'll report the car stolen."

Will stepped back onto the flagstoned entrance of the hotel. He looked at the car, covered with Haven logos and stickers from all the secondary sponsors. He noticed that hidden among the mix was a Greens sticker somebody had slapped into an open space. "No," he said, "Deeds will report a circus wagon stolen. No self-respecting cop would call this a car. Besides, I left him a note. By the time he sobers up and finishes with the police, I should be well over the border and heading for Paris, picking up my gear and jumping a train for Lille, Roubaix and Cucamonga."

"Why?"

"Why? Jesus, where have you been? Colgan. Tomas. Merkel. How many more folks around here have to die before you lose your taste for this sport? And frankly, I'm not waiting around till my pillow explodes and the maid plays soccer with my head just so I can say that I helped the Haven brothers choose the proper CEO for the company."

"What about Tomas?"

He stopped and stared at the ground. "It's not a question of Tomas."

"You bet your ass it's a question of Tomas. I don't really give a rat's butt about Colgan. After what you told me about Merkel and his phone-sex buddies, I don't really care much about him, either. I do feel bad about his head, I'll admit, but after three you start to get just a bit cold to new and interesting ways to disassemble the human body. But don't you stop thinking for a second that this isn't about Tomas. This is personal, Will. They've made it personal. And, frankly, I can't sleep with the thought of a chump in a suit deciding which of my friends should live and die so he can get rid of the cycling team and sell more vitamins."

"What?"

"What?"

"No. What. Your what. What did you say — about the team?"

"Jesus. You are out of the loop. The rumors are all over the place. Bergalis wants to kill the team."

"He's doing a good job of it."

"No. He wants to shut it down. Rumors are he wants to invest in American football in Europe. Get his own football team."

Will was quiet. Jablom had said that. Henri had intimated that. Why the hell hadn't he caught any of the hints? Maybe because Kim had said he couldn't take a hint if it were laid out on a billboard right in front of him. And Kim. What the hell did Kim have to do with this? And the letters — what did Kim have to do with those letters Godot had flashed in his face and threatened him with? And *plastique*. Plastique had killed off three good people. Well, one good person and two good riders.

People, paper, plastique. The three keys. He had one. He knew the letters from him to Kim had been forged. Godot knew that. Godot knew the why and how, if not who. He knew who — Kim and her little buddy Martin — but there was no way to get into the corporate offices of Haven without showing his hand and skinning his knuckles.

And then there was the plastique. And the person behind it.

Fight or flight? He had felt the question before, but now it reached up and strangled his guts. He had his mother's spastic colon. The twist in turn three of his lower GI tract was making him wince and bend over at the waist. Fight or flight? Then, it had simply been a question of getting on the bike. Screw up their plans. Ride to win. See? I wasn't as bad as you thought. Sorry.

"You always hated to be told no."

Will paused his internal debate and looked at Cheryl. "What?"

"You always hated to be told no. You'd always throw a fit, wouldn't you?"

This was an amazing woman. "Yeah, all that does is piss me off. Always has — mostly."

"Well, that's what they're doing now," Cheryl said, moving up close and getting in his face. He stared at her gray eyes, focused, angry and pointed at him. "They're telling you 'no,' Will. Don't go on. Don't do. Don't rock the boat. Don't ride. Don't get upset about Tomas. Just let us kill off the team and leave the whole of you in the lurch. You've fought back on the bike pretty well. Are you ready to fight back on your feet and make them pay a bit? You've already paid a pretty hefty price."

Will stared at his feet. The Italian tennis shoes had red and blue striping. Under the odd fluorescents it became green and purple. He should've stayed in bed in Avelgem, he thought. They'd all still be alive. Except Colgan, which was no big loss. Still, one rather than three. And yet, he had grown tired of being drunk. And he'd grown tired of not riding smart, of not riding well. And, more than anything, he was tired of being pushed around. He was tired of being told 'no' by Kim and the Bergalis boys and the cold and bony figure of whoever was sculpting little party favors out of modeling clay.

Modeling clay. Plastique. The second key.

Will looked at Cheryl. He was thinking. His eyes were shuttered. His brow furrowed. He spoke quietly and slowly, almost rhetorically.

"If you were hiding plastic explosive, where would you do it?"

"Well, not in the basement next to the furnace, if that's what you mean."

"Exactly. If you were hiding plastic explosive, you wouldn't hide it in your house or garage or apartment, because police could find it, or it could kill you, given the right set of circumstances. You wouldn't keep it at the office, either, because — well, because of the same reasons. So, you'd keep it someplace where you could get at it easily. Someplace, where, if it were found, there would be lots of people around to suspect, and you'd have time to make your getaway. And — if it went up — it would actually help your cause, because it would be just another nail in the coffin of the team."

"Perhaps the whole team. At once," Cheryl said, her voice as distant and muddled as Will's whisper.

They found the answer at the same time.

"Senlis," they said in unison.

Will turned and walked to the driver's door of the Peugeot.

"Where will you be? I'll give you a call to let you know what I find."

"Just turn to your right and say, 'Howdy, Chester,'" she said, pulling open the passenger's door and strapping herself into the seat before Will had a chance to say anything about it. "I'm your goddamned shadow."

"What would your mother say?"

"Same as always. She's crazy about you."

"What?"

"Just drive."

Will turned the key and the Peugeot rattled to life. He rolled out of the driveway and began the 300-kilometer drive south. The small white car, belching exhaust and covered with company stickers and carrying an ancient bicycle on its roof, was quickly swallowed up by the murk of a Belgian night.

⌘

LASARGE COULDN'T CONTAIN HIMSELF AT THE EARLY MORNING, LATE IN THE graveyard-shift kaffeeklatsch.

"I not only solved Godot's computer problem, but I solved his case for him as well."

Aron Benedict, an ancient detective who made even Godot look like a newcomer to the force, rose to his defense.

"You've worked disposal. Godot has never worked explosives. Usually domestic homicides. Cut him some slack."

"What?" LaSarge said incredulously.

"Cut him some slack. Give him some room. Don't be so hard on him. He doesn't have your experience."

"Cut him some slack?"

"Augh," Benedict said with disgust, "I heard it on 'Dallas' last night."

"Ahhhhh." The other detectives in the room nodded and smiled. They understood the cultural connection. America. It was a creeping cultural vine that no one could seem to kill.

"So, who is the bad guy?" the old detective asked.

LaSarge pulled the folded photo print out from the inside pocket of his suit coast and spun it in the air over to the table. Benedict looked at it for a moment and looked up to find himself surrounded by every other inspector in the room.

"Who is this?" he asked LaSarge.

"La Bombe. Serial bomber. Demolitions expert in the Legion. Specialized in plastique. Likes to maim even more than kill. Very good. Very ingenious. Very messy."

"Hmm." The old detective nodded and looked back at the computer printout. Carefully. Not only did he want to make sure that the man he was looking at was who he thought he was, but he was also letting the dramatic tension in the room build to a breaking point. And it was, as each head in the room turned toward him and leaned forward, just a bit, in anticipation.

"Well, then, he has changed his name. And his line of work. At Christmas, he was introduced to me as chief of security."

"For who?"

"Haven Pharmaceuticals," the detective said flatly.

The room was very quiet.

Finally someone said, "You'd better go get Godot."

WILL AND CHERYL MADE THE DRIVE FROM MEERBEKE TO SENLIS IN JUST OVER three hours, and as they pulled up to the two-meter-high cyclone fence surrounding the decaying velodrome, night was still upon them, but the feel of the sky had begun to change, as the day prepared to break. Now, the only problem they faced was finding the way inside. The gate was wrapped shut for the night with a heavy-gauge chain and padlock. The only way in, it seemed, was up and over a two-and-a-half-meter gate with 20-centimeter spikes spaced 15 centimeters apart.

"Wait here," Will said over his shoulder to Cheryl and clambered up the fence. The tricky part was not up and not down, but over, getting his gonads up and over the spikes without serious gouging.

At the apex of his climb, Will tried to position himself so that as he swung his leg over the top, his crotch was over a gap between the spikes.

He made the move smoothly, but even so, he quietly wished that he had descended from a race of longer-armed people. Every male relative Ross had known had to stretch to scratch his nose. Great time to remember that. Great time to notice, as well, that each spike across the top of the gate had an edge to it, so that if Will's elbows did give out for any reason, he'd likely slice open an artery in his leg and wind up featured above the fold of the evening editions of the Paris papers with some headline like: Senlis Refuses to Remove Christmas Decorations! Elf Turns Disgusting! Will shifted his weight and tried to catch a toe in the chain link of the inside of the fence. Despite the cool of the morning, he was sweating heavily. He caught the toe, put his weight on it slowly, then began to bring his right leg over the spikes. Three quarters of the way over, with victory in sight, his toe slipped and he began to drop over the fence, catching his foot between the spikes. He pulled himself up and tried to twist the foot free. He was at such an odd angle that he couldn't seem to get it loose. And now, the loop of his knot was caught in something. His hands began to sweat. He couldn't hold this much longer. One last time, he pulled himself up and twisted his foot. Hard. The shoe came free, but as he leg swung down, it threw his weight off and he lost his grip, skinning his chin on the fence and falling at an angle toward the ground. He sat there for a long moment and then looked through the fence for Cheryl. She was nowhere to be seen.

"Hey!" He whispered in a loud, conspiratorial voice. "Hey! Miss Big Help!"

"What?"

The voice was behind him and made him jump. He turned himself quickly and pressed his back up against the chain link. Cheryl looked down at him grinning with a wise satisfaction. From his side of the fence. Looking none the worse for wear.

"What the ... hell ... are you doing in here?"

"Well, while you were busy playing The Crimson Pirate, I just remembered that they never finished the fence around the track. The gate you just climbed over — so gracefully, I might add — is basically to keep people from parking their cars too close to the door or on the infield. I just walked around it. Took maybe, oh, 45 seconds."

"Sometimes, I just really, really hate you."

"Thank you. If this was sitcom-land, that would mean that we'd be in a clinch real soon." She smiled evilly. "Don't count on it. Men with road maps for faces who don't know enough to look for an unlocked door have never really done much for me."

"Before I catch my breath, go to a window, and break in," Will said, "you wouldn't happen to know a way inside, now, would you?"

"Door to the tower is unlocked. I already checked. There's a spiral staircase inside. Shall we?" She stretched out her hand to him.

Will took it and pulled himself up. He straightened his jacket and shirt and brushed his pants smooth. Without a look or a word, he walked over to the external stairs leading up to the velodrome tower.

This, he thought, wasn't the way it was supposed to work at all.

GODOT LOOKED AT THE COMPUTER SCREEN THAT LASARGE HAD BROUGHT UP through magical manipulations of his keyboard. On the screen were three pictures of Godot's mystery man. Three different pictures with three different names.

"*Voilà*," said LaSarge.

"This is damned strange," said Benedict.

"Oh, *merde*," said Godot.

THEY HAD BEEN STUMBLING THROUGH THE VELODROME BUILDING FOR NEARLY an hour, not sure what to look for, with little or no light to look for it, running out of time and energy and patience.

"What does this stuff look like?" Cheryl asked.

"I think it looks like modeling clay — either gray or olive-colored. It should have some writing on it. You know, military symbols and such. Beyond that, I don't know."

"It could be anywhere in here."

"Well, even if you believe 'The Purloined Letter,' it wouldn't be in a high, high traffic area. People might ignore it because it's obvious, but somebody could stumble over it pretty easily. I suppose it could be in some kind of storage locker. But, again, if it's with other stuff that other people use, maybe they'd muddle into it — open the box to see if it was something they needed. So ... no. Are there any rooms you remember that people just didn't use? Didn't need to?"

Cheryl thought for a moment. The slowly brightening dawn made it easier for him to see her in the gloom, her head cocked off to the side as if an angle would make the ideas drop from one side of her head to another. "I suppose this building is full of them. But I've been in them all, at one time or another. Except the drying room."

"What drying room?"

"It's just off the changing room and the showers. We never used it for much of anything. Usually, it stayed locked."

Will remembered it well. On his first day with the team, he had broken into the building by climbing through a window in that self-same drying room, then dropping to the floor and smashing his shoulder against ... against what? A box. A wooden box. Covered with a green canvas tarp.

Will looked at Cheryl and said quietly, "I think I may know." They walked off in the darkness toward the changing room. Streaks of dawn were now beginning to fill the high windows and cover the ceiling of the room with a morning glow. Will and Cheryl crossed the room quickly, their excitement growing with each step. They stopped at the door and Will reached for the door knob, turning it slowly. It stuck, then released. The door was unlocked. He pulled it open and they walked in together, the shadows of the room filling with the sunlight spilling through the open door. Will quickly scanned the floor, starting on the opposite wall from the window, his eyes running up to the low, rectangular shape still in position under the window, still covered with a tarp. They walked to it carefully.

"This stuff won't blow, will it?" Cheryl asked with just a shade of a quiver in her voice.

"No, I don't think so. I think you need a detonator of some sort. An electrical connector. A blasting cap."

He pulled the tarp aside and in the gray light, they saw a pine box with a blue compass star stenciled on its lid.

"What's that?"

Will had seen this symbol before. He had ridden past the headquarters in Brussels.

"NATO. Bingo."

"Stolen?"

"They don't sell this shit." The box had a padlock on it, but the back hinges seemed loose. Will took his pocket knife, opened the screwdriver, and, using the flat edge, worked the screws free, opening the box from the rear. Inside were blocks of what appeared to be clay, in six-centimeter-square strips about 20 centimeters long. Each was wrapped in what appeared to be wax paper.

Cheryl began to reach for one of the bars of clay and Will stopped her. He didn't know enough about this stuff to fool with it. And besides, clay and wax paper would hold fingerprints like nobody's business. They were in deep enough already. Using the edge of his knife, he slowly peeled back a corner of the paper. On the surface of the gray-green clay he could read "U.S. Army C4" and then a strip of warnings and code numbers. This was it. The real magilla.

Four blocks seemed to be missing. Jean-Pierre. Tomas. Hans. And — who? The second key was in the box. Death was in the box. Will closed the wooden lid and with his screwdriver pushed the screws back into the soft wood. He then pulled the canvas back over, trying to recreate the look of the room when they originally stepped in. Replacing the dust they had stirred up was another problem.

"Time to call in the cavalry."

"What time does Godot get in?"

"Who knows? But this stuff has been sitting here for months. I doubt it's going anywhere soon. We'll call him from the café down the street."

"You sure it won't go off?"

"Naw. Like I said. It needs a detonator. A switch. An electrical charge or a blasting cap or a battery or ..." he paused for a moment, looking past her shoulder toward the door of the drying room as if in thought, "... or Philippe."

"Philippe? Why would it need ..." She turned, following his eyes toward the door. She saw a figure and a hand, holding a gun, sideways, not at the proper angle. The arm of the figure, the arm holding the gun, snaked out quickly toward her face. She felt a pop and the pressure of cold steel along her left cheek, from the base of her jaw to the bottom of her eye. Then, her head exploded in a profusion of bright lights. Her last conscious thought was that the floor was pulling her down quickly and that if she didn't put her hands out, she'd wrinkle her Laughing Cow sweatshirt.

Her shirt got wrinkled.

❁

GODOT, LASARGE AND BENEDICT STARED AT THE COMPUTER SCREEN.

"Who is he to you?" Godot asked.

LaSarge answered first. "La Bombe. Philippe Champeau. The Camel. Ex-Foreign Legion. Demo' expert turned mob bang-boy. Can blow anything big or small. Isn't averse to using his talents to assassinate anybody, if the price is right."

"Where is he?" Godot asked.

"Don't know. Dropped from sight maybe nine months ago. We figured someone just decided it was his day in the barrel."

Benedict chimed in. "Nine months ago, Philippe Champeau reappeared, quietly, but not without notice, at Haven Pharmaceuticals as director of security. Philippe Sournois. The Sly. After being introduced to him at the club of the chief inspector, I have not seen or heard of him."

"The 'him' I know as Philippe Graillot," Godot said. "Team assistant for Haven Cycling. Which, oddly, can boast of two dead, both from plastique."

LaSarge reached behind him and in a detached manner, tossed Godot a copy of the morning paper. "Three. One in Belgium last night."

Godot quickly scanned the article, looking för Ross's name. He didn't know this Merkel. Someone else had questioned him after the death of Colgan. Will wasn't mentioned. Godot breathed a sigh of relief. Ross's luck continued to hold. For the moment, anyway.

Isabelle arrived for her day to see her boss staring intently at a computer screen. An old dog, she thought, has found a new trick. Two colleagues sat with him staring at three pictures. Godot turned when he heard Isabelle walk into the room. She shuddered. He looked horrible. Gritty beard. Bleary eyes. Rumpled clothes. A thoroughly disgusting cigar butt hanging from his mouth.

He picked up the paper and tossed it to her.

"Call that Meerbeke hotel mentioned in that article." He stabbed the paper with his finger. "Get Will Ross on the line for me. Wake him up if you have to — just get him."

He turned back toward the screen.

Isabelle Marchant escaped the sweat- and smoke-filled room happily to do the bidding of her boss.

✺

DAWN HAD BROKEN IN SENLIS, BUT THE TOWN WAS STILL NOT MOVING. At least not in the region around the velodrome. Will had hoped that a passing cop, or someone walking their dog or going for bread at the *boulangerie*, at least *somebody* would be out on the street, but everything pretty much deadended at the velodrome. There was no through traffic. It left his hopes deadended as well.

Philippe held his gun, a Beretta 9mm, pretty much on Will, as they dragged Cheryl's limp body out to Philippe's car. Will had her feet. Philippe had his hands under her arms. The gun, in his right hand, trailed back and forth across Will's gut. Philippe's left hand cupped Cheryl's breast. He grinned at Will.

"You must take it when you can."

"Do you punch out the lights of all your dates before you begin foreplay?"

Philippe lost his smile. He left his fun and reached behind himself with his left hand to open the rear door of the Renault. He turned and unceremoniously threw Cheryl's head and shoulders on the seat, then motioned to Will to get her into the car. Will leaned over the lifeless face and looked for any sign of life. She was breathing, but she was out. Stone cold out. As gently as he could, he worked her body across the seat until she was completely in the car. He was crouched in the well in front of the seat when Philippe leaned into the car and swung the Beretta hard against his temple. Will had seen it coming and tried to move with the blow, but the back of the front seat held his head and he blasted into unconsciousness.

The last feeling he recalled was being covered and smelling canvas. Good God, he thought, he folded me up like a road map and put me in the box with the plastique.

✲

ISABELLE STUCK HER HEAD IN THE OFFICE DOOR. SHE REFUSED TO ENTER.

"The team manager says Ross stole a car and a woman last night and headed for Paris. That's it."

Godot shook his head. What now?

"Call downstairs. I'll want a car. I'll find him at his apartment. LaSarge — give me your cellular phone."

"First a computer, now a cell' phone. Aren't we rushing into the 21st century?"

"Just give it to me. I need contact."

Godot took the phone and slid it into a pocket of his trench coat. As soon as he stepped out of the office, he noticed the difference in the air quality. Perhaps, he thought, he should give up cigars.

Perhaps, Isabelle thought, as he walked past her desk, he needed to take up showers.

✲

PHILIPPE SOURNOIS-CHAMPEAU-GRAILLOT DROVE QUICKLY THROUGH THE MORNing traffic toward his rendezvous in Paris. His human charges were sleeping peacefully under a tarp in the back seat. His fourth plastique charge in as many months waited to greet anyone who happened to open the door to the apartment of Will Ross.

Philippe laughed heartily, thinking, "Whoever it is — I bet they'd be surprised."

CHAPTER FIFTEEN:

GOOD MORNING TO YOU

In their best races, everything moved in slow motion for Raymond and Will. Smooth and sweet and focused. On the other hand, when the races were out of control, they moved like Charlie Chaplin movies at 24 frames per second, all jerky and out of synch and faster than the human eye could comprehend. There was no controlling the pack. It was a state of sheer anarchy, with teams racing as individuals, no tactics, blown riders everywhere and who knows who would cross the line first ... only the guy who somehow clawed his way out of the pack early on and left the nonsense behind.

According to Stewart Kenally, it was their job to control the mob instinct. He was always there, leading, teasing, inspiring, cajoling, driving them through the murk of undisciplined riders toward a bigger goal.

"You're going to want to ride in Europe," he said, "and Europe demands control." Everyone knew he was talking to Raymond.

Will knew it. Will understood. Three years of hard riding on the team and training in his high school gym to the jeers of the other, established mainstream athletes, had brought him as far as Raymond's lieutenant; but it would take Raymond's departure for the big time, for the ACBB or another amateur developmental squad on the Continent, before Will got his chance to lead the team. And who knew if there would be anyone there to lead when Will finally got his chance?

But that was okay, because Raymond was good. He was strong. He was tactically wise. He played each rider in each race like a professional fisherman playing out a prize-winning sailfish. You're free. You're mine. You're free. You're mine. You're dead.

And Raymond was his best friend.

Raymond had reached the next step. National-team tryouts. He was going to do it all. Train with the best. Ride track. Ride road. Do it all. Lead the squad. Big dreams. Go to Europe and ride the Tour.

They were racing near the center of the state that Sunday, north and west of Detroit, near Mount Pleasant. And, as always in the middle of a Michigan summer, the heat was humid and oppressive, especially when you dropped between the ripening cornfields that captured any sort of breeze and stilled the air around you. It was like riding in a wet oven.

This was a good day. They moved fast, while life moved slowly past them.

Raymond and Will had left the pack far behind. Because of the humidity, no one's heart was in it today, other than Raymond's, and because he was there, Will was right behind him, pacing, drawing, falling in and falling out. There was just enough growth to the corn to make each road a dark green hallway with gray black carpet. Up ahead, at the T-intersection, Will saw the race marshal with his caution cones and red flag. He was looking to the left and holding his flag up for a driver. Raymond, who was on the pull in the two-man pace line, raised his right leg to the top of the stroke and dropped the bike to its side into the turn. Will, directly on his wheel, did the same, catching, for only a split second, a flurry of a red flag to his left as he dropped the bike over into the turn. And then there was noise and then there was green and rust and a horn blasting long and slow and cursing and Will feeling the bike accordion beneath him like a woolly caterpillar taking a leisurely crawl as his left arm and back slammed into and rolled off the moving wall of metal into the ditch and the fresh grass and the pussy willows that dotted the side of the road. Corn. He looked up and he saw corn. Row upon row upon row of dark green corn. Rustling and bending and screaming in the new breeze. Screaming?

Will turned to see the marshal, a grown man, at least 35, frantically waving his red flag and screaming, screaming, completely out of control. Screaming. And then, Will saw his bike. His new, first-season racing bike. Just out of the box. What, three races? Broken and bleeding by the side of the road. And Raymond's bike. Broken. And bleeding. Demolished. In the middle of the road. And then, Raymond, just his feet, across the road, in the ditch, just his feet poking up over the lip of the road. Will started to walk across the road, the cleats on his racing shoes sliding, skipping, skating across the graveled tarmac.

Will stopped in the center and looked at the screaming man. He pointed down the road. Will turned and looked. The faded green pickup truck had stopped, maybe 50 yards down the road. The driver, in overalls and a straw hat, was yelling and gesticulating. Will began to walk toward him, as if drawn. He had covered about half the distance when he could finally begin to hear. "You don't own the road I own the road I pay taxes and you don't own the road you little bastards!" and then the bottle glinted in the sun and broke at Will's feet. I know that label, Will thought. I've seen that one. And he looked up to see the truck moving away now, skittering back and forth across the highway like a gigantic pale green whale, back and forth, trying to find purchase in the wave trough between the sea of green.

Will turned back and began to walk toward Raymond. The man stood in the center of the road and pointed at him and screamed. And screamed. And screamed. And screamed. And time collapsed and Raymond's mother was screaming and crying under the tent and in the rain and clutching her children, one, after another, after another, and clutching Will, hard, and burying his face in her chest until he couldn't breathe and couldn't cry anymore.

The big-town papers that ignored their races didn't ignore the funeral. And they took picture after picture, with exploding flashbulbs, of the family and the children and the riders and Will. Who couldn't cry anymore.

He just couldn't cry anymore.

And yet, he was crying. Crying for Raymond and Mrs. Cangialosi and the pain. The pain that wouldn't leave his head and made his brain explode and his stomach heave. No more pain. No more. No more crying.

"Shhhh." Her hands softly caressed his face.

"You're okay. You'll be all right. Just take it easy."

Will heard his voice, very far away. "I'm sorry. I'm sorry."

"I know. I know you're sorry. I know you miss me, don't you?"

Yes, I miss you.

"I know. I know. Shhhhh. Take it easy. I'm here."

He felt his face fall deeply into her fingers, and then the softness of her chest. He swam to the surface of his mind, slowly rubbing his face in her sweater and her breasts. This was a safe place. This was a good place, he thought. And he slowly began to rub, like a cat, and surround himself with her scent. It was a rich smell. Deep and warm and ... and ... Lagerfeld.

He pulled away from her hands, frantically swimming to the surface of the darkness, toward the point of light in his mind. It grew colder and more painful, but he knew that if he sank down, back into the warm and the smell and the caress, he would die again a hundred times, so he pushed himself up, up toward the point of light that sheared his eyes and threw him hard back across the back of the leather couch.

He threw himself forward and retched, hard and dry. His left temple exploded with each spasm. He was hyperventilating now. Try to control your breathing. Try to calm yourself. He focused on the silvered edge of the glass table. One breath. Slow. Slower. Slower. Slower. His focus moved to a window. The Tower. Focus. One breath. Slower. Slower. Slower. It wasn't a window. It was a book. A huge book. The Tower. Paris. Slower. One breath. Slower. The book was on the table. The table was in front of the sofa. The buttoned leather. Sofa. One breath. Slower. Legs. On the sofa. Legs. He followed them up to a richly colored suit. Beautiful. Slower. His head started to rattle. His eyes were losing their focus. Slower. One breath. Up to her breasts. Oh, nice, he thought. And the scarf. Nice. Slower. Neck and chin and lips and eyes. And, shit.

Kim.

Kim. Kim. Kim. What are you doing here? Kim. His eyes started to blur and then refocused as he fell back across the couch and his head fell back and looked up at the ceiling and Kim was suddenly hitting him. Pop. Pop. Pop. Across his face. Damn. Kim. You got the dog. What more do you want? Pop. Pop. His head fell forward and he knew it wasn't Kim hitting him. It was Philippe. Philippe. You ... you....

"Fucking bastard!"

Pop!

Will's head spun around and he rolled toward the edge of the couch. He grabbed the heavy, covered arm and using his momentum, spun himself off the cushions and up, away from the next slap, which hit him only lightly against the back of his skull, until he was up and standing back against the wall. He used it for support, his head still spinning, slightly, and quickly surveyed the room.

It was an office, of some kind, up on a hill overlooking the city. The gigantic window had a beautiful view. Damn. Why did you need a big-ass coffee table book about Paris when you had this kind of view? Damn.

His view pulled back slowly from the window. There was a man sitting in a huge leather executive chair in front of the biggest desk Will had ever seen. Oh. Yeah. He must be the boss. What is his name? Damn. Philippe. Philippe was next. The short, balding and round little toad was standing in the center of the room, his arms crossed, his left hand, no, his right, his right fingers, they're all cross and screwed up, resting on the butt of a black pistol. I've seen that gun before. Nice gun. Beautiful workmanship. Where did I see it?

And then, there was Kim. She was sitting on the leather couch, next to something — a pile of rags or something, he couldn't quite see — crumpled up next to her. She looked at him with concern.

"How do you feel?"

"Uhhh. I don' know. I ... shit. Where am I?"

"You're at the office."

"You still want the dog, don't you, Kim? But you don't want the dog. I want the dog, Kim. Where is the dog?"

"The dog is dead, Will. I had the dog put down."

"What? Aw, shit. You bitch. You bitch. You and your two-bit fucking lawyer ..." He drunkenly walked across the floor, giving a wide berth to Philippe and the gun when he realized that this wasn't her lawyer at all. This was ... give it time ... this was ... the boss.

"Hey, chief. How you doin'?"

"Better than you, Mr. Ross. In every and all aspects."

"Damn. Really?" was all Will could think of to say. He thought about the B-flat sousaphone banging around just inside his left ear and realized he was probably right. Bergalis. Hen ... Martin Bergalis. The boss. Head of Haven. That's it. Jesus, dear sweet Jesus, stop the banging in my head.

"Do you know why you're here, Mr. Ross?"

"Uhh — urrr — no." He swallowed a hard burp that had picked up a hitchhiker.

"You are here, Mr. Ross, because you are a failure."

Will simply stared at Bergalis through heavy, red and watering eyes.

"You were hired because your ex-wife told me you were a failure. Nice, eh? That's why you got the job over hundreds of other, better riders. Because we knew that you couldn't do it. And you couldn't, could you?"

"I did okay. Het Volk — I got Richard up. What was that other race — Flanders. I did okay there."

"Please, you're embarrassing yourself. You didn't win, did you? Second is as bad as last, isn't it? Eh? But then — you played the counselor; the inspiration. Come on, Merkel ... ride hard for the team; win for the team. Don't listen to them. And now, he's dead. So, you are a failure there as well. By the way — you owe me for a cellular phone."

"So take it out of my pay."

"I will. Don't worry, Mr. Ross, I will."

Will desperately wanted to sit down. To sit down and sleep. This must be a concussion, he thought, or, more than 24 hours awake, seven hours of them in a race across Belgium. How long ago was that? Days. Years. He turned and looked in the room for an easy chair he could fall into, but there was none. Kim was sitting on the light leather couch to the left of the door, while Philippe had moved to the other, darker couch to the right, underneath what appeared to be a gigantic piece of black slate artwork. He sat and fingered the pistol, now back in its shoulder holster. Cheryl. He wanted to go see Cheryl, but his legs wouldn't move toward her. She was sitting, crumpled up at the end of the couch next to Kim. He could see her back rise and fall. She was alive. At least she was alive.

"Mr. Ross. Mr. Ross. I am over here."

Will swung his gaze back to Bergalis. He had only heard about half of what he had said so far, but, like fourth-grade geography, had caught the gist of it. South America is somewhere south of Michigan and looks like Charles De Gaulle. You are a failure, Will Ross, in everything you have tried to do and that is why you are here. He still had a fearsome headache, but the fog was lifting quickly. He knew where he was. He knew who was here. He was beginning to realize the depth of the shit he was wading through.

Bergalis waited until Will's eyes focused on him and continued.

"And then, you were a failure in trying to be a detective. You and your little friend." He motioned toward Cheryl, still silent and unmoving on the sofa. "You looked in where you had no business looking. You got involved where you had no business getting involved. You have held up my plans all along the way. This is not a good thing."

"What plans — getting rid of the team? So go ahead. They're your team," Will realized that he was sounding like the noisy drunk at the end of the bar. "Close up shop. Sell off the gear. You oughta make a mint on the jerseys and hats and bikes and shit. That's all donated to you, isn't it? In-kind sponsorship? Final-year issue of a team — that stuff would go for top dollar on cable TV shopping in the States. It's gotta be easier than killing us off one at a time. A lot less messy, too. Let us walk out of here," he motioned toward Cheryl, "and I can promise you, I'll never ride again. You can close up the team, and we'll never say another word. Honest. Really. We'll just disappear off the face of the earth."

"It's not that easy. You, both, are a part of this now. And, as for the team — I have a family to deal with. A father who created the cycling team and a brother who cannot read the future and insists on keeping it. I have to create a situation where dropping the team is the only alternative. And that's where you come in. You were a key as you began — and you are a key again today. That is, if you'd like to survive the day."

"Wait." Pieces suddenly dropped into place for Will. The gigantic jigsaw puzzle that had been the Haven team and his part in it became clear. Flashbulb time. The rebus was solved. The bell was ringing. And the picture was not of people and bombs and a crazed killer, but of corporate politics. You're a pawn. And as pawn, my pawn, I have a right to sacrifice you. He turned and looked at Kim. To the queen, if necessary. He looked at Philippe. To the knight. He turned to Bergalis. But always in service of the king. Your life is forfeit in the service of the king. Will's anger grew quickly, through the pain and the last bits of muddle inside his head. He was thinking clearly now, if not wisely. Wisely, and he would have kept his mouth shut. Nodded and gone along. No. He wasn't thinking wisely at all.

"So, you're telling me that you've killed off three people — three people — because you haven't got the guts to stand up to daddy and kill off the team? That's it? You haven't got the balls that God gave a garter snake, and so three people, including my best friend, are dead? I'm sorry." He stepped up to the front edge of the desk, reached over, and placed a sympathetic hand on top of Martin's. "No, man, I'm really damned sorry. I'm sorry this has all happened. I'm sorry you are a dickless wonder and can't find the guts to run your little vitamin company here and all the things that go with it. But that's your problem. And it continues to be your problem. Because I am not going to help you."

Kim lowered her head. Shut up, Will. You don't know where you're taking this — you don't know what he's capable of doing to you and this woman.

Philippe smiled. This was going to be a busy day for him.

Bergalis simply stared at Will for a long, long moment.

"Then," he said, quietly, without emotion, "you'll die. Here. Now. Today."

"Oh. I don't think so. First — it would mess up your carpet. Have you got the guts to call a carpet cleaner, then show Daddy the bill? And Christ, do you know what it costs to get blood out of ... what is this, four-ply beige industrial? It'll never happen. You'll always know I was here."

Bergalis leaned forward and opened a folder. In front of him were copies of the letters Godot had shown to Will, letters that implicated Will in the killing of Colgan, and, with a little imagination, of Tomas and Merkel.

"Let me tell you, Mr. Ross," Martin said, "how the scenario will play out across the rest of today. In a few moments, you will die here. So will she," he pointed at Cheryl. "She will simply disappear from the face of the earth. She'll fertilize a field east of the city. She will never be found. You will never be found, either. Not a bit of you. But, the police will be convinced that you are still alive. And that you are behind the horrible deaths that have plagued Haven across the season. You. Will Ross. Ex-husband of Kim Grady Ross, the head of the Haven Cycling Division of Haven Pharmaceuticals. Based on these letters — these letters pleading for a chance. These letters saying you'll do anything to get a chance to ride. Anything. Which, given the suspicious nature of some of my friends on the police force, could easily be murder. And that idea will be helped along with the discovery of the plastique that is currently hidden in a corner of your apartment. Complete with detonators. And oh, yes, no matter how much blood you spill — I can have this entire office redecorated — spotless — within two hours.

"Boy. The hardware stores must love to see you coming."

Kim spoke up from the couch. "Will. Listen to him. You have no idea what he is capable of — and he is serious."

He turned fast and hard and stared into her eyes, her head, her soul. "And what are you capable of, Kim? What do you get out of this? Five people die and you'll never have to waitress again? Think hard, kid. You really think he's gonna let you survive this? I know too much. You know more. I may be dead — but you're Milorganite right along with me."

He turned back to Bergalis, swinging his gaze back past Philippe, who continued to watch the proceedings with interest, hands spread out across the back of the sofa. Could Will make the jump? He quickly plotted the distance and the angle and realized he'd likely be dead within a step. Not good. Not yet.

"By the way, Bergalis — you've got a problem with these letters. I dunno who gave you my signature," he cocked his head toward Kim, "but you really should have taken a little more time with it."

He looked across the desk and saw a golden can filled with pens, including a black, permanent marker with a wide tip. Perfect. He snatched the marker off the desk, bounded across the office to Philippe's surprise and jumped onto the couch next to Kim.

"Look," he looked down at his ex-wife. "You watch, too. You might learn something that you can use when you try to frame your next husband."

He started writing, in huge strokes, across the wall, the black ink sinking deeply into the rough cloth wall covering.

"You see, when I was in ninth grade, my brother kept signing my name on lists: Ugliest Man Contest ... Girl's Volleyball Tryouts ... Audio/Visual Club ... Chess Club — which, by the way, I joined and liked — and, so, I decided, to develop a signature that couldn't be forged. And I did it. And that," he stepped back and swept his arm across the huge William E. Ross that was now imprinted in the wall, "was what I came up with." He glanced at Kim. "Check your wedding license, sweetie, you'll see it there. That's my 'official' signature." He looked across the room to Bergalis. "But that's not the signature on the letters."

Bergalis looked at the letters and then back at Will. His face showed the anger and the quickly disappearing patience that burned within.

"But you can't always sign your whole signature. Don't want to — especially when you're writing to your friends. So, you create a casual signature. Pay attention now, Kim, here's where you fucked up."

With the wide edge of the marker he swiped a loopy "wr" across the wall.

"This is how I sign letters that anybody but the government might see. Friends, acquaintances, ex-wives, you know." He looked hard again at Kim. "People I trust. But — as you can see, Marty, that signature isn't on the letters either."

Bergalis looked down again.

"Nope. What is on those letters is my third signature. And it's not a signature at all. It's an autograph. I didn't notice it at first when I saw the letters — but then, I remembered something. Odd. Fausto Coppi told me, in a dream, to 'write my name' at the Ruta. And I remembered it. Damned strange, don't you think, Kimmy?" He turned and pressed the marker deep into the cloth covering the walls. Deep enough so that it would stay there and face Bergalis for a damned long time. Long after Will had fertilized his first wheat crop. The letters were sharp, short and very different from those in the other two names.

"You should have paid closer attention, Kim. Because the police have already tossed these letters aside as evidence. What, they didn't tell you, Marty? Damn, I'm sorry. You should go to the country club more. Oh, yes, and by the way, Kim. When you take my autograph out of the GelSchweiz team handbook — you might want to make sure that the computer doesn't scan the extra bits of printing shit that come with it. Don't rush your work, miss. You tend to make mistakes."

He looked at Kim with satisfaction. He was gonna get his ass shot off in a few seconds, but damn, he was going out satisfied. Wrench-in-the-machine time. Kim was flushed and quietly hyperventilating. This had not been a good morning. She slowly turned away from Will and faced Martin. Will followed her gaze and watched as Martin Bergalis, the head of Haven Pharmaceuticals, slowly drew his hand across the top letter in the folder and crumpled it into a tiny ball, his eyes never leaving Kim. Oooh, Will thought, this is one pissed-off boyfriend.

"By the way — sorry about your wall, Marty." Let's see you redecorate that in an hour, asshole.

"They will still find the plastique in your apartment."

"Yep, they will. C-4. American-made. Out of stolen NATO stock. Read about that. Last year. When I was in Italy doing a horrible job of riding in the mountains. Lost a lot of Beretta 9 millimeters, too. Like the one Chumley is carrying." Philippe started, hearing himself dropped into what had been a fascinating conversation. "But even you've got to admit, it's going to be a stretch to put me with the plastique. It's a plant. Besides, I'm gonna bomb my own bike? Godot will make short work of all your little backup plans."

"Godot?"

"Yeah, Godot." Will suddenly didn't like the way Martin was smiling.

"Inspector Luc Godot of the Paris police?"

"Yeah."

Bergalis laughed.

"I have some sad news to report to you, Mr. Ross. When the police find the plastique, they will find it in the rubble of your apartment, in the rubble of your apartment building. It seems that someone, maybe even you, wired your front door — and when Inspector Godot and your landlady opened the apartment door, what," he looked at Philippe, "an hour ago, to search your apartment, to find you, it simply ... went up. Sorry."

Will stood as if gut-shot. The fourth brick of plastique. Now, he knew where it had gone. He could hear Philippe laughing to his side. Bergalis took the crumpled letter and slowly, carefully, opened it, smoothing the wrinkles flat.

"It saves me the trouble of demolishing the building. And perhaps I should be a little more careful with this — you never know when I may need it."

Bergalis smiled and looked to Philippe. He jerked his head toward Will. Oops. Damn. Shit. Think quick. Game over. All his mind would play was "game over." Game over. Bzz. Bzz. Bzzt. Again and again. Game over.

Philippe bent at the waist and put both hands on the edge of the couch to push himself out of its deep comfort. He rose, both hands down, head down, everything in him pointed at the floor.

Will heard it first. A deep animal roar. Then, a flash of white and red and yellow leaping across the room. A cow. A laughing cow flying through the room. A laughing cow had come to save him. Then he saw the cow had human arms and the human arms were holding a book, a huge damned book about Paris that swung up in an underhanded arc and caught Philippe Graillot under the chin just as he was pulling himself to his full height. The force of the blow snapped his head back and into the black slate wall hanging. There was a dull bang and his head split the slate and he fell forward again, the book coming down hard on the back of his already bloody scalp. Philippe crashed to the floor like a sack of rice falling off the back of a feed truck.

Cheryl Crane stepped over the body of her tormentor, picked up his gun, turned it toward the assembled masses and said, in a voice filled with pointed resolve: "Don't anybody fuck with me. I'm from Detroit."

No one in the room moved. Will felt a sudden and full relief that made him desperately want to go to the bathroom.

"My hero," he squeaked.

"Will, come over here, get out of my line of fire. If I have to vaporize that asshole's head, I'd rather not have to shoot through you to do it."

Will quickly moved toward the door, almost sneaking, on tip toe, across the carpet.

"Now you're blocking my shot at lil' Miss Kim. Take a step." He did.

"Not that I don't trust you, Kim-ber-ly, but I don't trust you." Kim started to move and Cheryl snapped the gun directly over to her. "Look, sweetheart, you've been pissing me off on a regular basis since January, so don't think I won't blow your damn head off right here and now. I'm tired. I'm sore. I need coffee. And you've been discussing grinding me up for plant food all morning like it was as basic as that foundation you use way, way, way too much of.... So — don't try my patience, Kim. Understand?"

Kim stood frozen and nodded.

Martin quietly said, "Where do you think you can run? Where do you think you can hide from me?"

"I'm not gonna run," Cheryl said, her voice still and steady. "I'm not gonna hide. Neither is Mr. Ross here. Our first stop once we leave here is a phone and one call to your brother Henri. And then one to daddy. Do you realize your father ... like I said, Kim, don't move, I'm in a crappy mood ... your father thinks I'm cute. Even gave me his private phone number. Never liked using 'cute' to get ahead — unlike some people I know — but in this case, I'll make an exception."

Martin was starting to sweat, his face glistening with concentration and a rapidly increasing blood pressure.

"Then, I think I'll call the cops — with or without Godot — to sweep up Mr. Phil and the rest of the 'Hee Haw' gang. And then go get a shower. And breakfast and a good night's sleep under something other than a tarp. And then — who knows — maybe I'll inspire my little cycling buddy here to ride one more time for Haven, kick some butt at Ghent-Wevelgem or, better yet, Paris-Roubaix and make a monkey out of all your little plans."

"Umm, Cheryl ... I really don't ..."

"Shut up, Will." She slowly swung the gun in a small arc between her two targets. Just behind her, Philippe started to moan. Cheryl glanced back over her shoulder, raised her left leg and snapped it back, catching Philippe just at the base of the skull with the heel of her running shoe." Urk," said Philippe, and fell silent.

"Let's go, Will. Fun's over." She looked at Will's name scrawled in various ways across the wall. "Love your decorator. You'll have to give me his number." Will opened the office door and stepped into the hall. Cheryl backed out of the room directly behind him. "Tell Philippe it really was something personal, would you? And the next time he tries to cop a feel from me, I'll bust his goddamned fingers off." She reached around the door with her left foot, caught the edge and pulled it shut. As the scene within the room began to close into a sliver of light, she said, "Thanks for having us. Have a nice day."

She was already running down the hall, toward the stairs and the lobby and the front door when she turned to Will. "Hurry up, pal. We've got a lot of work to do and people to call and plans to thoroughly screw up."

Will ran quietly behind her down one flight and into the tiled reception area and through the locked front doors and out into the street. The Beretta had disappeared into Cheryl's sweatshirt. The Laughing Cow was armed and dangerous. She stepped into the boulevard, took a quick breath and began jogging east.

"The Metro is only a few blocks from here and I need a phone."

"You were serious," Will said, jogging beside her. "You would have shot them. Where did you learn to use a gun like that?" His questions were quick, rambling and unfocused. She essentially ignored him.

"You're damned right I'm serious. I'm bringing jerk-face and his girlfriend down and down real hard."

Will turned back toward the chateau and in the second floor window saw Martin and Kim side by side staring at their retreating figures. He wanted to wave, but didn't. Once you've escaped the vipers, you don't stick your hand back in the basket to say good-bye.

❖

MARTIN WATCHED THE TWO FIGURES HURRY DOWN THE STREET. HE NEEDED time to think. To come up with a counter. He could block Henri, but not his father. And how the hell did she get his private number? Even he didn't have his father's private number. He looked at Kim — his mind working quickly, steadily, carefully — and then he knew. The answer was directly in front of him.

Kim smiled, a self-conscious, frightened smile in return of his gaze. Philippe moaned in the corner. Martin looked at the clock. Monday morning. 8:15. The office staff would begin arriving in the next 30 minutes.

"Wake him up. I need to talk to him."

Kim turned and walked quickly across the room toward Philippe, who pushed himself up and pushed her away. He didn't want or need her help. Martin watched Philippe slowly stand and sway, rubbing his neck and then staring, eyes full of hate, toward his king.

Martin Bergalis realized that he was in check, but not, checkmate. The deadliest piece on the board still belonged to him.

And it was his move.

CHAPTER SIXTEEN:

BREAKAWAY

Godot hated sleeping while sitting up. He tried to force himself awake, just so he could walk into his bedroom, but he couldn't seem to do it. And worse, he was sleeping sitting up, backwards, with his knees, stomach, chest and face pressed hard against the back of the world's most uncomfortable chair. God, when did Beatrice buy this thing? Before she left him, obviously. It must have been her last act of defiance, but who could blame her? He was never home. He had wanted it to end, but he didn't have the guts to say anything to her; he simply let it die and let her do all the dirty work.

This was horrible. The noise. The pain. He tried to force himself up from the depths of the nap and turn the damned TV off. What would the neighbors say? He forced one eye open and realized that his neighbors wouldn't care. This wasn't his house. This wasn't his house at all. This wasn't his chair or his room or his cut-glass, leaded window. With a bang and a whoosh, the TV screamed again. That wasn't his TV either. It was one of those big-screen jobs that brought life right into your house.

It wasn't just the mattress, this was the world's worst pillow as well. He tried to raise his head and found he couldn't. Oh, *merde*. He was stuck to it. Forcing himself to ignore the pain, he started from his forehead and began to peel his face back from it until his head was free and wobbled in the air like a cheap kootchie doll in a tourist shop.

Godot tried to fall backwards. He was still being held up, but he could fall to the side, and did, finally stretching out against the chained fence and looking up toward the sky. This definitely isn't my apartment, he thought.

Mine has a roof. He passed out just as the 11:15 out of the Gare du Nord hit full speed, screaming its way north to Brussels.

❁

THE LAST THING WILL HAD SEEN BEFORE HE HAD PASSED OUT WAS CHERYL, deep in conversation with Henri Bergalis about their experiences of the past 24 hours. He would have loved to stay and chat, been a part of it all, but he hadn't slept in more than 24 hours, with a seven-hour race and a ride under a tarp built into it. Just sitting on the edge of the divan was enough. The dark gods of sleep reached up through the mattress, took hold of the back of his head and pulled him down toward their domain.

He didn't struggle.

He didn't dream, except for a snapshot of Mrs. Cangialosi, standing in the rain at Raymond's funeral. Not moving. Surrounded by her army of daughters. Raymond had been her only son. Will walked over to her and was immediately chosen to fill the empty spot in her life.

The rain and the darkness enveloped the two and Will passed into the mists of sleep.

❁

CHERYL WAS ON THE EDGE, BUT STILL TOO KEYED-UP TO SLEEP. SHE HAD PUT her faith, her trust and their lives into the hands of Henri Bergalis. She hoped she was right. She hoped she was still thinking clearly. She, also, had been awake for 24 hours, had taken a shot to the face from the leading edge of a 9mm pistol and had an ugly purple and red streak across her face to prove it, had traveled to Paris on the floorboards of a Renault sucking exhaust most of the way, played Calamity Jane in the main office of a multinational drug concern and had called everyone she could think of for help in the matter: Henri; Stefano Bergalis; Deeds — never did get him; Debbie ("get out of the apartment"); and her best friend in the States, collect and in the middle of the night, for moral support.

The friend had listened thoughtfully and said, simply, "Stay in the pocket.

Make Ross stay in the pocket. If you leave, they win. Just watch your back."

Easier said than done, especially from 5000 miles away. Everything in her told her to run like hell, but she was also mightily pissed off, and, more than anything, Cheryl wanted to watch the world collapse around Martin Bergalis. So, she chose the brother. She had seen the two together. She had seen a chill, if not growing hatred, between them. Perhaps, she thought, she could use Henri as a shield to protect her and Will and Deeds and the rest of the team.

No more deaths.

"No more deaths."

"Excuse me?"

"What?" She shook her head clear. She was fading. Henri had been talking at a steady clip and she hadn't really been listening, lost in her own internal conversation. "Sorry. You were saying?"

Henri stopped and smiled. This, he thought, was a woman to love. Tough, smart, strong and beautiful in a quiet, simple way. Fresh, despite that purple line across her cheek. It almost gave her some character, imparting a dangerous look to her beauty.

"Why don't you just rest? You and Mr. Ross are safe here. This is one of my safe places. It is yours as long as you need it. Rest here. I'll send Bertrand to get your clothes. Something fresh. I'm sorry about Mr. Ross. Due to the explosion, everything of his is scattered over the neighborhood around his apartment. I'll send Bertrand out for some new." He looked Will over. "We'll have to check his sizes from the team's clothing list." He smiled.

She nodded. Slowly. Cheryl's eyes began to glaze over. Henri helped her stand and took her into the bedroom.

"Thank you," she said, her eyes moving from the bed, to the windows, to his face. "Are you sure your brother doesn't know about this place?"

"You never know about my brother," Henri said. "But this time, I do believe you're safe. He thinks you are staying at the George V. Besides, you have countered him. What you did threw his plans into disarray."

"He won't simply come charging forward and kill everyone in sight?"

"What do your football teams call that — a 'blitz'? No. He plays with a certain kind of deadly finesse. He has backed off now, looking for new avenues to travel toward his goals."

"Or to cover his ass."

"Well, yes. He would like his, uhh ... ass ... covered."

She had kicked off her shoes and pulled the dirty Laughing Cow sweatshirt over her head. She stood before him, unashamed, her breasts swelling with each breath. He tried not to look, but the lower third of his vision was drawn to them and with each breath he found her more enticing and delightful.

She had done it without thinking, and the cool in the room made Cheryl realize she was stripping in front of a man who was pretty much a total stranger. Even growing up in a huge family hadn't made her that bold. She smiled, took Henri's arm and walked him toward the door.

"I'll call Deeds," Henri said, staring straight ahead but working his peripheral vision for all it was worth "We'll pull Ross from Ghent-Wevelgem on Wednesday and see how he feels for Paris-Roubaix. Try to persuade him to ride Paris-Roubaix."

"I don't think that will be too terribly difficult. He's more into it now than he has been in years. Even Paris-Roubaix, which he hates even more than Mont Ventoux."

"Yes." He nodded. "I will leave your clothes for you here — next to Ross."

They both looked over toward the divan. Will was sprawled across it, one arm under, one arm behind, his legs bent like pipe cleaners.

"Perhaps I should make him more comfortable."

"Naw. Leave him. He'll figure it out." She turned to him. "Thank you. Thank you for your help and protection, Henri. You're sweet." She leaned to him, touched his face with her hand and kissed his cheek. He reached up and held her hand for a moment, then turned and kissed her palm.

"It's nothing."

They looked at each other for a long moment, before Cheryl pulled her hand away, stepped back into the bedroom and closed the door, watching him through the slowly narrowing gap.

The door closed with a snap. And Henri Bergalis smiled. This had been a great morning for him. He was on the verge of wresting control of his company from his brother. And — at the start of a new relationship with the American. All within a few minutes of waking up to her call.

Sleep well, my dear, he thought. After what you have done for me and to me this morning, there is no way I'd let anyone harm you. He turned and saw Will, snoring peacefully on the day bed, a little line of drool trailing out of the corner of his mouth, unshaven, unkempt, disgusting.

Henri sighed. Or you. I suppose.

❁

THE TRAINS WOKE GODOT UP. WHY THE HELL THEY HAD TO WHISTLE EACH and every time they blew past him was beyond his comprehension. But they did. And he did. And it capped a lousy night's sleep.

He stared at the sky for a moment, wondering where he was, then realized he couldn't really roll in either direction. The heavy hedge held him on one side, the chain-link fence separating the tracks from the rest of the world held him on the other. He slowly worked himself into a sitting position. His face was on fire. He ran a hand across it and came away with flecks of dried blood and leaves. Another train roared past, heading south, into the city. This was not, he knew, a good place to nap. Using the chain link, Godot pulled himself up. Everything inside him ached, and standing nauseated him. He leaned against the wooden rail at the top of the fence and gave the world outside his eyeballs a chance to stop doing a *pasa doble*.

He then turned, found a thin gap in the hedge and, ducking his head, pushed his way through. It was tougher than he thought, taking a true effort to push through the tight hedge and into the world beyond. That made him wonder how he got there in the first place. Standing free, he uncovered his eyes and began to quickly remember. He was standing in a small backyard, mostly dirt and mud, a little grass. In front of him was the shell of what appeared to be an apartment building. Most of the sidewalls were still standing, but the front and back were gone and the roof appeared to have dropped straight down.

Will Ross lived here. Did. Dead? Perhaps.

He remembered the landlady knocking on the door and LaSarge's cellular phone ringing. He answered the phone, but the connection was horrible inside the hallway. He walked down the single flight of stairs and out the back door. The connection cleared. It was a call for LaSarge. And then he was being carried across the yard by a giant hand and through the hedge and toward the trains. But his face stopped him by driving itself into a chain-link fence.

Smooth.

Police and rescue workers were crawling over the building like reporters at an open bar. Godot couldn't really hear them. All he could hear was the occasional scream of the express trains roaring past in and out of the city. He stood silently, watching, as the workers continued to cut through the roof of the building, digging, probing, looking for survivors.

The landlady must have opened the door.

Don't bother looking for her, Godot thought. There won't be enough to fill a demitasse.

He began to cough, shallowly, then deeply, and he was down on his hands and knees, flushing his lungs and his guts of the day. LaSarge and Benedict had been near the front of the building. Benedict was watching rescue efforts and waiting for word of his friend, LaSarge was watching the teenage girls in the dance studio across the street as they watched the events unfold through a picture window with no glass, when the uniformed officer told them about the trench-coated survivor in the backyard. They showed no interest at first, then began to walk, slowly, then faster and faster, down the narrow walk between the apartment buildings. As soon as Benedict saw Godot, even in the distance, he started calling for assistance. They ran up to the figure and, taking him by the shoulders, set him back on his rump in a sitting position.

"Luc — Luc. It's me. Benedict." Godot's eyes looked like those of a drunken St. Bernard. His nose and ears had been bleeding. Concussion, Benedict thought. His face was covered with scratches and whiskers and dried blood and criss-crossed lines. Whatever Godot had been in a fight with, Godot had lost.

LaSarge looked at Godot with the practiced eye of a man who had seen a lot of trauma in his day. Unless there was something deeply internal, Godot would simply suffer from a ringing in his ears and the devil's own headache for the next few days. That diagnosis became the basis for his defense back at the station later in the day, when he was criticized for his cold and brazen attitude in the backyard of a destroyed apartment house in the north of Paris.

LaSarge took Godot firmly by the shoulders, shook him, and said in a loud, piercing and forceful voice, "Where the hell is my brand-new cell' phone, you bastard?"

❂

HEAVEN WAS OBVIOUSLY OUT OF HIS REACH. THIS WAS MORE LIKE THE WAITING room of the Milwaukee bus station. It couldn't be heaven. He had expected so much more.

"This isn't heaven," Tomas said. "You can relax."

"What is it, then?" Will looked around himself, slowly and confused.

"Well, it's more like purgatory. Or limbo for adults."

"Did Philippe find me?"

"No, buddy — you're simply visiting. Traces of your concussion. He really tonked you on the noggin, there," Tomas said, leaning over and peering at the lump and bruise just high and ahead of Will's left temple. "You're lucky. You coulda been stuck here filling candy machines for a few centuries."

"Huh?"

"Penance. Minor things. Moral lapses. Language. Turning your back on your friends. Venial shit. Nothing mortal."

"I thought you said language."

"Yeah — oh. Taking the name in vain, that sort of thing. Far as I know, there ain't nobody named Saint Shit." He shouted though the hall. "Anybody hear of Saint Shit?" His voice reverberated through the empty chamber.

"See?"

Will looked around heaven's waiting room. The plastic benches and chairs. The candy machine with the cracked mirror. The grimy doors that led out to North Seventh Street in Milwaukee, he never expected it to be this way.

"I see an empty warehouse next to the pier in Corsica," Tomas said, looking around the cavernous hall. "My father sent me there each summer to work on crews with my uncle. I always had to wait here, in this warehouse, for the boat home. Sometimes days at a time until they decided to sail. What do you see?"

"No, man," Will said, sweeping his arm around, "it's the bus station. In Milwaukee, I think. I spent a lot of time waiting here. To go home."

Tomas smiled. "Purgatory. It's different for us all."

"I miss you, man."

"I know, Will. And I appreciate it. I'll remain alive as long as you keep my memory in your heart. Speaking of which — Raymond says hello."

"Raymond. Jesus."

Tomas quickly held up his hand. "Uh-uh. Name in vain. Name in vain."

"Oh, sorry. Where is Raymond?"

"He' s here. Kinda tweaked at you, though. Seems you turned your back on his family. His mother. Some friend, huh?"

Guilt and shame reached across a decade and hit Will full square in the back of his heart. He *had* turned his back. He had walked away from Mrs. Cangialosi. He had turned away from Raymond's entire family. He didn't know how to deal with death. Especially the death of his best friend right before his eyes. He didn't know how to deal with her need for a son to replace him. He was a kid. Sixteen, maybe 17. He just didn't know. And so, he turned away.

Will could feel the hot tears burning his cheeks, burning the scars that rode across his face like a surgeon's game of cat's cradle. He had turned his back. Sixteen years after the accident, 15 years after he walked away, his shame refused to turn its back on him. It returned to haunt him.

❋

WILL AWOKE ON THE DIVAN IN A ROOM HE DIDN'T RECOGNIZE, ROLLED ONTO THE floor, stretched, and went in search of a phone he couldn't find. Just go away, he thought. Stop ringing. It wouldn't. It was insistent. Will wandered through the semi-darkness of the room, semi-conscious. Daylight sneaked in through the edges of the heavy velvet curtains shuttering the rounded windows. His head wasn't banging any more, but his mouth felt like it was filled with the inventory of a high school gym bag. He tripped over a cast-iron dog and cursed.

The phone continued to ring.

Listen for the sound. He thought. Find the sound. He stopped, shut his eyes, and listened through the next ring. He promptly began to fall asleep. To the right. And close. He slowly stepped ahead, tripped over the cast-iron dog again, cursed again, and stopped. To his right a bit and ahead.

He stepped slowly, listening to the ring. Close. His thigh bumped into a rounded table. He opened his eyes, picked up the pearlescent French phone, and whispered a greeting.

"What?"

"Will?" It was a woman's voice. One he knew, even though he hadn't heard it on a phone in years.

"Kim?"

"Yes. How are you?"

"I'm really rather pissy right now." There was a long, uncomfortable pause.

"I've got to talk with you."

"Gee. Wasn't this morning enough?"

"This morning? Will — it's Tuesday noon."

Was it? Shit. Didn't feel like it.

"Will, I've got to talk to you."

"How'd you find me?"

"Will —"

"How'd you find me?"

"I have my ways."

He laughed. "Oh, man, I'm sure you do."

"Dammit, Will. That's not fair."

Will was losing his patience. The more his head cleared, the more he desperately wanted to get off the phone. Kim finding them meant Bergalis could find them. Bergalis meant Philippe, and Philippe meant back to the bus station in Milwaukee. For good.

"I know it's not fair, Kim, but you've played and won by your little game too damned long to be able to claim sweet and innocent when somebody throws it back in your face."

"I need your help, Will."

"How so?"

"They're going to kill me, Will."

"Who?"

"Martin. Philippe. They're going to kill me and hang this all on me."

"All what?"

"Colgan. Tomas. Merkel. Even Godot. I ran the team — so they're saying I used your signature. Your autograph. I tried to frame you. I tried to destroy the team."

"Well, you did."

"That's not the point."

"Of course it's the point."

"But on orders from Martin."

"Ahh, vat a gut Nazi frau yew'd mahke."

"Damn it, Will, I'm next in line. You cared about me. You loved me. I'm next, Will!" Her voice suddenly softened. "Doesn't that mean anything to you?"

Will was silent for a long time, then sighed quietly, "It did. It really did, Kim. Once. Maybe even recently. But the last few days and weeks...." Snapshots of Milan ran through his mind and his voice sharpened. "Hey — ever seen a man — a friend of yours, after an explosion of plastique, Kim? The human body, Kim," his voice quickly grew heavy with barely controlled anger, "the human body breaks apart, Kim, in pieces. Fingers. Forearms. Heads. Feet. Knees, Kim. Once you see it, it sticks in the back of your head. Forever, Kim. I saw that, Kim. I saw my best friend die. That's the second time I've seen that, Kim. You never get used to it. And you had a hand in it. Maybe you didn't say 'do it,' maybe you didn't plant the bomb, but your hand was on the trigger, Kim, right beside Martin and Philippe, because you knew. You knew, and you didn't say a damned thing to anybody. You ..." He felt his temper start to subside. "You killed Tomas as much as anybody. Don't expect me to feel a great deal of sorrow because your fingers got caught in the wringer."

"Tomas was a mistake. He wasn't supposed to die."

"No, Kim. I know. Tomas wasn't supposed to die. I was supposed to die! It was my bike, Remember? My bike that blew. Not Merkel's. Not Bourgoin's. Not Fred Smoot in Pawtucket. My bike. Jesus."

"No, I mean — Colgan was the only one who was...."

"What? On your calendar?" he said sarcastically. "Stuck in your index? Oh, here it is, 'Kill the world champion. Noon Sunday. Tennis at the club. 2 p.m.' God, the life you must lead. How do you sleep with all this going on?"

"Will, you've got to help me. They're going to kill me, Will." Kim began to cry, heavy, racking, frightened sobs. "They're going to kill me, Will. I'm sorry. I'm sorry. I'm sorry, Will, but they're going to kill me. I know it."

He listened to her for a moment, thinking what he could say. A part of him still wanted to reach out to her, but it was to a different Kim than the woman on the phone. A Kim he had felt something for and toward and with. But the other part of him burned with hatred and bitterness toward the naïve ambition that had eaten away her conscience and left her crying on the phone when the devil stepped forward and demanded payment on his contract.

He wondered what form her purgatory — no, her hell — would take. It wouldn't be pleasant.

"I can't help you Kim. I'm sorry. But there is truly nothing I can do."

"Meet me. Meet me tomorrow in Wevelgem. At the finish."

"No, Kim."

"After the race. I'll find you."

"No, Kim."

"Will, they're going to kill me!"

"Kim — you're not dead yet."

"What the hell is that supposed to mean?"

"Either go to the police and spill your guts and hope for the best...."

"Are you...."

"Or run, Kim. Run like hell and don't look back."

"You gutless bastard," she said, her voice dripping with venom. "It is true — all your little friends have always said it — you walk away when people need you. I'm amazed you have any friends at all."

"Well, that's true, Kim — but, then again, my friends aren't trying to kill me."

He took a deep breath, waited a moment for a response, and slowly hung up the phone.

He stared at the phone for a moment, then quickly awoke to the realization that they had to leave. Now. He hurried across the room to the double doors that led, he remembered, to the bedroom he had never reached. He pushed them open, ignored Cheryl's semi-nakedness on the huge bed, threw open the curtains, walked back and slapped a hand on her rump. She rolled over in a fright, grabbed the sheets and covered herself.

Will leaned forward on the bed and smiled into her sleepy and confused face.

"Let's get a move on, Miss DeMilo," he said, smiling, "they know where we are — and if they're going to kill us, I want to make it a challenge."

Cheryl woke up instantly, shook her head quickly, and stared back at him with quickly brightening eyes.

"No shit, Sherlock."

❁

DEEDS WAS FURIOUS. HE HAD BEEN MISSING A CAR, A BIKE, A RIDER AND A SOIGneur for 48 hours, with no idea if they were taking a leisurely stroll through the French countryside or had joined the elect in heaven forever. Then, without warning, all four had shown up at the team hotel in Ghent late Tuesday afternoon, battered, bruised, and broken.

Deeds looked horrible as well. He had been dealing with the Belgian police for two days trying to convince them that pillows blow up all the time and Mr. Merkel was just one of those unfortunate people whose heads detach easily. Between the police and the missing team car and the frantic calls from Henri and Martin Bergalis, he had never had a chance to return to his room even to brush his teeth.

The team was now under the control of Henri Bergalis. Kim Ross was out. Martin Bergalis was under investigation for one thing or another, no one quite knew what. Carl had driven to the Haven offices under Martin's orders Monday afternoon, only to find him gone, Henri in place and workmen swarming over the office changing the wallpaper. That expensive cloth stuff. Must've had a madman in here, Deeds thought, there's black magic marker scrawled all over the wall.

He was down a rider, with Merkel gone, a mechanic, with Tomas gone, and now, he was down a driver as well, with Philippe having up and disappeared. Deeds told no one, but given the events of the past few weeks, every time he opened a door he expected to find Philippe's head in a hatbox or hear a bang and find pieces of his balding assistant scattered over the hotel laundry room.

Deeds glanced over at Will, who had pulled a wing-backed chair to the window and now sat sprawled over it, his feet poking out the open hotel window.

"Will, I'm sorry. You can't ride Ghent-Wevelgem. Berga — Henri —

says you need the time off to prepare for Paris-Roubaix. I know you were looking forward...."

But Will was already asleep again, back in dreamland, back in the bus station, back in Purgatory. It was getting hotter.

This was not a good sign.

WEDNESDAY MORNING, WILL HAD SHOVED HIS HEAD OUT THE HOTEL WINDOW and wanted immediately to drive to Paris and personally thank Martin Bergalis and Kim and even Philippe for the past few days. There was a bitter wind whipping through the city courtesy of the North Sea. The riders would be fighting that all morning. He looked up and saw that the gray overcast had darker and lighter sections, which meant they'd be riding through rain most of the morning as well. A little water, a little wind, a little water. It was a great way to make a living. Butt sore from the weekend, back on the bike to face the midweek weather of Belgium with not a soul to watch you do it. Not me and not today, Will thought.

He smiled, but there was still a nagging feeling inside him. A guilt. The same kind of guilt you feel when you play hooky from school or work or ate meat on Friday. He ought to be there and be miserable right alongside the others who struggled with the wind and felt the burning in their legs and faced the never-ending road wishing they were anyplace else.

After the start, he leapfrogged the course in the team van, helping Cheryl at feed stations and listening to the race on the team radio. He'd better get used to this, he thought, if he stayed in the game; this was likely his future staring him in the face — second assistant flunky for filling water bottles.

Cheryl looked back, concerned.

"Are you all right?"

Will shut his eyes, hard, and rubbed his forehead.

"Yeah, sure, no problems."

Five hours into the race and Will stood by the side of the Kemmelberg, watching the first riders struggle up the hill. This wasn't the worst of it. The worst came 40 kilometers down the road, when the pack hit this same berg from the opposite direction. If the wind and the rain kept up, the irregular surface on the descent would make life hell for the riders who had survived this far, this long.

Will wanted to be a part of it.

"You sort of miss the anguish, don't you?" Cheryl said, quietly, stepping up beside him as the first riders passed.

Will smiled. "Yes. Damnedest thing, but I do."

"I know. That's what I felt at the end of last season when I lost my ride. I stood on the sidelines during a late-season women's criterium in the south of France and I bawled my eyes out. I knew most of the riders. And — can you believe it — they had the gall to be racing without me. Without me! Ripped me up. It takes you about six weeks before you really start getting over it. If, in fact, you ever do."

"Last year," Will said, staring down at the cobbles lining the road, then, into the endless gray of the Belgian sky, "I walked away. I had no problem leaving this sport. I just walked away from it all. Hitched a ride to Avelgem and that was it. Got the bike out and rode 50 klicks a day, basically for the hell of it. Out of habit. It didn't call me. It didn't speak to me. I didn't miss it for a second. But now — this," he swept his hand across the narrow descent of the Kemmelberg, "is just killing me."

"Welcome back...." A young Italian rider came flying down the descent, lost his balance when an unexpected dust devil pushed him sideways, regained control, caught his front wheel in a road gap, regained control, straightened out and rode straight as an arrow into a milk truck parked by the side of the road.

Will and Cheryl watched silently.

"Yep," he said, "I miss it."

✿

THE WEATHER HAD DECIMATED THE FIELD.

Bourgoin, Cacciavillani and Cardone had all dropped out of the race between the Kemmelberg and the return to the Kemmelberg. The wind was so sharp and fierce that recovery would take days and since the biggest spring prize lay just on the far edge of the weekend — Paris-Roubaix, the Sunday in

Hell — it made no sense to destroy yourself here, just to see yourself fold like a house of cards somewhere near the Forest of Arenberg.

Paluzzo was the only survivor, if you could call the agony filling his face as he battled the elements in a struggle toward the finish "surviving." He would learn. Next year, if conditions were the same, he'd bag it with the rest of his team. This year, it was something new. Something fresh. Something exciting. The challenge was a drug that he was newly addicted to, yet, one easily loathed in 12 month's time.

The finish crowds in Wevelgem were better than any Will had seen along the way. Some people were sneaking out of work early, the wind having finally died and the skies brighter, if only a bit. The colors of the day were still muted, but livelier than the black and white he remembered in his mind's eye at the start.

Looking down the finishing straight, Will saw the first riders come into view. The field hadn't broken up nearly as much as he thought across the Kemmelberg. The Italian and German teams were leading out the sprint, with Belgian and Dutch riders massed between. The locals had lost the last few races on home ground and didn't intend to lose this one.

Will tried to count the riders in the pack. He hit 20, but there was so much shuffling, stringing out, bunching up, that he wasn't sure. It was quite a peloton, tight and pounding hard. A few of the Belgian and Dutch riders were breaking early; not a good idea with the sprinters of this caliber sitting in close behind, sucking a wheel and waiting for a last slingshot surge toward the finish.

The pace was picking up now, the sprint was in earnest, the leaders back and forth across the street, blocking the inside move, making anyone trying to go around them go the long and hard way. Will could see Kosygin, the Russian, head down, concentrating on the back wheel of a young Belgian rider. That kid in front, Will thought, will never know what hit him. Five hundred meters out and the accordion of 20 riders had pulled back together again. At 200 meters all hell would break loose and there would be a mad dash for the finish.

And yet, there was something, something calling, just outside Will's consciousness. It was heard and unheard, a voice, his name, lost in the crowd. Reluctantly, he broke his concentration away from the sprint and looked around him, then across the street. He scanned the crowd for a voice he wasn't sure he heard, a face he wasn't sure he'd see. There, next to the timer's platform.

Kim.

She saw him notice her and smiled as if the past few days, or years, had never happened. She waved at him, then elbowed her way through the crowd, watching him closely, pushing aside anyone who slowed her progress until she was stopped near the middle of the barricade.

There was a shuffle in the crowd behind her. Kim Grady Ross broke her gaze from Will a moment, looked over her shoulder into the people straining behind her for a look at the finish line, and turned back to Will. Her eyes had changed from a false seduction to outright fear.

"Kim?"

She wormed her way, frantically, toward a gap in the barricade, but the crowd slowed her progress. She looked over her shoulder again and her movement, quick at first, became mindless and hysterical, an animal fighting its way out of a trap. Philippe Graillot stood perhaps six people from her, slowly moving through the crowd.

Will caught her eye from the opposite side of the street, her look panicked, pleading, and then, surprised. Shocked. Outraged with the turn of events that brought her to and through an opening in the fence and into the street as 16 men, at nearly 70 kilometers an hour, arrived at the same point in space at the same moment in time.

"KKKiiimmmm!"

Will screamed, but his voice was lost in the shouts and cheers and exhilaration of a Belgian crowd exploding in joy as the sun broke through the overcast of Wevelgem for the first time in nearly a week.

CHAPTER SEVENTEEN:

A SUNDAY IN HELL

The headlines screamed for the rest of the week.

Crash... Death... Haven...

Death... Haven...

Haven.

Kim. Fear, made flesh by Philippe, had chased her onto the course, where 200 pounds of man and bicycle at 45 miles an hour had killed her. *Quelle tragédie!* For the riders, of course. For Kim, public sympathies were something else altogether.

She had once told Will that her greatest dream was to be headline copy. She should have been a touch more careful in her wishes, for now she was center stage in the greatest scandal in the history of professional cycling: murder, money and destruction of a team, all laid neatly at her feet.

Will smiled grimly. He could see Martin Bergalis, fresh shirt, Armani suit, immaculately groomed and tailored, playing the choirboy at the news conference.

"If only I had known, if only I could have stopped her ... saved the team ... all these people ... Would anyone like more wine? Something to eat? Please — help yourself."

And the guardians of truth, justice and the French way would descend upon the catered lunch, eat their fill and beyond, and later wonder aloud in their newsrooms how sad it was that such a magnificent Frenchman as Martin Bergalis could get sucked in so completely by an American whore.

Kim.

The preliminary autopsy results said there were traces of cocaine, apparently injected. One two-franc tabloid went so far to say enough cocaine to easily kill a 250-pound man in excellent health. It didn't surprise Will that she was trying to escape that way. She was a great escape artist.

Then again, in the end, it wasn't drugs that killed Kim Grady Ross. Or the deadly hands of Philippe Graillot or the deadly business of Martin Bergalis.

It was a 170-pound Russian sprinter who hit her full square on the side and drove her out of Will's view like a Barbie doll hit by le train à grande vitesse.

The Russian's arm was broken, his season put on hold.

Her neck was broken, her season done. Permanently.

And somewhere, deep in the background, Will could hear the great Haven vacuum cleaner sweeping up the mess. He wondered if he was still one of the crumbs in the corner.

❁

"HOW IS HE?"

"It's not my day to watch him."

"Cheryl, dammit. How is he?"

Cheryl Crane was shocked. Deeds seemed genuinely concerned. After three months of badgering, baiting and trying to destroy the man, Carl Deeds spoke on the phone with an actual emotional tremor in his voice as he asked about Will. She sighed heavily. She was concerned as well.

"Honestly, Carl, I don't know how he is. In fact, I don't know where he is. I saw him in Wevelgem. Talking to the police. That was Wednesday. At the crash. That was nuts. You know that. And then, I didn't see him. By the time I got back to the team cars, his bike was gone, the junky one that was still stuck on the top of the Peugeot. So, I don't know, Carl. Since Wednesday afternoon he's been gone. Riding. Somewhere."

"Will he be here on Sunday, Cheryl? Can I expect him for Roubaix?"

She paused for a long moment.

"I don't know, Carl."

"Well, find him. Bourgoin won't ride without him."

She hung up the phone with disgust. She might have known. Deeds's concern went as far as his roster for the next starting line. Cheryl turned to face Henri Bergalis, sitting comfortably in the tattered easy chair that made up a corner of her apartment.

He looked at her with sad, tired eyes. "Can we expect him for Roubaix?"

"God, Henri, I don't know. I don't know how his mind is working right now, or even if it is at all — after everything that has happened, he watched his ex-wife get whacked in front of him. Maybe he just blew."

She picked up her glass of wine carelessly and a splash of dark red jumped the edge of the glass and fell onto her blouse, just above her heart.

Damn, she thought. Nothing harder to get out of a white blouse than wine. Except blood.

❁

EVERYONE HAS A PLACE WHERE HE FEELS SAFE, TOTALLY SECURE, protected from the world, from worries, from strife. Will's was on a bike, he realized, pounding down an unknown road, through a blind corner, maneuvering in traffic, facing problems with no more than six meters in which to solve them, hammering, gliding, hammering, pacing, hammering, thinking, hammering, hammering.

He pulled the torn and mottled Michelin road map from his jersey. It was a cold and ugly Saturday morning. He had been riding. Nearly 150 kilometers a day since Wednesday. Thinking, pedaling, feeling the anger inside him rise and grow, then burst through as extra speed, spreading out across the rough pavement faster and faster, and then disappearing as if he had crossed the line. Crossed the line with Raymond.

He had felt every emotion known to man in the past few days: guilt, anger, joy, desolation, but mainly, self-pity. Everything he touched, it seemed, had turned to shit. Everything he was, it seemed, was false. Everything he had done since Leonard's call in January, had gone to hell.

Everybody he had ever cared for was dead.

He never should have picked up that phone. It had been a death sentence for Tomas and Merkel and Kim and Godot and his landlady, Mrs. Tonoose. And true to form, he had turned his back on them all and ridden away. Kim designed her own death, he thought — maybe Merkel as well — but he still felt small, somewhat less of a human being, for what he felt, and what he did.

He left.

He rode away into the sunset, once more leaving behind him the chaos that he had taken a hand in creating for others to sweep up. It was his sanctuary from the demons, for as he rode, the guilt and hatred would grow and overwhelm, then fade back into an easily controlled creature lurking quietly in a dark corner of his mind next to an old pile of *National Geographic*s.

As Will felt the emotional pressure settle within his chest, he looked down the unbroken ribbon of road, endless klicks in either direction, bordered by bare-limbed trees, silent sentinels to the coming spring, and realized he didn't recognize anything.

That was bad.

He had to find a way to the team hotel near Compiègne by that afternoon.

Sometime during his ride, sometime when he wasn't truly paying attention to the world outside his mind, he had come to a decision. For perhaps the first time in his life, he wasn't turning his back.

Not this time.

PHILIPPE GRAILLOT REACHED UNDER THE BED OF HIS APARTMENT, TOUCHED the handle and pulled the long case forward. He didn't remember it being this heavy. He stood, swung it onto the bed, and keyed in the numbers on the roller locks: 007. 007.

The professional killer in him smiled. Good joke.

He looked at the heavy metal stock of the Heckler & Koch PSG1 sniper rifle. Others in his line had stripped their weapons down to the barest essentials, cutting weight wherever they could. He kept his heavy for a purpose: It steadied his shot, especially over the distance he'd have to cover tomorrow. A moving target at 130 meters. Through trees. Interesting. Difficult, given conditions. Certainly not impossible.

Not for him.

He checked the scope. The latest in optical technology. He checked the stand. Precision ground to his specifications. He checked the silencer. Handmade in his own workshop. He checked the ammunition. .308 Winchester. Three clips. Fifteen shots. More than enough.

He'd only need the one.

He thought for a moment. No. Two would do nicely.

He hadn't even needed one for the American woman. Merely seeing him at the finish in Wevelgem had made her panic. And for no reason. Philippe had no intention of killing her. He had merely been sent to keep an eye on the long-term romantic investment of Martin Bergalis. But once she saw his face in the crowd she lost her composure, completely, and committed suicide with a bicycle. Amazing. Tragic. Comic, in its own way. He smiled. Oh, well.

C'est la vie.

He closed the case, snapped the latches shut, turned off the light and left his apartment for what he knew would be the last time, heading for a secluded cottage in a forest near Wallers, in northern France.

By Monday, he'd be in southern Greece, enjoying a whole new view and a whole new life with yet another whole new name.

IT TOOK ISABELLE MARCHANT 20 MINUTES TO GET PAST THE HOSPITAL SWITCHboard to the phone of Inspector Godot.

"They were simply protecting me."

"Well, tell your guard dogs that if they don't want to end their shift to discover their cars towed away, they had better let me through when I tell them I'm calling on official police business."

"You are plucky."

"I hate plucky. Look — I found what you were looking for: Haven owns 20 parcels of land generally along the Paris-Roubaix course. Most of it under the name of SB Development, a construction company."

"Are they building?"

"No, much of it seems to have been bought by Stefano Bergalis to preserve it. I guess the bricks and cobbles on the road are disappearing — being paved over — so the company bought a lot of the farmland, preserved the roads, the homes, the barns and leased it back to the previous owners to work. That way, there's still *pavé*, cobbles for Paris-Roubaix."

Godot thought for a moment. "When the father dies — Martin takes control. And those things that make northern France special disappear under a bed of concrete and behind brick walls."

Marchant said nothing. Her family had owned property along that route.

Near the Forest of Wallers-Arenberg. She had sold it to SB Development two years ago for a very healthy sum.

"How soon can you be here?"

"Twenty minutes."

"Stop at my apartment. Bring me a change of clothes. Then, stop at the office. My keys are in a coffee cup on my desk."

"Which cup? The one with no handle or the one with mold growing in the bottom?"

"The one with the little bald-headed American detective on it. The one with the keys in it. The small key opens the lower right-hand drawer. Bring that."

"Bring what?"

"My gun. I'm going hunting."

❖

CARL DEEDS HAD SEARCHED EVERYTHING CONNECTED WITH HIS LIFE, TRYING to find his vanished American Express Corporate card. His wallet. His bag. His suitcase. His passport folder. His day book. His briefcase. Nothing.

The clerk at the small hotel in Pierrefonds was growing impatient. She could have sold these rooms at a much higher rate to racing fans and spring tourists, but had been forced into saving them for Haven Pharmaceuticals at the "industrial" rate. Now, it appeared, they couldn't even pay that.

Will Ross wormed his way through the crowd of riders and gear filling the tiny lobby and tapped Tony C on the back of the neck. When the sprinter turned to the right, Will ducked past him on the left, next to Deeds.

"Got a problem?"

"Gee, nice of you to show up. Yes. I don't have my card."

"Aw. Don't worry." Will turned to the desk clerk. "Here, put it on mine." He tossed the American Express Gold card on the register. "Give me a room up front, will you?"

Deeds looked down to see his card staring back at him.

"What the...?"

"Don't break a sweat, Carl. I filched it in Wevelgem. You know what's great about these cards? There's no limit. That's great. Although they may consider one on your card now. You know?"

Will scribbled his name across the register, took a key, shouldered his gear and looked at the still unbelieving Deeds.

"See you tomorrow, bud. Don't look so shocked. Bergalis is paying and the asshole owed me a week in the country."

Everyone stared as Will walked down the hall toward the ancient elevator. Tony C reached for the American Express card just as Deeds slammed his hand down on it.

"Isn't it my turn?" Cacciavillani asked.

"No. No," was all Deeds could think to say.

✲

THE PELOTON ROLLED SMOOTHLY OUT OF THE CROSSROADS AT COMPIÈGNE, quickly picking up speed, riders throughout the pack already resigned to their fate of riding seven or more hours through a cold and wet and grizzly hell today, only to see themselves arrive in Roubaix nowhere near the leader board. Those who knew the race, hated the race. Those who didn't, like children jumping in excitement at their first visit to the dentist, would certainly learn quickly enough.

Cardone had ridden in the lieutenant slot for Bourgoin at Ghent-Wevelgem, but the chevrons hadn't fit him. He had chafed under the obligations of the job and so the matter fell to Will in Compiègne. Not that he wanted it either, as this was a race of slinging the leader forward, sticking with him as long as possible, then falling back, only to thrash like hell for the shore in order to save yourself, but he was glad for the company. He had been riding alone for the past few days and it felt good to be in traffic made up of something other than automobiles. He looked toward the sky. The overnight rain had given way to a crisp, cold sunshine that was already beginning to give way again to gray clouds.

Such fun. Roubaix and its damned reputation.

Just north of Compiègne, the pack split for the first time, two riders shooting out ahead in a bid for cycling immortality and a chance to hit the cobbles first. Wary eyes glanced up to watch them go and then settled back into the routine. They'd be blown out and recaptured, sucked in and discarded by the pack by Troisvilles, before the first of the 22 sections of pavé.

Other races had cobbles. Other races had pavé. Other races had the rough hewn bricks as road coverings, but Roubaix was different. This was a race that took pride in its ever-changing face. As city fathers widened roads and laid down concrete to facilitate automotive and farm traffic, the race committee searched deeper and deeper into the backwaters of the French countryside to find roads that even cattle wouldn't travel: slick, irregular, out of line, and dangerous.

Perfect.

It led to a ride that wasn't just bouncing, wasn't just jarring, but a ride that compressed your spine and forced the rider into a daylong fight with his handlebars, his concentration, his nerve and his power. One hundred years of rain and snow and war and cattle had deformed the blocks and their seating, until, no matter from which angle you approached them, there was no clear line longer than 10 meters in any section of the road. Dry, they would grab, pinch and puncture tires, dent rims, knock bikes out of alignment in a second's time. Wet, they would push and pull, slide a rider sideways and out of line and slam him to the ground, reaching up to shatter a shoulder, a hip or a spine. In any condition, wet or dry, they were fearsome. Impossible to ride cleanly.

Some riders, in fact, ignored riding completely, and, in the worst stretches, merely carried their bikes through to higher ground. Some went beyond that and refused to ride the race at all. While Merckx and Moser and De Vlaeminck made it their own, Anquetil hated it. Hinault complained it was nothing but a 270-kilometer cyclo-cross, won it, then turned his back on it forever.

Will didn't have that option. He couldn't turn his back on Paris-Roubaix, as much as he hated it, as much as he wanted to abandon. This was what he was getting paid for, after all, and, deep down, there was a certain satisfaction in knowing that the better he did, the harder he made life for a drug store Dweezil in downtown Paris.

Will smiled. He picked up the pace, took position in front of Bourgoin, and began to weave through the pack, moving them closer to the front.

The pace was steady and Will found that in the smooth asphalt, despite his attempts to focus, he was lost in the week, the month, the season. The face of Tomas rose up in his mind, then Merkel and Colgan and his landlady — I didn't like you until you died, he thought — and Kim.

Kim.

Everyone, he thought, has a blind spot in life, a person who misuses, mistreats, but is always forgiven. Kim was his blind spot. He couldn't help but feel sorry for her, despite the fact that she likely would have stood by calmly and watched him and Cheryl die. She was the headline now. She would take the brunt of the Haven investigation. She would be the key. And she would have nothing to say in her defense.

And Martin. The smiling face of Martin Bergalis. He had made the unexpected move with Kim. Now, he controlled the board again with the help of his deadly knight, Philippe.

But what about Philippe? He had dropped off the face of the earth, according to Deeds, according to some guy named LaSarge at the headquarters of the Paris police. Nothing to worry about. He's gone. Forgotten. Out of the picture.

Yeah, right.

If there was nothing to worry about, Will thought, why in hell were the hairs on the back of his neck standing straight up? He zipped his team jacket up the final inch, hunkered down, and lowered his head toward the wind.

❁

MOST OF THE DRIVING HAD BEEN ALONG COUNTRY LANES AND COW PATHS TO reach the abandoned house. Philippe Graillot stared up at it and wondered how much longer Martin Bergalis would let it live. Not long. Once he had final authority from the local councils, once the proper palms had been properly greased, the house would come down, the roads would go in, the forest would be gutted and the homes would be built. Five-million-franc homes. Country living for the rich and their friends. Good-bye to northern France, good-bye to the farms, good-bye to the pavé, good-bye to Paris-Roubaix.

Good riddance, he thought.

He pulled the heavy case from the trunk of the car and carried it toward the door.

❁

CHERYL WAS MISERABLE. HER FACE THROBBED WITH A DISTANT ACHE. DEEDS was standing on the seat next to her, his waist and chest and shoulders and head reaching up through the sunroof, his body a living hood ornament for the car, buried inside a forest of spare wheels and bikes meant for on the road emergencies. He kept screaming down at her to pick up, slow down, pick up, slow down, get in position, get in position, but never told her exactly where to place Haven's lead support car. She was driving by the seat of her pants and from images she had of the race in the past. This wasn't her job. Deeds had sprained his wrist just before the start and needed a driver. He grabbed Cheryl before she left for the feed zone. Now, she was tense from following the peloton, tight behind, as it split and rejoined, hit the early cobbles, and riders flew this way and that. The fans along the side squeezed in and she was sure in one section that she had caught a child with a rear view mirror. In the back seat, the Belgian mechanic held a radio to one side of his face, a cigar to the other. She was going to throw up. She knew it. Everything she had ever eaten was going to spew out, fill the car and drown them all. She should have listened to her father.

Never raise your hand.

❁

GODOT AND ISABELLE HAD DRIVEN PAST THREE OF THE SB DEVELOPMENT PROPerties so far in their race north. Each was flat farmland just outside small towns, away from the path of Paris-Roubaix.

"What are we looking for?" Isabelle asked, her plans for a quiet Sunday in Paris already ruined.

"I don't know. It's a sense — a feeling. I'll know it when I see it. What's next? What's next on the list? Stay with the properties that border the course."

"I don't know if I can do that — these are only listed by towns. There is one south of Valenciennes. And one just inside the forest near Wallers."

Godot raced the engine of the small car and felt it jump ahead. Maybe he should get an American car, he thought, that always got more respect than his Peugeot. An American car. A Dodge. Dodge truck. That was a car that got respect on the road.

The Peugeot, almost in response, hit a depression in the road that forced them down into the seats and then up into the roof. Godot shook his head and fought to bring the car under control as it sped north.

Isabelle looked over at her sweating, balding boss. She had never seen him like this before, intent, intense and focused on a single idea. His face still carried the scars and lines from his encounter with the fence earlier in the week.

And somehow, she wasn't sure how, it all made him ... well ... kind of sexy.

❋

PHILIPPE TIGHTENED THE FINAL SCREW ON THE SCOPE AND RAISED THE SNIPER'S rifle to the window of the cottage. Looking out the open window, he saw three breaks in the forest that would give him additional shots, if necessary, at the target. Leaning hard to his right, he could also see the run up to the forest. With a spotter scope he could easily see his target approach.

Perfect.

Philippe Graillot looked at his watch. According to the radio, the field was at least 15 minutes away. He leaned back against the wall, lit a Gauloise and thought warm and wonderful thoughts about the Greek islands. By this time tomorrow, he'd be there. With more than two million francs and endless sunshine to keep him warm.

❋

GODOT RACED PAST THE SIGN ANNOUNCING WALLERS, 3KM.

"Which way? Which way?"

Isabelle hadn't been paying attention to the map.

"Uhmmm. Uhm. Right. No. No. Left. Left. Here. Here!"

The car screamed around the corner, through a shallow ditch and onto a dirt road.

"Are you sure?"

"Yes, I'm sure. There's a house out here," Isabelle said. That it was the house she grew up in, that she had sold to SB Development against her mother's wishes, was left unsaid.

WILL COULD FEEL THE SURGE IN THE PACK. RIPPLES OF ENERGY RUSHED THROUGH the peloton, back to front. Without knowing where they were, he knew where they were. The pavé was approaching. The forest. The place with the worst cobbles and the tightest crowds and the least room to maneuver.

The pack strung out as teams and individual riders fought for the chance to meet their doom quickly.

"STAY TIGHT. FOLLOW THEM IN," DEEDS CALLED DOWN TO CHERYL.

"What about the crowds?"

"They'll move."

FROM A RISE BEHIND THE COTTAGE, GODOT EXAMINED THE CAR PARKED IN the small clearing behind it with his binoculars. Shifting his glance, he looked at the crowd lining the course perhaps 100 or 150 meters beyond the cottage, through the trees. Perhaps it was just a spectator who had figured a way to park close. An assassin, from there? No. Impossible shot. Then, he noticed the breaks in the trees. And the angle of the house. And the license plate and the sticker beside the plate.

Rental.

This was it.

Reaching into his pocket, he pulled out the Smith & Wesson 9mm revolver. A classic. Fully loaded. He took a deep breath and began walking toward the cottage.

Without looking over his shoulder, he growled, "Stay here."

Isabelle Marchant waited a moment, looked around at the empty expanse of field and forest, shuddered and quietly started following Godot.

There was no way in hell she was staying alone.

Besides. She had to find a bathroom. And she knew there was one here.

❂

THE PACK STRUNG OUT AS IT APPROACHED THE PAVÉ. WILL STEELED HIMSELF for the first shudder up his arms. He caught a quick glimpse of the skies and realized it had been misting for the past few moments, giving the pavé just enough slickness to make it deadly.

He took a deep breath and plunged over the infamous train tracks into the forest, just ahead of Bourgoin.

❂

THERE.

Philippe found Will in the pack leading into the forest perhaps 30 riders back, just behind three bright yellow jerseys of the Regio Possanza team. Those were his markers, he thought. Watch them through the first gap, mark the spot, hit him in the second. Use the third as backup.

Simple.

What was the American phrase? Ah, yes. Like shooting eels in a bucket.

He took one last glance in the spotter scope before setting it aside and going to work. What he saw made him smile.

In that split second, he decided to change his target.

❂

JUST FEWER THAN HALF THE RIDERS HAD SHOCK ABSORBERS ON THEIR FRONT forks to deaden some of the brutal jarring of the day. They had grown in popularity since LeMond introduced them a few years before. Everyone had laughed then. Those were for mountain biking. No one was laughing now. Including Will. The chances of winning without the shocks was dropping dramatically. The best riders had them. Will looked down at the front fork of The Beast.

He didn't.

Will tried to follow the line of the Regio riders directly in front of him, but they were having a hard time riding the crown of the road. As the lead Regio rider lost his back wheel, Will decided to pull off toward the side, and, if necessary, find a dirt path through the crowd. Two boys saw what he was doing and shouted to the fans on that side, clearing the way, for their heroes, Bourgoin and Cardone.

GODOT STOOD IN WHAT HAD ONCE BEEN A FRONT HALL. THE DOOR HAD SEEMED to fairly scream when he pushed it open, but as he listened now, he could hear nothing. Then, a rattle, as if something metallic, a pen, a screwdriver, a bullet, had fallen on the wooden floor, one floor up, toward the back of the house.

Godot pulled the hammer back on the 9mm and heard the reassuring click. He took a deep breath and stepped on the first of the stairs leading to the second floor.

THIS WAS A STRANGE POSITION FOR PHILIPPE GRAILLOT. HE HAD NEVER BEEN at this juncture before. Which target? The man or the woman? He couldn't believe his good fortune. He couldn't believe he couldn't decide.

The money was for the man. The revenge would be for the woman. He had never been bested by a female and, certainly, never knocked cold.

Revenge won out. He could always catch the man. The man was a fool. It would just make for a longer day.

He swung the rifle toward the first gap. The Regio team had yet to appear, but, there was Bourgoin and a rider in front of him, deep inside the crowd. Was it Ross? No idea. He couldn't see. The pack was obviously broken and improvising its way through the forest and pavé.

No shot. Which? Wait for the next gap? Try your luck? Or go for the sure thing? Prince Albert in a can?

He swung the rifle back across the field of fire to the beginning of the first gap in the forest, the first moment he could pick up his target, in her car, behind her wheel, in her coffin.

❁

GODOT WAS TWO STEPS FROM THE TOP WHEN THE STAIR GROANED. HE FROZE. He lifted his foot slowly off the step and raised it to the next, gently, slowly, putting pressure on it. In the moment of silence on the stairs, he had heard the rustling continue in the back room and felt a breeze coming through an obviously open window. He hoped to God he wasn't drawing a bead on a photographer out for an unusual shot. He took a deep breath and stepped to the top of the landing.

❁

"THROUGH THE CROWD, THROUGH THE CROWD," DEEDS WAS SCREAMING.

Cheryl flashed her lights and tapped the horn, working the wheel with one finger, back and forth through the wall of humanity that had closed the course down to a path wide enough for only single riders to pass, a gauntlet of pushes forward and sideways and slaps of encouragement and detestation.

Out of the corner of her eye, she saw a gap in the trees to her left. The road came up to a small rise beside it. There was less shadow here. More light. And the crowd was thinner. She smiled. It would give her room to breathe, if only for a second.

❁

PHILIPPE EXHALED SMOOTHLY AND CAREFULLY. HE COULD SEE THE FLASHING lights of the lead car coming through the forest to the gap. He placed the crosshairs of the scope just beneath them and waited. The car rose up into the gap. He adjusted his aim quickly, without hurry, without panic, settled his cheek into the smoothed stock of the rifle and identified his target, an area directly through her right breast. Slowly, gently, Philippe Graillot squeezed the trigger and felt the surge of power as he sent his gift hurtling through the cool air of a Sunday afternoon toward the chest of Cheryl Crane.

C.O.D.

CHAPTER EIGHTEEN: ROUBAIX

There was an instant of sunshine in the gap for Cheryl Crane, an instant of diminished crowds, an instant of easy driving, an instant of golden diamonds playing off against the windshield as it shattered into a thousand pieces with a roar and she heard a sound like a small melon exploding and felt thousands of small impacts across her chin and neck and chest as if a child had carelessly thrown a handful of pebbles at her just as the window to her left simply disappeared with a pop and whoosh.

And then she heard Deeds.

From above the car, his torso still through the sunroof, he screamed with the deep angry bellow of a wounded beast. She turned to her right and looked to where his knee had been. All that was left was a gaping joint with no hinge. The hinge, she realized, slowly, almost in a daze, being nothing more than the red and white flecks playing off against her chest.

Oh, my God, she realized, and she wanted to throw up.

❁

PHILIPPE PEERED CAREFULLY THROUGH THE SCOPE. THE SHATTERED WINDOW didn't help, he wasn't quite sure. He caught a glimpse of Cheryl, her chest covered in blood, but couldn't quite tell what that thing was beside her. Hmmm. Better make sure. He settled in for a second shot.

❁

GODOT HADN'T BEEN EXPECTING THE BLAST FROM THE RIFLE. IN HIS SHOCK and surprise, his gun flipped out of his hand and into the hall opposite the open doorway.

❦

CHERYL STILL WASN'T SURE WHAT HAD HAPPENED. SHE KNEW SHE WAS IN A form of shock, but Deeds, Deeds, she knew, was in big damned trouble. He was trying to climb up out of the car through the sunroof in the madness of his pain. She fought with the car and she fought with him, driving with one hand and holding the pocket of his pants with the other. In the rear seat, Roger, one of the assistants, sat white-faced staring at the bloody gap that had once been Deeds's knee cap. Cheryl turned to him and said, simply, "Help me." There was no response. She let go of Deeds for a moment and swung her hand in an arc, reaching back and catching the side of his face with her knuckles. It wasn't much, but it was enough.

"Help me, damn you!"

Cheryl reached across the seat and shoved both of Deeds's legs out from under him. He came slithering down through the sunroof like The Incredible Boneless Man. He was in the car, but so was the noise, for now the screaming was maniacal. He could see what had happened to him. Beyond his initial shock, he could feel it as well.

In the few maddening seconds, Cheryl realized that she was approaching the second gap in the trees. Before crossing the train tracks, she had noticed a small farmhouse about 200 yards off into the field. A farmhouse meant a road. A road meant she could backtrack the eight kilometers into Valenciennes and get Deeds to a hospital.

With one hand on Deeds's chest, another on the wheel made slippery by the blood, she screamed at Roger, "Hold him! Hold him!"

Roger leaned forward and threw himself over the seat, pinning Deeds into the cushions. Cheryl grabbed the wheel, saw the second gap, downshifted into second, and, just before her turn, into the forest, through the crowd and into the break in the trees, put on her signal.

At first, the crowd thought the turn signal was a joke, but they moved, and quickly, when they discovered it wasn't a joke and that the steely-eyed driver was leaving the course to go cross country in a team car with a siren all its own.

❁

GRAILLOT WAS STUNNED. IT WAS AS IF HE HAD WOUNDED A BULL ELK AND the damned thing had turned to charge him. The small black, red and yellow team car shot through the high grass at the rear of the trees and careened across the open field. He looked through the scope — the passenger, a male, was in agony, writhing in the seat — while someone, it appeared, was trying to control him. At the wheel, face set and determined, sat the Crane woman. Bloodied, but alive.

Damn. He missed.

Oh, well, he sighed. Not this time.

He brought his cheek down to the stock and peered through the scope. Dead center. Over an inch. Heart shot. She'll never know what hit her.

He slowly exhaled to calm himself. He had grown excited over the thought of his good fortune.

❁

THE CAR HAD BECOME LIKE THE FLOOR OF AN ABATTOIR. THE SICKLY SWEET smell of blood filled the compartment, while the blood itself seemed to be everywhere. On the wheel, on the pedals, on the windshield, on the seats. Cheryl couldn't get a grip on anything. She yelled through the screaming in her head at Roger. "You've got to stop the bleeding!"

He reached in the back seat and came up with a T-shirt. He stuffed it into the socket that had once held Deeds' knee. Carl roared with pain, grabbed Roger and dragged him over the seat in his anguish.

Cheryl couldn't hold the ring of the wheel anymore. Blood covering the wheel had made it too slippery to control. She had to clutch one of the struts in order to drive the car with any semblance of direction. As she approached the farmhouse, she noticed a glint in an upstairs window. People. Good. People meant cars. Cars meant roads. Roads meant a way out of this field and into Valenciennes. The car hit a small ditch. Deeds howled and wrapped his arms around Roger who screamed with fear. Cheryl realized she was screaming too, screaming in the effort to reach the first goal — the house, then the road, the town, the help.

Dear God.

Again, she noticed the glint in the window.

She didn't notice the man behind it.

JUST A BIT, MY DEAR, HE THOUGHT. JUST A BIT. PHILIPPE BEGAN TO PUT PRESSure on his finger, to bring the rifle just to the edge of firing. It was difficult this time because he sensed another presence in the room, as if he was being watched. He pulled his face away from the stock for a moment as if to listen. He was so occupied that he didn't realize that with the foam plugs in his ears he wouldn't be able to hear much of anything. He turned back to the business at hand. The car was approaching nicely. Easy shot. Easy shot.

This time, he felt it. He felt pressure on one of the floor boards he was lying across. Whoever it was, he thought, had just punched a ticket to hell. He let go of the stock, smoothly reached into the holster under his left arm, withdrew the Beretta 9mm, and, as it swept the room toward the door, where he imagined his target to be, cocked it, ready for firing.

Godot saw the move. He had stepped into the open doorway to retrieve his revolver when he had felt the floor give. He turned to see Philippe Graillot already reacting. His hand shook fearfully as he aimed the Smith & Wesson in Graillot's general direction. The huge Beretta was still moving toward him as he shouted "Halt, police!" to no one but himself. He pulled the trigger on the revolver and pulled and pulled and pulled. It was an endless drag, he thought, as the hammer reached backwards toward the firing position.

The Beretta continued its swing toward him.

THE FARMHOUSE WAS RAPIDLY APPROACHING. FIFTY YARDS. FORTY. THIRTY. Cheryl saw a gap between the main house and a small shed. The ground finally grew smooth there. She pointed the car toward it as a door on the shed opened and a woman stepped out with exaggerated care and quiet.

"Heads up, lady," Cheryl shouted. "I'm coming through."

❀

THE REALIZATION CAME TO GODOT THAT HE WAS GOING TO DIE. HIS GUN WAS taking forever to fire; because of the way he was shaking, it was swinging back and forth across his target, and the Beretta was coming his way, quickly, surely, deadly. And then it went off. The revolver jumped in his hand as it fired and Godot realized that he had closed his eyes. He opened them, fully expecting to see the flash of the Beretta in his face. But, no. He saw Philippe Graillot holding a small spot at his waist, blood slowly seeping out of the gap between his fingers. Graillot looked at Godot with shock and surprise. He pulled himself upright in front of the low window and brought the Beretta back up into line with Godot. Godot wasn't even sure he still had his gun, it felt like he was simply pointing a finger at Philippe.

And his finger went off.

A small red flower blossomed on Philippe's chest and he stumbled backwards, falling against the aging window frame that held, then gave way, the window, the frame and Philippe Graillot falling backwards toward the ground.

Isabelle Marchant had been inside *le petit château* went she heard the first shot. She finished her business quickly and huddled in a corner. When she heard nothing more, she carefully opened the door and stepped out into the yard of her childhood home, only to be very nearly run down by a circus car driven by a madwoman, filled with madmen apparently doing some kind of Jerry Lewis comedy routine, all covered with red paint, and then, to hear another shot, then a pause, then another, almost a pop, followed by a crash ... and the body of her brother, Philippe Givre, falling in a heap at her feet.

She was greatly surprised. Her brother had left home nearly 25 years before, vowing never to return.

And now, here he was. Sleeping in his own backyard.

❀

WILL AND BOURGOIN CROSSED THE EDGE OF THE FOREST AND ROSE UP ONTO A narrow country road. There wasn't much room, but at least it was concrete. Will felt his forearms relax and the pain slide slowly out of his shoulders. How many zones of pavé had that been? Seven? Ten ? He had lost count. He still had far too many of the damned things to go, and in this weather, with this kind of mist in the air, the worst were yet to come. The bricks weren't so irregular, so deformed, as those in the forest had been, but there would be mud and water on the course, right up to the crown of the road. It would be treacherous.

They were still about 75 kilometers from the finish when a new breakaway of three riders formed and shot away from the leading group of 30. Will and Richard were sitting in the middle of that pack, perhaps 15 riders back, all working to get the mud out of their eyes, their faces, their gears.

Will had ridden this course four times before. It had never been this bad. Bourgoin had ridden it six. He agreed. One farmer at the start, he told Will, claimed that conditions hadn't been this bad since the war. The first one.

Bourgoin gasped. Will saw that the blood had once again left his leader's face and that time was running out on Bourgoin's day. A supreme effort was out of the question, probably for both of them. Survival was the only option.

Surviving to Roubaix.

They swept off the concrete onto a short stretch of cobbles that hardly merited the name. Will laughed to himself. When they were hideous, he whined, as if he was being murdered. When they were easy, he whined, as if he had been cheated. Men, he thought — we're never happy.

They turned again, this time onto yet another narrow, concrete road, and dropped in behind two riders, sucking wind and mud off their back wheels. Will felt the pace increase as the riders toward the head of the pack began to stretch forward and reach across the gap toward the breakaway.

Will noticed that Bourgoin was playing with his ear.

"What's wrong?"

"I'm not sure. I haven't heard from Deeds since we entered the forest. I have no idea what is going on behind us."

"Maybe his battery's dead. Maybe he's out of range." Will thought for a minute. "Which means that we're out of range if we need any kind of help."

"There's neutral support."

"Yeah, but God only knows where that is, or who they're willing to help first. Remember Duclos-Lassalle and Ballerini? They punctured at the same time and Ballerini had to fight them for a tire."

"Don't worry. I'm French. They love me."

"Worry. I'm American. They won't serve me in restaurants."

Bourgoin laughed, but there was no feeling, or energy, in it. He was beginning to fade.

"Richard, drop in behind. Let me pull for you."

Bourgoin fell in behind Will, struggling to regain the fire he had felt in the first 100 kilometers of the day. It was gone, he thought to himself. Gone for today.

*

CHERYL REALIZED THAT SHE WAS DRIVING LIKE HER UNCLE, HEAD OUT THE window, shouting names at passers-by for directions.

"Infirmerie!"

A woman on a Valenciennes street corner pointed.

She passed a gendarme.

"Infirmerie!"

He pointed straight and then made a left turn with his hand.

She floored the Peugeot and it shot ahead toward a small blue sign with a large "H" and an arrow pointing left.

Home free, she thought. Deeds was quiet now. He had passed out perhaps halfway between Wallers and Valenciennes. It was probably shock and loss of blood. Perhaps a reaction to the pain. Whatever.

She only hoped it wasn't Death telling him to shut up before the long bus ride to the netherworld.

*

THEY WERE IN THE WORST OF IT NOW, THE SHORT STRETCHES OF PAVÉ BEFORE and after Seclin, the pavé that replaced those closed down by the new express train lines though northern France and under the Channel and into London. The race directors had searched for suitably difficult roads and cow paths to follow toward Roubaix. As he struggled back and forth across a muddy stretch, trying to stay on the crown of the road, constantly sliding down into the water and mud along the shoulders, Will thought to himself, "Gentlemen, you have outdone yourselves. Soddy bastards."

They were just beyond the 50-kilometer mark now, about 30 miles left, when Will noticed that they were sliding off the pace. Where the pack was reaching forward toward the finish, they were falling back, slowly, toward the start. It was a gradual thing, hardly to be noticed, almost like remembering falling asleep, but Will knew. He tried to pick up their cadence, but he could feel Bourgoin falling off, dragging him back. Richard was not going to see Roubaix on a bike today.

They turned again onto a dry, solid mud road. The pace picked up again.

Will dropped back to Bourgoin's side.

"Are you okay? What do you need?"

Bourgoin was fiddling with his ear again. "I don't know."

"Don't know what?"

"Something has happened in the pack. Something happened to Deeds's car. We don't have a No. 1 car anymore. We've got neutral support — but that's all."

"What happened?"

"Something in the forest. I don't know. They're saying shots — and blood — and...." He paused, long enough that Will desperately wanted to rip the earpiece from him and listen himself. "It's really confused. The car ran off the course, through the forest and disappeared. No one is sure what happened."

The realization struck Will like a shot from an elephant gun. His breath came in short gasps. He needed to ask the question he couldn't ask. "Who ... who was ... driving?"

Bourgoin looked at him. "Cheryl. Cheryl was driving. Deeds and Roger. She was driving them."

Will felt his heart fall out of him. "Is anyone ... is anyone...?"

"I don't know, Will. I don't."

Bourgoin realized they both had stopped pedaling and were coasting, the mud and dirt along the road grabbing at their tires and pulling them quickly to a stop.

"Will. Will. Come on. Will. We must ride. We must keep going. We can't go back. The soonest we can help them is in Roubaix. We've got to go forward Will. Will! *Mon dieu*, Will! Look at me!"

He grabbed Will's face and turned it hard to him. Will's eyes were vacant, but hard, strangely hard. He said one word, blinked his eyes, looked at Bourgoin as if waking from a deep sleep, and said the word again.

"Bergalis."

"What?"

"Goddamned Bergalis. Goddamn. Bergalis. Goddamn. Goddammmmit!"

Will looked back, toward the forest and Compiègne, then up the road, toward more pavé and Roubaix. He turned toward the finish and began to pump The Beast furiously, back and forth, back and forth, trying to gain purchase in the wet soil, trying to rebuild his pace and regain the slowly splintering pack.

Bourgoin was surprised by the quick shift in emotion. He stood alone on the country road for a moment, his left foot in the pedal, his right in a mud puddle. He had never seen anyone act like this. Anyone sane. He pushed off with his right foot, forced the muddy cleat into the pedal and struggled off to catch his teammate.

*

WILL REACHED THE BACK OF THE PACK. LESS THAN 40 KILOMETERS OUT. THE pavé would end soon and the dash for the line would begin in earnest.

Bergalis. It had to be Bergalis. And his damned roach, Philippe.

Will dropped into a hard left turn, going through the middle of a mud puddle. Not a good idea. No idea what he might hit or pick up in there. Didn't matter, though, now did it? Roubaix. Roubaix was the goal. A phone. And information. And his hands, his hands around the murderous damned neck of Martin Bergalis.

He could hear someone struggling behind him. He knew those gasps. Richard. Richard had caught up. Must push harder now. "Hang on. Hang on," he shouted back. He shifted to a bigger gear and picked up his pace again. He could vaguely feel a burning in his legs, along the tops of his thighs, and the scars along his cheeks began to sing, but it was distant, almost as if he felt it in a dream. He came up behind a paceline of three riders, their jerseys a rainbow of colors against a gray-green sky. He passed them along the right side without a pause. He could hear Richard wheeze behind him. Hang on, man, he thought, we're going home. We're going home. A single rider was ahead, sliding back and forth from the crown of the pavé to the right side. He was sliding down, now, and Will timed his cross to take him to the top of the road as he passed. Just beyond the rider, while still on the crown, Will realized he had crossed over the peak and was sliding down toward the left shoulder. Too late he saw the hole where two cobbles had disappeared after years of service to the farmers of France. Given his speed and conditions, it was too late to avoid the hard-edged hole. He tried to lift the bike, but hit it with his front wheel, dead on, full power.

He immediately felt the change, the loss of control, the gain in resistance. He had punctured. Perhaps bent the rim as well. He was furious. Out of control. He rolled to a stop on the side of the road and immediately leapt off the bike, releasing the wheel and yanking it from the front fork of The Beast only to hurl it far into the field beyond. He immediately held up his hand for assistance.

It was unnecessary. The front wheel was already off Bourgoin's bike. The leader of the Haven team was fitting it smoothly into the fork of The Beast and tightening down the release, saying, over and over, "Go, just go, just go, go go go go!"

Mindlessly, out of years of training, Will's leg was back over the bike and he was already moving forward as Bourgoin slammed the release into place and pushed Will forward toward Roubaix and the finish line. "Go, just go!"

Will immediately stood up on the pedals and quickly regained his pace, the change happening so quickly that the three riders he had just passed immediately dropped in behind the American madman for a draft.

Richard Bourgoin, team leader of Haven Pharmaceuticals, the successor to the mantle of Jean-Pierre Colgan, watched his teammate ride off into the gray mist. He pulled his bike to the side of the road and sat down on a small tuft of grass. Now, he waited for the race to come to him.

He was in no hurry.

✲

WILL FELT THE POWER OF SPEED RETURN TO HIS LEGS. FROM HIS MOMENTS OFF the bike, he realized he was largely out of the range of any kind of help or support now, as crashes behind had tied up the neutral support motorcycles, and team support vehicles were trapped behind the main pack. The only motorcycles he saw now carried photographers. And they had no wheels. They were no help.

Then again, he thought, as he dropped right into a turn, beyond the pavé and back onto solid ground, everyone else was in the same boat. They faced the same dangers. One puncture, one problem, and the race was out of reach.

He approached the rear of a group of perhaps 10 riders. There had to be more ahead, he knew. There had been 14 or 15 ahead of him and Richard earlier. The pack was breaking up under the pressure of constant attacks and counterattacks. If he stayed here, he thought, his day was done, but the pain along his spine was starting to overwhelm him. Earlier, it had released at the end of each stretch of cobbles. It wasn't anymore. It was a constant reminder of the day. If he stayed here, it might release and give him a chance to breathe. The thought drew him toward the back of the group.

Until he remembered Bergalis.

There was one picture in his mind and it forced the thought along his spine and through his back and into his legs until he realized that he had broken through the pack of 10 and was bridging the gap again, toward the next group and toward whoever rode beyond and whatever lurked beyond the next corner, the next turn, the next section of cobbles, the next bank on the track in Roubaix.

With no idea of where he stood, Will shifted into his largest gear, set the metronome in his head and increased his cadence until he saw the gaps in the concrete snap along under his wheels faster than he ever remembered them doing before.

✷

MARTIN BERGALIS SAT INSIDE HIS SILVER MERCEDES LIMOUSINE INSIDE THE VIP section of the Roubaix track. He was watching the final 20 kilometers of the race on Eurovision and didn't necessarily like what he saw. There was Ross, bridging the gap to the final group before the three leaders, at a pace that was surprising, especially for a man who was supposed to have died nearly 100 kilometers before. He wondered what had happened and why one of his team cars had driven madly through the forest only moments after it all was supposed to happen.

Questions.

They bothered him, but only vaguely.

He had achieved his goals. He already had what he wanted.

And still with one surprise left in reserve.

✷

IT WAS A SURE AND STEADY APPROACH TO THE REAR OF THE LEADING CHASE group. The smart thing to do, Will thought, was to drop in behind and ride their draft in toward the track at Roubaix. Something else, however, something over which he had no control, drove him directly through their tight pack, scattering them across the road like skittles in a London pub, gaining him curses and three riders directly on his wheel.

Screw you, he thought. No riders. Screw you.

He shot over to the side of the road and then back across again. He lost two. The Belgian held on like grim death, sucking air at Will's wheel like it was mother's milk. Fine, Will thought. One I can live with. Hang on.

He put his head down, heard the metronome in his mind, and focused on his cadence, one after another after another, the pace of his feet and the silvered crankset hypnotizing him beyond the pain he felt in his legs, his hips, his back and his arms.

The Hell of the North was over. He crossed over the last section of pavé, so smooth it hardly merited the term. Now, it was a concrete sprint to the finish, racing through the suburbs and the tight turns into the track at Roubaix. Will glanced over his shoulder. He had lost his lamprey, the Belgian falling off to rejoin the chase group and finish high in the standings without destroying himself in the process.

Reality on a bicycle. It's a hard concept.

And yet, this was not reality. This was not Will Ross. This was a demon on two wheels.

On the outskirts of Roubaix, Will caught the breakaway. He thought about blowing through them and ending this charade, but he kept hearing the voice of Stewart Kenally in his head, Stewart, who had ridden this race in the late 1940s against the great Coppi and Van Steenbergen. Stewart, who kept hammering into his head, sprint from the back, sprint from the back. After a chase of he didn't know how long, Will dropped gratefully into the slipstream of the three-man leading group and arrowed his way toward the finish line.

It was a maze of city streets leading up to the track, right, left, right and left again, and then right into the gap. Will sat third in the paceline onto the track, one-and-a-half laps to go. The fourth rider fell off almost immediately, settling for whatever scraps came his way on the other side of the finish. The lead rider, Henderson, of the Boschavie team, began his sprint early, trying to build a gap between the Dutch rider in second and Will in third, but no gap is enough to survive a lap-long sprint. The Dutchman caught the jump and fell in close behind, Will directly on his wheel.

Hold.

He wanted to jump. He wanted to jump. Hold. Hold. Watch for the Dutchman's twitch. He'll twitch before he jumps. Hold. Go. No. Hold. By sense he rode the wheel of the rider in front. He watched the Dutchman's head. Three quarters of a lap. Watch. Not yet. Wait. Coming on half ... the twitch. He saw the twitch as the Dutchman jerked before pulling right and around. Will was there first. He jumped from the rear and shot past the Dutch rider, boxing him in behind the German, Henderson. The Dutchman cursed and dug in behind Will, hoping to find a final burst to shoot him across the line. Henderson was sprinting hard, but had led out so long, so far, so hard, that he couldn't seem to find one, last, final surge.

The finish rose up. Head down, sprinting furiously, unaware of the Dutchman on his right or the world around him, Will read: La Redoute — Redoute — Redoute — painted across the track before one last gap of grayish brown concrete and....

The white line.

The damned, cursed, beautiful white line.

CHAPTER NINETEEN:

TOO LATE THE HERO

Somehow, he had expected more than this. A party. A celebration. Tomas. And his grandparents, his dogs, the French teacher who didn't know the first damned thing about the Tour, his phys-ed teacher, who had always made fun of cycling as "something for kids," the English teacher and her forest of parking meters, Colgan and Merkel and Anquetil and Coppi.

The hall of the bus station was empty. Will couldn't breathe. He was passing out. He frantically spun, looking for someone, anyone, a reason to be here again, when he saw a lone figure in an expensive, well tailored, Italian suit. Stefano Bergalis stood in the background, his face stern and set. "Pieces are still in play," he said without a trace of emotion, and, oddly, without his electric larynx. The room grew distant and the pictures in Will's mind began to smear.

"He's coming around."

Everything Will could feel was cold, except for the tropical rain forest around his mouth. It was suffocating him. He struggled to rouse himself and opened his eyes to a forest of faces, all wide eyed, frantic and ... and ... close. Jesus were they close. The face he wanted to see, the face he needed to see, was not there.

Cheryl.

He thrashed an arm and the faces moved away. He clutched at the oxygen mask and ripped it from his mouth and nose to inhale the cool, wet air of a Roubaix Sunday.

"You collapsed," the attendant in white said. "You needed oxygen."

Will was panting. He looked at the oxygen mask, held it to his ear, and listened.

"Thanks. I appreciate it. Next time, turn it on."

He handed it back to the pint-sized paramedic who stared at the mask in disbelief.

Cheryl.

Will stood in the crowd, which pushed and pulled him toward the podium. The race continued to finish on the track around him. Watching the riders on the slick, wet concrete, the bikes themselves desperately gripping the slick surface, he stopped, turned and went back to where he had fallen. He carefully picked up The Beast and rolled it toward the podium.

A silver-haired man in a suit and tie, covered by a clear plastic rain slicker, stopped him.

"Take a moment. You need to talk with your team." He pointed at a staging area just off the apron of the track. A boy tried to take The Beast, to help, to roll it to the cars for Will, but he shook him off as gently as possible.

They were going together.

After all the emotion and the effort, walking through the stadium in Roubaix was a letdown, physically and emotionally. It was as if he had taken two Valium with a glass of wine.

Cheryl.

He needed a shower. He needed a chair. No. No sitting. Not for a while.

Bourgoin rushed up to greet him. He wasn't smiling.

"First — okay? Congratulations. Second. She's okay."

"What? What happened?"

"She's fine. Shook up, but fine. She's on her way here, now, with Henri Bergalis."

"From where?"

"The hospital in Valenciennes. Deeds ... uhh ... Deeds lost his leg. Somebody shot at the car and hit Deeds in the knee. Pretty bad. He lost a lot of blood. Cheryl saved him. *Sang-froid*. Exceptional woman."

"Who? Who shot?"

"The police are investigating. The shots came from a farmhouse near Wallers."

"The forest. The shots were in the forest."

"Yes."

"In the gaps in the trees." Will thought back to the forest, to the bursts of sunlight that came through the trees like the picture on a religious postcard. He remembered the rise and the break and the light and the crowd thinning at the gap and the entrance to the forest, where on the left, he could see the cottage clearly in the distance. Set the shot at the entrance, take the shot at the gap. Unless the target was out of position, riding through the crowd on the opposite side of the road. So take the backup. Take the shot at the woman who made a fool of you in front of your boss.

"The assassin is dead," Bourgoin said. "A policeman shot him. They haven't identified him yet."

"It was Philippe. Our Philippe."

"No ... no, impossible."

"Rest assured, Richard. It was our boy." Will smiled, sadly, thinking back to the policeman who had been so diligent on the case and had, in his own strange way, become a bit of a friend. "Too bad the policeman couldn't have been Godot."

"Godot? I heard the name today — I think it was."

Will laughed. "That's good shooting. Heaven to Wallers. Boom. In a wind. Boom. In the dark." He felt the crotch of his riding shorts begin to bite and fester between his legs. "I've gotta get outta these."

Bourgoin pointed to the team's soigneur who was standing at the base of the grandstand. "He'll wipe you down — he'll give you your gear."

✵

WILL FINALLY FELT CLEAN, COMFORTABLE, AND SOMETHING HE HADN'T BEEN in years — a champion.

In a sense, it was an exotic flower he couldn't get enough of, a drug, a narcotic, an addiction that drew him toward its center and embraced him in a way long since forgotten.

Winning.

He held the marble base onto which was set the heavy stone cobble of Paris-Roubaix above his head, straining to keep his balance atop the podium, straining to keep his smile and his poise within his exhaustion and concern.

A reporter ran up behind the crowd of photographers and TV cameramen, the reporters, the press groupies, the racing fans who had cadged a pass, and said something, in a stage whisper, that ran through the assembled media like news of an open bar.

And they were gone. All that remained behind was a girl, perhaps 10 years old, snapping pictures of Will with a disposable cardboard camera.

The rest had run off toward the end of the track, where Martin Bergalis was holding court.

Will lowered the trophy and stared across at Bergalis, surrounded by the international cycling media, hair, suit and style perfect. Calm. Cool. Collected. How many people had to die each day to keep his picture of Dorian Gray fresh and young? How many people suffered and buried their friends and children so he could get what he wanted? How many hearts were broken because he didn't have the guts to run his own company on the square with his old man?

How would Bergalis look, he wondered, with a 15-pound brick sticking out of his perfectly done hair, above his perfectly shaved chin and his perfectly tied cravat?

Carrying his trophy, Will stepped off the podium and began to stride across the infield, slowly, then faster, his pace growing with his anger, his hatred of the man before him, closer, now closer, doubling with each step.

Cheryl.

She stood before him, pale, unsmiling, a woman who had survived a longer and harder day then he would ever know. She put out both hands and stopped Will's march toward the crowd.

"He's won, Will."

"What? Hi. What are you talking about."

"Bergalis has won. Come on. Come with me."

"I don't know what you mean with this 'won' shit, but you will have to excuse me — I have a weapon that I need to insert about six inches into the top of his head."

"Will ..." she held him in a firm, yet gentle grip, "it's over. Please, come with me."

Will Ross stared into the eyes he had found so fascinating on the first day he had seen them. He looked at the face that had seen and felt and done much today. He saw his friend, his confidante, the person who had helped him rise up through the ashes of his life and given him a reason to feel and trust and ride again.

He put down the trophy that he thought meant the world to him and desperately hugged the woman who did.

She returned his embrace, broke it, and calmly pushed him back.

"Henri and I must talk with you, Will — now." She took his hand and pulled him toward the gate, the entrance to the velodrome he had ridden through less than an hour before, across the asphalt to a burgundy BMW limousine. Cheryl opened the door and stepped inside. Will followed.

He was amazed at the size and the accouterments that finished the interior. It was like one of those cartoon houses that was a shack on the outside and a palace just inside the front door. Cheryl turned and sat next to Henri Bergalis.

Will folded down a jump seat and sat across from the two as Henri Bergalis gently put his arm around Cheryl.

"Oh, shit," Will thought, "too late. Too late. Shit on a shingle. Too late with too little."

"My father," Henri said stiffly, his voice working to hold its emotion in check, "my father died this morning."

Will thought back to his visit to the bus station. "Yes. Yes, I know. I'm sorry."

Bergalis seemed a bit startled by Will's statement, but went ahead. "As of that moment, with the full support of the board of directors, my brother controls the company. Completely. I am second in command, but merely a voice on the board of directors, little more."

"So, what does this mean to me? Or ..." he said, spreading his arms to include the two of them, "to us?"

"It means that Kim was behind a conspiracy to destroy the Haven team. Martin has documents."

"I'm sure he has," Will muttered.

"Documents he found in her files — he says — after her death — that prove — he says — that she was responsible for the deaths of Colgan and Tomas and Merkel and Godot."

"Godot's not dead."

"He died this week at your apartment."

"No. Godot killed Philippe today after he took a shot at you. You shouldn't have pissed him off, Cheryl."

"Damn — you're joking, right? That was the — that bas ... I should have known, I should have.... How did you know?"

"I've heard just enough — Bourgoin told me — that it's the only way any of this makes any sense. Philippe was still on the board. Kim was your brother's queen, but he sacrificed her so that his knight would win the check."

"Checkmate," Henri mumbled. "The king is dead. Long live the king."

"Well, I'm not so sure about that — I haven't had the chance to show him my trophy yet. So, what now?"

Henri tapped his finger against the leather-covered armrest at his side.

"Now. Now, we see the end of Haven. The reporters who ran from your award ceremony were chasing the biggest story of the season. As of today — Haven drops from 30 riders to 10. Support staff is cut by 75 percent. There will be one team, a minor team, riding small races, maybe Le Tour, out of tradition, simply to finish out the season. Then, no more."

"No more Haven?"

"No more Haven cycling. Haven American football, perhaps, but no Haven cycling. He's won. He's won everything."

"Jesus."

Will shook his head in wonder.

"God — you know, I'm actually impressed. The guy is a goddamned miracle worker." He realized that Henri and Cheryl were staring at him in shock. "No, look at it — he's been countered every step of the way. Every time he tries to pin it on one person, who wiggles out, he finds another patsy. He is never suspected by the authorities. Not once. And after it all goes down and there are bodies everywhere — your old man kicks and he walks away with everything he wants free and clear and with lily-white skirts."

Will shook his head again.

"Amazing."

Cheryl's mouth hung open.

"You amaze me, Will. Five minutes ago you wanted to kill that son of a bitch — and now you want to give him the Businessman of the Year award."

There was a tap at the glass of the car.

"No awards. But you've gotta admit — what a pro. He makes Catherine de Medici look like Pee Wee Herman."

There was another tap at the glass. Cheryl leaned over the long seat until she was almost parallel to it and released the door latch. It swung open to reveal Martin Bergalis, and, behind him, an army of journalistic darkness.

"Hello, children. And how are you on this glorious day?"

Cheryl slid back as gracefully as possible into the crook of Henri's arm. Martin turned to Will.

"Care to join me in my chat with the press?"

"No. Not particularly."

"Oh, come now. It will be fun."

Will stepped out of the car and into the broken sunshine of a late afternoon in Roubaix.

"Ladies and gentlemen," Bergalis announced in a loud and pompous voice, "may I introduce to you the new team leader of Haven Pharmaceuticals — Will Ross."

Will was caught off guard.

"Though the team will be reduced in size, Mr. Ross will lead our team to more glory — as he did today."

Will's mouth worked frantically. He desperately worked to find the word, the thought he needed.

"Ably assisted by Richard Bourgoin — and the rest of the leading squad of our old team. The rest of the roster ..."

Will found it. "No," he said quietly.

"... will be determined in time. And this," Martin held up a small package, "is a special gift that my father commissioned for Mr. Ross — before today, before his win — to celebrate his 'never-say-die' attitude ..." Will blanched at the words "... on a bike this entire season. So, for your strength and style and fortitude — we of Haven present you with this ..."

Bergalis shoved the package roughly into Will's hand, hard enough that the wrapping tore. His mind lost in a forest of faces and thoughts and emotions, Will ripped the rest of the paper away. It was small, but heavy. A golden cyclist on a black acrylic base. The journalists leaned forward, cameras whirring and snapping, fighting for a look at the magnificent present delivered into the hands of a man who was saved from the pit of mediocrity by the munificence of the Haven team.

Will stared at the cyclist. He turned and looked at the empty faces of Henri and Cheryl, then looked at the smiling, triumphant face of Martin Bergalis and finally said it loud enough that he could be heard above the rattle and chatter and clutter of the media frenzy.

"No." He stuck his finger through the frame of the golden cyclist and spun it on his finger. "No, you two-bit, piece-of-shit bastard, I will not lead your team. Not now, not ever."

"Now, Will," Bergalis chuckled darkly, "you have a contract."

A laugh jumped from Will's throat and fell upon the ground.

"I've heard that before. Fine. So sue. But I'm out of here and I'm out of your games. Bourgoin is the leader on this team. He deserves it. And Paluzzo deserves the chance to play lieutenant. And Cacciavillani deserves the chance to sprint hard and chase teen-age girls. They all deserve the chance to build on what has been an outrageous start to the season. But that's not what you're doing. You're not building. You're destroying. A team this size with no support — they'll be destroyed. They'll all be one year closer to an early retirement with nothing to show for it by the time you toss them aside and go play football. They'll have to struggle to find a ride, each and every one of them. You know it, too. This is just end game, isn't it, Marty? Game's over — let's see how many more lives I can screw up before they put away the pieces. Right?"

The reporters slowly turned to look at Martin Bergalis, to gauge the reaction of the great man to such obvious ingratitude and buffoonery.

Bergalis said nothing. The smile never left his face. Only the edges grew hard.

"I can't stop you. You're too damned good, Marty." Will took a deep breath and plunged toward his immediate goal, something he had vowed never to do again, but was, today, the only exit toward sanity. "But I won't be one of your pieces today. Or tomorrow. Or ever again. I'm out of here. Now. This moment." He scanned the area quickly and saw The Beast leaning against a Haven Team van, ready for loading and transport. "And, I'm leaving on that bike.

That one right there. If you want to sue me for that — or charge me with theft — fine, go ahead. It's your legal system, isn't it, Marty? I'm going to turn my back on you — hoping you don't shoot me in the back — and ride away. From it all."

"Kim," Bergalis said the name slowly, gently, "Kim said you walked away from just about everything in your life. Ran. Some things never change, do they?"

Will looked at the ground for a long, hard moment. "No, Marty, some things never do. But I can live with that now."

"Too bad," Martin Bergalis said aloud to the crowd of reporters, "he was a major talent once."

"Don't fool yourself, Bergalis," Will said quietly, "we were all major talents. Once. Somehow. In something. But nobody is a major talent forever. You grow old. You fall off. There's someone new." He sighed. "It's called life. Live it. And in the future, let other people do the same."

Will turned away from Martin and looked at Henri and Cheryl, both framed in the door of the car. Henri had his arm around Cheryl. Will put out the same hand.

"Thanks, Henri, sorry it didn't work out."

Henri Bergalis shook Will's hand. "I liked it better when you called me Henry."

Will smiled and turned his gaze to Cheryl.

"See ya, kiddo. Thanks for everything."

He could see in her eyes that the day was almost over for Cheryl, her face red and drawn, and collapsing under the weight of what she had seen and felt and heard.

"You'll never ride again, you know that, don't you?" Bergalis said it with just enough venom to make it itch, just enough volume to reach the back of the press mob. All heads turned as the ball shot back on to Will's side of the court. "You may not ride, but I'll hold you to your contract. No one will be able to touch you. You'll be 33 next year. Who wants an old man riding for them?" He smiled, showing sharp, pointed teeth.

"True, true," said Will, in a diminishing voice. He took Bergalis by the hand and turned him, walking him slowly away from the press mob and toward the team vehicles. Under his breath, in a voice filled with a quiet, understated power, Will whispered, "But remember, Marty — I am your worst damned nightmare. 'Cause I'm the guy who knows where all the bodies are buried and how they got there. And you don't know if I'm going to just ride away, or ride to Godot and spill everything I know. You may try to keep Henri quiet. Or even Cheryl, who, once she's rested, I think will likely tell you to go piss up a rope. So, she'll be out of your control as well. You'll never know if or when we'll rise up and make your life miserable. And, believe me, I am going to continue to ride, Marty.

"You've given me a great gift, pal. My sense of self, Marty. My sense of what I am and who I am and why I am on a bike. So go play your games, Marty. I'm going to ride — and, best of all, I'll always be just inside the edge of your mind. Making you wonder. Making you cringe. Making you sweat."

"What is to keep me from killing you?"

"Simple. Who the hell would you blame? Everybody's gone, Marty. Face it. All your pals, your squeeze, your suspects are dead. You kill us — or anybody else — and even your tennis buddies at headquarters are going to start wondering.

"It's not exact, but I thing it's something akin to a Mexican standoff."

Will spun the golden cyclist once, like a gunfighter. With a quick, backwards glance toward Cheryl, he pushed his way past Martin Bergalis toward the van. His gear bag sat beside the bike. He opened it, slipped on his riding shoes and gloves, still wet from the day, threw the duffel over his shoulder in the manner of a backpack and sat on the bike. He had spent a long Sunday on this seat, and his southern hemisphere let him know it immediately.

"I'm stealing your bike, Martin. There's a gendarme over there. You may want to call him."

Bergalis stared with a furious, impotent power. This fool had swept the pieces from the board. Just go, he thought. Get into Henri's car and go. Go to your hotel with Henri. Now. Just go.

"Let's discuss this tomorrow."

"Discussion's done, boss. I be gone." He leaned forward. "And, Martin," he whispered with great care and precision, "if anything, anything, happens to Miss Crane or your brother, if they get a pimple, or a car filled with orphan children misses a turn and crashes into them, or they fall down the stairs, or slip in the shower, remember something: I'll be in your face. Because I'll know you had something to do with it. Understand?"

Bergalis said nothing.

"Thanks, Marty, you've been swell." Will patted Bergalis's cheek, then pinched it. He spun the cyclist on his finger one last time, snapped his right foot into the pedal of The Beast and slowly pedaled off toward the exit, toward the road, toward Avelgem and his life.

A life that lacked something he wanted, but held what he needed to survive.

And he was riding it.

WILL QUICKLY DISAPPEARED AS THE CROWD SURGED AROUND MARTIN BERGALIS, who, a number of reporters noticed, was still smiling easily after the obvious rudeness of the American. What they didn't notice as Bergalis glanced at his watch was that he fingered a small, but long-range, radio trigger in the other pocket of his beautifully tailored Italian suit.

Unpredictable.

"'Marti.'" Hmph, he thought. He hated that. His father had always called him that.

WITH THE EXCEPTION OF THE FACT THAT HE HADN'T BEEN ABLE TO GET THE golden cyclist statuette off his finger, it had been a great exit, Will thought. He had made a turn, just outside the view of the reporters, and stopped to tug the trophy off his finger. With some twisting and a grunt and slight tearing of skin, it came off. Will looked at it for a long moment.

It was a beautiful thing. But it wasn't worth the lives behind it.

A silver Mercedes sat along the road. The chauffeur of Martin Bergalis had the trunk opened and was carrying a box of advertising brochures back toward the press area. A few had fallen onto the floor of the trunk. Will rolled to the side of the car and looked over the edge.

The New Haven, the headline cried.

Every great fortune, he recalled, starts with a crime. Maybe, Will thought, they continue with them as well.

With a flick of his wrist, he tossed the golden cyclist into the trunk of the limousine.

He slowly pedaled away and did not look back.

CHAPTER TWENTY:

END GAME

Within 10 minutes of the velodrome, within 10 minutes of riding to the north and east, toward the outskirts of Roubaix, toward Avelgem and home, Will realized that reality had struck and struck hard.

He was not pedaling The Beast, he was pedaling an ox cart that was dragging a drunken wildebeest. There was nothing left inside him, no drive, no energy, no life. He had made his grand exit from the Roubaix velodrome on sheer adrenaline and anger, but now, he had to find a place to rest and do it quickly. He turned onto a main street and faced the traffic for a block until he found what he had been looking for: a small, elegant hotel, set back from the street, its ornate and elegant design boasting of fine rooms at a top price. Will stepped into the small lobby, pushing his bike beside him, and startled the sneering desk clerk.

"I need a room."

"We are full."

Will proceeded as if he didn't hear.

"A room with a bath."

"They are expensive."

"A room in the back."

"They are very expensive."

"Put it on this." Will tossed the golden card on the silver plate before the unctuous hotel manager.

The thin, balding man in the tight suit with the boutonniere looked at the card for a moment, then directly at Will.

"Of course, Monsieur Deeds. Immediately, sir. Do you need some help with your bike?"

Will shook his head. Carl should really be more careful with this thing.

TEN MINUTES LATER, WILL DROPPED HIMSELF INTO A STEAMING TUB. BESIDE him, on the table was a huge bottle of beer packed in ice to near-freezing, a concession to his plebeian American tastes. He raised the bottle in the air and said, to no one in particular, "Here's to me."

He looked over at The Beast, leaning against an incredibly expensive oak chiffonier in the corner.

"And to you, my friend." And to Carl and Tomas and Richard and Raymond and Tony and Cheryl and Henri and Jablom and Godot and Philippe — may you roast in hell on an acid spit, you son of a bitch — and to Stewart. Stewart who started it all — hell and heaven and all.

He took a long, deep drink and felt the sharpness of the beer reach back and jangle that little punching bag at the back of his throat. Will watched the last rays of sunlight play across the ceiling of the bathroom, heard thunder in the distance and decided that was good. Despite the fact that he had ridden in it all day and hated it with every crank, he loved to hear the rain at night when he slept.

THE BUS STATION WAS EMPTY, WITH THE EXCEPTION OF WILL AND TOMAS sitting in the single wooden pew in the center of the great hall.

"You gotta tell me, Tomas, am I doomed to this?"

"Good God, Will, how many times do you have to watch 'Mr. Magoo's Christmas Carol'? You're alive. You can change."

"I wish you had been there today, man."

"You don't know how much I did. Even for a moment."

"I understand."

"No. No, you really don't. Not really," Delgado said, gently. "When you're dead, then you will. You really will. But now, it's like telling your mother you understand how she feels when you drive a soccer ball through her grandmother's collection of cut glass. You're alive, Will. You're living. You're doing.

You're trying and hurting and touching and loving and living. You're living. I'm dead. End of story."

"I'm sorry. I suppose you're right." There was a long, awkward pause. Will suddenly brightened and turned to his friend. "Look, you're dead. You know all and see all now, right? Well, I've got a question."

"Go ahead."

"What's the deal with Anquetil? Why doesn't he cut Colgan some slack? The poor guy wanders through my dreams with a handful of toaster being called a putz by his hero."

"Ask him yourself."

Tomas Delgado nodded and Will turned to see Anquetil in a corner, staring into a candy machine. He pulled a lever, barked an oath, then kicked the machine.

"Somehow, I expected more from heaven!" the French champion shouted.

"Jacques," Tomas said, "has never really accepted his fate."

"Go to hell, Tomas."

"With your mother, Jacques."

Will looked around quickly for a cop or some kind of ethereal hall monitor. There sure was a lot of cursing going on for purgatory.

"And you," Anquetil snapped, bringing Will back quickly into a stare down, "you are as much of a putz as Colgan."

Will reacted on sheer instinct.

"Screw you, pal. At least I won Paris-Roubaix. You never did."

Tension flared in the Frenchman's eyes, then flushed and the great man smiled.

"You are right, Delgado. He will do."

Jacques Anquetil, five-time winner of the Tour de France, world hour record holder, leader of the peloton more times for more races over more miles than just about anyone other than Merckx, gave Will a crooked smile and disappeared in a puff of rainbow-colored smoke.

"You mean, that's it? Standing up to him? Winning his respect? That's all it takes?"

"For the most part. He lived in a world of sycophants. He respects those who give him a challenge. On the other hand, we must face reality, Will. Jean-

Pierre Colgan really is ..."

"A putz."

"Exactly."

"I've got another question."

"One more — but don't ask me who really killed Kennedy or what happened to Amelia Earhart."

"Naw. Simple one. What's the deal with my English teacher and all those parking meters?"

❁

WILL'S EYES SNAPPED OPEN. HE LOOKED AT THE CLOCK. 9:25 A.M. HE HAD SLEPT in. A whole two hours. Just five more minutes he thought, five more minutes, and he would have heard Delgado's answer. Five lousy minutes. Damn.

He lay in bed, staring at the ceiling, trying to focus on the stucco design and the day, the life, ahead. He knew, quickly, what he had to do first.

He picked up the phone and dialed the hotel operator.

"Yes, Mr. Deeds?"

"I need to make three calls to the United States. To Kalamazoo, Michigan, Mr. and Mrs. Harold Ross, and then two to Detroit. Mr. Stewart Kenally and...."

"Yes, Mr. Deeds?"

"Mrs. Rose Cangialosi. Try her first. Here's the number."

He hoped that 16 years hadn't fried his memory.

❁

BY NOON, CARL DEEDS HAD CHECKED OUT OF THE HOTEL IN ROUBAIX, leaving a large bill and a generous tip to be puzzled over by the accountants at Haven Pharmaceuticals, and William Edward Ross was on the road again, fresh gear, fresh air, fresh attitude. He rolled slowly out of Roubaix, crossed the border just north of the city and began a leisurely, roundabout tour to Avelgem. He was in no hurry to cover the 25 to 30 kilometers to the village. He was meeting no one. He had nothing pressing to accomplish. Besides, he'd get paid by Bergalis, just out of spite, right up to the end of the season.

So, he took his time. Smooth roads. No potholes. No cobbles.

Still, there was a certain disappointment in his travel. Somewhere, in Roubaix, he had left his trophies: the marble base and huge cobble for Paris-Roubaix and that golden cyclist he had tossed away too early with too much the air of the uncaring cavalier.

It had been given to him by the father of the devil himself, but the devil certainly does tempt you with your greatest desire and that was his, the beauty of the piece still speaking to him a day later, despite the fingerprints of Martin Bergalis.

Within an hour, he was on his usual course, his shortened training ride, the one he had fought so weakly in early January, as Colgan died and he was reborn. He was close now, close to home and rest and even more training and a chance to decide what to do with his future and to that of Martin Bergalis.

He crossed into the village and waved through the window of the bicycle shop. It caused quite a commotion. Monsieur Vanderarrden and at least three children burst through the door waving and shouting, "*Chaussettes rouges! Chaussettes rouges!* Hurrah!" Will smiled and lowered his head. Two months ago, that would have been an insult; now, he raised his head in pride.

Damn square. I won. Damn square.

He rode through the village as people stared and pointed and clapped. There was a champion in their midst.

And that champion was him.

❁

HE POKED HIS HEAD INTO HILDA S FOR A MOMENT, JUST TO WAVE, SAY HELLO and feel their praise. There was none. Leo was drunk, head down on a plastic-topped table. The tavern reeked of smoke and stale beer and old urine and that strange electrical smell that a TV set left on too long gives an entire room.

The atmosphere, the smell, the memories of himself there pushed him out the door and into the brightly lit street. He took a deep breath to clean himself and remounted The Beast to begin the slow ride home.

A door had opened. A door had closed.

He turned the corner and saw the warehouse up ahead, and the house of Madame Nola, his landlady, and his own house, tired, worn, at a bit of an angle, and yet, inviting.

Hmph, he thought, just like the man who lived here.

"Madame Nola, hello," he sang, as The Beast swept past the house. He heard a screech and, "Hello, Will!" in answer from a deep corner of the house. Will lifted the front wheel at speed, jumped a ridge and brought thc bikc to a stop in front of his steps.

Something had been added.

A marble base with a cobble, a big, damned cobble, on point at its center, sat full square in the middle of his steps, the steps leading to his door, the door that opened, slowly, to reveal Cheryl Crane.

"Hello, stranger."

"Hiya. You left in a big damned hurry yesterday."

"I had a guaranteed reservation in Carl's name and I didn't want to lose it."

"Took your own sweet time in getting here."

"Sorry. I can only bust my ass two or three times a week now. I'm old."

"Well, grandpa, you missed all the fun."

"Jesus, what now? A day without Haven is a day without the three lead stories on the evening news."

She tossed an edition of *Le Matin* at his feet. It took him a moment to read the headline upside down, but eventually, he deciphered it.

"Bergalis Dead!"

"Jesus ... Henri?"

"No, thank God — Martin."

Will gave a low, long whistle. The king had been swept from the board.

"Who got him? How?"

"Police aren't sure. His car blew up. A bomb. In the trunk. Set off the gasoline. He didn't have a chance."

"Like he gave Tomas a chance. One last gift from Philippe?"

"Don't know. Interesting thing, though, Henri says police found a radio detonator in his pocket. Almost as if he set the damned thing off himself. Suicide. Who'd have thought it?"

Suddenly the image of a golden cyclist, on a heavy, black acrylic base, spinning through the air and into the trunk of a beautiful silver limousine, filled Will's mind. He took a deep, ragged breath. Yikes.

"Yes," he said, "who indeed?"

He stepped off the bike, leaning it against a tree, before, as gracefully as possible, clacking across the concrete in his riding shoes to the wooden steps of his home. He pulled the heavy duffel off his back and dropped it to the side, sat down, and put his hand on the Paris-Roubaix trophy separating Cheryl and himself.

"So, what's next? No offense, but there's gotta be more to your being here than a traveling news service."

"There is. I'm here to bring you back."

"What? To lead a major team down the road to mediocrity? No, thank you."

"Stop. Henri is in charge. The team stays at 30. Full support. Three squads. No football. Bourgoin is screaming for you to ride shotgun for him at the Giro, the Vuelta and the Tour."

"Gosh, Richard has planned my whole damned vacation for me, hasn't he?"

"You brought it on yourself."

And he had, he knew. The thought of where he was and where he had been and where, after years of trying, he might actually go, made his throat feel tight and his face flush.

"Who's ... uh," he fought back the rush of feeling and emotion that came over him, "who's in as directeur sportif?"

"Deeds. Deeds will live. He'll lean, but he'll live. He should be back in six weeks, as joyous and beautiful a human being as ever."

"Yes, but now we can run away from him."

"I dunno. Some orthopedic dude from Denver has already been in touch with his wife about rehab and a prosthesis."

"Shit. Buttinsky."

Now, it was her turn to laugh. As Will heard the sound, he steeled himself to ask the question he didn't want to ask, to hear the answer he didn't want to hear, but knew, in both cases, that it simply could not be avoided. He took a deep breath and plunged ahead.

Cheryl beat him to it.

"I'm not sure what I'm going to do. Henri wants me to stay around, continue as soigneur and begin to learn the job of assistant directeur sportif. He's a very nice man, but just a bit cracked. Wouldn't the cycling press have a cow over that one? A female assistant on a male team. Europe would faint."

"Entire continent. Dead away."

"I've also got an offer from the States. A friend of mine is setting up a mountain bike team. He's offered me a ride — a chance to go up against Furtado, Ballantyne, Matthes. The best."

"That's great."

"You might have heard of him. His name is Stewart Kenally."

Will smiled.

"I wondered when we might get around to this, Miss Don't Fuck With Me, I'm From Detroit.'"

Now it was Cheryl's turn to smile.

"My mother raised us to survive."

"Yes, I know. By the way, CharLouise, your mother says 'hello.'"

"She said you called. Thanks. It meant a lot to her. She's always been crazy about you."

"Why didn't you say anything? Tell me about being changing your name?"

"Because, at first, I didn't like you. Hated your guts. As far as I was concerned, you were a loser. A chump."

"I appreciate your kind thoughts."

"Hey, what did you expect me to think with your ex-wife calling the shots? Besides, it was none of your business why I changed my name. You turned your back on my mother and my family and on Stewart when Raymond died. When they really needed you. And you needed them, I might add. They both told me, always told me, to forgive you, to give you room, but I really hated the thought of you."

"What changed your mind?"

"Who says I've changed my mind?" She laughed at the stricken look on Will's face. "Relax. Took me a long time not to. Tomas helped. The Ruta helped. The way you rode. The way you fought back. Ghisallo. Tomas." She wagged a finger at him. "My mother warned me about boys like you." She took a deep breath and exhaled very slowly.

"And, then, there came another reason. Another reason I didn't tell you."

"What?"

"Hey — who wants to kiss his best friend's little sister?"

She looked at Will with warm, open eyes.

Slowly, in the middle of a Belgian street, as the warmth of spring finally began to unfold around him, William Edward Ross raised his hand.

ACKNOWLEDGMENTS

My thanks, first and foremost, to John Wilcockson, Tim Johnson, Charles Pelkey, Chas Chamberlin, and Mike Sitrin of *VeloNews* and Velo Press for their support and willingness to support this project. Tim Johnson not only put up with endless phone calls, but also bought me gallons of a caffeine-rich Indian tea at a local restaurant that was always good for three chapters within an hour's time. John Wilcockson's insights into the workings of the European cycling community have been invaluable. My thanks also to Chris and Raetta Webster, who gave freely of their own insights into both riding and mysteries. Their friendship is a cornerstone of my life. As is the friendship and support of Reynelda Muse and donnie betts. Thanks also to Debbie Stabio, who helped me with my French; Steve Youngerman, a wizard with weaponry, who basically armed everyone in the story; Rich Ryer, whose Colnago inspired "The Beast," and Tony Cacciavillani, who allowed me to use a magnificent name for one of my characters.

And yet, my deepest thanks must go to writers Stephen White, who gave freely of his time and criticism and knowledge as the book neared its end, and Clarissa Pinkola Estes, Ph.D., who sparked the creative fire more than a year ago and kept it burning with her friendship, even after I think I stiffed her for lunch and my answering machine cut her off. Friends like this are almost impossible to find.

And, finally, to Becky, Devon and Brynn, with whom I share a life and a home and a boatload of dreams. They keep it all real and daily help me find the joy in life.